Mary Elizabeth Coleridge

The King with Two Faces

Mary Elizabeth Coleridge

The King with Two Faces

ISBN/EAN: 9783743400252

Manufactured in Europe, USA, Canada, Australia, Japa

Cover: Foto ©Andreas Hilbeck / pixelio.de

Manufactured and distributed by brebook publishing software (www.brebook.com)

Mary Elizabeth Coleridge

The King with Two Faces

BY

M. E. COLERIDGE

AUTHOR OF

"THE SEVEN SLEEPERS OF EPHESUS"

NINTH IMPRESSION

LONDON

EDWARD ARNOLD

37 BEDFORD STREET

1898

CONTENTS

CONTENTS

NOTE

THE writer owes much to Mr. NISBET BAIN'S most interesting work, *Gustav III. and his Contemporaries.*

THE KING WITH TWO FACES

——◆——

CHAPTER I

IN WHICH THE HERO IS EXPECTED

FOUR horses, saddled and bridled, stood ready. Four loaded pistols lay on the table.

A. had a book in his hand, but he was not reading.

B. was writing a letter, but the regular scratching of his pen had ceased some time before.

C., with his hands in his pockets, was trying to sit listlessly before the fire, but he was not sitting listlessly.

D. had thrown himself on to the sofa and closed his eyes, but he was not asleep.

Very lightly and slightly, apologetically, as it were, because his ears were tired of long listening with nothing to listen to, *B.* began to whistle a tune from *Thetis and Peleus.*

"Be quiet, cannot you?" *D.* said angrily.

And *B.* took up his pen again, while the speaker shut his eyes in the resolute manner of a person who *will* not remain awake.

The slow ticking of the clock seemed to each one of them like the beating of a hammer on a bare nerve.

Yet, when at length it struck eleven, three out of the four started, for there is nothing so sudden as the arrival of a long-expected moment. In the interval between the first stroke and the eleventh, each man saw sharply defined before him a different picture— different and yet the same. Each man beheld two figures—one dead, one living. The dead man was the same in all the pictures; the living man, who stood over him, varied.

A. saw this picture on the open page of his book, *B.* on the blank sheet of letter-paper before him, *C.* in the glowing embers, *D.* on his own eyelids.

When the last vibration of the last stroke had died away, the silence settled down again more leadenly than before. Three out of the four men began to wonder where they would be this time to-morrow.

" It will not do," said *B.* abruptly. " He ought to keep time."

" He will keep time," said *A.*

" Hark ! "

D. started up and curled his hand over his ear.

" What ? "

" Hush ! It's coming nearer."

" Thank Heaven ! " cried *B.*

" You left the gate open ? "

" Yes."

" And there are lights in the avenue ? "

" Yes, yes."

" Unbar the door, somebody ! "

D. ran to do so. The cold, keen, peaceful stillness of the air without refreshed him after the full, feverish atmosphere in which he had been breathing. But there was no sound.

He waited a second or two, and then, oddly frightened lest he should be the first to hear what they were all waiting for, he shut the door again and rejoined his comrades.

" A false alarm ! " muttered *A.* " I thought so."

" I tell you I will bear this no longer," cried *B.*, after another interval of palpitating dumbness. " A man's nerves won't stand it. I am no coward, I hope, but I tell you fairly, *A.*, the thing is not possible. If he is to be shot, in Heaven's name challenge the poor young fellow, and do it decently ! No adversary of yours has ever been known to escape. This is too much like murder for my taste."

"It is murder," said *A*. coolly. "There is always a certain element of chance in a duel. I have never fallen, but I might fall ; and the fate of my companions demands that I should not fall—yet. Murder, if managed well, is certain. What right have you to object to murder? May I ask you to recollect your oath?"

"You forget that I am a gentleman," cried *B*. hotly.

"You yourself have no right to remember it. You have vowed to the gentlemen of your country not only all you have, but all you are. It is of the utmost importance to those whom you represent, that the King should not receive the message, whatever it may be, which this young man carries. Messages to the King by his special messenger are never written ; they are—I thought you knew this—transmitted by word of mouth. Therefore, as we cannot take the despatches from him, nothing but his treachery or his death can avail us ; and he comes of too good a stock to turn traitor."

"Why not imprison him?"

A. gave a short laugh.

"Where is the prison?" he said. "Find that, and we will make a prisoner of him by all means! This house is ours for to-night only. There is no other that we can claim within fifty miles. Where is the prison?"

B. dropped his head upon his hands and made no answer.

"Why not fire on him in the open?" suggested *D*. "It would be easier. He would have no more chance of escape, practically speaking, than here, between four walls, he being defenceless and we leagued together against him. Bah! you may say what you like, *A*., but I am of *B.'s* opinion ; it smacks too much of common murder. We shall never fire steadily."

"It is not to be risked," said *A*.

"Why?"

"Because I say so."

D. was silent.

"'Tis an abominable business," muttered *C.* "Of all the accursed courtiers, why choose the only one that's worth his salt?"

A. turned on him fiercely.

"Because he is the only one likely to thwart our aim. The others are but a pack of cards; he has the mettle of a hero. Adonis has found it out too; he showers his favours upon him. He knows when a fish is worth catching."

"So do you, for the matter of that; only you bait your hook with fear, not with favour," said *C.* "There's an extraordinary fascination about fear. I fear nothing in this world that I am aware of, *A.*, except yourself; and I follow you because I am afraid of you and would rather be afraid of you than in love with another."

A. nodded his head.

"You do well," said he. "The fear of me will carry you farther than the love of anyone else. I am doomed. I go straight as a cannon-ball to the mark."

"Are you sure he will come to the house to-night?" asked *B.* "He might go on. He has but five miles farther to ride in order to reach the village, and he may think that he can do his errand here to-morrow, and still rejoin the King in time. In that case"—

"We shall hear him galloping past the gate; we shall mount and follow. Every objection has been foreseen and answered, as you are, by this time, aware; else I should not have allowed this conversation to proceed. The horses are standing ready, but I am much mistaken, or they do not leave the stables to-night. There he is!"

The last words were spoken as quietly as all the rest.

The three accomplices sprang forward.

A. raised his hand deprecatingly.

"Be seated, gentlemen!" he said, in a tone which had the effect of physical force. "Let the groom open the door. Do you not see that, if one of us went out to meet him, he might hand in the letter without dismounting? It is our object to decoy him into this room. When he enters, bow to him, but take no further notice. The shutters are bolted. While I am speaking, *C.* will lock the door and secure the key. I shall try to get him into the garden. If it can be done there, so much the better. If not, the business must be finished here. Remember that no one sees whose shot it is which takes effect. Have you your weapons? Good! When you hear me say *The King*, fire!"

In a second the pistols had vanished from the table.

D. was asleep again upon the sofa.

B. was writing as if he were writing for a wager.

C. sat before the fire, the picture of indolent reverie.

The galloping hoofs came nearer, the sound grew louder and louder, and stopped short suddenly just outside.

There was a thundering knock on the door.

CHAPTER II

" IS Colonel Engeström's cousin at home?" said a
fresh young voice, broken and panting, for the
rider was out of breath with the speed he had made.

"He is, sir."

"Ask him to speak to me at once. I am pressed for
time."

"My master gave me the strictest injunctions that
you should be shown into his private room, sir. I dare
not disobey him. If you will step this way"—

"Be quick, then!" cried the voice, as, with a hurried
oath, the rider dismounted. "My business is urgent;
I cannot wait."

The servant ushered him in.

A., who had turned out the lamp just before, so that
the faces of himself and his companions might not be
recognised, rose courteously and bowed; the rest,
excepting for the slight inclination which politeness
required, kept their positions.

How is that we can, nay, that we *must* see, whenever
we do not wish to look? Is there some other sense
than that of sight, by which, in moments of intense
excitement, the bodily image of a man is transferred
to the brain?

They all beheld the person who had just entered the
room. Not one of them but would have cried, had he
been questioned at the moment, *I did not know he was
like that*; and nothing could have shaken their nerve
more. For he was handsome; there was nothing
about him which could have led to any repulsion—

14

rather a certain careless nobility of air and gesture, that did not solicit but commanded admiration. And above all he was young—they were all, except their leader, about the same age.

"To what circumstances do I owe the honour of this visit, so late at night?" said A.

The young man answered with frank impatience.

"To no desire of mine to make your acquaintance, sir," he said. "I was entreated by Colonel Engeström to bring you this letter. You are his cousin, I presume?"

"The presumption is quite correct."

"He begged me to deliver it into no hands but your own. Will you bear witness that I have performed my commission? I am in great haste, and shall be glad if you will not detain me any longer." He tendered the letter that he held.

"A cold night!" said A., leaning his elbow on the mantelpiece and his head on his hand. "A very cold night! The stars are strangely brilliant. I do not remember that I ever saw so many in the group of the Pleiades excepting once before." He spoke slowly and deliberately. Had the young man been quick of apprehension, he might have noticed that a figure which was more immediately in his shadow, as he stood there, stole to the door and back again.

"As a rule," continued A., without pausing, "only a limited number are visible to the naked eye; but on that occasion, it was the anniversary of the birth of"—

"Pardon me!" interrupted the young man. "The history of the stars visible in the Pleiades on the occasion to which you allude would, no doubt, interest an astronomer. My present business is with earthly and not with heavenly bodies. And I am engaged in an affair of life and death."

Again he might have remarked a simultaneous movement of all the men in the room at the very moment when he began to speak; but it was over directly, and he was too much absorbed in his own sensations to take any heed.

"You are engaged in an affair of life and

death?" said *A*. "Good! I am much obliged to you," and, with a murmured word of thanks, he took the letter.

The young man lifted his hat and went to the door.

The handle turned but it would not open.

He looked for the key; there was none.

Again he tried the handle.

"What does this mean, gentlemen?" said he.

"It means," said *A*., looking up from his letter, "that you will not leave this room by the door."

The young man shrugged his shoulders.

"I am at a loss to comprehend you," he said. "Be so good as to explain."

"There are certain words which explain a good deal," said *A*., "your own name, for instance. I have the honour to address Count Ribbing, have I not?"

"I have no need to be ashamed of my name, sir. It has been borne for over five hundred years in Sweden by men who have done nothing to disgrace it."

"Just so," said *A*. "It has been borne for over five hundred years in Sweden. High time it should die!"

Ribbing changed colour suddenly. He recollected that he was quite unarmed, that they were four to one, and the door was locked. He glanced up at the windows; they were shuttered and barred. There was no possible means of retreat. He thought of all this before it occurred to him to wonder why his life was threatened.

A., having paused an instant to let his words take effect, continued—

"We wish you to understand that we have no personal grudge against you—that we are, in fact, not persons at all, but representatives. The cause we represent demands your life—except on one condition."

"The condition?" said Ribbing, in a voice that was perfectly calm, but sounded to himself like some-one else's.

"I ask your forgiveness for mentioning it before-

hand. You comprehend that my doing so is the merest
formality. It is a condition which no gentleman
could accept, namely, that you reveal to us the
message with which you are charged."

"I thought," said Ribbing, in the same voice, though
he was angrily conscious that his heart was beating
louder and faster than usual, "that I was among
men of honour. It is my good fortune, apparently,
to have fallen in with a band of assassins."

"Do not take the name of fortune in vain, sir,"
said *A.* "Destiny is but another title for God. See
that your last words are not of such a light and
frivolous character, that they move the celestial
powers to darkness at the very moment when most
you need their help. I have been young myself; in
years, even now, I am not old. Although your
eyes are steel and your voice unshaken and you play
the man well enough for a boy, I know your heart is
beating so that you are afraid we shall hear it ; I know
your breath comes unevenly, and I have marked your
hand closing and unclosing twenty times in the last
minute. It is useless to pretend before me. I know
that you would, at the present moment, give anything
except honour to be able to reveal what you will never
reveal because honour forbids it. Further than
this, I know that you would give anything—would you
not?—for the mere chance of an impossible make-
believe of resistance, so as to get your blood up and
die with a little more colour about it ; but we are
all armed men and you are utterly defenceless. If you
will be guided by me, you will make no foolish and
undignified struggle ; you will give me your word not
to attempt escape. In that case, I shall use no force.
I shall not bind you hand and foot, as I shall be compelled to do if you show yourself obstinate. I shall
only ask you to accompany us to the garden, and to
place yourself with your back to the wall. These
gentlemen are all good marksmen ; we shall not hurt
you."

"This condition at least I can accept," said Ribbing
grandiloquently. It vexed him to feel that he was

2

turning theatrical to avoid the semblance of cowardice ;
but to act well is difficult, when once the audience has
reminded a man that it knows he is acting.

D., who was but a boy himself, experienced a sudden
impulse of indignant, irrepressible pity.

" If the Count has any last wish that we could
fulfil " —he whispered nervously to his chief.

" It is unlikely," said *A.* " The Count knows that
our friends are not his. Still," — he turned to his
prisoner,—" if you have any wish of the kind, speak ! "

" I have a wish of the kind, and it is very simple,"
said Ribbing. The timid murmur of sympathy had,
in some strange manner, recalled him to himself ; he
no longer felt as if his intellect were paralysed. " This
house stands on the highest hill in the neighbourhood,
does it not ? "

" I believe it does," said *D.*, surprised at the
question.

" Will you allow me," said Ribbing, addressing
himself to the leader, " to go to one of the rooms on
the upper floor and to look out of the window ? "

" No," returned *A.* drily.

" If I give you my word that I will not attempt to
escape ? "

" I will send one of these gentlemen, if he can
pleasure you by going."

" That will do´just as well," said Ribbing. " All
that I wish to ascertain is, whether the light of a
bonfire can be seen on the summit of a hill three miles
due east from the spot on which we are standing."

" You can go, *D.* Be as quiet as you can ! Lock
the door after you. We will await your return here."

The leader seated himself and signed to Ribbing to
occupy the place left vacant by the person he called
D.

" It will take him five minutes at least to go up and
five minutes to come down again," thought the young
Count. " He has some heart in him."

The door was unlocked and locked again. The
light, swift footsteps were heard ascending the staircase all too fast. Then they were lost above. When

they were heard once more, all hope would be over. Ribbing knew well enough that there was no light in the direction which he had indicated ; he had asked for the assurance simply because he could devise no other means of gaining time.

Time ! Time ! Time ! It was more than half up by this, and still his mind was a blank. In desperation he opened his eyes—he had closed them that he might think more connectedly—and gazed around him.

The room was bare of furniture, with the exception of a few chairs, an old couch, a wooden table in the centre, and a forest of branching antlers, which covered the walls in every direction, interwreathing their fantastic, angular shadows in the firelight.

It seemed to him that he could do nothing for the tracery of the shadows of these deer's horns ; from those of the great elk over the door to those of the gazelle over the chimneypiece he tried to disentangle each one separately and to get it clear, but it was no use. They were thickest over the clock. He could hear the loud ticks, but he could not see the face. He went on still at his work of disentangling, and this although he knew the minutes must be counted by seconds now. If he could only have seen the clock instead of hearing it—if he could only have known the limit of the time at his command, he could have thought. But the clock stood in a dark corner, and, so long as he did not know, he could not think. Time ! Time ! Time ! "And there shall be no more time." The words possessed him.

"I wish I had never wished at all," he said to himself. "Why did I insist upon dying, when I was offered death without it ? I must be as great a coward as that man thinks I am. Fie upon all such ! I might as well be dead already and down among the shades, for all the light there is, or the conversation either, in this grave of a room. What will it feel like, I wonder ? *We will not hurt you.* As if he knew !"

"You are wondering what it will feel like," said A., lifting his eyes from the book that he was reading by the fire. "That plan of sending someone to the top of the house was only an expedient to gain time. You are not quite what I thought you."

A blush of hot shame and anger tinged Ribbing's pale cheek, but he contained himself and said nothing.

"You are wrong," went on *A.* "You do but lengthen your own suffering. *D.* was wrong too, although he meant well. *B.* and *C.* would have thought me cruel had I denied his request; but the real cruelty lay in granting it. I regret the last few moments more than you, who are not responsible, can possibly regret them. Reassure yourself, Count! A sudden pang, no worse than that which you experience when a tooth is drawn, and then a sudden sleep; death means no more than that. But if you think about it, it grows mysterious and dreadful. Try rather to distract the mind! I feel for you. I know you wish to preserve your dignity to the end. Do you take any interest in subjects of this kind?"

He handed Ribbing the book on which he had been engaged. The Count took it mechanically, and even at that pass, could not forbear a smile at the grotesqueness of the incident, when he read the title: *On the Proper Cultivation of the Coffee Plant in the Island of Ceylon.* He was about to give it back, when an idea occurred to him.

There flashed before his eyes the recollection of an old woman poring over the grounds in a coffee-cup, as she had been described to him a day or two since.

He almost laughed aloud.

On that old woman depended his one thin chance of life.

It was a desperate move indeed, yet he was quite resolved to play. He was not one of those who throw over the chessboard when once checkmate appears to be inevitable.

CHAPTER III

IN WHICH THE HERO RIDES AWAY

EVERY energy of Ribbing's mind was bent to the move. Holding the open volume like a shield between himself and his enemy—for he had an instinctive fear that the latter would read his thoughts, even by that dim light, as easily as a printed page, if he did not interpose a solid, substantial non-conductor—he wondered whether this man were superstitious or not. It seemed hard to be within whispering distance of him, and not even to know what his features were like, so as to have some clue; but Adolf dared not risk so much as a glance. He was a revolutionist of the type then called *Illuminé*—so much was clear —and he took an interest in coffee-planting and agriculture. Beyond that the Count knew nothing; but he determined to play as boldly as if he did. It was some comfort to him to reflect that he could not make his case more desperate than it was already.

One slight circumstance fanned the spark of hope that a chance word had kindled, and one alone. Dangling upon the chief's watch-chain, as he hung thoughtfully over the fire, Ribbing saw a little fork-shaped piece of coral, such as is worn by peasants in Italy, to avert the Evil Eye from their persons. He knew what it meant, for his mother possessed an amulet of the same kind; but he could not allow himself to build much upon so trivial an indication.

A moment more, and the messenger was heard descending the staircase with heavy and slow steps.

The key groaned in the lock, and the door creaked as it turned on its hinges, thrust open by an unwilling hand. The critical moment was come, and Ribbing braced himself to meet it, and thought resolutely of nothing.

"Well?" inquired *A.* "Was there a bonfire burning on the summit of a hill, three miles due east from the spot on which you are standing?"

D. shook his head.

"Have you any more last wishes?" went on *A.* scornfully. "Would you like to know whether there is a bonfire on a hill three miles due west?"

"No."

"Once more, then, and for the last time, will you betray the King, or will you follow me?"

"I will do neither," said Ribbing, with a sudden audacity. "I will not betray the King, but you—if you are a wise man—will do me no harm."

"Why?"

"Because," said the Count, mimicking as well as he could his enemy's *sang-froid*, though he felt conscious that the imitation was but a clumsy one, "it is by my hand that the King will fall."

"Are you mad?" said *A.*, with some contempt. "Do you yourself believe what you are saying?"

"No," said Ribbing; and this time his voice had the ring of conviction. "If I did, I should entreat you to fulfil the sentence which you have just pronounced immediately. But you will believe it. It was spoken by Noorna Arfridson."

The person whom he addressed gave a slight start. Was the move indeed a successful one? Whether it were or no, to have shaken the equanimity of that man of ice, even for one instant, was nothing less than a triumph; and death would come easier.

"What proof have you to give of this?" said the leader abruptly. "We have only your word for it."

"I should never have dreamed of asking the present company to rely on the word of a man of honour," said the young Count, shrugging his shoulders. "But it so happens that I have in my pocket a letter addressed to my mother, which contains a detailed account of the whole transaction. It is perhaps just possible that you will credit me, when I tell you that it has not been forged during the last ten minutes. As the first part of it refers to family affairs, I shall be obliged if you will consider it in the light of a private communication, only reading aloud that part of it which concerns the visit of His Majesty to the Sibyl."

A. took the letter, glanced rapidly over the first page, and began to read at the second, bending still lower over the embers to enable himself to decipher it.

"His Majesty is in excellent health. Were it not for the modesty which I inherit from you, my dearest mother, along with my brown eyes and my little straight nose, I should be tempted to sinful pride. His kindness knows no bounds.

"Yesterday, as I was crossing the North Bridge, I was surprised to meet him on foot and unattended, except by the Grand Chamberlain. I had often heard that he traversed Stockholm thus *incognito*, in order to find out as a man what is hidden from him as a king; but at Court we say more than our prayers occasionally, and you cannot accept everything, so I confess that I felt surprised. He made a sign to me not to take any notice of him, nodded to the Grand Chamberlain, who went on his way immediately, drew my arm within his own, and walked along by my side for a minute or two without speaking. Then he gave a low laugh, and said, with the arch, half-mischievous expression that is so charming when he condescends to be familiar, 'If I did not know what an excellent heart you have, my dear Count,—if I did not know that you are a man of high principle,—I should do well to be very much afraid of you.'

"In vain I begged him to explain his meaning. He only laughed.

"At last I became seriously uneasy, for I thought that some chance word or action of mine must have been misrepresented. You know what an atmosphere of scandal and backbiting it is; one is never safe for an instant.

" When he saw that he had alarmed me, he changed his tone at once.   Much as I have always loved him— indeed, after yourself and one other, there is none for whom I entertain so deep an affection—I think I never loved him so much as at that moment.   It was as though he were my elder brother, and could not, even in jest, cause me a moment of real pain.

"'Come, come!' he said, 'I was only in fun.   Tell me, Count, do you believe in soothsaying?'

"'No, sire,' I answered, more readily than my dearest mother would perhaps have thought right.

"'There is something in it, notwithstanding,' said he.   'But, in the present instance, I think the witch reckoned without her host.   Did you know that Fröken Arfridson was a witch, Ribbing?'

"'All fair ladies are witches, sire,' I replied.   'I must admit that I have never heard of this one.'

"'Fröken Arfridson is neither fair nor a lady,' laughed His Majesty.   'Pah, the horrid old hag! Yet, when I entered her dirty room, disguised as you see me, she got up instantly, made me three curtseys down to the ground, and said, " Be seated, sire ! " at once.   How did she know?'

"'There are portraits of your Majesty in every other shop window in Stockholm,' I observed, 'and the portraits are very like your Majesty.'

"'Sceptic!' pursued the King.   'She told my fortune in the grounds of a coffee-cup.   That our fate is written in the stars, I can easily believe—that were a royal thought—but the bottom of a coffee-cup, my dear fellow !   Even prophecy is become democratic. What dreadful days we live in !   When she had done, she sat for a long time, with her eyes shut ; then she screamed ; then she said in a whisper, so low that I could scarcely hear her, " Sire, 'tis a cruel end ! "

"'"What end?" I asked her.

"'"I dare not, sire ! "

"'"I insist.   Speak ! " I said, adopting the air with which I say to the Diet, " Be dumb ! "

"'She hesitated, or pretended to hesitate.

"'At length she said, trembling, " Sire, you will one

day be assassinated by the first person whom you meet on the North Bridge, after you leave this house."

"'I need not tell you, my dear Count, who was the first person I met.'"

Directly the reading stopped, there was a dead silence.

Ribbing watched intently, though without the intolerable sensation of suspense which had before oppressed him. He had done something. The weight of utter helplessness was gone. Be the result what it might, he felt happier. Some kind of change had come over the face of the leader, but whether the change betokened anger or relief, he could not feel certain. The rest were holding their breath. All about the room the shadows seemed to grow thicker.

At last a voice spoke out of the darkness : "I war with kings, not with the King of kings. Young man, go free !"

Count Ribbing's impulse was to rush towards the door, but he forced it back and merely rose from his chair, overmastered by the fear of showing that he had been afraid. He thought of nothing else at that moment.

The leader took the key from his lieutenant, and ushered him, with grave courtesy, into the hall. They might have been parting after a formal visit.

"Can I assist you to mount ? " he inquired.

"No, I am much obliged to you," said the Count, returning the other's dignified bend of the head.

But he had hardly sprung into the saddle before he was a boy again. Rising in his stirrups, turning half round in the direction of the house, and making a hollow of both his hands so that the sound should carry, he shouted with all his might in the courtly language that was, as he knew, best calculated to rouse the indignation of those within—

"Vive le Roi !"

CHAPTER IV

IN WHICH THE HERO REFLECTS

THE night was cold, the day was not yet born, but the sun at noon in midsummer had never shone upon Count Ribbing with such celestial radiance as did these fading stars.

Life danced in his veins and flushed his cheeks. Laughing aloud, singing and shouting, mad with the reckless joy of a caged animal set free, he raced along the high road, marking his fiery course by the sparks that flashed from the hoof of his excited steed.

"I am alive!" he cried; it was the first time he had ever felt surprised at that simple fact. The boughs of the sycamore trees, planted in long, straight rows on either side, in imitation of the poplar avenues of France, quivered as he went under, the rocks resounded, and the hills echoed his voice.

"I am alive!" he sang; then, with a sudden change of tone—

> "'We were young, we were merry, we were very, very wise,
>   And the door stood open at our feast;
>   When there passed us a woman with the West in her eyes,
>   And a man with his back to the East.'"

He had heard a beggar chant this once, when he came upon the man unexpectedly, in one of the lowest streets in Stockholm, returning from his day's work. The image of the jolly old fellow, caught at such an unprofessional exercise, just crossed his brain like some faint, thin impression saved from the forgotten experiences of a former life; but the words rose to his lips of their own accord, as doggerel will after a solemn crisis.

"Who sings my song?" exclaimed a thick, harsh voice. A ragged figure rushed instantly across the road at great risk to itself, and seized the horse's bridle, forcing it back with such haste that the startled beast reared on its haunches, and Ribbing had much ado to keep his seat. "Who sings my song?"

"One of the King's servants," said Ribbing.

"You lie," returned the voice. "A beggar sings it— a beggar at the Sign of the Black House, a beggar at the Sign of the Three Water Lilies, a beggar at the Sign of the Knight of the North. An alms of life from the Black House, an alms of love from the Three Water Lilies; but when the Knight of the North refuses both, sing that song where you will within a mile of St. Brita's Cross, and the Beggars will come to your aid!"

"Let me go!" said Ribbing, who scarcely noted this oracular speech. He thought the man was mad, and flung a piece of money upon the road to loosen the claw-like grip of his fingers from the rein.

"No," said the man. "You should not have sung my song. I take no money from those of my own trade. Good-night, beggar!"

The voice grew lower instead of louder as he let go, and Ribbing, who had raised his whip angrily, hesitated for full a minute; then he set spurs to his horse and galloped on and on, until the strange figure of his would-be associate mingled with the darkness behind him. "Good-night, beggar!" The expression, coming from the quarter whence it came, was so absurd that he burst out laughing. He thought of the black, bony figure, the black, long nails, and laughed the more; but his laughter broke short off in the middle.

On a sudden, the terror which he had doggedly resisted for the last dreadful half-hour within doors, not daring to look it in the face, raised up its face and looked at him.

There was nothing—no reason—only a scare and

panic ; the overbalancing of courage, which had hung
suspended, on the wrong side. For the first time in
his life, he felt that he was a craven ; that nothing on
which he had been accustomed to lean for support was
of any avail. All things, material and spiritual, seemed
to have melted into one hungry, brooding enmity.
There was no escape ; his young untested strength
was altogether cowed.

Rather the shadowy chamber ; rather the dark, un-
manlike men ; rather the sense of imminent doom and
that tight bracing of the nerves to meet and to endure
to the utmost ; rather anything than this empty, insignificant horror of a mere void—and no one by, not
even his worst foe, to shame him into the semblance of
self-respect.

Such a dizzy faintness overcame the lad, that he was
fain to dismount because his head was swimming and
his flaccid hand could no longer hold the reins.

The horse, after its wild career, was glad to stand still,
panting, by his side, where he lay in the frosty grass,
unable to breathe except in long-drawn sobs of stifled
vitality, sick with a sickness of heart which only the
fear of death causes, and that not more than once or
twice in the lifetime it would otherwise shorten.

He had the sense to soak his handkerchief in the
rime—for the feeling was, after all, more than half
physical—and to bind it loosely round his forehead.
After [a few moments of perfect stillness, of clinging
with all the energy he possessed to that one delicious
sensation of cold, the weight rolled off him, and he
remained, how long he knew not, in a blissful trance
of comfort, the world his friend, certain that never
again in life should he fear anything, unless it
were to break the spell of this perfect peace by any
movement.

The sensation, however, drifted off painlessly, and
he became his normal self and sat up, dazed, as though
he had but just returned from a journey into the
ultimate seat of consciousness of some unknown nature,
and scarcely recognised his own.

What was he to do ? Go on—that was obvious ; and,

climbing wearily into the saddle, he urged Sleipner forward along the hard, unending road. Out of the dim haze of his perceptions, certain definite images . floated up to the surface and grew distinct. He shivered yet, although the sickness was past, when he remembered those twisted antlers round the wall. He saw the firelight gleam upon the little fork of coral.

It was at once the most real and the most dream-like experience through which he had ever passed—the most real in after imagination, the most dream-like in its actual happening. It was so distinct that the process by which he recalled it appeared to be far more vivid than memory, yet so unusual, that he could hardly persuade himself he was awake. He repeated out loud the message to the King with which he had been charged, to make sure that he was still master of a formula which could give him the clue to his own identity. Until he got through this ordeal, it seemed to him that he recollected it only as people recollect a poem without the words or a tune without sounds. The young man who rode away from that door was a very different young man from the one who had ridden up to it; so different indeed, that he fell to considering next how things would have stood had he accomplished the greatest change of all—and died.

Never having seen a dead man, he had recourse to fancy, and quickly he beheld himself divided, his body stretched stiff and straight under the wall in the garden, while something that could not be seen, something that had no eyes, something more impalpable than a breath, more intangible than an essence, escaped.

He pursued his body. He saw it lowered into the grave; he went down with it, and, shuddering disgustedly, he saw what would happen there.

"But only for a time," he said. "After that, flowers."

He pursued his soul.

But that is a pursuit which none but the very young

undertake, and this same night had made him too old.

"Nineteen!" he thought.   "And Tala!"—

He rested on the word.   "If I were dead now, she would be living here without me."

"Tala!"

Some names are a perpetual prayer; this, whenever he thought of it gravely, was thanksgiving.   That night it seemed to be the only thing which had suffered no change at all.

Tears started to his eyes for the first time, as he bethought him of the tears that he had never seen in hers.   Had the danger been but a little farther off in space and time, he was capable of having wished himself dead to deserve them, for sentiment had more than its due share in his composition; but for the moment, fact held him fast in her grim claws, and he knew, as he did not always know either before or afterwards, the full value of mortal existence.

He recollected his mother too; but it was not the same egotistic luxury to ponder on her grief, for she had wept too much before, and was too well accustomed to sorrow ever to mourn as a girl mourns, when it is new.   The breaking of broken hearts is a poor achievement.   It might be worth while to leave the world to make Tala cry; the reflection that that pistol-shot would probably have killed her to whom he owed his being gave him but little pleasure.

Lastly he thought of the King.   Would the King have cared?   The answer was not long in coming.

"No."

And he worshipped more devoutly than before.

CHAPTER V

AT this point in his meditations, an indescribable sound, so faint that at first it was possible for him to think he had imagined it, struck on his ear.

He rode a few steps farther and heard it again — more distinctly this time.

A few steps farther yet, and it turned into music. Then, before he could make out what manner of music this might be, it was lost.

He had come out of a world of dreams into a world where things were beginning—in a lame, tentative way—to be real again. Now he passed a cottage, and another cottage. No queer faces grinned out of the window ; no strange, dark figure stood at the door. He looked hard to assure himself of this, for he felt an odd conviction that, if he had not looked hard and close, he should have seen them.

Each cottage that he passed, however, seemed less fantastic than the one before. When he came to two or three, huddled together at the entrance of an untidy village, he almost thought that human beings might inhabit here.

A voice confirmed the impression.

" Half after twelve at night, and a fine evening ! "

It was the old watchman, going his rounds with a lantern ; for the oil lamp, swung on a creaking chain across the little street, existed but to make darkness visible. The rough, homely voice was pleasant ; there was nothing unnatural about it ; and Ribbing stopped

an instant to ask the shortest way to the Castle of Carl
de Geer—although he knew this well enough—simply
for the pleasure of hearing it again.

"You are a late guest," said the old man, raising
his lantern, "but Carl de Geer never turned man or
beast from his door. Keep along by the lake side,
and a few minutes will bring you to it. Good-night,
young master !"

"A more fitting salutation than that of my friend on
the highway !" laughed the Count.

He had left the village some way in the rear, when
he stopped to reconnoitre ; it seemed to him that the
air was a thought less keen.

"I have ridden near upon three miles by now," he
said. "This must be the lake."

The wan glimmer of something that was not land
soon assured him that he was right. In spite of the
violent impatience that sprang up in him at the sight,
kindling the lifeless obstinacy, like that of a person
dreaming, with which he had hitherto pursued his
way, he compelled himself to ride with care, for it
was long since the path had been mended, and the
horse was but too likely to stumble upon the rough,
uneven ground. Young as he was, he had learnt
caution ; haste made him slow.

Yet it was all he could do to restrain a wild, ringing
cheer, when, rounding a corner suddenly, he saw,
straight in front of him, the Castle of Carl de Geer.

It stood on a small promontory, overlooking the
lake. He had expected to find it black and desolate,
the inhabitants all wrapped in slumber ; he beheld it
gleaming with light from every window. The music
was now clearly audible.

"Violins !" said he to himself. "It is the *Menuet
de la Cour* they are playing. I thought it had been a
merry tune. Out here it sounds like a dirge."

But sound has its perspective as well as light, and
that which distance makes pathetic, becomes, as we
approach it, familiar and practical. The wonderful
strain changed when he found the gate open, and,
hungry and weary as he was, the Count inspired

himself afresh with the recollection that he was the
bearer of great tidings. It was to a tune of triumph
that he rode gaily up the steep ascent and under the
heavy archway.

The archway also was lighted up; he could distinguish the well-known sign of the Three Water
Lilies, embroidered on the faded banner waving over
his head.

The door stood open ; no need to knock.

Within, the hall was filled with young men and
maidens, all in gala attire, the stiff brocade and the
powdered head-dresses of the girls showing in high
relief against a background of darkest oak, blazoned
with the shields of many different generations, amongst
which the Three Water Lilies held the most prominent
place. At the upper end stood she whom his eyes
sought, his cousin, Tala, in the act of stepping
forward to meet her partner, her hand held high in
his. She was one alone among her snowy-haired
companions, for the thick auburn tresses, which distinguished her, were raised in shining masses from
her white brow and drawn up from her little
neck, curling and coiling with devious grace, in
all their bright perfection of colour. Happening
to turn her head at that moment, she saw the
dark form upright in the doorway, the pale face
framed in the blackness of night, and, dropping her
fan in her hurry, rushed forward, with arms held out,
to meet him.

"Dolf! Dolf!" she cried. "His spirit! I knew
that he would come."

The groups of dancers divided, in consternation, to
let her through ; but when she had reached the
middle of the hall her courage failed, and she stopped
short—self-conscious—frightened by their wondering
eyes.

For a single instant Ribbing had hesitated. What
did she mean? Was he on this side death? Smiling
at himself for his bewilderment, restraining as best he
might his longing to take her in his arms and still the
outburst of nervous laughter to which she had given

3

way, he walked quietly up the hall and dropped on one knee before her.

"Very well done, upon my word!" sneered Tala's former partner, Baron Essen, to the lady beside him. "The fellow might get an engagement at the Theatre Royal, might he not? His Majesty likes that kind of thing."

"How now, you Wild Huntsman?" cried Ribbing's uncle, Carl de Geer, advancing to greet him. "The little one is weeping, I declare. What need to frighten us all by arriving in this costume? And at such an hour too!"

"What need indeed?" said Adolf, rising to his full height with the calm assurance of one who knows that the tidings of which he is the bearer are strange enough to make amends for whatever may have seemed odd in his behaviour. "What need indeed, when the Danes are besieging Gothenburg and threatening Stockholm—when the King himself is gone to rouse the peasants of Dalecarlia—when, unless we burn the fiery beacon on every hilltop, our homes and hearths will be the blazing torches, to light us on our way to exile? Come, fiddlers, strike up 'The Song of the Sword'! Give me your hand, sweet cousin. I myself, and all these gentlemen present, may have danced the Dance of Death before we meet again."

He had been carried beyond himself, and spoken as a young man never means to speak but sometimes does.

There was a momentary pause.

Then the violins struck up "The Song of the Sword," as though the King himself had commanded it; the gallants raised their weapons, inclining them until the glittering points touched in an arch of glory, and underneath he passed with Tala as lightly as though he had been the ghost that she thought him.

CHAPTER VI

A HOUSE DIVIDED

"AND now," said a dry voice, immediately on the conclusion of the dance, while the fiddles were still vibrating, "may we be privileged to inquire into the real sense of the masquerade? I, for my part, have no great taste for private theatricals, when public interests are at stake. Before I follow this infant Cupid to Gothenburg, whither he apparently proposes to lead myself and every other gentleman in the room, I should wish to inspect his credentials. Who knows whether he has been duly authorised by the Diet, or whether this is only another of the King's benevolent schemes for ridding Sweden of the flower of her nobility? Hästesko may be in prison, but we have not forgotten him.'"

There was a murmur of assent. Colonel Hästesko had refused to lead the troops in the war with Russia, but the nobles considered that the King had not been justified in undertaking it, and his arrest rankled freshly in the memory of many of those who were present.

Adolf stepped forward with blazing eyes.

"Gentlemen," he said, "you hear the accusation. It is to you that I make my defence. My orders are not signed by the Diet—there was no time to confer. It is but a day since the news was brought to His Majesty at the château de Haga, where I had the honour to be in attendance. In an hour's time he had despatched all the available troops to Gothenburg, had formed the citizens of Stockholm into a garrison, entrusting to their guardianship the Queen and her children, had started—accompanied only by two of his most intimate friends among the officers—for Mora, where he appointed me to meet him. You have heard all that there is to hear. The beacons must be lit upon every hilltop; the rendezvous is at Mora. Those of you who decline to obey the summons"—he turned slightly in the direction of Baron Essen—"will do well indeed to remember the fate of Hästesko."

"More heroics!" said the Baron, shrugging his shoulders. "It is as I thought. He has no authority from the Diet."

"He has no authority from the Diet!" echoed about the room.

"Traitor!" cried Adolf, and stamped his foot upon the floor. Several of those who were standing near him crossed over to Baron Essen.

"Nephew," said Carl de Geer, bending his brows, "the Baron is my guest—in consequence, he is yours also. Your youth alone, and your infatuation, can excuse an insult offered to one who is under the shelter of your own roof-tree. I demand that you instantly retract the offensive expression, which you made use of in the heat of the moment."

"I will not retract it," said Adolf indignantly. "I will repeat it, if you like, and with interest. Baron Essen is a traitor to his King and to his country; furthermore, he is a coward. He knows that he is free to insult a man who is bound on the King's service, and cannot stay to demand satisfaction. I call no roof-tree mine that harbours such people. Farewell, sir! I am your debtor for one night's loan of a horse. Saddle me the fastest in the stables, Bru, and be quick! My man will be here with the dawn; he will bring Sleipner to me to Mora and restore you your own. Adieu, Tala!"

Here it occurred to Adolf that the most provoking thing he could do before Baron Essen would be to embrace Tala, and he did it accordingly, with no emotion whatever except a calm desire to infuriate that person. As his cold lips touched her forehead, she whispered—

"The summer-house on the Reindeer's Crag!"

He touched her hand in token that he understood, strode out of the hall, followed by many threatening glances as he went, waited sullenly until the horse was brought round, flung himself on to its back, and rode off at a gallop.

He was very angry—so angry that he was not in a passion. When indignation hoists her white flag, not her red one; when she turns to ice instead of to fire, she is dangerous. Baron Essen had good cause to remember "The Song of the Sword." Adolf himself rode for a while like a man who has taken food and a draught of strong wine and is much refreshed, but the sensation, new and absorbing though it was, wore off after a little, and he began to feel light-headed, as if thinking were unaccountably easy and movement impossible. It was ten hours, at least, since he had tasted anything, and for the greater part of that time he had been on horseback. Eager as he was, he felt that he could not go farther. He had been delicately reared, and this was his first experience of privation. It was well for him that Tala thought of the hut on the Reindeer's Crag. The ascent was not hard, comparatively speaking, and at the top he knew there was a little deserted shelter, in which they had often played at keeping house together when they were children. There, at anyrate, he could sleep until daybreak, without the risk of being frozen on the bare ground.

Fastening his horse to the tall flagstaff outside, from which the Three Water Lilies were still floating, as he remembered them of old, he lifted the latch and went in.

The hut contained nothing but a few rough logs, standing on end, by way of chairs, and one larger than the rest, which did duty for a table in the centre. It was, of course, quite dark, but so much he distinguished by means of the bruises which he inflicted on himself as he stumbled about amongst them.

The first that came to hand was rolled over on the ground to make a pillow, and he wrapped himself up in his cloak and lay down.

Altogether overcome by fatigue, he was on the point of falling into a sound sleep, when a light tap at the door forced him back into consciousness. He closed his eyes obstinately, resolute that, come what might, he would not be defrauded of his hard-earned repose.

But the tap was repeated.

Now a person who is bent on slumber may, if he will, ignore a thunderstorm or an earthquake, but a little persistent noise, occurring at uncertain intervals, is enough to wake the Seven Sleepers of Ephesus; and Adolf sprang to his feet, with a muttered cry of "Go to the crows of Odin, whoever you are!"

The ungracious exclamation failed of its due effect, for the door was timidly pushed open, and an apparition, so like his dreams that it was better than the best of them, revealed itself on the instant.

There stood Tala, clothed from head to foot in snow-white fur, one or two locks of auburn hair straying from under the soft edges of her hood—the light of the torch she carried gleaming upon her flushed cheeks and in her radiant, red-brown eyes.

"Dolf! Dolf!" she said, half laughing, to conceal the pretty shyness, dearer to him now than all the dear familiarity which had existed between them almost ever since he could remember, "did you not hear me? Why did you not say 'Come in'?"

CHAPTER VII

A HOUSE AT UNITY

IF Adolf had been remiss about saying " Come in ! "
before, he certainly could not be accused of any
desire to keep the hut to himself a moment longer.

"How cold it is ! " said Tala, shivering, for all her
furs, as she put down the basket she carried. "My
poor, poor Dolf ! "

"Do not call me '*Poor* Dolf ! '" he said, with a
joyous laugh, taking the torch from her and thrusting
it sideways into a chink in the wall. "There's another
word that is better."

"What do you mean, dear Adolf ? "

"As if you did not know ! Tala, I thought you were
honest. Say it again, as if you did."

"I shall do no such thing. Give me your hand ! "
She stooped till her cheek touched it, as if by accident.
"You are as cold as ice. Put on these gloves
directly."

She pulled off the loose gloves, lined and trimmed
with fur, which were worn by the ladies of the North
in those as in these days, and tried to thrust Adolf's
fingers into them, laughing as she did so at his
awkwardness. "There ! That is beautiful ! But you
ought to be ashamed to find that they fit you, all the
same, a grown-up man like you ! Never mind ! I like
small hands. Baron Essen's are big. Oh, if we could
only make a fire ! Why, why did I not bring the
tinder-box ? How could I forget it ? "

"I have got a flint and some tinder in my pocket,
but what's the use of that ? There is no wood."

"You great gigantic stupid!" said Tala. "Don't you remember that the wood is always stacked here? Have you quite forgotten our wedding when you were ten and I was nine, and how we roasted potatoes to celebrate it? You faithless husband! Why, this is worse than my forgetting the tinder. There it is in the corner, faggots and boughs and all! It has got its dry leaves still; it will make a fine blaze. Not all at once like that—break it up, silly fellow! Now then, where is your tinder-box? Why, there was the torch all the time; we never thought of it! If we had something light to put at the top— Oh yes, I know!"

She pulled a book out of her pocket.

"What is that?" cried Adolf, trying to seize it; but the fur gloves made his hands feel like paws, and she held it behind her when he attacked in front, and over her head when he went round to the rear.

"Be quiet, Dolf! I brought it for you to read, because I thought you would be dull up here by yourself; but it's a stupid book—nothing but Voltaire's poems— and you had much better be dull than cold. Besides, Baron Essen gave it me."

"Allow me to help you tear it up!" said Ribbing; but Tala had made short work of it already, and the fire was beginning to crackle, and the smoke to curl up through a hole in the roof.

Then she turned to the basket.

"There's half a turkey, Adolf," she said apologetically. "I was very sorry I could not find a whole one, but the greedy people had eaten them all up."

"Ravenous though I am, dearest," said Adolf, "I think that I shall have enough with half. How your little arms must have ached! It weighs a ton at least."

"He *was* heavy," said Tala, with self-satisfaction. "It's Gobbo, the turkey-cock; he used to fly at you last winter. You recollect him, do you not? And there are some oatcakes and a jug of mead. Oh, I am so glad you have got a knife! I did not remember to bring one. Is it a very long time since you had anything to eat, Adolf?"

"It is a long time," said Adolf, pausing, with a

slight sense of shame, in the midst of his tremendous assault upon Gobbo, but falling to again instantly.

Tala seated herself on the log he had taken for a pillow, beside the fire. It did not give much warmth yet, but it gleamed brightly on her bright hair, and the flames leapt up as if her hands had a magnetic power of drawing them.

"You looked as if you were half starved," she said compassionately.

"Oh, a man soon gets used to that sort of thing!" said Adolf, with affected carelessness, charmed to have made an impression. "Are you quite convinced that I am not a ghost now?" he added, laughing.

She nodded, with some significance.

"But why did you think I was?" he continued, more gravely.

"Oh, I don't know!" said Tala, her shyness returning. She hesitated. "I—I had been thinking a great deal about you, Dolf."

"So had I been thinking a great deal about you, Tala, but I never thought you were a ghost."

"I do not know why it was," she said, her eyes filling with tears. "I could not bear it, if you were to die."

"But did you think I was in any danger to-night?"

"Oh no, of course not! How should I? I thought you were with the King at Stockholm."

He felt a sudden chill. To speak the truth, that wild cry of hers had delighted him; now the illusion was dispelled.

"I am very sorry I was so foolish," Tala said meekly.

Adolf sighed.

"Are you angry with me?"

"No. But how dreadful it is to think that you or I might be very ill—dying—and the other not know."

"I should know," said Tala softly; "I should know. I dream so often."

"But you do not believe in dreams?"

"No, because you told me not to; but they come all the same."

"I do not wish you to believe in childish superstitions

of that kind," said Adolf pompously.   " I am a follower
of the light of pure reason."

Tala was silent.

" Did you ever hear of Noorna Arfridson ? " he
asked.

" Yes."

" She told the King that I should kill him."

Tala shrank back in horror.

" Do you not believe that I should kill myself first ? "
said Adolf, with an imperious gesture.

" I do, I do," said Tala, flashing her great eyes full
upon him, as if to let him read in them the perfect
confidence she could not trust herself to utter.   " *You*
kill the King !   Why, you would die for him !"

Somehow or other, her words recalled the twisted
shadows of the antlers on the wall, the firelight playing
on the fork of coral.   If it were all to happen over
again— ?

" Yes," he said, with grave deliberation, answering
his own thought rather than her speech.   " Yes, I
would die for him."

It was not spoken as Tala had expected.

" What do you mean ? " she said quickly.

" All that I say."

" There is a change in you, Adolf.   You are older."

He smiled.

" You speak as people speak when they are old, when
they do everything by weight and measure."

" Is not that wise ? "

" It may be wise," said Tala.   " I will not love you,
if you do it.   I loved you first because you were
foolish."

" Indeed ?   That is a compliment, madame !"

" Baron Essen is wise ; he would never risk his life
for anything in the world except to save it.   It was he
who made them all wise to-night, so that they would
not listen.   I hated him."

" It is not for me to say you were foolish, then."

" I had another reason.   He looks behind my eyes
as you do.   If only he and I had not been dancing when
you came in !   He looked into my eyes ; he saw what no

one else but you has seen. He had no right to see it.
It was taking away what is yours. And in a
moment I knew it, and I hated him. I hated him so
much that I forgot you, Adolf."

"Poor mean beast!" said Adolf, with contemptuous
pity. "I do not hate him."

"You will some day."

He had never heard her speak so low except once;
and that was when she answered his first passionate
avowal.

"Do you think anyone ever fell in love with anyone
before—I mean like this, Adolf?"

"Yes," said Adolf promptly, "everyone."

"You must be wrong," she said, between jest and
earnest. "If it had been the same with everyone,
why should I mind his seeing? Oh no, we found it
out, you and I!"

"Your father and mother and mine found it out
first."

"But, Adolf,"—the note of suffering made her silvery
voice ring sharp,—"my father is wise too."

"Will he be angry with you for to-night?" said
Adolf, with some anxiety.

"I hope so."

He gazed at her in blank surprise.

"I never deceived him before. I do not like deceiv-
ing. I wish women could fight. These men could
go to-night to help the King and they will not.
Cowards! cravens that they are! But it was all
Baron Essen. If he had not been there, they would
have gone. He is a coward, Adolf—a coward, I
tell you!"

"If he be, I am sorry for him," said Adolf slowly.
He could not have spoken thus the day before.

"And I am sorry for him," said Tala, "sorry as the
Scotch General was for the coward in his army. I
cannot pronounce his name. Knut Hamilton told me
about it, the other day; he served in the Scotch war
more than forty years back. The coward was the son
of an old friend of his; the first time he ran away under
fire, the General sent for him, told him that he had no

business to be a soldier, and urged him to go away and be a merchant, a shopkeeper—what do I know? —some stupid, peaceful thing. The young man fell at his feet and wept, and prayed for one last chance. At length the General yielded. But when the swords clashed once more, and the balls whistled, and the shot fell, the coward was a coward again. He had turned his horse to fly, when the General came up with him. 'Your father's son is too good a man for the Provost Marshal,' said he, and he raised his pistol and fired, and the man fell dead to the ground. That is what should be done to all cowards."

"After all, they have wives and children," said Adolf, enjoying the sensation that he could afford to be magnanimous, as he took another long pull at the jug.

"Wives and children!" cried Tala scornfully. "What sort of wives can they be? No, no! They call it *wives and children*, but it is fear. Why are people afraid, Adolf? When you are far away, I often come up here by myself, and think and think how it would be to die. That is because I want you so. If I were dying, I should think of you. If what you say is true, and everybody has one to love, how can they feel afraid?"

"Shall I tell you a secret?" said Adolf, looking curiously at her. "When you are dying, you think of only one thing—how not to die. I know. I thought I was dying myself once—not lately,"—he saw the alarm in her eyes,—"a long time ago."

"You never told me. How was it?"

"It is not worth talking about. Do not look terrified; I am sorry I spoke of it. I thought you were afraid of nothing. Take care! What are you about? Your dress will catch fire."

She had sprung up from her seat, but stood gazing as if spellbound, until he dragged her away. The fire had caught the thin boards behind, whilst they were talking. A moment more, and the hut would be in a blaze; it was beginning to fill with smoke already.

"The first fire that we lit together will burn our

first house down," she said.   "This is the beacon that you wished to light upon the hilltop, Adolf."

"One toast before we go," he cried, lifting the jug to her lips.

"To the health of the King!" she said, just touching the edge.

"To the health of the King!" he shouted, draining it to the last drop, before he flung it over his shoulder.

They hurried out together, Adolf grasping the torch, which he had plucked from between the boards.

It was not a second too soon.   The little summer-house was dry, and burned quickly.   All at once the roof fell in with a crash, and the great tongues of flame shot up to heaven.

"Glorious! glorious!" he cried, brandishing the torch over his head in his excitement, and shouting until the mountains rang again.   "Everywhere they will see it.   They cannot fail.   The country will be up in arms to-morrow.   Glorious! glorious!"

He got no answer.   The fire in Tala's eyes went out; tears overbrimmed them.

"We lived together there," she said.   "Shall we ever live together again?"

He turned and looked.   She stood there, cold and white, in the fierce red gleam of the flames.   She took the torch and silently reversed it.   That was his last vision of her.   In the moment that came after she was too close for any vision.

Nor did he see a dark figure creep from behind the flagstaff and follow her, as she went down the hill.

CHAPTER VIII

THE rest of Adolf's journey was accomplished without misadventure. When he looked back on it in after-days, it shone out from his life, before and after, with a peculiar radiance. For the full delight of being young is not experienced till youth has received its first shock, and the full glory of independent action intoxicates for the first time then, when defeat, at the very outset, has been turned into victory.

It was autumn in the great woods. Everywhere their green was lightening into gold, deepening to crimson ; but man in his own springtime knows no change of the seasons, and if Adolf marked it at all, as he rode singing through them, it was only to rise in his stirrups to strike the highest bough that he could reach with his whip and make the leaves float down in golden showers around him, while he essayed to catch one here and there, in memory of an old game that he and Tala had played as children, when every leaf thus intercepted in its passage to the dark earth was called a "happy day." And many a "happy day" he caught, and the vision was not brighter than the present reality.

For he was not received in other houses as Carl de Geer had received him. It was the great nobles who hated the King of Sweden. The tenants of the large, outlying farms, to whom he was directed more especially to appeal, greeted him with enthusiasm, and promised help in men and money with all the eagerness that even Tala could have desired. They knew it was the King alone who had made the desert land flourish. They knew that the King alone could secure them, whether against foes from without, in the shape of the invading Danes, or enemies within, whose dissensions in the Diet of the realm had not seldom proved even more fatal.

One brought out an old stocking, and poured the money it contained into Adolf's hands, saying, "Take it! It is the life of my wife and children, when I am gone, but I would give it all for the life of the land The King's life is the land's."

One farmer's wife brought him her bracelets, another the silver ornaments she wore in her hair. "It is because of the King that I have them," said each in turn. "Let them go back to the King."

Where the men of the family were young and strong, they spoke little, but bent their heads gravely, and asked the time and the place at which the King expected them to meet him.

"We love the land; we know that the King loves it."

Where they were old and feeble, on the contrary, they talked so much that it was hard to get away. Adolf's sense of the ridiculous was sometimes sorely tried. In their anxiety to hear the latest news and their extreme credulity, no tale was so wonderful that it might not find due acceptance. On one occasion, he told the tiresome patriarch of the village through which he happened to be going, that the Court physician had certified that already the wings of an angel were growing out of the King's shoulders. Within an hour, five or six persons came to make inquiries concerning the length of the feathers.

One and all treated him with distinction, as an honourable and an honoured guest, a gentleman in whom the King reposed confidence; who was therefore worthy of every trust.

Here and there he met a man who had been decorated by Gustav with the Order of his greatest ancestor, revived by him to encourage, throughout his dominions, the pursuit of that honest alchemy which turns clay into precious metal. Then indeed he was welcomed almost as though he had been the King himself. His passionate admiration of the master whose very name had become a talisman in the most distant parts of the kingdom gained in intensity with every step he took.

For, whatever Gustav's private vices may have been, there is no doubt that he was a good lord to the people. The first, for generations, who had been born and bred amongst them, and could speak to them in their own language, it was he who had broken, without bloodshed, and at a single blow, the hated tyranny of the two great parties of the Hats and the Caps, under whom nothing could flourish except the base intrigues fomented by Catharine of Russia and Frederic the Great; it was he who had signalised his triumph by the abolition of torture; it was he who had filled the fields with labourers, the mines and factories with busy workmen.

As Adolf rode farther and farther into the northern province of Dalecarlia, as nature and man alike grew visibly wilder and wilder, he found that the sentiment of loyalty became more and more enthusiastic. In one rough village the peasants knelt before him, and almost kissed his horse's hoofs, weeping for joy.

"Look at our potato plots!" they said. "It was the King who taught us how to plant potatoes, where nothing else would grow. What should we have to eat, if it had not been for the King?"

And it was all that Adolf could do to refrain from laughter. As he looked at the earthy faces of those men, furrowed with black lines like the unyielding soil in which they worked, as he touched (not without secret repugnance) their hard, misshapen hands, he thought with wonder of the dainty and at times effeminate appearance of "the little gentleman with the scarlet heels," and marvelled, not once nor twice, how such an one could have learnt the secret way to their hearts.

The scenery around him recalled the stories which he had read as a boy of the wanderings of Gustav

Vasa. It seemed to him that he was riding not only far away from everything he knew, but far, far back in time. The face of the earth had not altered. The peasants spoke the rude lingo of their forefathers.

The rivers had not yet begun to freeze, and boats were still needful to ferry over the lakes; but as he crossed the Lillelf the thin ice covered it already to the eyes of his fancy, and broke once more beneath the weight of the uncrowned King. Once again Barbara Stigsdotter let him down from the window by a long towel, that the treachery of Brun Bengtsson and of her husband, Arendt Persson Ornflykt, might be defeated; and once again the audacious driver carried him at full gallop across the frozen waters of Lake Runn, and the smoke from the copper-mines of Falun veiled him from the sight of men, as though a second Elijah were ascending the bank in his chariot of fire.

The memory of all these things was in the air. In the desolate country, where there is little or no progress in thought, life may stand still for centuries and yet keep fresh and strong. It is but yesterday in such places, though it may be long ago in the towns. Adolf, who had always thought that it was long ago, began to feel the romantic past close round him. All that he saw and heard encouraged the illusion. The solemn wind that swept the sound of the sea from the pine branches had lifted Gustav's hair, had murmured thus in Gustav's ear, when he lay sleeping below them three nights together, hungry and thirsty but for the food the peasants brought him of their own scant substance. On "The King's Height," above the wild, wide, reedy marsh, still stood the tall fir itself that had sheltered the outcast. Here was the very bridge under which he lay hidden. Speeding northward and ever northward, and flying far before himself on the wings of the Muses' galloper, Adolf crossed the ridges of the hills and saw the whole earth white with snow, while over it, on their wooden skates, glided the two dark figures of Engelbrecht and Lars of Kettilbo, the fleetest skaters of all the countryside. Over the Western Dalelf he followed them, into the lonely

4

village of Sälem, the last upon its shores, into that miserable hut at the foot of the grim Norwegian Mountains, where lay the King who was about to place them as an everlasting barrier between himself and the ungrateful kingdom that had failed to respond to its lord.

The rocks and trees, even the thundering waterfalls, whose arrowy shafts shone bright beneath the moon, were yet instinct with loyalty. The men and women kept something of the fixity of the great forests in which they had been reared. They had not changed their minds and forgotten, like the people in cities ; to them Vasa was still alive in the young and gallant son of his house, who bore his name, who spoke his language and their own. Little need was there for Adolf to set forth to them that the Danes were the enemies of Sweden ; for more than two hundred years they had never thought the Danes anything else.

They laughed with savage joy when they heard him speak, they groaned at the very name of Denmark, they caught up stones from the ground and flung them southwards, they came in crowds to swear that they would lend a hand in the destruction of their ancient foes. They thought it was but the other day that Swedes had beaten them. The triumph of Gustav Vasa's men at Sönnebohed was a recent occurrence here. At night Adolf heard them singing in their huts—

" We drove the Danes to Brunbäck's wave,
Thus, thus, and thus !
And Brunbäck's waters were their grave,
Thus, thus, and thus !
Out upon Christian, dog and slave,
No Christian king for us ! "

The words fell upon his heart and stuck there. He remembered the old legend of his house : how the tyrant, Christian, had ordered the execution of the two children of Sir Lindorm Ribbing, the elder of whom was eight, the younger six ; how the little one, not understanding what had happened, said to the headsman in his baby accents, " Dear man, you must not stain my collar as you have stained my brother Axel's! Mamma will whip me, if you do." The headsman flung away the axe and fled, but Christian's soldiers completed the work for him; and ever since, in times of tyranny—so ran the tale—the spectre of a child, unseen by any save the destroyer, had warded off mischance from the chief of the Ribbings. He never believed the story before. Now, in the long, dark aisles of the forest, where no sound but the weird singing of the peasants roused the echoes at nightfall, he had no choice but to think it true. Was it the spectre of the child that preserved him in the Black House, where the firelight shone on the antlers and on the little fork of coral?

He was nearing the mines now. The trees were growing smaller and scarcer, the ground even more sterile. It was morning when he left the last of the firs behind him, and rode across a dreary tract of burnt and blackened heath. Such men as he met were little, swarthy, thick-set, with bony, long arms, and dull, blinking eyes. They were not likely soldiers, so he thought, but they were all going one way.

"To Mora?" they said, when he asked the road. "Yes, yes; to Mora, to meet the King!"

"It was just such creatures as these who travelled miles and miles to hear Vasa speak — to win his battles for him," reflected Adolf. "I could think that I was going to hear him myself. What was his famous speech in the churchyard at Mora?"

As he was taxing all his powers to recollect, he came to the crest of a plateau, across which he had been riding for some time, and saw below him such a strange realisation of the scene his imagination had conjured up, that he stopped short, out of breath with surprise. The ground was black with human beings, and from the open doors of a quaint little stone church with a copper roof to it, more and more came pouring out every moment. A single figure was standing, slightly raised above them, on the summit of a hillock just outside the boundaries of the churchyard. It appeared to be that of a miner, wearing the rough costume of the Dalesmen—a short black jacket, grey stockings, a round cap with a silver lining. He knew it all well. Many and many a time he had seen it in his boyish visions.

" *Right over the hills of Essund, lying directly south, stood the low noonday sun. His dazzling light was cast upon the fields of snow. A fresh north wind was blowing, and the men of Mora think the north wind a good sign.*"

The words of the old history that he had learned as a child came back to him. There lay the hills of Essund directly south ; there was the low noonday sunlight upon the fields of snow, and the wind blew steadily from the north. There stood the strong deliverer.

Scarcely knowing what he did, between dreaming and waking, Adolf leapt from his horse, and, flinging the reins to a boy on the outskirts of the crowd, plunged into the thickest of it, eager to see and hear. The King's side face was towards him. He caught the magnificent profile clear against the sky, he heard the ringing tones of the commander.

"Men of Mora," said the King, "I speak to you on sacred ground. The voice of Gustav Vasa is the voice that you hear to-day. Once more the Danes are upon us ; the stranger defiles the holy places. Once more the nobles have betrayed their trust. Once more the King appeals to the nobility of his people. He needs your hands to fight for him, your hearts to support him. Say, will you give them ? "

There was a moment's silence, for something in the attitude of the man, something in the proud humility of his utterance, called for tears rather than for applause.

Adolf's own eyes were wet.

Then there arose a cheer, the like of which he had never heard, and never heard again. The earth rocked beneath him, and the sky over him.

It had hardly died away, and he was yet dizzy and bewildered with the wild echo of it, when a broken voice behind him exclaimed—

" The face of the King is as the face of an angel."

"Ay," said another voice, the tones of which recalled something to Adolf, though what it was he could not define, "the face of an angel! But he has two faces, you know."

"What do you mean?" said the first voice angrily.

"No offence," rejoined the other. "An accident of birth, that is all. But the two sides do not correspond. Look!"

The King turned round to speak to someone, and the fact that one side of his face was indeed different from the other struck Adolf for the first time.

CHAPTER IX

TWO GENTLEMEN LAY A BET

WEARIED as he was, for he had had but little sleep for some nights past, and had risen before daybreak, Adolf repaired immediately to his Colonel, who showed him a written order from the King, to the effect that he was to give him the verbal message from Stockholm, and to deliver up the papers and other effects with which he had been entrusted, as well as the diary of his reception in every village. This he did faithfully—though in his secret heart he was much vexed that the King had not sent for him in person. Two incidents, however, were omitted from the diary. He did not mention his uncle's conduct, nor did he allude to the strange encounter with the four men at the Black House, as he had called it, without thinking, ever since his interview with the beggar. He had promised Engeström that he would say nothing about the letter; and besides, it would have been difficult to account for his escape, without misunderstandings. This was the reason that he gave himself; perhaps another and a deeper one underlay his reluctance to speak.

The Colonel was standing, notebook in hand, in a large barn or cow-shed not far from the church, busily enrolling those miners who had come forward, after the King's speech, to offer their services—the magistrates having resolved to equip a body of twelve hundred volunteers at their own expense. The atmosphere was heavy and malodorous, and Adolf had to wait some time; for the enthusiastic recruits were hustling and

jostling each other in their eagerness to assume the
white scarf, and some confusion prevailed. When his
turn came, he was simply informed that his papers
would be taken to the King at once, and that a lodging
in the town had been reserved for him, whither he had
best betake himself at once to await further orders.

There was an unacknowledged disappointment, a
feeling of flatness about all this. It was hard to be
spoken to once more as if he were a boy at school, hard
to give up the rôle of knight for that of an insignificant
pawn in this tremendous game. He had ridden into
camp, conscious that he was a highly important person,
without whom the war could not be carried on. Now
that nobody seemed to think there was anything
extraordinary about what he had done, he began to
wonder why he had ever thought so himself, and to
bless his stars that thoughts are not audible. A certain
sense of humour was latent in Adolf Ribbing, which
circumstances afterwards developed—he used to say
that he had been frightened into fearing no one—but at
this time he was keenly alive to ridicule, and there is no
form of it more dreadful in the eyes of a sensitive young
man than that which attaches to one whose pretensions
are out of proportion to his achievement. He had honestly
believed that nobody else could accomplish what he
had accomplished, and lo and behold, any fool could do
it! Other aides-de-camp were spurring in from all
parts of the country. They looked weary as he did.
As for their lists, there was no difference that he could
see ; they had beaten up as many recruits, or more.

He mounted his horse again, and rode slowly into
the town. His thoughts were all confusion. So late
as yesterday he had been his own master and ruled
many others into the bargain ; now, even as a servant,
no one on earth appeared to need him. A dim,
unjustifiable suspicion of ill-usage fought with a growing
conviction that nature had made him insignificant—
that he never could be anything else. He found no
stable seat upon the see-saw of his youth ; now he was
sent suddenly flying into mid-air, and now he strove in
vain to rise an inch from the ground. He had no

confidence in himself, and too much.   A child gives, a man sells; but between the two there is a creature who flings away all that he has, and finding that he gets no acknowledgment because he has not set a price upon it, begins to wonder if his all be really what it seems to the world in general—a mere nothing—and to base such self-reliance as he may possess on what he will do in the future, not on what he has done already.   He does not know—for only experience can teach—the worthlessness of the most magnificent promise compared with the smallest actual fulfilment, but he is irritably conscious of building on a foundation that must be invisible to others, strong though it may appear to himself.

The crowded streets were lonely indeed to Adolf Ribbing, after the blissful solitude out of which he had come.   The world was unaccountably full of people, he thought, and of noises; it made his head ache.   The friendly indifference of a fir tree cannot wound, but the indifference of a fellow-mortal soon becomes hostile. Here, every man was a fortunate rival; he knew, at least, who he was and what he had got to expect. And Adolf, who knew neither, longed for the fir trees again.

It occurred to him to feel forlornly glad that Tala was not there.   He recollected his little display of boastfulness to her.   At this moment, probably, she was sitting upon the Reindeer's Crag, picturing to herself his glorious arrival, to the sound of trumpets.   Of course he should never marry her now; he should die neglected and unknown, where all the neglected and unknown do die, in a garret.   Much better so!

He found out his lodging at last—it was in a back street, with a back window that looked out on a back court; not a bad substitute for the garret as he conceived it.   He threw himself on the bed, and fell fast asleep, rather expecting never to wake.

By the time he did awake, however, he was himself again—not the conquering hero who had got up in the morning, nor the abject beggar who had lain down in the afternoon.   A good meal still further restored him to his usual condition; and he had gone so far as to wonder whether there were such things as theatres in the good town of Mora, when a note from the Colonel was handed in to him.

With a fluttering heart he broke the seal and read—

His Majesty desires to see you at 10.30 *p.m. at " The Vasa Arms."*

His Majesty desires to see you.   Whether this form of speech signified approval or disapproval, Adolf had no means of finding out, as he was too shy or too proud to ask.   His nervous diffidence returned upon him with twofold force.   He had looked forward to a special summons on his arrival, but nothing occurred; now, all these hours after, what did it mean?

He tried to reason with himself, but to small purpose. At his first introduction to Court life, a few months earlier, he had behaved with perfect ease.   Brought up at a Military School in Berlin, where public opinion was by no means favourable to Gustav III.—returning for his brief holiday to a home where he was accustomed to hear his father's ironical remarks—Adolf had come prepared to find his sovereign's character fit food for mirth and mockery.   Perhaps the very want of sub-servience with which at first he had conducted himself, attracted one whom flattering speeches wearied.   In any case, the King treated the boy with marked dis-tinction, and Adolf, yielding quickly enough, became convinced that all the rumours which he had heard to the disadvantage of this "Prince of good fellows," were quite unfounded.

His father was dead.   His mother, gratified in spite of herself by the kindness with which her child had been received, and not unwilling to let herself be conquered by his urgent representations, began to give way.

Then came the war with Russia.

Prevented by transient illness from following the King to the field, Adolf fumed and fretted at home. He was one of those who had heard Gustav boast that he would write his name on the pedestal of the statue of Peter the Great in Peter the Great's own city.

When the defection of the troops rendered the fulfilment of the threat impossible, at the very moment of
triumph, Adolf had no words in which to express his
contempt for his fellow-soldiers, his ardent admiration
of the man whom even such reverses as these could
not daunt.   He had joined the King immediately—with
what consequences we have seen.   Loyalty was become
a consuming passion.

He longed and dreaded to be near his leader, almost
as a lover longs for and fears his mistress.   A word, a
look of commendation would be heaven ; but this he
dared not hope for.   In vain did he assure himself that
he had done his best, that it did not become him to
think of results.   Enthusiasm had sapped his independence.   He felt as if a frown from the King would
annihilate him.

It was some consolation—not much—to perform an
elaborate toilet.

He reached "The Vasa Arms" long before the
appointed hour, and hung about the gate of the
courtyard miserably enough, thinking that he would
give a hundred thousand riksdalers to go in and
get the interview over, until the moment approached
for him to enter, when he discovered that he would
have given two hundred thousand only to stay without.

The yard was full of servants hurrying hither and
thither with torches in their hands, their long flowing
streamers and the glimmering candles in the lanterns
which some of them carried striping and blotching the
darkness.   Overhead in the gateway, an old oil lamp
swung to and fro.

Adolf was about to try and force his way through,
when a couple of lacqueys ran full tilt against each
other just in front of him, stopping the road.

"Out of the way, you fellows," he cried imperiously,
not sorry to vent his over-excitement in abuse.   "Be-
gone, I say !   There's no room for you here."

"The more angels, the more room," said the same
voice he had heard in the morning.

Adolf looked round, but it was impossible to identify

anyone in such a crowd, and the lacquey had swiftly lost himself among lacqueys.

"Room! room for His Royal Highness the Duke of Sudermania!" shouted the sentinel who was guarding the gate, as he saluted.

Adolf doffed his cap and stood aside.

There was nothing for it but to wait now.

The brother of the King was to start that night for Lexand; so Adolf gathered from the remarks of those about him. His horse stood ready at the foot of the steps, a groom holding it. He came down booted and spurred, chatting affably to a gentleman of his suite, and got into the saddle; but no sooner did the groom let go the bridle than the horse, frightened perhaps by the glare of a torch that was suddenly whisked past its eyes, made a violent plunge and threw the Duke, who was not yet firm in his seat. He would have landed head foremost on the pavement but for Adolf, who caught him in his arms and thus broke the force of the tumble. In the hurry and bustle all round no one else had observed what it was that frightened the animal.

"I am much obliged to you, sir," said the Duke, laughing, as he extricated himself. "You have saved me from a bad fall. May it be my good fortune to save you from just such another, one day!"

He lifted his plumed hat and rode off over the Platz, the people cheering as he went, for the hero of Hogland was just then, for the only time in his life, deservedly popular. (They recollected how, at a critical moment, he had seized the match from one of his artillerymen and threatened to blow up his ship then and there, if he could not get help.) Adolf was left staring stupidly after him.

"It is never permitted to anyone in heaven to stand behind another and to look at the back of his head," said the voice again. "It stays the influx from the Lord. Besides, that angel has one face, not two. You keep a diary; put down in it the date on which you saved him from a fall. It is to your advantage to remember; but he may think it is to his advantage to forget."

"It would be much to my advantage to know who you are," said Adolf, speaking rather loud and gazing now in one direction, now in the other. "This is the third time I have heard your voice, but you have the fairies' fern-seed—you walk invisible. I shall not look for you again. If you wish to continue the conversation, I must ask you to show yourself."

"You are wrong," said his interlocutor. "This is the fourth time you have heard my voice. You have looked for me twice, and the third time is lucky for looking. But not to-night, I counsel you. Wait until the moon has changed, say, for her three-and-twentieth changing. Look for me then, the third time!"

Of course Adolf looked immediately, but in the crowd behind he could distinguish no one, and he was too much afraid of being late for his audience to do more than glance round before he made his way in.

He found the King upstairs in the best parlour, seated at a rough wooden table near the fire, reading letters. He did not even turn his head as the young lieutenant was ushered in, and from this fact, Adolf, while he bowed profoundly, augured ill, and instantly began to feel a desperate kind of satisfaction, as if he had got over the worst and should not mind now, happen what might.

"The new tenor at the Royal Opera has a bad cough," observed Gustav abruptly, after the lapse of some minutes. "They will not be able to mount Gluck's *Armida* for a week or two."

"Indeed, sire."

Adolf took no manner of interest in the new tenor at the Royal Opera. It was as if the King had said, "You are a silly boy, not fit for the serious business which I entrusted to you."

"The old Duke of Richelieu is very ill," continued the King, after another pause, still without looking up.

"Really, sire?"

The old Duke of Richelieu interested Adolf, if possible, even less than the new tenor. It was as if the King had said, "You are a silly boy, not fit for any serious employment in the future."

"You have never been in France, I think?" said the King.

"No, sire; nor have I any desire to go there at present."

"Why not?"

"Your Majesty has made Sweden too enjoyable."

Adolf was half amused and half annoyed to find himself repeating a sentiment which he entertained with the sincerity of his whole heart in the glib compliment of a professed courtier.

The King smiled.

"You are quite right. It is not a good moment. The treasury is paying three-fifths of its obligations in money and two-fifths in paper."

"Sire, if the treasury were paying a hundred per cent., I would not change this country for any other."

The King lifted his large blue eyes, the pale colour of which contrasted oddly with the vividness of their expression, and fixed them full on Adolf.

"The Queen of France has wept," he said.

There ran through Adolf the same electric shock which had startled the rough populace but a few hours before. It tightened and stiffened his figure, so that he grew visibly taller, and stopped his breath.

"When may I go, your Majesty?" The words were scarcely audible, but they cried aloud in the eyes that answered Gustav's.

"There spoke the true son of the North," said the King. "Not yet! Not yet! We must see to our own borders first. Look to the *Groschen* and the *Thalers* will look to themselves! How have you sped? The contribution in money is larger than I hoped for. What was the disposition of the people?"

"Sire, they have but one wish—to beat the Danes—to die for your Majesty."

"Well!" said the King, with a careless gesture of the hand; "those are two wishes, and quite distinct. How many from Lake Runn did you say?"

Adolf was taken aback. He could not remember, but he guessed boldly.

"Five hundred, sire."

"Four hundred and ninety," said the King, knitting his brows. "You must be more exact, young man. Still they are coming in on all sides. We shall have three battalions at Mora. How did Carl de Geer receive you?"

Adolf blushed and remained silent.

"Forgive me, sire," he said at last. "Carl de Geer is my uncle."

"Oh!" said the King quickly. "He has a daughter, I suppose?"

Adolf looked up in surprise, but recovered himself almost at once and said simply—

"It was she who fired the beacon which brought many of the country folk to the royal banner, sire."

"Is it even so?" said the King. "Then is she a good daughter to Sweden, although a bad one to Carl de Geer. Was she alone?"

"Not, sire, upon that occasion."

"So Mercury played Cupid by the way," said the King. "I should advise you, for the future, not to confound those parts. Were there any other gentlemen present when Carl de Geer chose to insult my messenger?"

"There was one gentleman present, sire, to whom, in my judgment, the refusal of all the rest was owing."

"In *your* judgment!" said the King, with the faintest possible shade of irony; faint as it was, though, Adolf caught it, and would have given all he had to recall the expression. "Who was this gentleman?"

"Baron Essen."

"In my judgment, sir," said the King, "you make a mistake. Baron Essen is one of my few friends. He was with me in Italy. Times must have changed indeed, if he be found among my enemies. Tell me what happened?"

As baldly as he could, Adolf related all that had passed, while the King sat cross-legged, playing with the fringe of the long blue scarf of the Order of the Seraphim, which fell in a becoming manner across the silver brocade of his overcoat.

"You are not a good *raconteur*," he said, when Adolf paused, not because he had come to the end, but because he did not know how to go on. "I should doubt your having made a good speech. Some people can make speeches"—he glanced down again at the blue scarf—"and some people cannot. For myself, I distrust the people who can. For this reason, among others, I believe all that you say. Baron Essen has, without a doubt, gone over to the enemy. Whatever his price may be, it will have to be paid. I cannot afford to lose him ; his estates are too large."

"Your Majesty has many worthier friends," observed Adolf.

"Where are they?" said the King, shrugging his shoulders. "I was but a few years older than you are, when I thought myself very clever for saying to Monsieur de Marmontel, 'Men have few friends—men who are kings have none.' But I have proved the truth of it since, as I never intended to prove it."

He sighed heavily.

Something told Adolf that he ought to have gone down on one knee and protested ; but he withstood the inclination and—the next moment—wished he had followed it.

"Have you any uncles at Gothenburg?" said the King, in the tone of one who resumes business. "Any uncles with daughters, I mean?"

"No, sire."

Did this imply that he was to be sent on to the beleaguered city? The blood sprang to Adolf's cheeks and the fire to his eyes. He waited impatiently.

"A good thing too!" said the King. "Gothenburg, I may tell you in confidence, is in very great danger."

"Sire"— the young Count began eagerly ; but the King went on, without noting the interruption.

"I have just received the last despatches from Duretz. He begs for further instructions, but he must get on as well as he can without them. I dare not go yet myself; I am bound to Lexand—to Great Tuna—to Falun—to rouse the peasants there. I do not despair of fifteen thousand volunteers in the end, but I shall have to work hard; and the messenger would run too great a risk. There is no one whom I can trust."

"Sire," said Adolf,—and this time he found it easy enough to kneel,—"trust me! I will carry your instructions safely. I will defend them with my life."

The King smiled good-naturedly, and shook his head.

"That is too precious to be thrown away on any such wild-goose chase," he said. "Your mother is a widow, is she not, and has no other child? Young men are selfish; I have always observed that."

"When your Majesty first risked life itself for Sweden, your Majesty's mother was a widow."

"Well answered, upon my word!" said the King, laughing outright. "He quotes my example against my precepts. And how about your uncle's daughter, Sir Malapert? What would she say to it?"

"My uncle's daughter is heart and soul with my father's son, may it please your Majesty!"

"And how about myself?" said the King. His voice was gentle.

The room swam round with Adolf. Was it possible that the King really cared for him?

"Sire," he cried, "if you knew"— He could get no further

"I do know," said the King gravely. "Forgive me, my dear Count! I wished to see if you were in earnest. I am convinced. You have appealed to me by my own youth; when I look at you, I see myself as I was. I can no longer resist your entreaty. Go, in the name of fortune, and may the luck of all the gods go with you!"

"You shall not regret the confidence that you have placed in me, sire," said Adolf, finding his voice with difficulty.

"Of that I have no doubt," said the King. He took up a flask which was lying beside him, uncorked it, and poured out the wine it contained in a stream on the table.

"This is the route," he said, tracing a zigzag line

of crimson with his finger, upon the wood. "This red blot here is Gothenburg. There you will cross the river. If you meet the enemy, you must trust to your own wits to get through. They have not yet effected a landing, but they may contrive it before long. At this point you had better stick to the road; I have been told that it is wisest to do so, although it seems to be a round. You take me?"

"Perfectly, sire."

"If you stay long enough at Alengsab, remember to get a pair of silk stockings; they are the only wear for soldiers—in case of accidents, you know. Ask to see the Grand Chamberlain, Marshal Levenhaupt, at six to-morrow morning. He will provide you with money and give you the despatches for the General. Tell Duretz to hold out till I come, if the Danes batter down every spire in the city. You understand? The place is hard pressed, and Duretz is a sack of potatoes. I tell you this because you will have found it out for yourself an hour after your arrival. I look to you to keep up their courage. There is one true man among them, Lieutenant-Colonel Hans Axel Fersen, the son of my old enemy, Senator Frederick. Take him this letter from me. Point out that it is sealed with the *fleur-de-lys*. Commend me to him! This"—he took an envelope from a half-open drawer at his side— "contains the brevet which makes you a captain. It was destined for that one of my lieutenants who should bring in most recruits to our army. I have much pleasure in presenting it to you, sir. If you can make Duretz hold Gothenburg till I come, you may ask what you will of me afterwards. No thanks! Thank me with deeds, not words. Farewell, my Mercury! The watchword at the gate will be *The Queen of France*. Remember!"

"You do me too much honour, sire," said Adolf, quite overpowered with joy. He kissed the hand which the King extended to him, and left the room hurriedly. As he was going downstairs, he met one of his acquaintances, Count de La Gardie, arm-in-arm with another gentleman of the Court.

5

"Ha, Ribbing!" cried the young Count. "Where are you off to?"

"To Gothenburg, with despatches," said Adolf, in a much louder voice than was necessary.

"Alone?"

"Alone."

"Lucky dog!" said his friend. "When shall we get there, I wonder? Well, good-night, and a prosperous journey to you!"

The door had hardly closed on Adolf, when the other gentleman turned to the Count, and said, holding out his hand as he did so, "My seven hundred riksdalers, if you please!"

"I do not understand you."

"Is not that Count Adolf Ribbing, who told us the story of the prophetess?"

"It is."

"Did you not lay a bet with me, after Count Ribbing had left, in consequence of a disagreement between us as to his prospects? I said that they would be materially affected by that story; you, I believe, held otherwise."

"I do not see that you have proved your point. On the contrary, my dear fellow, it is you who owe me seven hundred riksdalers. The King has promoted him."

"The King has promoted him; yes. But he goes alone to Gothenburg. Have you never read the Second Book of Samuel, 'Set ye Uriah in the forefront of the hottest battle'? You will find the words in the 11th chapter and at the 15th verse."

"I never heard that David followed Uriah to the forefront of the hottest battle himself; that seems to me to alter the case."

"Oh, if you think David is going to pursue that line of conduct, I withdraw my demand for the present," said the other. "I am quite content to wait for a while. We shall see."

Gothenburg! Gothenburg! and *The Queen of France!* rang all that night in Adolf's ears. However, he was a prudent as well as a romantic young man, and before he went to bed he got pen and paper, and—smiling as he did so, at the recollection of the airy voice whose behests he was following—he made a memorandum.

14th September 1788.—Caught the Duke of S. in my arms as he fell from his horse. H.R.H. expressed the hope that he might one day save me from misfortune.

This he enclosed in a letter to his mother; there was no need to ask her to keep it.

The King, meantime, remained where Adolf had left him. When he had finished his despatches, he sat a long, long while, his gaze fixed thoughtfully on the fire. Sometimes it was full of marching armies. More often he only saw one face in it.

"The prediction is false," he muttered to himself. "The prediction is false."

When he was quite certain of it, the King seldom said a thing twice.

CHAPTER X

A HAPPY man was Count Ribbing to take the road again. Travelling suited his restless mood just then. It gave him plenty of leisure for long dreams of the King and of Tala.

He was prepared to meet with tremendous difficulties ; he met with none. Nature and man seemed to have entered into a conspiracy to send him gladly on his way. By day the frosty sun shone steadily ; by night the people in the towns and villages sheltered him as though he had been their own child instead of a stranger. As he drew nearer and nearer to the coast, the equinoctial gales began to blow, and he fancied that he could taste already the saltness of the strengthening breeze.

Impatient as he was to arrive, he followed the King's directions to the letter, even when they appeared to lead him out of his course. It might have been about five o'clock one evening when a soft, full, intermittent noise broke heavily upon his ear, and he knew that he had come within sound of the Danish guns, the army lying far to the north. The spirit of silent fury braced every nerve as he rose in his stirrups and shook his clenched fist threateningly at the sky ; it seemed as if he had heard a shot fired at his mother.

He pushed on eagerly, and came within sight of Gothenburg about twenty-four hours later. A city of grey, flat air, relieved on still and dusky fire, lay before him. Above, a single star peered in and out of thin, torn, flying fragments of fleecy cloud. Tower

upon tower, spire upon spire, soared up from the
surrounding houses and drew the whole mass nearer
to the low, overhanging sky. Beyond, the great grey
waters stretched away and away to meet the dull
horizon.

The sentinel, who was walking up and down in
front of a drawbridge that led to the ancient fortress
in which the General resided, hoisted his musket and
uttered a challenge, when he saw Adolf approaching.

"*The Queen of France!*" said Adolf promptly, recall-
ing his instructions.

The sentry lowered his musket, and signalled to the
man in charge to open the gates. The bridge was
quite deserted at that hour, except for a tall, dignified
person, who stood leaning over the rail, gazing far out
to sea. As he was close to the gates, he overheard
the challenge and the reply, and, turning quickly
round, confronted the King's messenger as he came
through.

Never did Adolf forget the keen impression of that
moment. The stillness, the brooding twilight, the
ethereal spires, had filled him with a sense of happy
awe. The face that looked upon him out of it all bore
stamped upon the beauty of the features the mark of
silence unbroken, of an inveterate melancholy. With
the swift egotism of the young, Adolf thought that he
himself should look like that if Tala were dead.

"Pardon me!" said the stranger, removing his
broad-brimmed three-cornered hat. "I think you
come from the King? It is possible that you may
have some message for me. Hans Axel Fersen, at
your service!"

"I have a letter for you, sir," said Adolf, producing
it. "The King bade me commend him to you.
Further, he asked me to point out to you that it is
sealed with a *fleur-de-lys*."

"Did he indeed?" said the other, shrugging his
shoulders. "His Majesty is often pleased to jest."

"More often than you are, I think," said Adolf, for
the icy chill of Fersen's tone had not failed to strike
him unfavourably.

"Did you mean to imply anything more than the literal sense of your words, sir?" said the Count, laying his hand on his sword.

"Nothing in life," said Adolf, laughing. "Your pardon, if I have by chance offended you; though why the King should not seal with a lily or with ten dozen lilies if so it pleased him, I am at a loss to imagine. What do you think of the state of the town?"

"That it will fall within a week, if the King does not come to the rescue in person. Duretz is only waiting for the first opportunity to surrender without loss of personal credit."

"You do not say so," cried Adolf. "The white-livered, black-hearted brute!"

"I am not displeased to hear you use that expression," said Count Fersen, still very gravely. "It is, however, the duty of a subordinate to speak respectfully of his superior officer."

"Do *you* mean to imply anything more than the literal sense of your words, sir?" said Adolf, offended in his turn. He let the butt-end of a pistol peep out from his breast-pocket.

For the first time Count Fersen smiled.

"I am not acquainted with your name, sir," he said, "but I have told you mine, and I know you now, as I hope you know me, for a plain, honest gentleman, that means what he says and no otherwise. It was I who set you the example of distrust; but I am losing that candour which is the natural birthright of a gentleman in this accursed mouse-trap. Allow me to apologise."

He held out his hand.

The other took it with great cordiality. "My name is Ribbing, Adolf Ribbing," he said. "I think my father was an old friend of your father's."

"Then let their sons be friends also!" said the Count, bowing.

"With all my heart. It is indeed ridiculous that every word we say to each other should be a challenge, and every other word an apology, when we are going to be shut up together like two men in a lighthouse." And Adolf laughed.

Count Fersen did not follow his example. He was by nature far too serious to be amused by anything, but the charm of his dignity was such that those whom he honoured with friendship never complained of the want of mirth in him—especially as he was careful to treat their jests with beneficent toleration.

"I have despatches for the General," continued Adolf. "Can you tell me whether I shall find him within the fortress or no?"

"You will certainly not find him anywhere else," said the Count. "He will no doubt accommodate you there; but should you have any time at your disposal, after your interview with him, I shall be much gratified if you will pay me a visit. My rooms are on the highest floor of the tower belonging to the town hall—the tower with the little dome and the gold cross on top of it. Do you see?"

"I see," said Adolf. "You have chosen an eagle's nest. That is the highest tower of all."

"The air is good," said the Count simply. He turned away. Adolf, looking back as he rode off, saw him still standing by the rail and gazing out to sea, the letter, with the seal yet unbroken, in his hand.

CHAPTER XI

THE streets through which Adolf passed were desolate. Early as it was, the shops had closed, and there were few loiterers to be seen by the way. Those whom he met wore long, pale faces, and led him to wonder if everybody in Gothenburg had a bilious complexion and a lantern jaw. They followed him with a languid stare of curiosity, but asked no questions, and answered as briefly as possible, or contented themselves with merely pointing a forefinger, when he asked them to direct him.

The Governor, General Duretz, a feeble, boastful man, with an eye like a weasel and an inanely beneficent smile, made such a negative impression, that Adolf, as soon as he had quitted his presence, began to feel doubtful as to whether he should know him again when they met the next day. Everyone about him spoke in subdued tones, and appeared to be in low spirits. The King's message which, even as he delivered it, roused the speaker himself "like the sound of a trumpet," was received with nothing but a silent shrug of the shoulders. No one uttered the word *Surrender*, but it was written on every countenance.

They were all very polite, and made a great show of regaling the ambassador on various dainties which, they assured him, were not to be procured every day. He had the best rooms in the fortress—after the Governor's—and two servants were placed at his disposal. When he contrasted the luxury of the whole place with the poverty-stricken appearance of the streets without, his heart misgave him. An utter absence of all curiosity as to the doings of the outside world struck him over and over again in those about him. They took no interest in anything.

"It is like a scene in a dream," he said to himself. (Adolf was not, as a rule, fond of his dreams, and used the expression in an unfavourable sense.) "It looks like life, but there is none. It is all unreal."

Involuntarily he lowered his own voice until he could scarcely hear himself speak. He felt as if some heavy morphia in the air had dulled his senses. There were frequent pauses in the conversation, and he grew dimly thankful when the long supper came to an end. Even then he was detained on one foolish pretext after another.

Some hours later he found himself standing on the threshold of the tower, which Count Fersen had pointed out as his abode. He was hungry for sleep, and yet he could not go to rest till he had seen once more the form of the only man in this dreary city who seemed to him a man indeed and not a shadow. He was weary, and yet, as he climbed flight after endless flight of cold stone steps in the dark, he pleased himself with the thought that he should see human eyes at the top and hear the voice of one who was not afraid lest his own ears should hear him.

The steps ceased at last, and he came to a small landing, in the opposite wall of which, after he had groped about for some time, he discovered the handle of a door.

Once, twice he knocked, but there was no answer; then, emboldened by the silence, he opened it for himself.

A draught of air from a French window that stood open down to the ground immediately blew it to, and the noise brought the colour to Adolf's cheeks; but there was no one in the room. It was bare of all ornament, as he had, somehow or other, expected to find it. A gun hung over the mantelpiece, and a case of pistols and a sword lay on the table. Over the door a branch of sweet bay was suspended. The fire had gone out, but fragments of charred boughs remained, and the room was full of a faint, spicy odour, as if someone had been burning leaves of the same plant.

Adolf went at once to the window, which led to a small balcony. There, leaning over the fragile parapet, up at a dizzy height above the pointed roofs and gables all around, stood the Count in the same attitude as before, gazing out to sea, southwards. A field-glass lay beside him, but he was not using it. His thoughts, whatever they were, absorbed him to the exclusion of everything else, for he had not heard the banging of the door, nor did he note Adolf's presence, although the latter was close beside him.

All through these long, spiritless hours, Adolf had been trying vainly to recollect Tala's features. At once, and without the smallest effort on his part, they flashed before him, and he forgot the stars, the sea, and Count Fersen.

For a few minutes he stood entranced. Then, with the vision in his heart, he stole away, trembling lest any spoken word should break it. Safe through the darkness of the night he bore it home to his lodging, and lost it only when he lost the consciousness of his own being in sleep.

CHAPTER XII

BESIEGED

THE days that followed were dreary days enough. Adolf worked hard at the fortifications, where there was more than enough for anyone to do that had a mind ; but it was hopeless labour. No one appeared to think that the city could, by any manner of means, hold out beyond a week at farthest. A cloud hung over the whole town. The garrison murmured against its leader. The citizens grumbled at the unusual contributions expected from them, when meat would soon be a rare luxury and bread itself was growing scarce. The few who did not complain let it be seen with sufficient clearness that this was only because they no longer thought that their representations would be of any avail.

One thing alone made amends to Adolf for the general depression, and that was the friendship of Axel Fersen. The two young men were opposite enough in character to become intimate almost at once, from a correct though unreasoning instinct that, if they did not, they could never afford each other any satisfaction as mere acquaintances. Yet there was a sense of mystery about Fersen, which only deepened as time went on.

During the day they seldom chanced to meet. Why he was in Gothenburg at all, Adolf could not even conjecture. He seemed to have little or no intercourse with the Governor, and he was not to be found on the outworks nor among the fortifications. Once or twice, when they came across one another by accident in the

neighbourhood of the river, Adolf thought the reasons
that he was particular to give for being there somewhat eccentric.

But this was only while the light lasted.   Evening after
evening they held long discussions up in the tower.   It
was usually Adolf who talked for the two, but Axel
had a conversational way of listening ; and neither of
them remarked this.   Axel had seen plenty of active
service ; Adolf had a lively imagination, was well read
for his years, and a keen politician.   When he had
asked Fersen a few questions as to the American
War of Independence, for instance, he would launch
into picturesque descriptions of the battles he had
never seen, his friend cordially assenting, merely
revising a detail here and there ; and what time the
stars were well on their way towards midnight, and the
lamp had begun to burn low, Adolf would retrace his
steps, with a gratified sense that he had acquired
more knowledge concerning that episode in history ;
while Axel went to bed reflecting on matters that
were as far from Gothenburg—or from America, for
that matter—as is the North Pole from the South.
And yet to both, night after night, the keen contests
waged in recollection and in fancy offered strange
compensation for the slack, disheartening warfare in
which they were engaged all day, and more than once
or twice the little room was grey with dawn before
they could make up their minds to leave off fighting.

"Is it true," said Adolf, "that you and His
Excellency, Count Stedingk, were the only two of our
nation whom the United States had decorated with the
Order of Cincinnatus, and that the King would not
allow you to wear it ? "

"Quite true," said Fersen.   "Poor old Stedingk
minded the prohibition more than I did ; but then he
was badly hit in the leg at the storming of the fortifications of Savannah.   He wanted something to prevent
people from looking at his crutches, I suppose.   But,
after all, what is a bit of ribbon—when a man gives it
you ? "

Adolf laughed.

"Half the theatres in Paris decorated Stedingk in effigy with all the Orders under the sun; and as for me, the King wrote me a letter, which I prize far more than any plebeian honour of that kind," Fersen continued. "He said the Americans were in revolt against their lawful sovereign; that I had no business to accept a favour at the hands of such people. He was perfectly right. In the nine years that have passed since then, I have become convinced of it. But I was only twenty-four at the time—not so very much older than you are now, my dear Adolf; and if a man is not a fool at twenty-four, he will never be wise at forty."

"What did you think of the English?" said Adolf.

"Oh, good enough for soldiers!" said Axel, "but they have not a single general amongst them. Even Cornwallis makes the most unaccountable mistakes. I wonder they did not shoot him as they did poor Byng, *pour encourager les autres.* There's a young man in the navy who will make himself a name some day or other, though."

"Who is that?"

"Nelson—Horatio Nelson, I think the name is. He is three years younger than I am, and the bravest little fellow alive—boarded an American letter-of-marque, when the sea was raging so that nobody else dared attempt it; boarded a Spanish battery at the head of two or three seamen and took it—goes straight ahead and never obeys any orders except his own. There was but one opinion about him among all the men that I spoke with."

"I wish we had him here," said Adolf, with a sigh. "And I wish with all my heart that the third Gustav would take a leaf from the book of his brother and cousin, the second George, and shoot Duretz."

"Amen!" said Fersen, inclining his head gravely.

As they became more intimate, the two friends drew nearer home of an evening.

Sometimes they spoke of quaint, stork-ridden Strasburg, where Axel was a student, comparing it with Berlin, where Adolf had grown to manhood

under the somewhat oppressive shadow of the Great
Frederick.

Sometimes they wandered to Italy, whither Fersen
had accompanied the King, discussing the famous
occasion when he compelled the pope to receive his
visit on Christmas Day, and caused Mass to be
celebrated in Stockholm and the Lutheran service in
Rome, at the very same hour.

"It was strange to see the face His Holiness made,"
said Axel, laughing at the recollection, "when His
Majesty, who had just been present at the celebration
of High Mass in St. Peter's, invited him to assist at our
service on equal terms, because he was the head of
the Swedish even as His Holiness was the head of the
Italian Church.   I thought one of the cardinals would
have died.   Upon my word, I was sorry for the old
fellow."

"Did you see Bonnie Prince Charlie?" asked Adolf.

"I did," said Axel significantly.

"And what did you think of him?"

"I thought the English had some reason to object to
him—almost as much, indeed, as the Countess of
Albany."

"Do you think he is really Grand Master of the
Templars and head of the Teutonic Order both in one,
though nobody knows it?"

"So they say."

"Why should the King have courted him as he
did?"

"How can I tell?"

"They say he wanted the Count of Albany to make
him Coadjutor, and then, at his death, our King would
have united both dignities in his own person.   He
would have got back Livonia again from the Russians,
because it properly belonged to the Teutonic Order,
and given it to Duke Charles for a duchy?"

"Maybe."

Adolf felt that he knew all about this affair now.

Sometimes he questioned his friend upon the brilliant
fête which took place when he was a youth of twenty.
Then the whole Court of Sweden had represented the

Fair at St. Germain, and Axel, disguised as an English jockey, exhibited a knowledge of horsemanship which bewildered all his contemporaries But Axel was more inclined to be communicative about the performance of *La Rosière de Salency*, two months afterwards, in which he and the lovely sister whose hand Duke Frederick desired in, vain appeared as a shepherd and a shepherdess, their father enacting the part of a country bumpkin, and their uncle, the Grand Venerer, that of a bailie. It was the same year that Axel held the field against all comers in a tournament which lasted three days, but of this he seemed to recollect very little.

Adolf was full of curiosity about the French Court also, but on this subject Axel was more reserved than on all the rest put together. "He would answer one question, perhaps he would answer two," as someone said of him at a later date, "but not a third."

"What sort of man is Baron de Staël?" inquired Adolf one evening.

Axel gave a peculiar smile.

"Baron de Staël is Baroness de Staël," he said. "And Baroness de Staël is Mademoiselle Necker—worse luck for the Swedish embassy! Among ourselves we call her Madame de Chicogne," and, as if he felt that he had said too much already, the Count changed the subject.

Those were pleasant hours when they talked, but as time wore on the shade of melancholy which Adolf had noticed on his friend's face from the first grew deeper and deeper, and even his own mercurial spirits failed to hold out against the all-pervading mournfulness.

September passed into October.

The sky was darkened, the rain fell in torrents.

The Danish lines were drawing closer and ever closer ; still invisible as they were, they seemed to coil themselves round Gothenburg and stifle it.

The great East Indiamen lay silent and lifeless in the docks, no longer answering with a single gun the thunder of the Danish warships as they passed by.

From the Danish camp loud shouts and cries of

triumph, the cause of which was quite unknown, filled the hearts of the defenders with terrified foreboding, when the scouts came in with the news. Was it only a ruse, a trick of war, to cheat them into believing that their last hope was gone? Or had the besiegers really heard of some tremendous defeat, and was this the reason that the scouts looked in vain for any trace of the King?

There was no active fighting as yet. The Danes were clearly trusting to time, to famine, and to a certain influence within the walls, to do the work for them.

Duretz had withdrawn almost all his outposts, and concentrated the troops on the citadel. He seemed to have but one thing at heart—that was the defence of the New Bridge, by which Adolf had entered, by which alone retreat was practicable.

On the night of the first of October, Adolf confided to Axel, rather shyly, that he had urged Duretz to give him fifty men, and let him attempt a sally.

"Ah!" said Fersen, showing considerable interest. "When did you ask him?"

"It must have been about ten o'clock. He had only just come out of his room, lazy hound!"

"I put the same question to him an hour before," said Fersen; "but I found him in bed. Of course he refused?"

"Of course."

"You were wrong to think you could do it with fifty, though. It would take two hundred to be effective."

"It might take two hundred to be effective, my dear Cincinnatus; but if there were more than fifty, it would not make me a knight of the new grade of the Order of the Sword which the King instituted the other day. And be a knight of the new grade of the Order of the Sword I will, or I'll die for it!"

Fersen smiled at the younger man's enthusiasm.

"Is that the Order which the King declared that neither his brothers nor himself would accept unless the army decreed that they should do so?"

"The same. Duke Charles got it for the battle of Hogland, you know."

"A queer fellow that! Do you think that he is really loyal to his brother?"

"I never thought he was his brother's brother at all before," said Adolf; "but I confess that Hogland has changed my opinion. It was a fine action, was it not, Axel? You know more of these things than I do."

"Very fine indeed," said Fersen quietly. "You are restless to-night; what is the matter?"

Adolf had risen for the third time since he entered the room, and strayed across to the window, as if he found it easier to breathe there.

"You will think me very foolish," he said, without turning round. "I should be ashamed to confess it but that I can say more to you, Axel, than to anybody. You recollect that great big private, who always whistled when he was on guard in the morning? He was the only man who ever whistled or sang in this God-forgotten place."

"I recollect him perfectly."

"This morning I never heard the whistle. I saw his wife afterwards. That is all."

Fersen was silent.

"I talked nonsense about the Order of the Sword. It was that which made me speak to Duretz," continued Adolf. "It seems as if I could not go on with this, unless I have a chance of shooting and getting shot at."

"You will have plenty of chances of that kind very soon, I should think, without troubling Duretz about them," said Fersen, rising and laying his hand kindly on the young man's shoulder.

"It is very hard to wait," said Adolf. "I was sorry for that woman. And what can a man say to a woman, Axel? It is of no use. She declared that he had not enough to eat."

"She should not have been here at all," said Fersen. "Most people sent their wives away before the storm broke. Quite right too."

"Mine would never have gone."

"Your *wife*?" said Fersen, with a puzzled look.

6

"My wife that will be," said Adolf. "I always think of her as my wife. I could not call her by any other name to you ; you know things as they are. And when I have been talking to you, I often dream of her, though never at any other time. Why is that, Axel ? "

But Axel did not answer. His hand had fallen from Adolf's arm, and he was gazing out to sea again, southwards.

CHAPTER XIII

THE SEALED LETTER

IT was not the first time that these sudden fits of absence had surprised Adolf. Any allusion to the Court of France was almost sure to bring them on, and Ribbing leapt to the conclusion that his friend was head over ears in love with some beautiful French lady, whose dainty, delicate name he would have given the world to discover. At the same time, he was baffled by the fact that Axel would, now and again, fall into deep abstraction, when there was nothing whatever in their talk, so far as he could see, to account for it.

One day, partly in the hope of probing this mystery, partly from the eager desire of sympathetic discussion which is common to youthful poets and lovers, our hero, blushing a good deal and feeling more like a fool than he had done since his arrival at Mora, submitted to Fersen a copy of juvenile verses addressed, of course, to Tala de Geer. The effect was different from anything that he had expected. Fersen read them through with the utmost gravity, returned them with the assurance that they were quite beyond criticism, that he considered Count Ribbing a first-rate poet, while he felt himself honoured more than ever before by his friendship, and requested a copy immediately.

"I would give all my experience in the field to have written one of those stanzas," said he.

For a moment Adolf thought he was joking, and then he recollected that Fersen never made a joke. He was much gratified, for Tala had laughed at the verses—and Fersen knew more of the world than did Tala

On the other hand, it is to be said that Adolf had
not often seen him with a book in his hand, unless
it might be a treatise on Military Tactics.   He did not
recollect this at the moment, but that cunning vanity
which lures us on to desire the repetition of a compliment, led him to say—

"Nonsense, old fellow !"

"I meant what I said," said Axel, frowning.   "I am
not in the habit of saying things that I do not mean."

· And Adolf felt abashed and ashamed at his patron's
simplicity, copied out the verses for him in his neatest
and spikiest handwriting, and ransacked the Swedish
language for rhymes to " friend."

This took place on the night after the conversation
recorded in the last chapter.   On the following evening
Adolf entered Fersen's little room, hot and excited.

"Duretz is a traitor—a traitor !" he cried.

"I thought we were agreed as to that on the first
occasion when I had the pleasure of meeting you," said
Fersen, as if the announcement did not very greatly
concern him.

"What do you think I have just seen, down by the
New Bridge ?"

"Duretz's household gods, going across it in cart-
loads ? "

"The very thing !   How did you know ? "

"I did not know.   I guessed."

"I learnt what they were by the handle of a great
china vase that was sticking out.   I saw it in the
corner of the room, the night I dined there.   If there
had been anyone else on the bridge I would have tried
to stop it, but there was nobody.   So I picked up
a stone, and broke the handle of the vase off.   He
won't adorn his banqueting hall with that any more,
anyhow."

"And you got away without a word ?"

"It was too dark for them to distinguish ; and
besides, I ran for it," said Adolf.   "There were about
twenty of them, so far as I could see."

"That looks bad," said Fersen reflectively ; "besides,
it is not the only thing."

"I went straight to Duretz to demand an explanation, but they would not admit me.   Duretz is ill."

"Oh!" said Fersen, "he is ill, is he?"

"Very ill indeed.   I should not wonder if he were dead to-morrow, and buried the day after that—with military honours—in Denmark.   But, jesting apart, Axel, how long shall we endure this?"

"Until it pleases His Majesty to arrive, I suppose. You do not propose to desert, do you?"

"I do propose to desert the Governor.   What has he ever done to make us faithful to him?   Why not organise a rebellion among the soldiers, Fersen, turn out Duretz and take command of the place yourself? There would be some hope for us then."

"Rebellion in face of the enemy?   Impossible."

"Why?"

"It is against all the rules of war.   For my own part, I would no more consent to such a measure than I would consent to offer terms to the Danes.   Oblige me by not alluding to the subject again."

"But the King's orders!"

"Duretz has obeyed them to the letter.   Gothenburg has not fallen."

"But if it falls?"

"Then we fall with it.   We shall have done our duty."

"You sit up here between the sea and the stars, Cincinnatus; you are too deep and too high for me," said Adolf.   "I cannot, for the life of me, understand why we should treat a man who is a Dane at heart and a traitor to his country with any regard whatever. If it were not for you, I would shoot him down the next time he showed his weasel face in the streets."

"And you would deserve to be shot yourself as a traitor for doing so.   By a parity of reasoning, you would be at liberty to shoot the King, if his idea of what was for the good of the country did not happen to coincide with yours.   A subject has no right of private judgment.   You must respect authority as constituted by law."

"Well," said Adolf, "you have more experience

than I have.   I yield my private judgment to you, who, on your own confession, have not got any.   I may be the last of patriots—I think I am—but you must allow that I am the first of friends, Axel?"

"I will tell you one thing for your comfort, if you will give me your word of honour not to reveal it."

"Agreed!" said Adolf.   "But is it worth wasting a word of honour upon?   To whom could I possibly reveal it, when I never speak to a soul except yourself —unless I had the fancy for taking vegetables into my confidence, which possessed that barber who told the reeds King Midas had ass's ears?"

"I never heard of him," said Fersen.   "It was highly impolitic.   Spies are often lurking in desert places.   I see the sense of all you say; but I must, nevertheless, request you to give me your word."

Adolf laid his hand on the cross hilt of his sword, and gave the oath at once, as required.

"There was a sealed enclosure in the letter from the King that you brought me," said Axel.   "It is only to be opened in case of Duretz's serious illness or death."

Adolf rose and saluted, as if in the presence of a general.

"That alters the case," he said.   "We can afford to wait."

"There is nothing else for us to do," said Fersen, sighing; "my appointment would be highly irregular, since I have the honour to hold a commission in the French Army at the present moment.   Only extreme necessity and the absence of anyone whatever qualified to undertake the post could justify it.   I cannot, under present circumstances, assist at any council of war. The position would be an awkward one, and you are witness that I do not desire it.   But I warn you that nothing can preserve us eventually.   We might prolong the struggle, you and I; the King himself could not save the town now.   The time has gone by for that.   It is only a question of falling with honour or falling without it.   The rations are running short. Three days of blockade, and they will have to kill all the horses. I do not want to discourage you, Count, but if you have anything to leave, I should advise you to make your will. There is an excellent notary living at No. 5, Torbern Strasse. I drew up mine with his assistance yesterday."

"But—if the worst come to the worst—could we not cut our way through?" asked Adolf, breathlessly.

"Cut our way through twelve thousand men?" said Fersen, shrugging his shoulders. "We can cut our way through to heaven, if you mean that."

"Are they really twelve thousand?"

"Duretz gives out that there are twenty thousand, and as long as I could get anyone to listen to me I gave out there were nine; but twelve thousand is probably about right."

Adolf had never before heard his friend speak so cheerfully nor at such length..

CHAPTER XIV

THE THIRD OF OCTOBER

THE morning broke, gloomy and overcast. Adolf began to think that he hated the autumn.

It was with an anxious heart that he went down the long corridor and inquired after the health of the Governor.

" His Excellency has passed a good night, has eaten a good breakfast, and is feeling considerably relieved."

Adolf, who had passed anything but a good night and eaten anything but a good breakfast, did not participate in this sensation.

He went straight to Axel, whom he found on the balcony, sweeping the far horizon with his glass. All at once he seemed to concentrate his attention on a particular point in the middle distance.

" Look there ! " he said, handing the glass to Adolf, and pointing.

" What is it ? " said Adolf. " I see a man running— running as hard as he can go. What is that in his hand ? A white flag ! What does it mean ? "

" We should have watched the bridge," said Fersen. " Fool that I was, not to think of it ! Duretz has got a message through to the Prince of Hesse. The white speck is a handkerchief—a flag of truce." Fersen sank his voice nearly to a whisper, as he added, "For Heaven's sake, keep it quiet ! "

" I should say rather, proclaim it upon the house-tops, as we have a good opportunity of doing up here ! "

" No," said Fersen. " I have thought the thing over, and we must wait. Duretz has thoroughly corrupted the troops under him, and we do not know how many others besides. If we spoke now, we should be overpowered at once, and the people, whom he would try to bribe with promises, would believe that we had calumniated him out of jealousy; it would take the heart out of the few who still remain faithful, and they would relax their vigilance. Besides, Duretz has just written to me to say that the Prince of Hesse threatens to set fire to the town unless we surrender, and to ask my advice. I merely quoted the King's last words to you in my answer, and he will not have the face to propose it again just yet."

"But if he announces a capitulation without consulting his officers?"

"We will denounce his treachery and seize the gates. Unless the people rally to us, we shall be arrested and shot for mutiny; but we must risk that. After all, die we must, one way or the other — whether by the Danish guns or our own signifies little." He laughed cheerfully.

Adolf, who had not enjoyed making his will so much as Fersen, wondered whether the lady in France were married. It appeared that a man who loved a lady in France looked upon death in a very different light from a man who loved a lady in Sweden.

"Could you draw up some sort of proclamation, in case we wanted it?" said Axel. "You write so easily, and it is difficult work for me. I have reason to think that the offices of the *Gothenburg Star* would print it for us, if we put a little pressure upon them."

The proclamation was drawn up, and the rest of the day passed just as many and many a day had passed before.

Adolf admired and envied the way in which Fersen went about his usual avocations in his usual manner, quite undisturbed. He himself was restless and could not settle. All the vague impressions of dislike and discomfort that had been floating in his mind since he arrived took definite shape. He had thought that he could never weary of the sound of waves,—for he loved the sea as one born and brought up beside it,—but now he was tired of that monotonous chorus to his own

monotonous thought, and would have done anything to
stop it, if only for five minutes. Every yellow, hollow
face in the streets filled him with loathing, so that he
wished he were in a desert; and the very noise of a
footstep jarred on his nerves as if it had been a blow.

He longed most ardently for the moment when
Duretz would announce the capitulation and put an end
to this state of suspense; but Duretz did nothing of
the kind—and as no one, except Fersen, had observed
the departure of a messenger for the Danish camp,
there was no stir nor excitement in the town.

Only the rations were rather less than they had been
the day before—and Axel pointed out to him that the
soldiers hardly grumbled at all.

"I wish the King would come," said Adolf, with a
sigh, that stormy evening, when he and Fersen had sat
silent longer than they were wont, whilst the wind,
which rose as darkness fell, howled in and out among
the towers and spires, and drove the rain in fierce,
gusty splashes against the window. "I could die better
if he were here."

"You need no king to help you to do that, I should
hope."

"Your old Republican of a father is strong in you
to-night," said Adolf, seizing the shadowy pretext for
a laugh. "What a strange sentiment for you, who
are *plus royaliste que le roi*!"

"Ah—h! But not *plus royaliste que la reine*," said
Axel, smiling in his turn.

"The Queen? The poor old *Statue du Com-
mandeur*?" said Adolf, alluding to Sophie-Madeleine
by the title which her shy rigidity had gained for her
throughout the kingdom. "What can you mean?"

"I spoke French," said Fersen.

"I do not know French as well as you do, my friend,
but I never supposed that you were speaking Swedish."

"Who, when he says *la reine*, could think of any
except?"— said Axel, with lightning in his eyes.

"I for one," said Adolf, in a low, happy voice. He
was thinking of Tala, her bright eyes and her white
furs. "Every man has his queen. Were the Queen

of France Helen herself, she could not prevent that. Depend on it, Hector thought Andromache fairer! You have a queen, Axel; I know you have."

"Yes," said Axel. "If we live to get out of this hole—but that, after all, is impossible—I shall show her to you, one day. Then she will be yours also."

"To my mind," said Adolf, "the world is divided, not into Royalists and Republicans, but into men who follow a king and men who follow a queen. I knew, from the first moment I saw you, that the thought of a woman guided your life. It was because the thought of a woman guided mine already that I understood it. Ah, how the wind shakes the tower! What a free thing it is! Liberty, liberty!"

"I cannot bear the word," said Axel, with sudden fierceness.

"I think it is the king of words. When the great free breath without calls to the little free breath within me, I long for freedom more than for anything else in the world—'A free king of a free people.' That's why I love our King."

"And that is why you will cease to love him," said Fersen bitterly. "Kings are the laws incarnate, and liberty is not for earth—nor for heaven either. The devil made it, to be the law of all the lost."

"Then would I rather be the devil's freeman than the slave of God," said Adolf.

"Hush! What was that?"

"Nothing."

"It sounded like a cry."

"Only the wind."

They were silent for some time longer.

"You cannot think of death when the King is by. He makes you feel three times more alive than anyone else that ever I saw. We should not have to die at all, if he came here," said Adolf, with an outburst of candour.

"Do you think the King himself will live to be old?" said Fersen. "I do not."

"Why?"

"There is a doom upon the race."

"You believe that rubbish?" said Adolf scornfully,

"I do not say that I believe it, but many people do ; the King himself among the number."

"How can you be so credulous ?"

"I come of a Scotch family, and the Scotch hold many of these opinions.   Our name was Macpherson originally."

"Fleming told me, the other day, that he was descended from Titus Quinctius Flamininus, the Roman Consul," said Adolf sarcastically.   "Perhaps that's why his hair is red.   For me, I am descended from Adam."

"Laugh as you will !" said Axel.   "It is not on such a night as this that you will make me give up the old prophecies.   Was it for nothing that I mistook the wind's voice for the voice of a human creature just now ?"

"I know what you mean," said Adolf, more thought-fully.   "I felt it when I was riding through the woods of Dalecarlia.   I could have believed anything, if you had told it me then—'Wild Huntsman' and all !   But what is this story of the doom on the King's family ?   I never heard it."

"You never heard the vision of Charles XI. ? Impossible !   Every child in Sweden has learnt it by heart, these hundred years."

"You must remember that I went early to school.   I never knew it.   Tell me !"

"I have heard the King tell it himself," said Fersen, "and that was something to hear indeed.   But I have not a good memory, and you must pardon me if I do it scant justice.   Stir up the fire !   The wind blows through the chinks and crannies of the walls, and these old stories make one cold."

Adolf vigorously thumped the coal until the sparks flew up the chimney, and Axel began—

"It was an autumn evening like this, and old King Charles XI.—peace be to his memory ! (the King always says 'Peace be to his memory !') — was sitting by the fire, as we are sitting now, with his dressing-gown and his slippers on, in a room of the old palace overlooking Lake Mœlar.   Count

Brahe, his chamberlain,—the ancestor of the present man,—was with him, and his doctor, Baumgarten, and they were talking of nothing particular — very idle talk."

"Much like ours, if you will forgive me!" said Adolf.

"Suddenly the great hall of the estates, which is situated, as you know, in the opposite wing, began to shine resplendently, as if there were a light in every window. They all three saw it at once, but no one spoke.

"'I will go into the hall myself,' said the King at last. He had turned pale, but was quite composed. The Count and Baumgarten followed, each with a candle in his hand. They roused the porter, who found the keys and showed them into the gallery, which was always used as an antechamber. To their astonishment, the walls were hung with black.

"'Who ordered this gallery to be hung with black?' demanded the King.

"'To my certain knowledge, no one has entered it since the last time I had it swept out,' said the porter. 'And then it was panelled just as it had always been.'

"A confused noise made itself heard from the hall.

"'Stop, stop, sire!' exclaimed Count Brahe, as the King stepped forward.

"'Allow me to go and fetch twenty of your life-guards,' cried Baumgarten, as a gust of wind blew out his candle."

"Axel, you invented that on the spur of the moment," said Adolf, trimming a candle which had been put too close to the window and was guttering dolorously.

"The King never heeded the words of his companions. He took the key from the trembling hands of the porter and said, 'Let us go in!'

"The hall was lighted with an immense number of torches, and hung in black from top to bottom. Every bench was crowded with senators all dressed in black. On the raised throne in the centre sat a dead man with a crown on his head; the blood was flowing from his wounds. To the right of him stood a child, and on the left was an old, grey-haired man. At the foot of the throne stood a wooden block, and an axe lay beside it.

"At a sign from the President the door opened, and several young men came in, their hands tied behind their backs. An executioner, veiled and masked, followed them. Their leader stopped when he came to the block in the middle of the hall, and looked at it with supreme contempt; but the dead body quivered, and fresh blood flowed from the wounds. Then the young man knelt down and stretched out his head, and the axe glittered and fell with a thud. A jet of blood spurted out on to the steps of the throne and mingled with that which streamed from it. The head, rebounding on the bloody pavement, rolled at the feet of Charles.

"Hitherto he had kept silence, but now he regained his power of utterance.

"'If you are of God, speak!' he said, addressing the President. 'If you are of the other, leave us in peace!'

"'Charles the King!' said the phantom slowly, 'this blood shall not flow under your rule, but it shall flow when five reigns have gone by. Woe! woe! Woe to the House of Vasa!'

"The forms grew indistinct and gradually vanished. The torches went out; the hangings, the head, the block, disappeared.

"But when the King looked at his slippers, they were stained with blood."

Fersen made an impressive pause.

"But when the King looked at his slippers, they were stained with blood," said Ribbing, in the absent tone of one whose ear had apprehended, but not his brain. "Hark! what was that? Your phantom had a real voice, Axel. I heard it cry."

"I heard nothing," said Axel testily.

"Again, again! Listen! It is a cry. It is not the wind. You were right. Someone is calling. Hark!"

"I hear," said Fersen. "It is not the wind. Unbar the shutters!"

"It comes from the west gate, down by the Castle drawbridge," shouted Adolf, trying to make himself heard above the clamour of the storm, as he threw open the window and held it with both hands to prevent it from being smashed.

"Are you sure? Is it really in that direction?"

"Quite sure. If it came from the other, we should hear more distinctly. The wind blows from the sea. Axel, Axel, if it should be a messenger!"

"The sentries must have heard it. Why do not they let the man in? Stay! what was that?"

"The great clock of St. Bridget's striking twelve."

"This is no living voice we hear," said Axel, in low, awestruck tones. "None hears it except you and I."

"But they *shall* hear it," cried Adolf vehemently; and, making a trumpet of his hands, he screamed with all the force of his lungs, "*Gustav! Gustav! Gothenburg!*"

A faint cry was borne back to him, but no words could be distinguished.

"Do not make a fool of yourself," said Axel, who had shaken his mind free from the influence of Charles XI. by this time. "If it is a messenger, we had better go to the Castle and see why they have not let him in."

Ribbing dashed madly down the hundred steps which led from the top of the tower to the bottom.

"The door is locked," he cried, "the door is locked! They have bolted us in." He stamped his foot with fury.

Fersen, descending more leisurely, tried the door in his turn, but the lock would not give.

"I shall climb down from the balcony."

"You will do no such thing. Try the other doors first. The rooms are empty, I know, but they may be open, and we might make an attempt from the lower windows."

"They are all locked," cried Ribbing, as he rattled one after the other, in vain.

Fersen had gone quietly upstairs again, and was making a rope of his bedclothes.

"It is not more than sixteen feet to the next balcony," he said. "You must let me down by this; if it holds—if I get down in safety—I will unlock the door for you."

"Forgive me, Axel, I must go first," said Ribbing passionately.

"We will draw lots," said Fersen, with imperturbable politeness. "One of us must be left behind, you see. There would be no one to hold the rope steady, else. I have two sous in one of my clenched hands. If you choose the hand in which they are, you go down first—if not, I. Right hand or left?"

"Right," said Adolf, in desperation.

Fersen opened his hand. There lay the two sous.

"Good! Here is my pass-key. Put it in your pocket. Run round—unlock the door with it before you go—that is all I ask!"

Adolf took the end of the improvised rope, and let himself cautiously down over the railing.

"Do not think about it," said Fersen, "and do not look down. Shut your eyes! Let go when you get to the end of the rope!"

Adolf did as he was told, recommended his soul to Heaven, and was surprised to find it still in his body a moment after.

"Scramble down by the pipe!" shouted Fersen, leaning far over the balcony. "Wave your handkerchief when you get to the bottom!"

Adolf found the pipe, embraced it valiantly with arms and legs, and slid unhurt to the ground.

Having got thus far, he waved his handkerchief as directed, receiving a congratulatory cheer from his imprisoned companion, rushed round to the front of the tower,—unbolted—flung open the door, threw the key inside (for it would not stand open against the wind), and dashed off at full speed to the Castle. He thought that he had heard a distant shout at the very moment when his feet touched the earth. Others must have heard something too, for by this time all the world was awake, and people were pouring out from every house; but they could know no more than he did. He did not wait to ask questions; he ran.

Just as he came within view of the west gate and the quay, a loud, unmistakable cry went up.

The crowd surrounded on all sides a solitary mounted figure, bowing to right and left of him. He rode a gaunt, bony hack, and his cloak was draggled and splashed with mud. His uniform was that of a common soldier. A man with a torch ran in front.

By the light of it, Adolf saw the face, and as he saw it, his heart almost stopped beating.

It was the King; but he looked like a king who had come to die.

CHAPTER XV

FERSEN WATCHES

ABOUT an hour later, Axel and Ribbing were both in attendance at the palace, where the King was holding a consultation with several of the leading officers, who had been summoned in haste to meet him. He had promised to address the Municipality on the morrow, that he might lay before them the results of the marvellous activity displayed in the course of the last month, during which he had moved from place to place with such swiftness that the British envoy, who came to Stockholm to look for him, lost eleven days in the search—Gustav's own Council not being able to tell where he was. Arriving late at Alengsab, he had left his carriage there and ridden on, post-haste, alone ; but he had been compelled to wait by the drawbridge for an hour in the furious tempest, before anyone recognised him.

Wild excitement prevailed throughout the town. The common people, who were gathered together in crowds without the palace, sent up cheer after cheer. Within, the agitation of those present was better controlled perhaps, and even more poignant.

The most exaggerated rumours were everywhere in circulation.

Duretz was to be fined—exiled—imprisoned—beheaded in the public square.

The King had mustered seven thousand—nine thousand—sixteen thousand Dalecarlians.

The Danes were breaking up their camp.

There would be a battle on the morrow.

There would be a *sortie* this very night.

So the tongues wagged, and the younger and older courtiers alike conjectured and predicted. A whole band of them, including Baron Wrangel and his friend, La Gardie, arrived shortly after the King, but they seemed to know little more than the denizens of Gothenburg—beyond the fact that this delay had been caused by Gustav's tremendous effort to enlist fresh forces in every direction—which forces were expected to come up on the morrow. They themselves had been sent on in advance, but the King had ridden straight through their camp in the night, *incognito*, and without stopping.

They appeared to be in the highest spirits. The many corridors of the palace, long empty and silent, resounded with their uproarious laughter and their snatches of noisy song.

As for Adolf, he was half mad. After the endless days of wearisome depression and monotony that he had spent of late, this strong dose of life went to his head. He laughed, talked, sang, shouted, boasted of his escape by the window, until Fersen stood aghast, scarcely able to recognise his companion. Men's ears were open for any marvellous tidings. The tale was listened to, demanded again, rapturously applauded. And all the time he was making a buffoon of himself for the rest, Adolf had an odd sensation at the back of his heart that the world would come to an end that night.

From time to time the door opened, and one of those within issued forth. Many were the attempts made to extract information as to what was going forward there, but in vain. Each officer shook his head and hurried away. Two or three conversed together for a short time and then returned; their faces, when they came out again, were graver than before.

The feeling at the back of Adolf's heart took on a sharper edge. It seemed as if there were two creatures in him—a wise man and a fool. The fool talked louder and more absurdly every moment, the wise man smiled and whispered, "Let be! It will all be over

to-morrow. I only shall survive." The fool found
other fools around him; the wise man sat alone.
Adolf wondered whether there were any other wise men
behind the other fools,—men who had seen the King's
face as he saw it,—but he did not ask questions, from an
instinct that the world would crumble to bits at once
if he began; and he avoided Fersen, seeing that there
were no fools in Fersen.

Some time had elapsed when the King's valet brought
out a message that he did not require the attendance of
his suite.

Curiosity got the better of fatigue for a little while;
then fatigue overmastered it, and the group began
to melt away, one by one. Wet through and weary
with the long ride, they withdrew to their several
apartments.

Among those who were left, the talk became more
and more ribald, the laughter more frequent; Adolf was
still the first to lead it.

Axel stood with folded arms, leaning against the
balustrade, looking down into the hall. His reputation stood high enough to protect him, though it
might have gone ill with any other man who chose to
abstract himself in this way. If he had few friends at
the Court, he had no enemies; he was, indeed, universally liked and respected, in spite of a reserve of
manner which forbade intimacy.

His keen eye noted the different councillors as
they went in, and he had no difficulty in identifying
them as they passed out again, singly or in pairs.

"They must be all gone now," he said to himself, as
he saw a man in a furred cloak slowly descending the
staircase. "That was the last to enter. It is like
Duretz's walk, but surely he would have recognised
me. Hullo! There goes Oxenstiern. The council
must be over then, in sober earnest. Good-evening,
Count!"

"Good-evening," returned Count Oxenstiern, and
hurried down the steps as fast as possible. It
was very evident that he had no desire for conversation.

Axel resumed his position.

A few minutes later Count Bonde-Trolle came out, leaning upon the arm of Baron Sparre. They were too much preoccupied to return Axel's bow, as they passed swiftly down the staircase.

"There is only Lœwenhielm left now," said Axel to himself, as he continued his idle watch.

He had not long to wait.

The council chamber door was violently slammed to, and the President of the Senate strode from the room, his brow dark and an angry flush on his cheek. As he did so, a burst of laughter from the young people round the fire at the end of the corridor made the roof ring again. Whether he heard it or no, Axel could not have told ; but he pulled his hat down over his forehead and descended the stairs rapidly, as the rest had descended before him. Shrieks of mirth followed.

Axel turned round, displeased by this unseemly behaviour. Only his cousin, La Gardie, Adolf Ribbing, Baron Wrangel, and a young fellow named Clas Horn were left.

"Baron Wrangel," he said, addressing himself to the eldest among them and pointing to the door, "the King is in there, alone. Have we the right to disturb His Majesty?"

It was as if he had pricked a bubble. The laughter and the loud talking stopped instantly ; no one attempted to revive it. All the fools fled, and the wise men sat still in their places.

Adolf, though he would not have lifted his little finger to bring on that moment, experienced a sense of lightness and relief now that it had come. He was lying at full length on the floor, his head on his hand. Glancing up, he admired Axel's superb attitude.

"When you have died the glorious death that you are always dreaming of, my dear Cincinnatus," he said lazily, " how handsome you will look !"

"Yes," said Baron Wrangel. "He is not dependent on colour. His profile is magnificent. Men with regular features look remarkably well when they are laid out.   Are you practising for a monument, Count?"

"No," said Adolf.   "If I were, I should lie like a crusader.   They understood the profession best;" and he suited the action to the word and crossed his legs accordingly.

"Bravo!" murmured Clas Horn.   "But I intend to have a bust on mine."

"Your legs are not your strong point, my dear fellow; we are all aware of that," said Wrangel. "How did you know that the King was alone, if I may ask, Count Fersen?"

"I noticed everyone who went in; I have seen each man come out again."

"It is very odd that the King should stay there all by himself," said La Gardie.   "He must be tired out. He has ridden two hundred and fifty miles since the day before yesterday.   Perhaps he left the council chamber by another way."

"There is no other exit," said Adolf.   "I know the room well.   He must come out by this door."

Silence fell upon the little group.

Clas Horn rose and bid them good-night.

"What o'clock is it?" said La Gardie, after a long pause.

Wrangel pulled out a huge gold watch, and consulted it.

"It must be about one, as nearly as I can reckon."

"Then you mistook the hour of the King's arrival," said Axel to his friend.   "It must have been eleven, not twelve."

"I daresay," said Adolf, smiling.   "I was in no condition to count the strokes carefully."

Another quarter of an hour went by.

"It is very strange," said La Gardie.   "Did you ever know the King shut himself up alone like this before?"

"Never," said Fersen.

"After all, what are we waiting for?" inquired Wrangel.

No one answered the question, but no one stirred.

Adolf could have borne to wait indefinitely. The luxury of keen emotion after the blunt despair of the last week delighted him—the end would come soon enough. He was almost sorry when the handle of the door turned, and the King stepped out.

CHAPTER XVI

THE KING SPEAKS

THEY rose respectfully and made way for him, as he came towards the fire.

Gustav was naturally of a full colour; even the fatigue of the last month had not diminished it, although his eyes, usually so bright, were dull and void of any expression. He went straight to the mantelpiece, leaned both arms upon it, and hid his face in his hands, as if he saw no one and fancied himself alone. It was but a moment, as time passes on a clock, before he raised it again, but that moment seemed longer than all the hours that had gone before. Adolf, who stood facing Axel, lifted his brows; Axel shook his head mournfully.

"Ah!" said the King, in a whisper, glancing round him as he spoke, "so the rest have gone. The rats and the sinking ship! They do well."

He paused; then added, as if it had struck him, for the first time, that he was talking not to himself but to others: "If anyone had told me that I should find four men faithful to their King in his hour of adversity, I should have named those whom I now see before me. I am gratified; I should only insult you, gentlemen, were I to say surprised."

All four bowed low. Adolf dared not trust himself to speak. La Gardie said, in a voice that he could scarcely control—

"You may depend upon us, sire."

"I am convinced of it," said the King. " Let me request you to be seated."

He seated himself, and signed to Wrangel and to Axel Fersen to take the two arm-chairs opposite. La Gardie drew a three-legged stool, which stood near, into the circle; Adolf sat down in the shadow of the chimney corner, and, resting his elbow on his knee and his chin on his hand, watched the King's face intently.

"I desire to hide nothing from you," the King continued. "Our position is desperate."

The words fell like lead on the stillness; yet, the next minute, Adolf recollected that he had known this all along.

The King went on as if he were rehearsing a lesson, the meaning of which did not concern him.

"England and Prussia are the only allies to whom we might reasonably look for help. I have sent special envoys to each Court, but I have not as yet received any answer from the respective Cabinets—nor do I expect it. Hugh Elliot, the British envoy who came to me at Carlstadt, is full of hope. England, however, has not recovered her full strength; she is still bleeding from the wounds given her by her unworthy sons in America, and she will do nothing to involve herself in war. As for the King of Prussia, he is, you know, my blood relation." The King smiled.

Adolf, in the chimney corner, shook his clenched fist. A great longing to shoot the King of Prussia overmastered him.

" France ? "—

It was Axel Fersen who spoke.

"France is too busy with her own affairs." The King sighed. "She is in a position to need assistance rather than to give it. My six thousand Dalecarlians are brave fellows, but even so we are far outnumbered, and it is doubtful whether they can arrive in time to effect so much as a momentary diversion. What is your advice, gentlemen? Shall we remain here and die? Or shall we surrender?"

Adolf bounded upon his seat.

"That is a word I never thought to hear your Majesty pronounce," said Axel.

" It is impossible for us to save Gothenburg," said the King, weighing each syllable, as if he wished to let it sink far down into the hearts of his hearers.

" It is impossible for us to leave it with dignity," Fersen rejoined.

" Yes, yes, impossible ! " cried Adolf, finding relief at last.

" Impossible ! " echoed La Gardie.

" Impossible ! " said the Baron, more leisurely.

For the first time, a transient smile flitted across the King's countenance.

" This is a very different council of war from the last that I held," he observed.

" There cannot be two opinions upon this matter, sire," said Fersen gravely.

" You would not have said so, my dear Count, if you had been with me in the earlier part of the night. Duretz implored me to surrender ; there is no word but that strong enough to express his abject entreaties. When I found that all the other officers were unanimous in favour of his proposal, I felt myself compelled to hold a Diet, at which only one person was present."

" But that person, sire, was a host in himself," said Adolf, laughing. "And the Diet he held came to the same conclusion as that which is now sitting ? "

" *Parbleu !* " said the King, and snapped his fingers.

He threw back his head proudly ; again the lightning shock of those blue eyes set Adolf's heart dancing. He asked for nothing but that life should end, then and there, before that moment ended. In a flash, he thought of the room with the twisted shadows of the antlers, the firelight gleaming on the fork of coral, and wondered at the difference. Now, death appeared to him as full of glory as though it were his marriage. He heard the King's voice like some sweet instrument of music, tuned in a heavenly dream.

" If we die," the King was saying, " we will die like men of a royal race. We could not fall in a more noble cause. We are born to a high destiny ; the eyes of Europe are upon us. In fire we vanish like the Phœnix, and from our ashes new fire will arise. Our mother, Sweden, shall bewail us ; we will have such a funeral pyre as becomes the sons of the Vikings. Your ancestors, Baron Wrangel, have sat upon the throne of Pultava for two-and-twenty generations. Your burying shall not shame them."

"I have not lived like twenty-two kings, sire," rejoined the Baron, with a bow. "It is honour enough for me to share the funeral expenses of one."

Something ironical about the tone in which this was said jarred upon Adolf, but the King smiled.

"The expenses will be borne by the larger number of the citizens, I believe," he said. "I have given orders that all who value life above honour should leave Gothenburg to-night, and on foot. I am curious to see who remains."

"But is it possible, sire, that they should leave to-night?" asked Fersen.

"It is much more than possible, it is necessary. They were very willing to leave, I can assure you, but they disliked the notion of walking. When they found that I was inexorable on this point, great pressure was put upon me to consent to the passing of carriages ; but that would take too much time. I was compelled to refuse, though I incurred the risk of becoming more unpopular than I am. No matter ! If we give our lives, the *canaille* may well give their legs. Even then, the bargain is far from an equal one. I have decreed that all who wish to leave must be on the other side of the New Bridge by three in the morning, that is, in two hours' time. Five minutes later the bridge will be no longer in existence. I hate those cowards—I cannot breathe freely till they are gone."

"You have held it out as a threat, sire? You do not really mean to blow up the bridge?" inquired La Gardie, with a startled air.

"I mean to do what I say," returned the King. "The bridge will be blown to atoms before sunrise."

"It is mad," Wrangel muttered, half to himself.

The King waved his hand towards the door.

"There is still time," he said, with suave politeness.

"You mistake me, sire," Wrangel answered haughtily, "if you think that anything would induce me to cross that bridge, except in your company and that of my—friends."

He had noticed the quick shrinking back from him of the three other young men.

"I have reason to believe that my brother-in-law, the Prince of Hesse, will attack in a few days' time," the King went on, as though there had been no interruption. "He is sure to have got wind of the approach of the army from Dalecarlia, and he will not wait to let them come up. Now, if we demolish our only means of retreat, he will see that we are in earnest, whatever happens. The train of gunpowder is laid, is it not, Count Fersen?"

"It needs but a match, sire, and the bridge will be blown to pieces."

Adolf looked at his friend with amusement. So this was the meaning of his long and mysterious visits to the neighbourhood of the Göta!

"Who will set fire to the train?" said the King. They all sprang forward eagerly.

"I claim it as my right, sire," Axel said, in his most musical tones.

The King waved his hand, as though he deprecated enthusiasm.

"One is enough," he said. "Count Fersen, I cannot give you the preference. These other gentlemen have not had the same opportunity, but their devotion equals yours. The risk is great, of course; but scarcely greater than that which we all accept by remaining here. If I survive to-morrow, let him who carries out the task successfully—if he survive to-night—ask of me whatsoever he will, even to the half of my kingdom! How long does it take to reach the place where you have laid your train, Count?"

"Not more than half an hour at most, sire."

The King mused.

"Come to me in the chapel, when the clock strikes again," he said. "I must request you to enter one by one, at an interval of five minutes. I shall make my choice there."

He bent his head with a grave salutation, including all those who were present, and strode away down the corridor in the direction of the steps which led to the chapel.

The young men remained standing, until he had closed the door behind him, when La Gardie said, laughing nervously—

"His Majesty might have chosen at once, I think."

"His Majesty has chosen," said Wrangel, *sotto voce*, to his companion—and glanced at Adolf.

La Gardie shook his head impatiently.

"You are insane on this subject. Why should he keep us all kicking our heels here, if that were the case?"

CHAPTER XVII

THE KING CHOOSES

" HOW shall we go in?" inquired Wrangel.

"You take precedence," said Fersen quietly. "You have royal blood in your veins. I follow. La Gardie, your ancestors on the father's side had land in Sweden before the time of Christian the Tyrant, had they not?"

"If all my mother tells me be true," La Gardie said.

"Our friend must go before you, then, Count Ribbing."

Adolf laughed and agreed.

He had strolled over to the window. The prolonging of this strange night was very welcome to him. There was a sudden lull in the wind, and the storm had fallen. The stars shone here and there, not large nor full, but very clearly.

"It is as if someone had pricked the sky with a diamond-pointed pen," Adolf said to himself. He threw the casement open, and leaned far out, sucking in the damp, soft air with delight. To his surprise, he saw two lights down below, and they were moving forward evenly.

"Look, look!" he exclaimed aloud. "There is a carriage driving round to the steps. The King said none was to pass."

His companions crowded instantly to the window.

"He must have known of this one," said Fersen. "They would not dare to bring it out here else."

"Whose can it be?" cried La Gardie.

110

"Bring the lamp!" called out Wrangel. "The courtyard is full of people. What's that?"

"A detachment of the Guards?"

"It is, it is," cried Adolf. "Those are the Blues. Nobody could mistake them. But how silently they are forming up!"

"What can it mean? Who is it?"

"Who is this coming out, cloaked and muffled like an old woman?"

"I can tell you who it is," said Fersen meditatively. "You are quite right, Adolf. It is an old woman. It is Duretz."

Ribbing glanced at his friend, and laughed out loud again. This King did things as he liked them to be done.

"He was going to have surrendered to-night. The Prince of Hesse had threatened to burn the town if he did not."

"They are taking him safely across the river. It is more than he deserves; upon my word it is!"

"He ought to have been shot like a dog," observed La Gardie.

"That happy lot is reserved for us," said Baron Wrangel, with a sneer. "I suppose the King thought that he must make a distinction."

They watched the carriage roll away, closely surrounded on all sides by the silent Guards, and then returned to the fire. A heavier stillness seemed to have settled down upon the doomed palace.

"I wish we had some wine," continued the Baron, yawning. "I shall never be able to keep awake."

"I have a flask of brandy at your service," said Fersen, producing one from his pocket and handing it across.

"Does the King never go to sleep, and does he never want anything to eat and drink?" asked Adolf.

"He wears us all out, I know that," said Wrangel. "Imagine what we had to go through at Falun! We had been riding day and night, night and day, posting about in all directions, making speeches, seeing illuminations, dancing till we had not a leg to stand on, because the filthy miners must needs entertain us at a great ball; and just when we thought it was over, for a few hours, anyhow, nothing would suit the King but to put on a blouse as black as a chimney-sweep's, and go down the worst of the copper-mines, deeper than anybody had ever gone before, to drink success to the money-grubbers at the bottom! Yah, how foul it smelt!"

"But how they shouted, when he came up again!" cried La Gardie. "How they dragged the horses out of the carriage! I thought the poor beasts would have been strangled! How they tore round the town with him! And how the volunteers came pouring in afterwards!"

"Yes," said Wrangel, "there were twenty thousand all told."

"Twenty thousand!" said Fersen, in surprise. "His Majesty said six!"

"He was obliged to refuse fourteen thousand of them provisionally—*provisionally*, you understand," said Wrangel, with a sinister laugh. "There were no weapons. If you had seen them drilling with Charles xii.'s old muskets! My word, it was a funny sight! And his officers were as queer as the artillery. Two old captains that nobody ever heard of before —Willenkröna and Föberg—their united ages must amount to three hundred at least."

The effect of this spectral army was not enlivening, somehow. Again the conversation languished.

"What shall we do to keep our eyes open until the clock strikes?" said La Gardie, with nervous eager-ness. "Tell stories? You are a good hand at that, Axel. Begin, for goodness' sake! 'Once upon a time'"—

"You had much better go to sleep, if you will allow me to say so," Fersen replied. "We shall need all the rest that we can get. Do not be afraid! I am a light sleeper, and I am able to wake at any hour that I propose to myself. If you will trust the matter to me, I will call you five minutes before the time."

"Willingly," said the Baron, measuring his full

length on the ground at once. "I have been on horseback twelve out of the twenty-four hours. I never refuse a good offer."

"I should be another man if I could forget myself for a few minutes," La Gardie murmured.

"Here is an arm-chair for you," said Fersen. "Put this cloak over your knees. No, thank you! I shall not lie down."

The young man took it, and fell asleep almost at once, as did the other two. Adolf only remained awake. He was far too happy to need rest. A man who is blissfully dreaming, with his eyes open, dares not trust himself to the chance that he may go on dreaming when they are shut. But he was lost in a reverie no less deep than the slumber of his associates when Fersen touched him on the arm, and he understood, with a start, that time was up. La Gardie awoke readily, but it was hard to rouse Wrangel.

"Lead the way, Adolf," said Fersen. "You know the palace best."

They traversed the corridor in silence, and descended a stone staircase at the other end of it. The spirit of dumb excitement possessing Adolf was very strong. He did not say a word. La Gardie spoke constantly, in short, excited, half sentences, as if he must provoke someone else to answer. Wrangel took no heed of him whatever, and Fersen replied in monosyllables. A small door at the foot of the steps let them out on to the roof of the chapel, the foundations of which were laid considerably lower down the hill than those of the palace. They shivered and drew their long cloaks closer round them, as they felt the rush of the night air. There was only room to walk one by one. Some rough steps cut against the walls of the tower ended in a low cloister, lit by a torch that was flaring smokily in the draught, caught in an iron ring on one side of the entrance to the chapel.

In the doorway stood the King, a long blue mantle, worn only on State occasions, falling back from his shoulders. The jewels of the crown of Sweden flashed and gleamed on his forehead. On his breast

8

shone the bright silver star of the Order of the
Seraphim. A moment, and he turned back again into
the chapel. Wrangel followed him and the door
closed.

The other three waited, with chattering teeth, in the
draughty cloister.

"That was well done," Adolf whispered, with
exultant eyes.

"Yes," Fersen said indifferently.

"Are the dead as cold as that, Axel?" said La
Gardie, touching the wall with his finger.

"Not at first; afterwards—yes."

"I feel as if we were going to our own funeral," said
La Gardie.

"Another!" said the King's voice from within.

"My turn!" whispered Fersen. He lifted the latch
and entered.

"I am glad that it is my turn next," said La Gardie,
drawing closer to Adolf. "I would not be left here
alone. What shall you do?"

"I shall not be alone," said Adolf. "I have a
thought that is always with me." And he smiled
gravely.

"You said that like Axel. I could have sworn that
it was his voice."

"Perhaps it is."

"Where do you think that we shall be when we are
dead?" said La Gardie irrelevantly.

"Under the earth and over the stars, I suppose; but
it concerns us very little."

It pleased Adolf to feel how much older than La
Gardie he was, as he gave utterance to this magnificent
sentiment. But the voice from within spoke again, and
he was left by himself.

He wondered intently whether, at that moment, Tala
lay asleep, dreaming of him. He wished she might.
He hoped that she was not awake. Over her thoughts
he could not have any power; but if she were
asleep, might not this tremendous will of his to be
remembered compel an image of him upon her brain?
He set himself to desire it with such strenuous

endeavour, that when his own summons came, he felt, for the moment, bewildered and exhausted.

He entered the chapel quietly enough, however, closing the door after him as the others had done. A blast of chill air seemed to come down the nave to meet him and to fly howling up behind. The chapel was very old and rough and small, hung with faded, ragged banners—brown, crimson, yellow—that had waved in many a battle where Sweden's soldiers had perished and been victorious. It seemed as if they longed to flutter freely in the breeze again, to be once more the winged symbols of a host, instead of flapping, idle and purposeless, at the mercy of every chance gust. They smelt mouldy. As the wind blew one of them against his cheek, Adolf shrank back with disgust, as though a bat had touched him. The light from a small lantern, set upon the altar, shone through the rents and holes in them. His three companions were kneeling upon the altar steps, their heads bowed on their hands. In front, against a pillar, stood the King. The flag that waved above him was blazoned with the Three Water Lilies. Adolf advanced to the foot of the steps and there paused. The King addressed him in a low, clear voice.

"As you shall speak it when you stand, a few hours hence, at the bar of your Creator, I call upon you to pronounce His name."

A dead silence followed. Adolf returned the King's look.

"Speak!" said the King at length.

"Sire," said Adolf, "I have obeyed your command. I have pronounced that Name where only, at such an hour, it is meet to pronounce it, in the heart and in silence;" and he also bent his knee beside Fersen. It might have been a moment or two before those even, judicial tones fell on his ear again.

"Eric Wrangel, you have uttered, with a light laugh, that Word which is King of your King. I will have no hand in sending you one moment earlier than may be to the death for which you are so ill prepared. May grace be given you to repent, in the short time that is left! For you, Axel Fersen, you spoke it, as every true man should, on your knees. Yet there is an earthly name which you revere more. I dare not hasten an idolater before the great Tribunal. For you, La Gardie, you said that Name as though it were any other; you did not even understand the question put to you. You are yet a boy, and this high errand is not for you. You only, Adolf Ribbing, reverenced truth in the letter, as your friend, Axel Fersen, did; and in the spirit, as he did not. Yours be the task! Let us sing the Te Deum together before you go. I sang it after my first victory; I will sing it before my last."

He took the crown from his head, and laid it, with a gesture of deep humility, upon the altar. Was he thinking of the day, sixteen years before, when he led the Te Deum, standing in the midst of an enthusiastic Diet, called together after that bloodless revolution, by means of which he had mastered his realm?

The five strong voices were raised in perfect accord, but Adolf heard only his own. A kind of wonder filled him that he should never hear himself sing again. When it was ended, he kissed the King's hand, and left the chapel. At a sign from Gustav, Axel followed him quickly.

"Axel, this is almost certainly the last night of my life," said Adolf. "What did the King mean by that allusion to you?"

"His Majesty is often pleased to jest," said Axel, shrugging his shoulders, just as he had when Ribbing delivered the King's message to him at their first interview.

"It was an odd moment to choose for a jest," said Adolf; and suddenly there came back to him the words he had overheard at the great meeting, *He has two faces.*

.   .   .   .

"Will you give me my seven hundred riksdalers now?" inquired Baron Wrangel, somewhat grimly, as he came out of the cloister, arm-in-arm with La Gardie.

But the young Count shook his head

"Not till to-morrow. After all, Baron, it was a fair test. Had you been silent, you might have gone."

The Baron screwed his lips together.

"Had I kept silence, I should have been but a dumb dog. Had Ribbing laughed, he would have shown a proper spirit, fit for the enterprise in hand. I know these tricks."

The King remained alone by the altar, engaged in prayer.

CHAPTER XVIII

BELOW GROUND

THE streets were still full of pale, silent, terrified people, as Fersen guided Adolf through them.

Outside an empty, shuttered-up house, not far from the river, he stopped, removed a loose stone in the pavement, and led the way down a rough, wooden staircase into a coal-cellar beneath, motioning to Adolf to pull the paving-stone into its place above them and leave one end slightly tilted.

"It is like being buried first and killed afterwards."

Axel assented indifferently.

"*Fi donc*, how dirty! I could find it in my heart to wish that you were a housemaid, Axel."

"Hush! Stand on this step—so—there is no room for two."

"Is that the water flowing? What a strange, hollow sound! I cannot see a single step before me. Where are you, Axel? Was one of your ancestors a cat?"

"Here is the gunpowder," said Fersen, taking Adolf's hand and placing it on something rounded and small. "Here is the first barrel. Now for the match! You hold it so."

"How shall I know when to light it?"

"You will hear the hour strike. There is a church close by."

"Farewell, then!"

"No. I am going to stay with you."

Adolf felt annoyed. In very high wrought moments, the useless fidelity of another person is often irritating. He wanted the stage to himself.

"Listen," he said, speaking slowly, so as to control the least sign of impatience. "I have no intention of dying. The King promised me what I would. There is one thing that I want more than life, Axel, but I must have life to get it. *I have no intention of dying.*"

"I daresay not."

"Then leave me."

"I have no intention of leaving you."

"And what is to become of the King?"

"The King may fight his own battles."

Adolf reflected an instant; then he shot the last arrow that remained in his quiver.

"And there is someone else who needs you. Forgive me, Axel; if we were not buried alive down here, nothing should make me say it. Is she to fight her own battles too?"

There was no answer. A heavy sigh fluttered the darkness.

"Well?"

"Good-bye," said Axel; and their hands touched.

Crouched up in a heap by the side of the barrel, Adolf heard the retreating footsteps of his friend,—the cautious removal of the stone,—and, as he adjusted the roof of the prison again, conquered a wild, momentary impulse to call him back.

CHAPTER XIX

THE MAN IN THE BLACK CLOAK

NOT long afterwards, the people yet left in Gothenburg were startled by a terrific noise. A heavy cloud of smoke which hung over the river had but just dispersed, when one of the sentinels descried a man on horseback, in a black cloak, making violent signals from the opposite bank, close to the ruined bridge. He immediately reported the fact to his superior officer, who reported it to the King, who ordered that every assistance should be given, and that the man should be brought at once to the palace, if he succeeded in crossing.

Meanwhile, the signals of distress had become more and more impatient. It was clear to the little crowd which had gathered round the sentry-box, that the man in the black cloak, whoever he might be, was greatly agitated by the discovery that the bridge no longer existed, and desired that a boat should put out to him. But, not to speak of the fact that the current at that particular spot was deep and strong, no one cared to make himself a mark for a body of Danish sharp-shooters, who were now descried at some distance. The crack of their muskets was already audible. They had evidently ridden hard in pursuit of the man in black, whoever he was; and though they had not succeeded in overtaking him, a few minutes more must bring them up. The attack would begin soon enough. It was a pity to waste life beforehand. It was a pity to weaken the defence. It was a pity the man could not get across, but it would be a dreadful pity to risk anything now, when everything must be risked later on. So they contented themselves with watching. Already the balls had begun to fly about this dauntless rider. Presently his horse dropped.

For a moment they thought that he was killed. Disentangling himself as best he might, he ran quickly down the bank, threw off his cloak, and plunged into the stream. A hail of bullets made little fountains all round, but none touched him. Once—twice the waters closed over his head, but he emerged again, still swimming vigorously. The bystanders greeted him with a cheer, as he came safe to shore. The look with which alone he responded, seemed, however, to chill their enthusiasm, for the cry dropped almost as soon as it was raised.

The band of sharp-shooters cheered also, and rode quickly away, having failed of their object.

"Take me to the King," said the man in black, addressing the officer in command, who now came hurrying down from the Castle—"at once," he added, as he saw the disposition of the people to try and help him in their own way. Dishevelled and dripping as he was, there was that about him which made them yield instantly. They followed him, at a respectful distance.

"Essen!" Gustav exclaimed, as if he could scarcely believe the evidence of his senses. "You here, Baron Essen!"

"My King's life is in danger. Where else should I be?"

"My life was in danger some weeks ago; you did not obey my summons." Gustav spoke rapidly and severely. A man who is accustomed to use theatrical effect himself, is, of all others, the least likely to be impressed by it. The pale, exhausted features, the wet, muddy, disordered garments, making little pools on the floor, prejudiced him rather unfavourably than otherwise, though his astonishment had got the better of him in the first instance. Essen was quite prepared for this. But the people had seen him; the courtiers had seen him too. He maintained a dignified silence.

"I presume that you have not come for nothing," said Gustav.

"I have not come to be spoken to as if I were one of your Majesty's lacqueys," said the Baron.

The King was habitually courteous. Nothing but prolonged nervous tension could have made him rude. He was quick to see the error and to repair it.

"Forgive me, Essen!" he said, taking the other's hand. "I am harassed on every side. I am done to death. I thought that my old friend had become one of my new enemies."

"I am no man's enemy but my own, sire—and, it may be, the King of Denmark's."

"You bring me news from that camp?" said Gustav.

"News of the last importance."

"Indeed?" said Gustav, with the air of a man who is pleased certainly, though all too well accustomed to the rapid turning of Fortune's wheel to show any surprise. "We will hear it as soon as may be. But you say well, that you are your own enemy; you seem to have been doing your best to drown yourself, my dear Baron. We are not in Italy, now, you and I. We cannot face damp and cold with impunity. You must change your wet clothes first, and have some refreshment. My valet will attend on you. Return to me here, when you have all you need."

He said the words lightly, without apparent effort; yet it was one of the hardest things he had ever done in his life, to let Essen go at that moment.

It was not only solicitude for the welfare of an important messenger which compelled him to do so; he felt it needful on his own account. Once already his temper had given way; he could not afford to let it give way again. He sat stiff and upright in his chair, scarcely moving a muscle, for half an hour, conscious that if he only allowed himself to rise, the tempest in him would break out into something like madness. Essen's desertion had been a heavy blow to him, and he had suffered more than he showed at the time. He liked the man and trusted him; they had travelled in Italy together, when Gustav was at the zenith of his fame, and something of the happiness of that delightful time had been due to him. Was it possible that he had been misrepresented—that he was really faithful? No. His long, unexplained absence confirmed Ribbing's accusation only too well. If Essen had returned at this moment, it was not to die with the King; it was because the tide had turned, and was now running in Gustav's favour. It must be running strongly too; else he would not have dared to come. But how? Why? Rigidly controlling all emotion, Gustav went over every possible combination of events, every possible move wherewith to meet such a combination. By the time Essen reappeared, he was master of himself. No one, looking at the two men, would have supposed that they were about to engage in anything but the most ordinary conversation. The room in which they sat was a fitting scene for such an interview. It was hung with pictures of kings and courtiers—each face a mask.

"With your Majesty's permission," said the Baron, "I will state at once that I have come straight from the Danish camp, where I believed that I could serve your interests better than in your own. I have lurked about it in disguise for some days. I left it three hours since, having learnt all that I wished to know."

"Did you discover the hour at which they will attack?" said Gustav eagerly.

"Sire, they will not attack at all. They will not advance beyond Uddevalla. They dare not. The Powers of Europe are against them."

"England?" said Gustav.

"Elliot, the English ambassador, has ridden post-haste across country to threaten a bombardment of Copenhagen by His Majesty George III., if the Danish army is not immediately withdrawn from Gothenburg. He arrived this morning."

"And Prussia?"

"The King of Prussia is prepared to invade Holstein, with a body of sixteen thousand troops, if the Prince of Hesse advances a step farther on Swedish ground."

" France ? "

" Louis of France, although debarred from active measures at the present moment, has assured the King of Denmark that he will heartily support the policy of Prussia and of England."

" This is great news indeed," said Gustav, drawing a long breath.   " Ewart, the British Minister at Berlin, sent me a courier the day before yesterday, to inform me of the resolution of the Prussian Cabinet.   I was uncertain whether to believe it or not.   I was right after all when I said that my one chance of safety lay in the Danish invasion.   We shall recover the prestige we lost in Russia."

" We have recovered it already, my liege."

" You think so ?   To what do you attribute this sudden change ? "

" To your Majesty's determination to fall with Gothenburg, if Gothenburg fell.   It is the second town in the kingdom.   The other Powers had no desire to see it in the hands of Denmark ; they could not, for very shame, refuse to send help to one who, like your Majesty, was risking his life in defence of the common right of all."

" My life ! " said Gustav dreamily, as if it had not struck him before.   " My life !   Yes, I suppose so. Well, you have saved it, Essen ; not for the first time neither."

" I sincerely hope that it may be for the last," said the Baron gravely.   " I trust never to see your Majesty in such a desperate strait again.   You play bold games, my liege, and Fortune follows your lead ; she has justified you this once, but it was bold to the verge of rashness to reckon on the interference of other Powers."   He smiled a sinister smile.

" Nor did I reckon on it," said the King.   " I reckoned on the love of my subjects."

" May I ask whether they have responded to your expectation ? "

" Nobly," rejoined the King, " with a few exceptions—Carl de Geer, for instance—among the nobles."

Essen just perceptibly shrugged his shoulders.

"Your Majesty was unfortunate in the messenger sent to Carl de Geer, if I may venture to say so."

"Say nothing against him ; he is dead," said Gustav, in such a matter-of-fact tone that Essen looked up, alarmed. The vibrating melancholy of the King's voice, which had power to draw tears from the eyes of thousands, did not affect him ; but this was different.

"Your Majesty is well rid of the youngster."

"If all those of his class loved me as well as that poor boy, I could conquer the world," said Gustav, as though he had not heard or heeded.

"His father made it hard enough for you to conquer Stockholm, sire."

"His father? Ah yes, I had forgotten! He joined my mother's party afterwards, and I lost sight of him." He sat musing, as though the words evoked some painful recollection.

"And it is lucky for you, sire, that you have lost sight of his son. He was a very dangerous young man."

"You too, Essen? Surely you did not believe that rubbish?" said Gustav contemptuously. He was gazing at the fire ; he saw one face in it, and that face not a mask like the one opposite.

"I believe what I saw with my own eyes," said Essen, too intent on stating his case to show any surprise at the form of the King's question. "My young Count, not a month ago, descended upon his uncle, Carl de Geer, in the midst of all his guests, one fine evening, and summoned him to the meeting-place at Mora, as if he were a vile peasant of the soil—he, the descendant of those who ruled Gustav Vasa! I heard him taunt the old lord and his friends because they sympathised with the conspirators of Anjala. I heard him threaten them with the fate of Colonel Hästesko, if they did not obey his commands then and there."

"Well," said the King, bending his brows, "it was foolish, of course—he loved me too well to love me wisely, poor lad !—but, however old Carl de Geer may be now, he was young himself once upon a time—so were you, for the matter of that, Essen—and I see nothing in this grievance to justify his neglect of his sovereign."

"Carl de Geer had another grievance against his nephew, sire."

"What was it?"

"He has a daughter. He might have overlooked his nephew's conduct, but for the discovery that she spent the night with him alone on the hillside."

"What of that?" said the King, almost brutally. "He is dead."

"But she is living, sire. He has no other child."

The King seemed to be weighing the facts in his mind.

"It is absurd to hold anyone responsible for the actions of a mere boy like that," he said at length. "On the other hand, Carl de Geer is too powerful to be his King's enemy. We must bring him round, Essen, we must bring him round. Can anything be done?"

"Sire, it is the great wish of his heart to see his daughter well married."

"Well married?" said the King irritably. "Who is well married? I know of no one. She is beautiful, of course, poor child! There is a law that only daughters should be."

"I dare not pronounce on that point before such a connoisseur as your Majesty."

The King spoke with still greater bitterness. "I am no connoisseur. My Queen was not an only daughter. But we are wandering from the point. Beautiful or unbeautiful, what is to be done with her?"

"I am an old friend of Carl de Geer, as you know, my liege," said the Baron. "I think that I may say I am an old friend of your Majesty's. I am sincerely sorry for the girl. Were I to propose that she should do me"— he hesitated a moment—"the honour of accepting my hand, I believe that I might possibly be of some service both to her father and to the Crown."

The King shook his head. "You are too old for her, Essen. Bah! Why should you wish to marry?

Do you want to become the parent of four children, so as to avoid paying the taxes? Have you no other suggestion?"

"Every man for his own hand, your Majesty!" said the Baron, smiling. "If you will give me no assistance, I shall drop my suit, for I cannot succeed without it; but you will hardly expect me to further someone else's. I have known the girl since she was a child."

"Of what assistance can I be to you, Baron? On the one hand, you have a fine estate, I know, but Carl de Geer has a right to expect even more from his son-in-law. On the other hand, I am not possessed of the elixir of youth."

"Your Majesty is possessed of something very much like it. Money is always young. The Chancellorship of Linköping has just fallen vacant. Give me that post, sire, and I do not fear Carl de Geer. Give me a good word—his daughter is devoted, body and soul, to your Majesty—and I do not fear her. Not now, of course. She will grieve for her cousin a month or so —any woman would; but by and by—later on."

"Poor young Ribbing!" the King said, heaving a sigh. He sat silent for some moments, then rose deliberately and stood with his back to the fire.

"But it is past," he said. "I do not see what better she can do. It is of the last importance to secure Carl de Geer. You have great influence, I know, Baron. I have felt it myself,"—he smiled,— "but—granted that you had what you asked for— granted that you were in a fit position to sue for his daughter, are you sure that you can bring him back to his allegiance?"

"Sire, I would stake my head upon it."

"It is well," said the King. "The patent for the chancellorship shall be made out, and we will pay the old lord a visit on our way back to the capital. Nay, no thanks! It is a bargain, is it not? It pleases you to be Chancellor of Linköping. It pleases him to marry his daughter. It pleases me that he should be my faithful subject. For our own ends, we are all contributors; I find the money, he the maid, you the fidelity. It is a rule-of-three sum. Have I stated the terms correctly?"

"Your Majesty is exact."

"Enough," said Gustav. "There is a meeting of the Privy Council in the chamber adjoining this in half an hour's time. Till then, farewell!"

Essen was wise enough not to attempt any expression of gratitude. He bowed low and quitted the apartment. The King, who had dismissed him with a careless nod, rose and locked the door after him.

"Five minutes' truce!" he said. "An actor has as much between the scenes of his play."

He threw open the window and drew a deep breath. The Castle stood high. Far down below in the distance he caught sight of a moving figure that reminded him vividly of Adolf Ribbing. His first instinct was to avert his eyes, but he compelled himself to look.

"I am a fool," he said to himself. "Ever since Fersen came to tell me that the cellar had fallen in and crushed him, I see that poor boy everywhere, I hear his voice. And, after all, I am a fool. It was not my doing. We were all deceived. What mattered it, a few hours more or less? No one could have foretold; there was no other choice possible. Wrangel is rotten to the core, La Gardie loses his head, I dared not risk Fersen."

He covered his eyes with his hand. When he looked again, the figure had disappeared.

"No," he said, returning to practical matters with a sigh of relief, "Fersen must go to Paris. De Staël is but a broken reed. Besides, he has a source of information that is sealed to everyone else."

The King smiled as he thought of it.

"*Le beau jeune homme* disliked my allusion to that last night," he said, knocking the back of his hand against his knee, as his way was, when amused. "Ah, bah! we can make it up to him easily. And as for Carl de Geer's daughter, why, I thank my stars that poor young Ribbing is out of the way, now that Essen has set his heart on her! Oh, but he laid his plans well, the fox! I should have been hard pressed between them, had Ribbing lived. As things are—well! I long ago suspected the Three Water Lilies. It is worth while to bind Essen to my service—if he can bind Carl de Geer. Eighty thousand a year—and not a man did he send to Mora! It grows serious. The girl will make no difficulty, I suppose."

The King whistled a bar of *Vorrei e non vorrei*, and then fell silent.

"Is it worth while?" he said.

It is but a little step from the worthlessness of woman to the worthlessness of man, and thence to the worthlessness of all things. Weariness and disgust unspeakable overcame him. What did it mean, this interference of the Powers of Europe? Was it nothing but an imperative call to him to escape from his own release? Was he in truth glad—was he not rather sorry? He took a long look down into the depths of that gulf on the edge of which, until an hour ago, he had supposed himself to be standing.

"And at the bottom of it, there is rest," he said. "No more false friends—ah, how tired, how sleepy I am!"

He half stifled a yawn, and, leaning back in his chair, let his eyes close. Very haggard and worn he looked. He had not slept the night before. He had lain counting the hours, listening in spite of himself for the report of the explosion which should tell him that the bridge was blown to atoms—that Adolf Ribbing was dead. He had asserted and maintained repeatedly that he could not feel secure till all means of retreat were cut off. In his secret heart he knew that he could never feel secure till one face ceased to haunt him. Before this time, there were long periods when he had forgotten; now, ever since his interview with Fersen, he went on seeing it incessantly. Why, Essen, of all people, had worn that face when first he entered, and every picture on the wall wore it in turn! He was ill, nervous, he told himself. It was only that. He had had nothing to do with the boy's death. Was life so sweet to him? Was it worth while?

9

And even as he asked himself over and over again that dangerous question, to which all the wealth, the knowledge, the power and glory of this world can give no answer, he felt that it was. He stood upon the heights; he saw the Promised Land at his feet; the haunting face vanished.

"For I begin again to-day, the future clear before me at last—at last!" he said, speaking to himself in the low tones of ecstasy. "There it is, plain and straight. Sweden—my country—first! France next! And then—then"—

He did not finish the sentence. The sun had risen, bright and clear, in a sky of dazzling blue. The mists were all dispersed. The people had got wind of the news of deliverance; from every tower and steeple the bells rang merrily. It was Gustav who had set the bells ringing; for a moment it seemed to him that it was Gustav who had made the sun shine.

Excitement was lighting every face and flashing in every movement of the crowd when he stepped forth from the palace, followed by his suite, to harangue the troops assembled in the great square. Rumours had gone abroad to the effect that the town was saved; how, or by whom, people only conjectured. Nothing was known for certain; his auditors could hardly contain themselves when the King mounted the steps leading to a hastily constructed wooden platform and began to speak. The air he breathed was charged with the inflammable silence of a vast multitude, only restrained from venting its agitation in outcries by the still greater agitation that compelled it to listen.

He spoke briefly, and to the point. The safety of the realm, he said, depended on the success of the efforts of her citizens to save Gothenburg. It was, of course, open to them to surrender at discretion. If they did so, they would probably save themselves much suffering,—he could not and would not disguise from them the horrors of war,—but it would be at the expense of their country, prostrate at the feet of her foes.

A solemn murmur arose among the citizens, and their spokesman stepped forward.

"We are ready to suffer anything," he said. "We are prepared to undergo a bombardment—to see our children slain—our houses laid in ruins—rather than to surrender this town."

Then, amid breathless silence, the King announced that he had already received overtures from the Danish camp at Uddevalla, thanks, no doubt, to the firm resolve of Gothenburg to fight to the uttermost —to the powerful reinforcements that were approaching from Dalecarlia—to the intervention of Prussia, of France, and in especial of the very good friend of Sweden, His Britannic Majesty George III., the exertions of whose envoy, Mr. Hugh Elliot, he could not sufficiently commend. For the present, *as soon as the enemy became aware of his movements*—no sooner—he meant to demand a truce of eight days, to be signed on both sides; it was possible that the negotiations during that time would greatly modify the course of hostilities. If not, they were prepared for the worst that could happen. Taking Baron Essen by the hand, he presented to them the hero who had come through fire and flood to bring them news of the enemy. He it was to whose timely information they owed so much. The only spot that tarnished the gladness of this day, he continued, was his deep regret for the lamented death of one of the bravest of his captains, young Count Ribbing, who had perished in the act of destroying the New Bridge. His body had not yet been recovered from the ruins of the shattered vault, under which there was, alas, no doubt that it lay buried! Further research would, in all probability, bring it to light, enabling them to pay the last sad honours to one who had given his life for that of Gothenburg.

The King paused impressively. Adolf Ribbing was well known among the men, and had made himself universally popular. One or two of them wept aloud. Fersen, who was standing on Gustav's right, bent his head.

Suddenly there was a cry, and the ranks opened.

A slight, boyish figure made its way through them,

climbed the few steps up to the platform, and dropped on one knee before the King.

The features were pale, the brown eyes dimmed and sunk. They sought Axel's face, but Axel had covered it with his hands.

Only Baron Wrangel saw the instantaneous recoil of the King, and noted his change of colour.

The next moment all the world saw him come forward, raise the young soldier, and lead him to the front of the platform, crying, as he placed one hand in his and one in that of Baron Essen, "Behold our two deliverers!"

The Baron darted a look of intense hatred at Adolf, who had no strength to return it, although, confusedly, he heard its language above the thundering shout of all the troops assembled : "Long live Count Ribbing! Long live our three deliverers!"

CHAPTER XX

A TOKEN

THE scene in the great square was followed by a solemn thanksgiving service in the cathedral. On the ears of some of those who were present the words of the Te Deum fell with a different signification from that which they had borne the night before.

By the time it was over Adolf had such a violent headache that he was conscious of little except the bounding and thumping of millions of small hammers inside his skull. Everything seemed to be unreal. The fifteen hundred voices chanting round him were mere noise compared with the stern music of those five, breaking the stillness of the dark relentlessly, as human action breaks and disperses the silent, imminent gloom of death, into which, but a moment after, it must resolve. He only desired speech; emotion, urged beyond a certain point, becomes apathy, and it leaves a flatness which nothing except fresh air, or sleep, or friendly intercourse can relieve. His long, slim legs almost gave way beneath him as he came staggering out of the porch.

"Come to my tower," said Axel affectionately, laying a hand on his shoulder. "You cannot rest at the Castle; they are making hell's own din there. Come and lie down for an hour or so; you will never be able to appear at the banquet to-night unless you do. What? You did not understand that the King had invited you? *Ma foi!* you must be very deaf, my friend."

"I do not know what is the matter with me. I

can neither hear nor see. You look as if you had eyes all round your head."

"Come and lie down at once."

Adolf vowed that he could not sleep. He was feverishly excited and inclined to talk. On the other hand, Axel had never been more silent. At first he answered only in monosyllables. At last, finding that even the shortest of these failed to act as a full stop, he said he had an engagement at the Arsenal. Adolf cursed that building audibly. Bad language was of no avail where good proved impotent. His friend departed.

He had fastened the shutters to keep out the brilliant midday light, but it came streaming through the chinks in long, slant rays, filled with the drowsy dance of motes, barring the floor with faint gold. The shouting in the streets had ceased ; for a brief period there was no noise. A kind of holiday stillness brooded over the great town ; not even a murmur penetrated so far. A delicious feathery warmth settled down upon Adolf ; the elfin hammers bumped and thumped less persistently. His eyelids closed and closed again, and every time the interval between their closing grew less until at length he fell asleep.

Hours afterwards he awoke, with the startled feeling that somebody was looking at him ; but there was no one in the room.

The door stood slightly ajar. A chair had been drawn close to the bedside, and on it a little leather pocket-book was lying open. It was the daintiest thing on which his eyes had rested for a long time, bound in the pale, pearly blue of the first forget-me-nots, with a clasp of wrought gold and enamel. The writing on the page could not be Fersen's. It was round and loose, and so large and easy to decipher that Adolf had read the following verses before he knew what he was about : —

> " Qu'écrirez-vous sur ces tablettes?
>   Quels secrets leur confiérez-vous?
>   Ah ! sans doute elles furent faites
>   Pour les souvenirs les plus doux !

En attendant qu'à cet usage
Le souvenir soit employé,
Qu'il soit permis à l'amitié
D'en remplir la première page."

Underneath Axel had added the single word, *Trianon*.

The second page, immediately below, was blank, except for an entry which must have been made a minute or two before, for the ink was still wet: *4th October 1788.—My friend, Adolf, Count Ribbing, escaped death.*

Adolf lay smiling and thinking until he heard Axel's step in the passage, when he turned over on his side and pretended that he was yet asleep. His friend shut the door in a cautious manner so as to make no noise, took up the pocket-book, touched the words lightly with his finger to make sure that the ink had dried, fastened the gold clasp, and put it in his breast-pocket. The sun was sinking low by this time, and he moved over to the window to unbar the shutter.

"Your poetical friend has good taste in pocket-books, Axel," said Ribbing, from the bed. "Besides, the verse is charming. I would not exchange friend-ship for love, if I were you."

At first he doubted whether Fersen heard; next he felt sure that Fersen had, and wished he had not. The silence became uncomfortable. The room was quite light now. If he would only turn round! But Axel remained standing by the window, and a man's back is eloquent of nothing, even to his most intimate friend.

"Forgive me, Axel," he said at last.

Axel came quickly over to the bedside, took Ribbing's hand in his, and looked him full in the face. Now Ribbing felt that the owner of the blue pocket-book should have blushed; he was angry to find that his own cheeks glowed instead, that he had hard work to sustain the unflinching scrutiny. He tried to smile, but could not.

"Ah, you are awake!" said Axel. "You have been dreaming hard. You were dreaming when I came in. But we will not speak of our dreams?" The tone in which the last words were spoken, half a command, half passionate entreaty, was irresistible.

"I will never speak of mine—to anyone," said Adolf. "What a strange fellow you are! You take nothing seriously except what others would take lightly. But one loves one's friends for what they are and for what they are not; it's no matter."

"I do not follow you."

Ribbing laughed.

"I love you, in the first place, philosopher, because you are Axel Fersen, and in the second, because you are not Adolf Ribbing. That is all. Now tell me, had the King a dream, or why did he think I was dead? Above all, why did you think so? People are curiously ready to believe that I have gone to a better world, though I am still quite content to honour the old one with my presence."

"It happened in this way," said Axel. "The King sent me down to that house as soon as we had heard the report of the explosion. I found that the roof of the cellar had fallen in. The mass of masonry was so compact that three men could not move it so much as a finger's breadth. Naturally, I concluded that you were lying, crushed to atoms, underneath it; and why you are not, I fail to understand."

"Then it was not you who pulled me out?"

"I? I could as soon have pulled out the foundation-stone of the Castle."

"I thought it must have been you," said Adolf, with a puzzled look. "Who was it then, I wonder? Someone must have dragged me into the next house. The explosion stunned me, I suppose. When I came to myself I was lying alone in a room that I did not know. The chiming of the bells woke me up. I wanted to know what had become of the King."

"Did you get out easily?"

"Yes. The doors were not locked though the house seemed to be empty."

"There are empty houses on both sides," said Fersen. "I took care to ascertain that when I began operations. I cannot understand how I could have

overlooked a secret passage in the wall.   I examined
the whole place most carefully.   As for the man, you
must have imagined him, Adolf.   No one knew where
you were except Wrangel and La Gardie, and they
were both on duty at the palace."

Adolf turned up his coat sleeve and showed Fersen a
violet mark high up on the arm.

"Did I imagine that?" said he.

It was growing late, and they had no time to discuss
the rescue further.   The King had told Adolf that he
would speak with him privately before the State
banquet.

CHAPTER XXI

BEFORE AND AFTER

AS Gustav sat alone in the early close of that autumn afternoon, his mind, released for a moment from the strain and tension of the present, went back to his childhood—perhaps because he saw in it a strange, picturesque allegory of his later years.

The day had been a day of violent changes, and his own calmness of demeanour was, after all, little more than apparent. The set resolve with which he rose, armed to face the probability that the last act of the drama was beginning—the feverish, triumphant exaltation of noon—both moods had vanished. The failing light disposed him to melancholy. The high spirit which, throughout his life, answered the call of danger as a bird answers the dawn, flagged and fell drooping in silence.

He smiled with infinite sadness, as he recollected the first scenes : his gay, careless father, a Jack-of-all-trades, if ever there was one ; the scornful words, the yet more scornful looks of his beautiful mother.

"I too love to play many games. I too, in my heart of hearts, disdain those who play at them with greater seriousness than myself. I am my own father—my own mother—and the father and mother of this great people ! "

He saw himself, a little eager boy, cutting his fingers with the sharp tools in his father's workshop at Drottningholm.

"And I have cut my fingers, playing with edged

tools, many a time since then!" he said, thinking of his fierce nobles.

He saw himself quarrelling with the unfortunate black child, who had been sent as a present to Louisa Ulrica, that she might make the experiment of bringing him up _à la Rousseau_, with no education whatever. The heir-apparent, who, in his own opinion and perhaps in that of some others, had only too much, wished often enough in those days that she had selected her eldest born for this delightful essay.

"But I have quarrelled with many a black child since," he said, "and ignorance loves me no more now than it did then. What work I had to destroy the Chamber of Roses!"[1]

He laughed aloud, as he thought of the description of himself which he had recently unearthed in a document bearing the signature of one of his tutors. "The Crown Prince is very stupid about writing, spelling, and grammar. He knows almost nothing of geography; he has an invincible horror of work. Far removed alike from serious thought and from religious sentiment, his heart is as empty as his intellect."

"Poor old Scheffer!" he said, speaking as though to someone else. "I must have played him many a trick before he wrote that of me. He lived to change his mind. We were good friends afterwards. He attributed my reformation to his own counsels, I suppose. But I owe him a greater debt of gratitude for his bad opinion. I should never have got the upper hand of my troublesome States, if they had not taken his word for it that I 'knew almost nothing of geography.' They might have been warned in time. I was only seventeen, when Voltaire wept—or said he wept—because someone told him that I had learnt the _Henriade_ by heart. They did not know that I was fond of Descartes, even then; _Cogito, ergo sum_. They did not think, but they existed all the same, the more's the pity."

His lips grew bitter as he thought of the one event of his life in which the nobles had been too strong for him

[1] The torture chamber.

—his marriage with the plain, dull, bigoted daughter of Denmark. Yet even the tragedies of youth have some little refreshing touch of youth's follies upon them. The diamond buttons, brought by special courier from Paris, as if they had been the most important despatch, that his costume might exactly resemble that of the Dauphin, pleased him now, as they had pleased him then—for a different reason.

They made him think of France. How he had plotted and schemed to get there; how he had rejoiced in his escape from bondage and revelled in the freedom of his inferiors! And what a pleasant place was Paris for the young Count de Haga, as he styled himself in those days! The King of Sweden laughed at the mere recollection. He had a smile for "the Dubarry" even, and the jewelled necklace he had given her little dog, and the disgust and contempt of the lovely Dauphiness, when she heard of his prudent behaviour. Marie Antoinette had not learned prudence then.

How many fair women there were in the world, twenty years since—how many witty and wise men! What had become of them all? Hard question! Some, like himself, had left their youth so far behind that it seemed like a nursery tale; and some were dead. He thought of these with tender, yearning regret. The tears stood in his eyes, as the vision of his Egeria, beautiful Madame d'Egmont, stood clear and sweet before him, clothed in the three soft colours, lilac, silver, and green, that he continued to wear long afterwards, for love of her. Thus was she dressed when she sat beside him in the box at the opera, on the night when he opened the despatch containing the news of his father's sudden death. He saw her delicate face and large, spiritual eyes; he heard her musical whisper, "Contentez-vous, sire, d'être absolu par la séduction, ne le réclamez jamais comme un droit."

"It was soon after that I signed the Constitution of 1720," he said, and his mouth grew stern again. "Some-one who was looking on told me that I did it with a smile, *qui disait bien des choses*. I have signed other documents since with something that was not a smile.

Old Fritz too! He thought his little nephew would be easy game. How his wrinkled brows drew together when I promised him that I would rule Sweden 'wisely and worthily,' and nothing more! Upon my soul, I was as glad to get out of the room as if I had been a beaten army! But afterwards—ah, that was the grand time! 'The Ides of March,' and all the rest of it. The wish was father to the thought in that case. Spite of his veneration for the classics, I think he could have found it in his heart to reverse the parts of the older and the younger man, and play Brutus to my Cæsar. He and the Empress Catharine reckoned without their host for once. Her Imperial Majesty will make a wry face when she hears of this day's work. How pleased she was long ago when I sent her word that I was about to ask leave of the Senate to travel! Travelling! why, it would have paid the Empress Catharine to pay my travelling expenses for the rest of my natural existence. Well, *Rira bien qui rira le dernier.* Who knows what the future may hold in store?"

Gustav's expression darkened. The past had been his friend. At times it seemed to him that his only real enemy was that future of which he and his foes were alike ignorant. His meditations became abstract as he sat leaning his head on his hand.

"Has the Divine Being who gave us memory to torture and to delight us given us indeed nothing whereby we may know the foretaste as well as the aftertaste, nothing whereby we may make the future our own? Has He given us eyes at the back of our intellect, and none whereby we may look forward? Believe it who list, that will not I! Some art there is, some way by which to see. The eyes are there. They make a great mistake who say such knowledge as that causes fear; if we could but be sure of it, we never should fear anything. The veriest coward on earth can face the inevitable. It is only the uncertain that we dread—and the bravest of us dreads that."

Here Gustav fell into a depth of thought which no words could represent. Gifted beyond many men of

his age with clear, practical views, he had never cared
to pry into the future from motives of morbid curiosity
—from a feeling that it was wicked, and therefore
agreeable, to force the secrets of his Creator.   He was
honestly annoyed by the one unknown quantity which
might, at any moment, alter the terms of the equation
that he was working out.   He honestly believed that
science, which was doing so much to annihilate space
already, would, in the end, annihilate time also—that
it was but a question of finding the right way.   He
had been present at solemn discussions of the theory
that any man had but to mount high enough in a
balloon, to descend in any country that he preferred,
just at the moment when the earth's revolution brought
it directly underneath him.   Why might not the daring
aeronauts of the spirit world mount above life, and see
its every phase mapped out before them, descending at
will upon the past, the present, or the future?   Meantime, he kept his mind open; nor was he easily
credulous.   When he first visited Paris, a clairvoyante
had told him to beware of firearms in the year 1792.
Her prediction was not so implicitly believed but that
he thought it needful to write a long letter, on the eve
of the *coup d'état* of 1772, full of instructions to his
brother as to the course to be pursued, in the event of
his death while it was still in progress.   Now, sounding
his own conscience, he asked himself whether the
recent warning of Noorna Arfridson had found him more
susceptible; he answered that it had not.   As for the
momentary impulse to shrink back when he saw Adolf
Ribbing again, that was mere surprise—overwrought
nerves—what you will!

And yet an unacknowledged feeling that he was
ashamed of the movement and would have recalled it
if he could, drove him on to make much of Ribbing.
He pondered long over the means of doing so.   His
memory was tenacious; when he recalled the conversation at Mora, he had little doubt as to the request most
likely to be preferred in the forthcoming interview.   He
wanted to convince himself that his attitude to this
young man was just what it would have been to any

other—if anything, even more generous and affectionate. How was it possible to do this, when the reward that would certainly be claimed was no less certainly promised to someone else?

"What if I were to break with Essen?" he said to himself. "Can I afford it? He is hand and glove with the nobles. He does not care for Carl de Geer's daughter, and my young Mercury does. Either way, I bind Carl de Geer to my cause; he has no other heir. And Mercury thinks me a god, whereas Essen knows me to be a man. True, Essen is a far more influential person. He thinks himself neglected too. I could see that in his manner. Neglected men are dangerous."

He summoned up a vision of Essen's sombre and brooding countenance, and turned from it with relief to Ribbing's boyish face. Yes—with relief—he was himself once more! Why not insist that Essen should give up his suit before he assumed the Chancellorship of Linköping? Why not throw the weight of his influence into the scale and persuade Carl de Geer to accept Ribbing as his son-in-law? He had not thoroughly liked Essen's plan from the first. It concentrated too much power in the hands of one. Yet how persuade him to abandon it?

"Well," he said to himself, with a smile, "are there no other feminine investments? It must be delicately done, but why should not I do it? By Heaven, I will! I sent young Ribbing to Mora. That was a dangerous task enough, and he came safely through. I sent him to Gothenburg: it was said that no one could reach Duretz—he reached him. It was Ribbing that I ordered to blow up the bridge. Any other man would have died; he escaped. If it be true that I behold Death in person when I see him, he bears a charmed existence until he has accomplished the purpose for which he was born. I wished to put it to the test; I have done so. Who is that? Ah, Wrangel!"

"A letter for your Majesty, forwarded by the Ambassador of France, *viâ* Copenhagen," said the Baron, as he presented it.

The King glanced at the neat, clear writing.

"Ah, Madame de Staël! That can wait," he said, with a half-sigh for his youth. Time was when a letter from Paris—an ill-spelt letter, full of long lectures on government and the morality of politics—would make him put aside important business for the laborious pleasure of deciphering it. On the very day of his coronation, he had answered one of these epistles with another, twelve pages long. But Madame d'Egmont was gone, and all the *bons mots* of the future Corinne could not make up for her.

"An audience is demanded, your Majesty. I heard Count Ribbing inquire when you would be at leisure."

Something insolent in the Baron's tone struck Gustav. He had noticed it on the preceding night, and set it down to jealousy.

"Let Count Ribbing wait!" he said. "Everything comes to him who waits—at least they say so in France. Be seated, my dear Baron! I want to ask your advice."

"Your Majesty does me too great honour."

Gustav crossed one leg over the other, and leaned back carelessly in his chair. To ask advice of any man is, as he well knew, the best means of flattering him. Wrangel would say, of course, that the appointment ought to be given to Adolf's rival. The King would demur at first — would then appear to be convinced.

"You are aware that Baron Essen and Count Ribbing have both rendered important services to the State?" he said.

"I have ears, your Majesty, and my sight is as good as ever it was, thank Heaven!"

The King was apt to confound impertinence with independence. Wrangel knew this, and made the most of it.

"The Chancellorship of Linköping is vacant," continued Gustav. "Baron Essen, I know, desires it. I have good reason to think that Count Ribbing will apply for it also. I cannot cut it in two, like Solomon's baby. With the best will in the world—for I should be the last to contest the justice of the claim on both sides—I cannot give it to both. To which of the two, then, shall I give it?"

"Sire, to Count Ribbing," said the Baron, without a moment's hesitation.

"Why?" asked Gustav, with as much indifference as he could throw into a question that he had not expected to ask. Wrangel's answer took him by surprise.

The Baron shrugged his shoulders.

"I have heard it said, your Majesty, that there are two ways of getting rid of a dangerous person: you must conciliate him or you must kill him. The last is the safest, but it is also the most difficult. It is not only cats that have nine lives."

"To what do you allude?" said the King. "So far as I can see, we were not speaking of dangerous persons at all. If circumstances were to make either of these two men my enemy—which Heaven forefend!—Ribbing is younger, he has but a few barren acres; Essen has great experience, and his estates are larger. You made a slight mistake, did you not? It is Essen that you meant to recommend me not to offend?"

"It is Essen, sire, if it was of Essen that Noorna Arfridson foretold a certain event."

"You have heard that foolish story?" said the King, laughing—he always laughed when he heard it mentioned. "Who told it you?"

"Ribbing himself. It seemed to amuse him even more than it amuses your Majesty."

"Indeed? I understand now that you should think him a person to be conciliated. Yet it may well be that he was amused," said the King. "I do not think I have a more faithful servant—in a good hour be it spoken!"

"It is to his interest, sire, to make a great show of fidelity. I do not blame it. I should do the same, were I in his place."

10

"Would you?" said the King drily.

"More especially," Wrangel went on, as though he had not heard the question, "if my father had been, like his, your Majesty's determined opponent."

"True. He was my mother's friend—that is as much as to say, her son's bitterest foe. I have been reminded of that once already."

Gustav sighed. Any allusion to his mother saddened him; she was the evil genius of his life.

"If your Majesty does not give Count Ribbing the Chancellorship of Linköping, your Majesty will no doubt bestow on him something of equal value."

"There is no other post vacant at this moment."

"Sire, there is always a rich marriage to be made."

"Did Count Ribbing hint at any such thing?" said Gustav, pausing.

"It is an open secret that he admires one of the beauties of Sweden, your Majesty. Fame says that his cousin has hair of the Venetian hue. Hair of that colour weighs very heavy—it might perhaps be found to weigh even heavier than the chancellorship. It *might*; I do not say that it would."

"Count Ribbing must manage his love affairs for himself," the King said lightly. "I will think over your advice, my dear Baron, but I cannot say that I am altogether prepared to take it. He deserves some reward, no doubt. But if we give him everything at once, we shall deprive ourselves of the pleasure of rewarding him over and over again."

"Everyone will agree that it is prudent in your Majesty to give Count Ribbing whatever reward he may ask for," said Wrangel doggedly.

"I have not always done what everybody would agree was most prudent. But I will give the matter my best consideration. In the meantime, allow me to thank you for your good counsel. Be so kind as to tell Count Ribbing that I am at his service. He has not the *grandes entrées*, as you have. Do you recommend that I should give him those also?"

"A superfluous question, sire! If I know our friend, he will take them without asking."

At that moment Adolf's voice was heard outside in the passage.

CHAPTER XXII

THE PROMISE

"BE seated, my dear Count," said Gustav amiably, as his lacquey lighted the candles. "I must ask your indulgence while I finish a despatch for the next mail. I shall be at your service immediately," and he drove a spluttering quill across the blank sheet of paper before him.

Had Adolf looked over his shoulder, he would have been surprised to see that the King was writing his own name again and again, with great regularity and swiftness. Meditations like those which Wrangel had interrupted were not usual with him; he resembled a woman, in that his thoughts moved more easily when his hands moved.

"So that is the reason of the rogue's disdainful manners to his sovereign! He thinks me afraid. There is no reason why he should not make others think so too. He is clever enough, in his own way. He would never have advised me as he did, had he not thought that I wished it. If I give this boy here his heart's desire—if I hopelessly alienate Essen, who is, as Wrangel is well aware, a much more important person—his conjecture will be turned into certainty. Dare I risk that?"

It was a curious dilemma. Afraid of his own fear, he had made up his mind to defy it; and the very action by which he meant to defy it, would, so it seemed, be construed into fear by everyone else. He made a long pause and dropped the pen. Adolf wondered into what foreign country those vague blue

eyes were gazing ; when not directly fixed, their empty
distance of expression was almost vacant.

"No." He took up the pen again. "The bargain
must stand as it is, for the present, at anyrate. But
what to do with Ribbing ? "

His eye fell by chance on the unopened letter beside
him. It brought back with a rush the old delightful
recollections.

"The very thing !" he said to himself. "I will send
him to Paris with Axel Fersen. They are great
friends ; there is no hardship in that. Hardship? Ah,
would that I could go myself! I will tell *Madame
l'Ambassadrice* to give him a taste of the life there.
If he does 'hot fall in love with her, a thousand
chances to one that he does with somebody else ; and
then I am quit of this coil. Anyhow, it will gain time."

The blue eyes veered round and flashed on Adolf
once more.

"I hope that you are quite recovered ? "

Once more it was hard to him to speak in the King's
presence. Since the journey to Mora, he had felt a
dumb, dog-like happiness in being near his master,
which only strong excitement, like that of the night
before, could melt into ease.

"We will not beat about the bush," said the King.
"Life is short—we have all heard that from our baby-
hood—and the fact that it seems a little longer to-night
than it did either to you, Count, or to me this morning,
does not authorise us to delay. You have deserved
well of the Crown. What do you want? "

"I want my cousin, sire," said Adolf, smiling. He
was not prepared for such an abrupt question, and the
suddenness of it left no time for diplomacy.

"I thought as much," said the King, shaking his
head. "How old are you ? "

"Nineteen, sire."

"Nineteen—and he wants his cousin !" The King
lifted up his hands in despair. "And does your cousin
want you, may I ask? Oh, very well ; your cheeks
have answered for you ! And does her father want
you also? "

"If he did, sire, I should not have troubled your Majesty."

"It is a delicate business," the King said, drumming with his fingers on the table. "You are aware—indeed, you told me yourself—that Carl de Geer is but a lukewarm friend of mine. I must ask you for your full confidence. Is there any sort of secret understanding between you and the lady?"

"We were betrothed as children. My uncle broke off the formal engagement, but my cousin and I have never ceased to consider ourselves bound by it."

"He countenanced the betrothal at the time?"

"Yes."

"On what ground did he afterwards refuse his consent?"

"We are not of the same way of thinking in religion and politics, your Majesty."

"Ah! when was nineteen ever of the same way of thinking in religion and politics as nineteen multiplied by three? But the old can never understand that the young are not old, nor the young that age is nothing but the absence of youth."

"I am willing to make every allowance for the prejudices of an old man," said Adolf stiffly; "but your Majesty would not wish me to give up my convictions."

"Certainly not," said Gustav, raising his eyebrows with an assumption of solemnity which, to anyone rather more experienced than the Count, might have implied, "They will give you up of their own accord soon enough, my dear boy."

The conversation seemed to come to a full stop. Adolf wondered why.

"You must allow me time," Gustav resumed, in a different tone. "Will you confide in me altogether? Will you trust your King to do the best that he can for you?"

"Your Majesty is too good," said Adolf, and in a moment his hope grew into faith.

"Remember that he is twice as old as you are," the King said, smiling, as a brother might, while he rose and laid his hand lightly on Adolf's shoulder, "twice as near death—*the last folly we can commit*, as a clever lady once called it—twice therefore, twice as foolish. Do you think you can trust him?"

Adolf raised the hand that fell on his and kissed it fervently.

"Is it a covenant between us? Well, then, promise me three things! First, that you will not tell anyone what has passed at this interview."

Adolf promised gladly.

"In the second place, that you will start for Paris with Count Fersen as soon as our affairs here are wound up, and that you will not attempt to come back to this country till I recall you."

Adolf glanced up, as if he thought that his ears must have deceived him and his eyes could report differently; but the King kept the same benevolent smile. It was exile where he had looked for home. Still, the King must know best. He mastered a rebellious feeling of disappointment as well as he could, and promised.

"Thirdly, that you will not attempt to see your cousin before you go, nor to hold any communication with her before your return."

As suddenly as hope had grown surprise fell to despair. Every trace of colour left the young man's cheek.

"I cannot promise that," he said.

"I am quite aware that the condition is a hard one"—the King's voice was almost womanly in softness. "Nothing short of necessity would make me impose it upon you. It is to save you from a condition harder still. You think now—you cannot help thinking—that you desire nothing in the world so much as to see your cousin before you go?"

Adolf blushed to find himself discovered. Was it so common then, this deep emotion of his? Was it so silly? He would not speak till he had his voice under control.

"I am not such a fool, your Majesty. If I could see that our meeting now would make it less easy for us to meet hereafter, I would give it up."

"I. will explain my meaning. I suppose that you have, from time to time, corresponded with your cousin?"

Adolf assented.

"And this correspondence has been kept secret from Carl de Geer? I thought so. He will be sure to find it out. Believe me! I have had as much to do with secret correspondence as any man."

"We would not continue it," said Adolf eagerly.

"You think not? Your cousin, if you see her, will soon change that opinion. You shake your head. You believe that she is one in a thousand. There is no such thing, my dear Count. One woman is another woman. I know them. We are wax in their hands; and they love to write letters—above all, to write letters in secret. If she sees you, she will know whither you are going. If she knows whither you are going, nothing will serve her but she must write. If, at the very moment when I am making overtures to Carl de Geer, he finds that he is being deceived by those of his own house, he will not give you his daughter, nor could I, in such a case, bring pressure to bear upon him."

"I could explain to Tala"—

The King shrugged his shoulders.

"If you see her, I can do nothing for you. I fully believe in the honesty of your purpose; but there is no such thing as a dual control. The greatest king on earth has no power where a woman steps in; and the humblest woman on earth thinks she knows better than the wisest man—were that man Socrates. If you see her, you will be her servant, not mine. You would begin by obeying my instructions, you would end by obeying hers. Make your choice. Manage your affairs your own way, if you will. You know best whether you have any chance of succeeding. But if you entrust them to me, I must have a free hand. I must be able to assure Carl de Geer that you have behaved in the most upright and honourable manner—that you have never, to my certain knowledge, deceived him. There must be no saving clause, remember, no private understanding. You must promise, and you must keep your word."

"Will your Majesty allow me to pay one visit— to write one letter to my cousin, before I go?" said Adolf. "How can she understand else? She will think that I have deserted her."

"Impossible! That one visit—that one letter would compromise everything. It is not that I do not see your difficulty, Count; but I intend to visit Carl de Geer on my way home from this place. I will myself explain your silence—your absence—to the lady. Does this satisfy you?"

Still Adolf hesitated.

"It is not likely that you will be away for more than a year, at the farthest. She must be very inconstant if she cannot wait so long for the chance of her life's happiness."

Still not a word.

The King frowned.

"Well, take your own way," he said, with a smile that hurt his devoted follower even more. "You may be right. I am but a broken reed to lean upon. My life itself is threatened every moment. Why should I expect, even of those who love me best, that they should believe in any power of mine to help them?"

"I promise," said Adolf desperately. His head was swimming.

"You do well," said the King, after a moment's pause. "There is one question more that I must ask you. The answer that you give I will not divulge to anyone; it is a mere form. But there are reasons why I must be convinced that I have heard the truth from your own lips. The line of conduct that I pursue towards the father may depend upon it. Have you ever—wittingly or unwittingly—done anything which might be held in any way to compromise the lady's reputation?"

The question, from anyone else, would have kindled Adolf's wrath; but it was asked in such a way that he could not feel offended.

"Never!" he answered solemnly. It did not occur

to him to think of the night on the hillside, for he was quite unconscious that Tala had been seen, and, even had he known it, knowing as he did his own innocence and hers, it would not have troubled him.

A curious gleam shone in the blue eyes of the King. It was open to him to believe Essen or to believe Ribbing. He did not see that it was open. Bitter experience had convinced him that what sounded bad might be untrue, but that what sounded good must be. For the first time, Adolf, as he thought, had told him a lie. He was not at all sorry.

CHAPTER XXIII

THE ARABIAN NIGHTS

THINGS went merrily in Gothenburg from that day forward. A wonderful change had taken place. Was it the same city? Adolf asked himself. Where were the shadowy creatures who could not be roused to take even those measures which were most needful for their own preservation? Where were those thin, starved wretches, who slid like ghosts about the streets? They were full of laughter now, echoing with jovial shouts and cries of enthusiasm. Those who had formerly refused all assistance were now eager to do everything in their power. The courage of one man had routed the cowardice of thousands, and the King was the life and soul of the defence. No one stirred without his knowledge; every detail was submitted to him, each difficulty reported the moment it arose. The fortifications were made secure. The artillery was repaired. Special directions were given with regard to the cannon, many pieces of which were choked with dust, and quite unfit for use, owing to the want of gun-carriages. The East India merchantmen gave up their own splendid horses for the service. The local militia was called out, and twelve hundred volunteers were enrolled from among the citizens alone.

The Dragoons and the Life Guards were among the first to arrive from without. They entered slowly, for, since the destruction of the New Bridge, there was no means of reaching the city except by boat or by the drawbridge. Day by day the advance companies of the Dalecarlians came pouring in, to the wild sound of horns and the blare of other uncouth instruments, that jarred upon the ear as strangely as their rough dialect. They would be terrible foes ; there was no doubt of that. Adolf, as he looked on, wondered whether they would be amenable to any control whatever—even to that of Armfelt, their adored captain. He had but little time to think of his own affairs—had indeed almost forgotten them in the absorbing interest of the present.

One morning as he sat in the anteroom, busy over the plan of a stockade which was to be erected on the north side of the town, a blast of trumpets caused him to look up from his work.

This was not the hour at which the troops were generally paraded ; he felt sure that it must portend something unusual, and was about to run downstairs to inquire, when Fersen entered the room hurriedly, with some appearance of excitement.

"News !" he cried. "News ! The Prince Marshal of Hesse has sent General Haxthausen, with two trumpeters, to summon Gothenburg to surrender."

Adolf sprang from his seat, seized the poker as the first thing that came to hand, flourished it round his head, gave a savage war-whoop of triumph, and burst into a fit of uncontrollable laughter, in which for once Fersen joined heartily. When the tempest of mirth had subsided a little, he continued—

"They are on the opposite side. The drawbridge has not yet been let down. Count Sparre has sent to me for instructions. Haxthausen says that he wants to see Duretz."

"He does not know the King is here then ?"

Fersen shook his head.

Again their laughter made the old walls ring

"But what are we to do ?"

"Why, ask the King, of course !"

"I dare not."

"*Dare not ?*"

"I dare not," repeated Fersen, slightly raising his delicate eyebrows. "His Majesty is reading *The Arabian Nights* for the first time."

For all his answer Adolf went over to the door leading into the King's apartment and knocked loudly.

There was no reply.

He opened it, Axel following hard behind to support him.

The King was seated in an arm-chair by the fire resting his head on one hand, while in the other he held an open book.

"Sire!" said Adolf, making no effort to restrain himself, "Prince Charles of Hesse has sent General Haxthausen to summon the town to surrender."

"Ah, I forgot to lock the door!" said the King, in a regretful tone. "Well?"

"General Haxthausen has asked to see General Duretz, and Count Sparre has sent for instructions. What answer does your Majesty wish returned? Shall we tell him to go about his business?"

"On no account," said the King quickly. He thought a little. "Is he aware that I am here?"

"No, your Majesty."

"Say that the Governor will see him at once. Be careful not to mention my name. Assure him of a safe conduct, but tell him that he must allow himself to be blindfolded before he is led through the ranks. Has he anyone with him, by the way?"

"Two trumpeters, your Majesty."

"Blindfold them also; let my steward give them some refreshment below stairs. Let me see—how much time have we? twenty minutes"— he turned the pages of his book rapidly, to see how many there were to the end—"no—say half an hour! On with your best uniforms, gentlemen!"— he turned to Adolf and Axel—"and request your friends to don theirs likewise! I am going to hold a *levée* in the great hall. I shall expect everyone to be present, in full dress. General Haxthausen will be as much surprised to see us, I think, as the fisherman was to see the genie come out of the sealed bottle. I am much obliged to you, Count

Fersen,—to you also, Count Ribbing,—for your extreme promptitude."

The two friends withdrew immediately. They heard the key turn in the lock as soon as they had shut the door.

"That is a most wonderful man," said Fersen.

"Is he a man at all?" said Adolf, laughing again. "He is two at least—sometimes I think he is ten. But this is excellent sport. Go you to the General, and I will tell Wrangel, Clas Horn, La Gardie, and the rest."

Half an hour afterwards he was at his post in the great hall, talking to the different members of the Court as they came in.

Punctual to the moment, the King entered, leaning on the arm of Baron Essen, and seated himself in the midst of the hall. He was daintily attired in blue and silver, and the sombre velvet which the Baron wore made an excellent foil. For all his hatred of Essen, Adolf could not but remark that he looked very handsome; his coal-black hair and dark features contrasted finely with the curling golden locks and forget-me-not eyes of the royal favourite, Armfelt ("the bonny general," as the Dalecarlians called him), who stood on the other side. A brilliant group of distinguished officers, amongst whom Axel's tall, stately figure was conspicuous, formed a half circle behind them. Clas Horn strode in, consciously magnificent in black and flame colour. Young La Gardie's crimson satin became his boyish face and fair hair.

"A pretty thing that we should all be summoned hither to play at blindman's buff!" sneered Wrangel, as he passed to his place. He was not so well dressed as the others. Adolf inclined to think that want of cash sometimes led to want of courtesy, and had become more lenient in consequence.

Presently the door was flung open, and the ambassador, who was well known, personally or by name, to most of those present, was introduced.

It was evident that the bandage had only just been taken off, for he advanced a step or two uncertainly, as though the light dazzled his eyes, then stopped, put up

his hand as he recognised the King, and fell back with
a little cry of dismay.

A low murmur of amusement, which even good
manners could not entirely repress, went round the
circle.

"Where did you think I was, *mon Général*?" said the
King, smiling.

"The Prince of Hesse believed your Majesty to be
at Carlstadt," said the bewildered messenger.

"Ah, well, I was there—a week since, I suppose, as
the Prince of Hesse reckons. It was there that I had
the pleasure of an interview with Mr. Hugh Elliot of
the British Legation. He should have reached the
Danish camp by now."

"He reached it two days since, your Majesty. He
assured the Prince that your Majesty was already at
Gothenburg, but—if I may say so—we did not believe
him."

"A very amusing man," remarked the King, "and,
as I have the honour to point out to you, sir, a true
prophet at the same time. I was never more entertained with anyone's conversation in my life than I was
with his. Now that the aspect of things has changed
so much, I will not conceal from you that I was in low
spirits at that time. In fact, I went so far as to tell
Mr. Elliot that I no longer counted myself a king.
'Lend me your crown,' said he, 'and I will restore it
to you with all its lustre.' The self-confidence of these
Englishmen is amazing. But in very truth I begin to
think the Danes equal them. Is it possible that the
Prince of Hesse really believed that the second city in
Sweden would surrender at discretion so soon as he
chose to summon it?"

"His Highness has good reason to think that
Gothenburg could not long sustain a bombardment,"
said the General, nettled by the King's tone of contempt,
and showing greater dignity than he had yet displayed.
"He wishes to give her citizens the option of mercy."

"He is quite at liberty to do so," said the King,
rising and going towards the window. "Call up
the trumpeters, La Gardie. There is a balcony here,

from which the General may make any proclamation he chooses. The great square is full of my
subjects, I perceive. If they elect to listen, let them
do so ! "

Haxthausen stepped forward with alacrity, and was
assisted out of the window by Fersen ; but the instant
he appeared, such a roar of execration rose up from the
infuriated multitude down below, that he turned back,
unable to face it.

" You will not try ? " said the King blandly. " Well,
perhaps it is wiser not ! They are hardly in the mood
to make a good audience. That being so, your errand
here is, I conceive, at an end. My guards will have
great pleasure in escorting you back again ; but, as you
saw nothing upon your first arrival, I hope you will
allow us, first of all, to make what amends we can, by
showing you various arrangements, which may be of
some interest, before you return. Count Ribbing, will
you kindly attend General Haxthausen round the fortifications, and take him over the Arsenal, the Armoury,
and the Commissariat Department ? "

If the General did not see all that there was to be seen
that day, it was by no means the fault of Count Ribbing.

They found the King still in the great hall, on the
conclusion of their rounds.

" You have inspected the new earthworks ? " he
asked.

" I have, your Majesty."

" You understand these things. They are in good
order ? "

" In excellent order, sire."

" You saw the field-pieces ? We have had some
little trouble with them. Should you have guessed as
much ? "

" I should not have guessed it, your Majesty. I am
bound to admit that the defences are in excellent
working condition."

" We have seven thousand now in garrison, and are
expecting reinforcements," observed the King. " All
the non-combatants have been dismissed ; that is in
itself a source of strength. As regards treasure-trove,

the bullion in the Bank was buried in a secret place,
known only to myself and two of the leading councillors,
the night before last. You may think it strange that
I tell you this; but I assure you, we are anxious
for the game to begin. General Armfelt informs me
that it is all he can do to keep the Dalecarlian regiments
from breaking the truce, even now. There is one
thing, however, which I fear the modesty of my young
captain here"—he smiled at Adolf—"may have
neglected to show you," and he pointed to the
ruined fragment of an arch, still standing above the
river.

"Do you see that?" he said, with stern emphasis.
"That is all that is now left of a structure which the
Prince of Hesse will find described in his map of
Gothenburg as the New Bridge over the Göta. We
can scarcely see it from here; you will get a better view
on your way through the Swedish lines. The bridge
was destroyed by Captain Ribbing, a few days since, at
the risk of his own life. It will not now be of much
assistance, either to the Prince of Hesse, if he wishes
to march his men in, or to me, if I wish to march my
men out. It is as impossible for us to fly as for you
to surprise us; and the citizens of the town are
unanimous that they will see it razed to the last stone
—like that bridge—before they surrender. I wish you
a very good-morning, sir! Convey my most distinguished compliments to the Prince Marshal, and say
that, whenever he honours us with a visit, we shall do
our best to give him a warm reception."

The General was ushered out of the Castle with great
ceremony, and the *levée* broke up, each member of the
Court resuming his particular employment.

Adolf lingered behind the rest.

The King drew from his pocket the little volume
which he had been studying earlier in the day, and
began to read again with avidity. He never used a
mark; the book seemed to open of itself at the place
where he had left off.

Adolf, who was still excited and rather inclined to
talk, smiled to himself at his disappointment, and the

11

King, looking up, caught his eye, and laughed good-humouredly enough.

"My dear young Count," said he, "you are diverted because I read fairy tales. It is, I own, a singular amusement for a man in my position, but they are the only stuff for times like these, when any attempt to pourtray Nature as she is appears flat beside the reality. I am like the princess who encountered all sorts of adventures with nothing but a smock and a casket of diamonds. My life is a fairy tale more strange than any one of them ; if it were written in a book, nobody would believe it."

CHAPTER XXIV

THE BEGGAR'S OPERA

ON the evening of the ninth of October, when it was definitely known that an armistice had been decided upon, an order went forth that the city of Gothenburg should be illuminated. The windows of every house were wreathed in light. Even the poorest people there bought one small candle, if they could not afford more, and set it in the centre and let it burn to the socket. From the balconies of the wealthy ship-owners swung great black cauldrons, filled with leaping flame. Others had fastened torches on either side the door. The High Street and many of the principal thoroughfares were outlined in brilliant rows of twinkling stars; on the topmost tower of the cathedral a huge cross of fire, tip-tilted by the wind, flared skyward, as though it would have soared up far beyond the clouds, and taken rank with Boötes.

The place was full of life and stir, crowded with eager citizens. Many of the fugitives had not gone farther than the neighbouring villages, and at the news that Gothenburg was saved they were all returning. Their friends were flocking to the gates to meet them. The streets were thronged. Fresh arrivals had become too common to attract any notice whatever. Among them were large numbers of country-folk, eager to hear the latest details. The inns were doing a brisk business, and there was much coming and going, especially at the most popular of all, which bore the emblematic Wheatsheaf of the Vasas, blazoned in flickering gold and crimson over its portal.

A motley crew was gathered in the bar, where, if drinking healths could make men immortal, the life of Gustav would certainly have been secured for ever. The King was everybody's hero. After him, in the estimation of the vulgar—but only a very long way after him—came Baron Essen and young Count Ribbing. The general opinion was that he had given these gentlemen far greater credit than they deserved. It was to him, to him alone, that the safety of the city was due. His wise foresight had controlled everything. He knew that the Danes must and would yield at the last moment. He knew there was no real risk in sending a man to blow up the bridge. Anybody could have done that. The fellow was but too lucky to get the chance. It was the merest superfluous generosity on the King's part to praise him. And at every fresh story and at every fresh instance of the King's prowess or sagacity, an old, white-bearded beggar-man, who sat boozing in one corner, cried out, in tones of tipsy exultation—

"Huzza for the King!"

The last comer was just concluding a sensational description of the King's ride to Gothenburg, when a young man, dressed in the English fashion, stepped inside, looked round him, and seemed about to withdraw again.

"And that is how the King reached Gothenburg!" the speaker finished up triumphantly.

"Huzza for Adonis!" shouted the old beggar-man up in the corner.

There was a general laugh, under cover of which the seeming Englishman turned back quietly enough, took a seat as far as possible from the beggar, and asked for something to drink. He might have been about twenty. He had a very fair skin, and large, restless grey eyes.

"What did you say *Adonis* for, old Whitehead?" cried a lusty cheesemonger, giving his neighbour a punch in the ribs ; but the beggar-man only chuckled foolishly, and the talk went on as before.

The young Englishman contributed not a little to its cheerfulness. England was very popular that evening, on account of the threatened bombardment of Copenhagen, and there was a national disposition to like anyone who hailed from that quarter. Hugh Elliot, the British envoy, who, on the apparent failure of his efforts to negotiate peace with the Danish princes, gave them a spirited warning to the effect that the result of their conduct would be a rupture with England and with Prussia, and repaired immediately to Gothenburg, had been hailed with enthusiasm. The English seamen then in the harbour had volunteered to help in the defence, and they were therefore on excellent terms with the citizens.

This boy (for he was little more) spoke Swedish fluently, only helping himself out with an occasional foreign word or two. He knew somebody connected with the Court, he said. The stories that he told about the King were even more wonderful than those which had preceded them, and he talked with a grace and fire which took everyone captive—everyone, that is, except the old beggar, who had fallen into a semi-intoxicated sleep, and only grunted now and then at inappropriate places, presumably when the story his own dreams were telling him required comment. He was muttering something about the power of Venus, when the door opened again, and two travelling musicians—one carrying a harp, the other a violin— appeared in the entry.

"Why, he is dreaming about Adonis!" cried the Englishman. "Venus must have been fast asleep herself before she took him for that gentleman. What do you say to it, friends?"

The company, never having heard of Venus in their lives before, otherwise than in the capacity of a vessel, laughed more loudly than ever, for fear of betraying the fact that they did not understand the joke, and the harpist and the fiddler joined cordially enough; but when this burst of merriment was over, one of the men round the fire, afraid perhaps of further mysteries in the speech of the story-teller, said—

"Come, we have talked long enough! Let's have a turn of the fiddle, eh, comrades?"

"I cannot oblige the company to-night," said the
fiddler, somewhat shortly.   "My fiddle is out of
order, and so am I, for that matter."

His answer caused some surprise.

"Out of order on a night like this!" cried the
man who had spoken first.   "Why, that is rank
treason!"

"If my poor instrument can make amends"—began
the harpist; but a sacristan interrupted him brusquely.

"No, no," said he.   "I do not know how it is; I
cannot abide the sound of the harp.   Maybe it reminds
me too much of the sackbut and psaltery and all those
dead things of music they talk about in the Bible.   A
poor, thin, twangling noise it is.   I would rather have
no music at all than that."

"And you are right," said the Englishman.   "The
harp is only cold metal, that comes from the dark
prison of a mine.   But the fiddle grew in a great wood.
The free winds of heaven blew over it, the free sunshine
passed into it; it drank the free rain wept by the clouds,
and the soft white snow mixed with its essence.   The
fiddle for me, any day!"

"Yes, yes; the fiddle!" cried all the rest of the
audience.

The fiddler's brows drew together.

"I have told you that the fiddle is out of order," he
said grimly.   "I cannot oblige the company to-night."

"Play us the National Anthem, and we will let you
off, more especially as it is getting late, by the same
token," cried he who had first proposed music.

"The National Anthem—yes, the National Anthem!"
exclaimed the other voices.

"The National Anthem—yes, the National Anthem!"
hiccoughed the tipsy beggar, with a very odd wink.
"If he plays the National Anthem, I will give him a
gold riksdaler."

"The National Anthem go to the deuce!" said the
fiddler.

There was a pause of astonishment, and then
indignant murmurs rose among the little group.

"May I ask you to lend me your fiddle for a

moment?" said the young Englishman, stepping forward. "I have some little skill, and I can promise not to hurt it. I am curious to try its quality."

The musician consented, with a shrug of the shoulders, and the other took the instrument.

A look of indescribable tenderness came into his eyes, as he fondled the poor, cranky thing, which was, as its owner had stated, to all appearance in the worst condition. He bent his head down to it caressingly, as though to coax a gentler sound from the rough, battered carcase. But he had hardly begun to tune it when he smiled. The tone was pure and sweet.

He played the National Air of Sweden first. The audience rose to its feet and cheered. So absorbed were they, that no one, except the fiddler, remarked the entrance of a dark-browed, gloomy-looking fisherman, who mingled among them unobserved. The shouts had hardly died away, when the tune changed or melted, no one knew how, into the strains of a certain funeral march, that was played throughout the country whenever a great man died. Following so soon upon the note of martial triumph, it sounded intolerably plaintive. It was a subtle, audible rendering of the closeness of two thoughts in every youthful mind —glory and death. There was something womanish in it. Every man began to think of his wife or his mother; it seemed to him that he heard an under-song of women weeping very softly and bitterly.

There were rough, seafaring people among them, superstitious by nature and education. One of these cried out hysterically, "No, no! Not to-night! Play something else!" but he was hushed at once. Two or three slunk away.

Those who were left began to find the room too stuffy and hot, the walls too narrow. The tune was growing—growing—it filled the whole apartment. It beat its wings against the ceiling and dashed itself at the windows. It had caught the unfettered motion of the winds, of which the player had spoken.

No one knew why he left, but there was a general exodus. Hurriedly the guests rose, paid their reckoning, and departed. The beggar, the two musicians, the sailor, and the Englishman were left alone at last.

"Upon my word, *A*.!" said the pretended Englishman, as he handed back the violin to its owner, "you choose strange baggage to tramp about the country with. That is a Stradivarius, or I am very much mistaken. Where did you get it?"

"It belonged to my father and to his father before him. No one has ever touched it since then. Ours is no family for music. Is it of value?"

"You hold three or four hundred pounds at least in your hands."

"I shall sell the instrument at once. Why did you play as you did? It was dangerous."

"That was it not, my son," said the old beggar, "not half so dangerous as your refusal to play. You wear disguises ill. Anyone with half an eye in his head (lucky that no one present had even that limited amount of vision!) could see that you were no more a strolling musician than I am the Grand Turk. Next time you try that sort of thing, you had better appear as an executioner. It suits your cast of countenance."

"The only part that I am fitted to sustain?" said *A*. gravely. "It may be so, perhaps."

Meantime, the others had gathered round the violinist.

"At anyrate, you have succeeded in emptying the church; and that is, I believe, the first object of a voluntary," laughed *B*.

"You all but drove me out of it, young sir," said the beggar, with the suave flattery of a high-bred gentleman. "May I ask where you acquired such skill?"

A dreamy look came into the young man's eyes.

"In another life," he said, "in another life." Then he roused himself scornfully. "May I ask whether we came here to talk about violins?" he cried.

A. was standing silent, with his back to the mantel-piece, as though it were not worth while to speak again till something of real importance should be mentioned. The beggar grinned from ear to ear.

"I caught your young spark on his way from the Black House," he said, "and I spoke to him words that he will remember. We do not forget the first we hear, when we are only just conscious that we have not spoken our last. As you had neglected to make sure of him in one way, I made sure of him in another. He will be one of us by and by. But why did you let him go? I would not have done so for all that I possess. He has saved the King twice, if not three times since, to my certain knowledge. It was he who brought half Dalecarlia to the rescue at Mora. Without that, Adonis could not have risked the march on Gothenburg. And, if he had not ridden hither at the imminent risk of his own life, Gothenburg would have fallen before ever Adonis entered the gates of it. Why did you let him go, I say?" and he struck his crutch on the floor, and peered up into *A*.'s face with his keen, red little eyes.

"He is dangerous to the King," said *A*. slowly. "Noorna Arfridson has declared it. We cannot afford to kill the King's danger."

The beggar raised his eyebrows.

"I thought that title belonged alone to you," he said expressively.

"It does. But henceforth he is part of me. He bears it also. I shield him as I shield myself."

"He is hand-and-glove with the King at present," observed one of the others. "What makes you think that he will ever be one of us?"

"The very fact that he is hand-and-glove with the King at present," rejoined the beggar. "How long will that last? Look at *D*.! He was the King's best friend once; each has better friends now."

"True."

"Besides, the King has been afraid of that young man for some time past. I have observed it. I did not know the reason. If this report of Noorna Arfridson be founded on fact, it explains all. The King has great confidence in her. He will lose his trust in

Ribbing, and very shortly too. One need not be a great prophet to foretell so much. The young man has a quick, sensitive nature, and he will resent it. I shall be the last to tell him that Noorna hated his mother, for more reasons than one. And we shall reap the benefit. Luck favours us in another way also. The Duke of Sudermania had a fall from his horse at Mora, one night, and Ribbing caught him in his arms, and kept him from cracking his skull on the spot. I whispered a word in his ear then, and he will remember it. If the Duke becomes one of us eventually—the wind is setting in that direction—he may do much for a man who saved that twopenny life of his ; he thinks far more of such a benefit than does Adonis. The boy is well worth winning. We must detach him from the Court, if possible. You agree with me there, do you not?"

"It is a matter of indifference," said A. "He will go where his fate leads him ; we have no call to interfere. If the boy is to be one of us, he will be one of us at the appointed hour—no earlier, no later. If not, we strive in vain. I agree with you so far as to consider it right that we should keep a watch on his movements."

"We might do better yet," said the beggar. "As to the prophecy, that, saving your presence, is all rubbish. He may be the King's enemy in time to come. I do not deny it. But for the present, it is evident that he is the King's valued friend, and his courage and his eloquence give him a certain amount of power. The King is sending him to France to-morrow. That gives us one more chance. It is a long way from Gothenburg to Paris. Supposing he never got there?"

"No, no !" cried D. impetuously. He, at the instigation of his chief, had saved Adolf on the night of the explosion, but no one else knew. "We have tried that, and it failed. Do not let us try it again."

"It might be well worth trying, nevertheless."

"Oh no, no ! Let me go after him to Paris. I will

watch him. I will see that he does nothing against our interests. Let me go, *A.*!"

The leader raised his hand, as though to silence both.

"The time is gone by for taking violent measures," he said, turning to the beggar. "What is not done when the clock strikes the hour cannot be done throughout eternity. Apart from this, if the boy goes to Paris, it must be in the company of Axel Fersen, who is starting to-morrow. I owe him nothing—he is a mere Court spaniel; but I have a great regard for his father, who has never ceased to oppose the King. I could not consent to endanger the life of that man's son; and if we did not kill both, we should kill neither. I mention this, not because it is of any validity, but because your faith is weak, and you lean upon reason."

"What motive has Adonis for sending him to Paris?" asked *C.*

A. shrugged his shoulders.

"I can enlighten you on that point," said the beggar. "Count Ribbing loves his cousin Tala, the daughter of the Three Water Lilies. Baron Essen loves her too; but there is a difficulty about that. The two cousins spent a night together out on the hill. Ha, ha! I saw the way the wind blew. I warned Baron Essen (I thought that he might have become one of us at the time; but, so far as I can see, he has returned to his old allegiance), and he went after them. Now both the lovers have besieged the King; and, I take it, he is going to give Essen the preference and send Ribbing to Paris, on some embassy of the highest importance, to learn to fall in love with somebody else—*Madame Capet*, perhaps, if Fersen will allow it. Ah, well! There are many fair ladies in Paris, and they are not all of one way of thinking. It is easy to forget what one has learnt there. He might do worse, from our point of view?" and the speaker looked meaningly at *A.*

A.'s indifferent manner had fallen off him like a cloak, and he was listening with deep attention. "That secures him to us," he said, in a low, musing tone, as he fingered the branch of coral on his watch-chain. "Count Ribbing is not the man to forget lightly." He turned to *D.* "Find out the route he takes, and follow him at a safe distance. Send your letters to the address you know of at Stockholm. I do not care to hear about the society he frequents; but if he should be in any danger, or if you should note any marked change in his opinions of which it would be possible to take advantage, send me word at once, and do your utmost to protect and encourage him. For the rest of you—remember that you must be back in time for the summoning of the Riksdag, whenever that takes place. According to the latest advices, it will not come off much before February; but we must all be in Stockholm at that time, to guard against the possibility of another *coup d'état.* You, *D.,* had better sleep here to-night. Give Ribbing a start of two or three hours to-morrow morning. You can easily make out his arrangements from his groom, who lodges in the next house. The rest of us must seek other quarters. Good-night, gentlemen!"

He strode out of the room without another word, and the rest went obediently, taking different directions.

D. sat half dreaming in his chair for a long while after they had left him. He still heard the music that his fingers had made; he would have given all the deeds that ever were done to have written one bar of it.

CHAPTER XXV

THE TWO QUEENS

" I BEGIN to think that you are a human being after all, Axel," said Ribbing, with a laugh.

And Fersen smiled. He was another man since they had left the city of towers behind them. Adolf became convinced that Paris was the home of the lady who had given him the blue pocket-book.

As for himself, he was happy enough. The King had promised that all should go well. All would go well, of course.

One cloud alone darkened the horizon. Anxiety concerning the fate of her son, during the siege of Gothenburg, had brought on a serious illness, from which his mother never quite recovered. She wrote to him still, but her letters were vague and rambling, and he could not rely on the information which they contained.

The cold grew more and more intense every day. Such a winter as was now drawing on had never been known in France within the memory of man. The people were without food, without fire. Not that this mattered much to Adolf, who enjoyed sharp frosts; beyond a little idle pity, he did not concern himself.

The first view of Paris excited him greatly, and his interest quickened rather than decreased as he entered more and more into the feverish life of the place. To him, as to young men since, the mere fact of existence in that stimulating atmosphere was as full of interest as a voyage over unknown seas.

We cannot follow him in this part of his story;

there are too many cross-currents.   The silent, heroic
influence of Fersen waned almost invisibly before that
of a woman who left her mark on the age.   Every part
of life became complicated.   Among the many things
that changed in him about this time two only remained
steadfast—his feeling for his cousin and for the King.

Not that there was any break with Axel—far from it !
—but Ribbing had learnt to talk, and the exercise of this
new-found art became indispensable.   If he was not
talking, he was listening to music or assisting at the
first nights of plays.   He went ardently to the opera,
heard sweet Rosalie Dugazon in Dalayrac's *Nina*
and Grétry's *Comte d'Albert*, and was ready to kill anyone who asserted that Piccinni was a greater musician
than Gluck ; in those days, there were many who did
assert it.   He found more to criticise at the theatre, for
he was an eager student of Jean Jacques Rousseau (on
whom Fersen looked with distrust) and a Romanticist
before the romantic movement.   It pleased him not a
little to think that he was very superior to other young
men about him, who saw nothing to object to in the
fact that Cornelia wore rouge—as she does to this hour
—and Seneca a powdered *queue* and Brutus a *panier*.
He kept, in after years, one ever-delightful memory of
lovely, laughter-loving Molé-Raymond of the *Comédie
Française*, as he once saw her, not on the boards, but
running along the street because she was late for
rehearsal, her curly hair tossed flying down her back, a
great hat with a waving feather set sideways on her
head, the ends of her muslin *fichu* fluttering behind her,
and her pretty hands hidden by a huge muff, the fur
of which quivered and shook in the wind.

At the suggestion of the lady aforesaid, he became a
fervent reader of many works, the names of which had
never attracted him before.   He got Addison's *Cato*
by heart, studied Plutarch, Cicero, Tacitus, and fancied
himself much consoled by the heroes of antiquity for
the disastrous dulness of the political period in which
his lot had been cast ; for of course there were no
public men worth speaking of in Paris at that time—
except Monsieur Necker.   He reflected deeply over

Emile, and drew up an elaborate scheme of education for his future children. He became enamoured of Richardson's novels, and shed burning tears over the fate of Clementina in *Sir Charles Grandison*. As for *Paul et Virginie*, it seemed to him that nothing so exquisite had ever been devised. *Sophie, ou les Sentiments Sacrés* delighted him beyond expression. He lingered long in that enchanted English garden, within sight of the urn surrounded by cypress trees ; and the word *death*, which had been as a trumpet in his ears, became an Æolian harp. He was nothing if he was not *l'homme sensible*. He burnt all his poems, and analysed all his feelings over again in prose ; many and many an hour did he devote to the composition of elaborate portraits and eulogies of Tala, in which there was nothing whatever about her person, but a great deal about the generosity of her soul and the *fêtes* which she provided for the children on her father's estate. Axel, as we have seen, read very little and wrote nothing except a diary ; there was an alarming want of sensibility about Axel.

Horse-racing, which was then a passion with many of his acquaintances, did not attract Adolf Ribbing. Luck was always on his side ; if he made a bet, he won it invariably. There was no excitement about that, so he gave it up. He acquitted himself well at billiards, whist, Boston, tric-trac, quinze, and many other games in vogue at the time. Wherever he went people complained very much of the triviality of the age. They did not guess—how should they ?—that the New Year's Day of 1789 was ushering in a year unlike the old indeed.

On the very first morning after Count Ribbing's arrival, Fersen announced that he meant to take him to dine with the Swedish ambassadress, Madame de Staël, in the rue du Bac. Of the Swedish ambassador nobody ever spoke ; he was *tout bonnement le mari de sa femme*.

The cold was piercing. The Seine had long been frozen over, slender icicles hung tapering from every window of the Tuileries and the Louvre. The weather

even forced itself on the attention of those fine ladies
and gentlemen whose minds were mainly occupied with
matters of less ephemeral importance. It was not
often discussed in that house which its admirers called
"the temple of Apollo," but on the night in question
"Zulmé" was not there to forbid the subject. Axel
and Adolf Ribbing, who had been trained in Courts
and knew that punctuality is the politeness of kings,
arrived to the minute ; they were welcomed by the
Baron de Staël, who at once apologised for the absence
of his wife.

"She is suffering from the cold," he said, taking
them both into his confidence, in the affable manner
which made him so great a favourite at the French
Court. "She did not go to dress so soon as usual
on that account," and he glanced nervously towards
the door.

They were standing in Zulmé's favourite boudoir.
It was not a large apartment, but so pretty and bright
that the eye rested with pleasure on every detail. The
flat whiteness of the unstained walls, illuminated as
they were by hundreds of small wax candles in gilt
sconces, might perhaps have appeared too glaring but
for the relief afforded by numerous pink-cheeked, pink-
footed infant Cupids, fluttering, dancing, throwing
wreaths of roses over each other. A gaily gilt bracket
held a little foolish china clock, that made Adolf smile ;
it had the sun, the moon, and the stars underneath its
ordinary face, and yet it was not the kind of clock that
could by any manner of means understand astronomy ;
the moon was wrong, of course, and that luminary
seemed to be winking. Over the mantelpiece hung a
resplendent mirror in a gilt frame. The floor was
polished till it shone. Very small tables on very tall
spindle legs stood all about. It looked like a lady's
room, Adolf said to himself. The Baron glanced at
the door again. The Abbé Barthélemy was announced.

Le Voyage du jeune Anacharsis was, at that time, in
everyone's mouth, and Adolf looked with interest at the
man who had persuaded the modern Parisian that he
was just like the ancient Athenian. There was nothing

particularly Greek, or particularly Gallic either, about him. He rather resembled one of the tight, buttoned-up Germans whom Adolf had seen in Berlin. The moments hurried by, and still no hostess appeared. The Baron consulted the clock, quite openly this time. The Count de Clermont-Tonnerre was announced.

His vivid rhetorical manner contrasted strongly with that of the abbé. He began to talk immediately about the foolishness of supposing that it is disgraceful to be hanged. It was no more disgraceful to be hanged than it was to contract a debt and then pay it; the man who had given society either his money or his life, in return for certain benefits received, had given it all that he could, and was to be respected accordingly. Adolf had a shrewd suspicion that this conversation wearied de Staël; he was listening to it with half an ear, while with an ear and a half he listened for his wife's footsteps. And still they did not come. Monsieur de Chamfort was announced.

The only thing Adolf noticed about this gentleman was that he was not at all noticeable. He began to wonder whether no ladies were coming, and to await, with some curiosity, the appearance of the mistress of the house. De Staël looked at the clock — then piteously at the door again, as if the action of the hands ought to have had some effect on it. This fussiness, well controlled though it was, annoyed Ribbing, and made him take the part of the priestess of Apollo, before she descended. Monsieur de Marmontel was announced.

He brought with him a new silver snuff-box, a present from the charming Princesse de Lamballe. The other guests came round him to admire it, and began to talk about the current value of silver. Adolf, who was not so well instructed in the subject as Axel appeared to be, had leisure to remark the growing irritation of the ambassador, and to excite himself still further on behalf of the brilliant girl, whose *Lettres sur Jean-Jacques Rousseau* had recently attracted so much attention. Still, he was getting hungry,—the fact is not to be denied,—and how long these favourable sentiments

12

would have lasted it is impossible to say, had not the door been suddenly flung open, and something, that at first he took to be a rush of all the winds of heaven, and then perceived to be a woman, blown up to him and greeted him with effusion.

The effect of this impulsive entrance was as magical as it was instantaneous. The atmosphere, which had been stuffy and close, changed at once. The listless talking ceased. Everyone crowded round her, everyone seemed to have found his centre—everyone, that is, excepting Axel, who never changed his position, and Monsieur de Staël, who said, in a low, flurried voice, "You have come downstairs too quickly, my love. You are out of breath, and you have torn the lace on your skirt, look!"

"Ah, well!" she said, laughing, "it·is no great matter, my friend. Our guests will pardon me; we love better those we forgive. I have such long sight, I can see what is going to happen in a hundred years' time—but not the flounce of my dress. Unlucky flounce that it is! It tore itself when I was making the last of my three curtseys to the Queen on the day of my presentation. I was never so frightened in all my life."

"And what did your present Majesty do, if I may be so bold as to ask?" said Monsieur de Marmontel, with an appearance of great interest.

"I have not the least idea. Where is the woman who knows what she is doing at the most important moments of her life? I am sure I did not know what I was doing when I married you, Erich. The Baroness Oberkirch, who is as spiteful as six cats put together, declared that I was exceedingly awkward — which makes me think that my conduct must have been really graceful. The Queen was very kind; she sent for her own maid to sew up my dress again, and the King said, 'If you have not confidence in us, you can have it in no one.' Ah, the dinner is served! Monsieur de Fersen, may I ask you to lend me your arm? You left the King of Sweden well, I hope? I have an old grudge against you, for keeping me so long without the sketches which he desired you to send. You see

that I have hung them in the place of honour? But,
as I told His Majesty, I have looked in vain for the
palace."

"I am afraid, madame, it is not represented in the
drawings which I had the honour to forward to you,"
said Axel stiffly. "They show the agricultural improvements carried out by His Majesty."

"Is it colder up in the north than it is here?" asked
Madame de Staël, turning to Adolf, who sat on her
left hand. "It is stupid to talk about what everyone
talks about, but when things come to such a pass,
they are not things any more, they are people. I hate
the frost as if it were the Comte d'Artois. I have been
ill from the cold all day. It makes me sick to walk
in it, and yet I cannot stay at home. But it is not
myself I think of. The babies are frozen to death in
their cradles,"—she paused a moment, and the tears
rose to her large, black, confident eyes, for she had
lost her eldest child (a little girl named after Gustav
of Sweden) but a few months before,—"the people
are starving—they come crowding into Paris from
every quarter. In Normandy, above all, the distress
is terrible."

"There are forty thousand workmen, and nothing
for them to work at, I hear," said Marmontel, holding
his snuff-box to the light, to catch the reflections on
its surface.

"Forty thousand!" She made her large eyes larger
still. "Ah, well! the fierceness of the storm shows
the true captain. Where would they be now, if it
were not for my father? Where would they be, I ask
you? He intends to make the provisioning of Paris
the great work of his life; he told me so himself only
yesterday. He is about to stop the export of grain;
he is importing it from America. The *Notables* are to
assemble again, we hear, the *Seven Bureaus* and all.
What will the *Notables* do? Bah, it is my father who
will do everything! What it must be, to stand, as he
does, between starvation and a whole realm of the
starving! Food for the mind, did you say? Ah yes!
You have read his *Importance of Religious Ideas*, of

course, Monsieur de Ribbing? No? Well, then, I
will tell you all about it, when we have fed our bodies !
Will you not take some *potage cultivateur*, Monsieur
de Fersen? We are nothing if not agricultural, you
perceive. We are as agricultural as the King of
Sweden. Monsieur de Rivarol opposes my father's
book. He thinks we are religious only from interest.
Never, never in all my life shall I be converted to such
a baseness as that ! I hold with my dear father—you
cannot build the palace of the virtues on the foundation
of nothing at all. You might as well say that a king
who has but his own interests at heart will rule his
people better than the king who is ready to give life
itself, if that would conduce to their welfare. You,
Monsieur de Ribbing, have such a king ; there is
nothing that he would not do for his subjects."

"You do not know how truly you speak, madame ! "
cried Adolf, his eyes shining, as the vision of Gustav's
entry into Gothenburg rose before him. In a few brief
words he made her see it. She seemed to grasp every
thought, every image, before it shaped itself on his
lips ; he saw her glorious eyes one moment lit with
fire—the next, suffused and veiled.

"But that is truly magnificent," she said, in ringing
tones. "Oh, to have seen such a man, at such a
moment as that ! The world is full of heroes, if you
like ; but it is unheroic. Is it not half a pity that he
was left alive? Where will he find again such a royal
death? No, he will die in his bed, as if he were you
or I, or any other common mortal."

"But you are not a common mortal, my love,"
observed de Staël mildly. "No one could say so."

The fatuousness of the remark baffled her for an
instant. For the first and only time during his long
friendship with her, Adolf noticed that she was at a
loss for an answer. Not thinking it worth while to
make one, however, she went straight on, as if she
had not been interrupted.

"Why must we die alike? Death is no king ; I am
very certain of that. He is a rank Republican. He
will not even give us tears of a different colour. If your

king were dead and I wept for him, my tears would look just the same as those which I should shed, if I were capable of crying over my torn lace flounce. (How my friend, at the other end of the table, wishes I were!) But the tears that we give to such a man should be purple—what do I say?—crimson."

"Too many crimson tears have been shed for the death of kings already, madame!" said the Count de Clermont-Tonnerre. "Heaven keep you from the fulfilment of your wish!"

"A needless prayer, Monsieur le Comte!" she exclaimed lightly. "There are no events nowadays—except in Sweden. Nothing happens; it comes to pass, that is all. Here am I, an old married woman"—she toyed with the spray of laurel that lay beside her plate—"I have been wedded three times already, if you come to think of it. I proposed to Monsieur Gibbon, when I was ten, because I thought that papa would like to have someone always in the house to talk to him—Monsieur Gibbon had been engaged to mamma, you know; and seven or eight years after, Mr. Pitt proposed to me, and I taught him French and he taught me English for six weeks at Fontainebleau, and we bored each other to extinction, and mamma said I was as good as his wife, and for six weeks I hated mamma—almost—and I cried, oh, how I cried at the thought of going to that detestable, foggy England, where all the women eat beef and are red! and—where was I? Oh yes! Here am I, an old married woman, and I have never yet seen anything worth seeing. The betrayal of Richardson's Clarissa was the only event of my girlhood. It shook me through and through; the solid earth trembled, and my heart with it. But I was young then—I am too old to feel anything like that now."

"It has taken you twenty-three years to grow old, madame," said Marmontel; "it will take you twenty-three more to grow young again."

"And twenty-three more to grow immortal?" she laughed, stretching out her beautiful white arm towards a dish of fruit. "It used to be said that I was always

young, but never a child. Let us hope they will say
that of me when I have numbered threescore years
and ten. What is it, then, to be immortal? Is it to
be no longer young, no longer old, no longer any age
at all? Is it quite to forget time? Is it"—and off
she flew upon an airy quest of definitions into some
transcendental space whither Adolf did not attempt to
follow her.

His saner instinct told him that she was talking
nonsense, but he was dazzled and fascinated. Love—
virtue—immortality; these were the themes which he
burned to discuss. Axel always fought shy of them,
having the most lamentable preference for facts. He
himself had avoided them with anyone except Tala,
partly because others were not sympathetic, partly
from a modest sense that the words were too great
to be uttered without an uncomfortable catch of the
breath. Now, to his astonishment, he heard them
bandied to and fro, like any other of the mere shuttlecocks of conversation. Whether he liked it, he
hardly knew. He had a general feeling of *remue-
ménage*, of someone bustling in and out of all the
secret recesses of his existence, turning them topsy-
turvy and inside out; but he seemed to have lost his
identity, just as everyone else in the room had lost it.
They were only parts and parcels of Madame de Staël.
Some drowned themselves willingly enough in the
ocean of that overwhelming personality,—for himself,
so far as he could make out, he enjoyed it,—others
rebelled and became stiff like Fersen, or fussy and
irritable like his host. It did not seem to matter in
the least to the lady herself.

"Nature," she was saying, when Adolf found his
place again in her talk, "nature is never so beautiful
as art, and yet art is always leading us back to nature.
Why do I wear my own black curls without any
powder?" She shook them out, with a bright laugh
of defiance. "Because Vigée-Le Brun, when she was
painting Madame la Duchesse de Grammont-Caderousse,
implored her to give it up. No, no; Franklin and
Rousseau are all very well! White muslin and a blue

sash look very pretty indeed in print; but women are each other's books. I happened to see the Duchess one night, when she had not had time to re-arrange her hair after the sitting, before she dined and went on to the theatre. She was an angel. I shall never forget it. No more powder for me, from that day forward!"

"Vigée-Le Brun!" said the abbé. "Ah, it was unlucky that she could not finish her picture of the Queen in time for the opening of the *salon!* You heard what people said when they saw the empty frame! *Voilà le déficit!*"

"Really!" said Madame de Staël. "They will soon say that of the empty frame of Vigée-Le Brun's own house, I should think. The King told a friend of mine that that Athenian supper of hers cost forty thousand francs."

"It cost fifteen, madame; I had it from her own lips—fifteen francs, *tout compris.*"

Madame de Staël shrugged her shoulders.

"Bah, how people exaggerate! I heard she served them up a peacock."

"I am afraid it was nothing more than a chicken and an eel," said the abbé. "True, they were dressed with Greek sauces, the recipe for which she got straight from *The Young Anacharsis*, and flavoured with wine of Cyprus, which she got straight from an old Etruscan drinking vessel, the gem of Monsieur le Comte de Parois' collection. Her little girl poured it out for the guests, and the poor gentleman was never in such a fright in any of his seventeen duels. He thought the child would break it."

"I have been told her rooms are so small that the marshals of France sit on the floor. Is that so?" said Madame de Staël.

"It is indeed. The poor old Marquis de Noailles was not intended by nature to take so low a place as that assigned him by art, and he found it mighty hard to get up again. I heard from someone who was there that he looked as if he meant to sit on the floor for the rest of his days."

"Charming! charming!" cried the young ambassadress, as she laughed and clapped her hands.
"But we are growing too fond of gossip. Monsieur
de Fersen does not approve of it, I know. He is quite
right. He thinks that it derogates from the dignity
of a marshal of France to sit on the floor. But, in
these democratic days, the King is only the first
democrat. For my part, though, I care not two figs
for grandeur of position; I have always wondered what
being humble means. Have you ever felt humble,
Monsieur de Ribbing?"

"Only once, madame," said Adolf, "that was when
I felt very proud."

She looked at him with more attention than before.
Suddenly he knew that she was talking, not to the
whole table, but to him alone, and held his breath
lest he should miss one of her words.

"I have never been humble; I have never been proud
either," she said; "at least—only for my father. He
has told me sometimes about his young days. Ah, if
only I had been young then—if I had not been his
daughter!"

"Poor de Staël!" thought Adolf; and, in a flash,
"Vile de Staël! Why does he not make this magnificent creature happy?"

"You have known what love is, young as you are,"
she continued. She paused and sighed. "We must
not stay longer at table now. Will you come and
see me to-morrow, at four o'clock?"

"With the greatest pleasure, madame."

"And you will be my friend? Remember, I have
never known what it is to be humble and proud both
together; but you will tell me?"

"If I could tell you, madame, I should never have
known that sentiment."

Adolf had not intended to speak thus—he had meant
to pay an ordinary compliment—but he used to say
afterwards, that Madame de Staël was the only woman
with whom, if a man once began to speak the truth,
he could not stop.

"But you will be my friend?" she said; the fire of

the great black eyes quenched all at once, he knew
not wherefore.

"To the death, madame!"

"Then let us go."

Fersen left early, and Adolf was not sorry to go with
him. He had had more than enough for one evening.
His head ached, his pulses beat feverishly. It was his
first experience of a woman of genius, and the overwhelming unlikeness of her to anyone that he had ever
come across fatigued while it enchanted him.

"Axel," said he, "Madame de Staël is the most
wonderful person in the world."

"What do you mean?" said Axel sleepily.

"Of course," said Adolf, answering the tone
rather than the question, "she is a theory, not a
woman."

"I prefer women myself; they wear petticoats
better."

"But what a queen she is!" cried Adolf enthusi-
astically. "They were all her subjects, those men.
They talked their very best—I never heard such
brilliant talk; but she outshone them all."

"I did not think that they had much chance," said
Fersen drily. "Personally, I have no great liking for
monologue. But our hostess was not at all brilliant
to-night. She is not well, I think. She can be really
amusing at times, but she repeats herself and talks
nonsense. I would not go to see her too often, if I
were you. There is nothing so monotonous as everlasting variety."

Adolf laughed.

"How witty you are now, Axel, and I have never
seen you so dull as you were *chez Madame l'Ambassadrice*! But you need not be frightened. I admire her
—she intoxicates me—I feel as if I had been drinking
champagne all the evening. I shall go and see her
to-morrow, and the day after that, and the day after
that, and the day after that, if she asks me—but if she
had been the only woman in the world and I the only
man, I should never have dreamt of making love
to her."

"I dreamt of it once—or someone dreamt of it for me," said Axel, with a smile. "I thank my stars that the dream did not come true. Good heavens! she would have driven me mad in a fortnight. You might as well marry a bundle of fireworks. A pretty life she leads poor de Staël! Upon my word, I think the most unfriendly act I ever did him was to withdraw in his favour."

"Where are we going now?" said Adolf, who had just become aware that they were not taking the homeward direction.

"To see the Queen."

"Axel!"

"It is her hour for playing billiards," said Fersen simply, and quickened his steps.

"I will wait for you outside."

"No. I have the *entrée* here, and it is right that you should be introduced. The King wished it."

Adolf made no further remonstrance.

The great clock of the palace struck twelve as they entered, but the Queen was not in the billiard-room. One or two people were playing, off and on. The rest stood about, chatting in little groups, and the King was not present. Fersen introduced Adolf to an acquaintance, left them conversing together, and went away, apparently to make inquiries. It struck the new-comer' that everyone was very dull. They seemed to have nothing to talk about. Indeed, they scarcely took the trouble to hide their yawns.

Axel was away some time. Several of the courtiers had withdrawn for the night before he came back again and touched his friend on the shoulder.

"This way!" he said, in a low voice, when he had taken a ceremonious farewell of all the rest. "We are not going home yet. Come this way, and I will explain."

Adolf followed him, shivering, down a long, dim passage that looked as dreary after the light, bright little house in the rue de Bac as the talk of the courtiers had seemed dull after that of Madame de

Staël. It opened into a bare antechamber, lit only by a single lamp, placed in one corner.

"Wait for me here!" he said; "I shall not be long. His Royal Highness the Duke of Normandy is ill; he has had a convulsion. The Queen is with him. I am going myself to fetch another physician."

"Is it dangerous?" asked Ribbing, frightened by the agitation of Axel's face and manner.

"I cannot tell. You know how delicate the Dauphin is. If this child—but I will not think it"—and he was gone.

Hour after hour struck on the great clock down below, and still Fersen did not return. Adolf fell asleep at last. He awoke with a start, to find that Axel was gently shaking him.

"What is the matter? You were so long, I"—

"Yes, yes, I know; the physician was out. I had to go to the other end of Paris for him. But the child is better now. The Queen will see us. Come."

"Impossible!" said Adolf. "How can I? It would be the utmost presumption." He glanced at his disordered dress.

"If you will not come," said Fersen, controlling his voice with difficulty, "*I cannot see her to-night.*"

Adolf looked at his friend with a quick fear that he was not quite in his right mind. But Fersen was calm, though deadly pale.

"She is surrounded by enemies," he said. "They criticise every word spoken in private. For her sake I dare not go, unless I have a witness. Will you come now?"

Adolf made no answer, but rose and went.

Axel, who knew his way about the windings of the palace as a bee knows its way in a hive, took him this time to an apartment which was even less cheerful than the one that he had quitted, inasmuch as there was no light at all, except what came from the corridor through a pane of glass high up in the wall.

"Here!" he whispered, "sit here! Remember, you could hear all that passed. If you will sit on this side, no one will perceive you."

He thrust Adolf down on a hard, wooden arm-chair, surmounted by the royal arms, noiselessly pulled aside a small curtain, which concealed a sort of peep-hole opening into the next room, and withdrew.

Gazing through the peep-hole, Adolf could see the tall, stately figure of a woman sitting by the fire, holding a little child in her arms. There was no other light. One or two maids, who were busy putting linen away in a cupboard, disappeared quietly. The lady by the fire was dressed in crimson velvet, cut low at the neck and trimmed with fur. Her white shoulders gleamed in the ruddy flame. She looked up as Axel entered. He fell on one knee and kissed her hand, but no word was spoken. From time to time the child wailed pitifully, and she tried to still it by moistening its lips from a silver cup, chased curiously, that stood on a small table by her side.

"If your Majesty would give him to me?"— said Axel.

But she shook her head, and rocked the babe to and fro, while she sang—

> "Ah, que je fus bien inspirée
> Quand je vous reçus dans ma cour!"

It was the sweetest voice that Adolf had ever heard, and in spite of all its sadness—for she sang low and wearily, in part to soothe the child, in part because she was worn out with long watching—there was a touch of irresistible gaiety, which made him laugh while the tears rose to his eyes. The fretful wail ceased, and the babe fell asleep in its mother's arms.

She rose, laid it down softly in its dainty blue and white cradle, and made a sign to Fersen, who took a cedar-wood match from a vase and lighted one of the four candles on either side of a tall cheval-glass, which stood by the dressing-table. The candle flickered a moment and then went out.

Adolf could see her face now ; he forgot everything else in the world. It changed, in some indefinite way, while he was looking.

Axel was about to light the candle again, when she

signed to him to try that on the opposite side. He
obeyed; but it went out even more quickly than the
first. She clutched the table nervously.

He lit a third. This too failed in an instant. She
clasped her hands together, and stood watching with
strained eyes.

He lit the fourth, but this also was extinguished.
Then she sank back into her chair, covering her face
with her hands.

"Dearest lady," said Fersen, in a voice which fell
on Adolf's ear like some familiar sound in a strange
land, "why should it distress you? They all have the
same wick; that is why they go out."

She made no answer; her low sobbing broke his
heart. If he had stood in Axel's place, he must have
thrown himself at her feet. But Axel did nothing of
the kind; he pointed to the cradle, and laid his finger
on his lips. She rose and held out both hands to him.
He held them in his own a full minute — and left
her.

Adolf was in no mood to talk, as they found their
way out again through the dark labyrinth. Excess
of sympathy held him dumb. He found relief from
the over-fulness of his emotions in curious, minute
observation.

As they returned home in the gloom of that grey,
wintry dawn, the snow was falling, steadily, giddily.
It made him think that only when it was snowing
could anyone have guessed from his own bodily sensations that the great world was round, was moving
round. It was at once fine and thick. He could not
follow the descent of the flakes, one by one, for they
were much too small, mere motes in a transparent mist
of white. They never seemed to touch the earth at
all, but to go drifting downwards or sideways through
infinite space. Some the wind stuck fantastically on
one side of a pillar, a bit of railing, or a chimney.
Some the wind carried up, so that the order of things
was inverted and it appeared as if the earth were
snowing on the sky. There was no sky indeed—
nothing but a dull whiteness, seen against which the

snow itself looked almost black, though everywhere else his fascinated eyes ached and rebelled against its terrible, unshadowed purity. It filled him with quiet excitement. He could not speak; it seemed as though his senses were confused and he were seeing music. His frame shook, his teeth chattered with cold. A spirit sat singing in his heart. "The Queen! The Queen!" it sang.

"What was that air?" asked Fersen abruptly, as they stood waiting for the night-porter to let them in to their lodging.

"Do not you know?" said Adolf, in some surprise. "The air from *Didon*, of course. I thought everybody knew that." And he began to hum it.

"Ah, que je fus bien inspirée
Quand je vous reçus dans ma cour!"

"No," said Fersen, looking him full in the face, "it was not that."

Adolf saw that there was something he did not understand.

"Very well," he said gravely. "It was not that."

A day or two afterwards, Madame de Staël told him the story of Axel Fersen's first introduction to the Queen, and the remarks that had been made by ill-natured gossips when she sang this song in his presence.

"It was the song that sent de Fersen to America," she said.

Even to Madame de Staël Adolf did not reveal that he had heard it. But to the day of his death, he could never speak of Marie Antoinette without tears in his eyes.

CHAPTER XXVI

THE MESSAGE

TIME was racing along with the young Count in Paris; with her who was dearest to him it stood still.

The Castle of Carl de Geer was at this season quite deserted. Tala saw no one except her father, and to him she was still a child, whom he never suspected of the treason of growing up. Perhaps it was this which made her shrink from telling him of her visit to Adolf. She had no wish to conceal it, and she could have faced his anger bravely; but she dreaded his laugh, his jesting allusion afterwards. When Adolf came again—when Adolf wrote—she would tell.

Meanwhile, she could hardly have been happier than she was; the joy that is purely fantastic is none the less true for that. Half child, half poet, as nature had made her, she whispered her secret to the fir trees, and, when the wind rolled through them the sound of the sea that Adolf heard, their answer filled her with delight. Everything reminded her of one whom she never felt to be absent, so long as she was out alone among the hills. The clouds, as they drifted over her head, were living armies. The wind was her messenger, carrying her love to him, bringing his murmured vows back to her. She was a thousand times more near to him then than she could ever have been in his actual presence.

This was at first. After the news of the relief of Gothenburg reached the Castle, moving even Carl de Geer to stinted admiration, the tremulous yet definite hope that, when Adolf next appeared, he might be led to look upon her cousin with less disfavour, began to take the place of this radiant abstraction. It was only natural that she should long for more distinct tidings ; hitherto she had hardly thought it possible that they could reach her. Still as the year went on, as autumn turned rigidly to winter and rain to snow, and neither letter nor message came, the longing grew.

Sometimes she would go and stand by herself on the site of the burnt summer-house, on the Reindeer's Crag, and dream with her eyes open, until she saw the very face of her lover, when she closed them, and heard his very voice. Then she would open them again, to find the dream still visible, still audible. Was the face but air, the voice only wind ?

One day, while she was leaning against the flagstaff, deep in one of these trances of vision, it was abruptly broken by the sound of a horse's hoofs down below on the highroad. A sudden impulse seized her ; she never doubted that he whom she loved was come. Without a moment's hesitation, she set off running down the hillside, calling, as she flew along, " Adolf ! Adolf ! "

She reached the bottom just in time to see the rider as he passed.

It was Baron Essen. He lifted his hat to her.

In a moment all her old hatred of him flared up, as though it had been a fire and his action the match that kindled it. Disappointment was none the less bitter because she had been unreasonably certain. On the contrary, it distressed her far more. Baulked calculation is bad enough, but baulked intuition causes us to doubt all things.

The sun was setting, and she went slowly home, tired and depressed.

In the evening, however, when they had withdrawn to the hall for dessert, she forgot her hostility in her eagerness to hear every detail of the famous siege. She sat listening by her father's side, white with excitement, while Essen described and re-described.

He was a good narrator. Scene after scene passed like a living thing between them. At last, over the roar of guns and the smoke—not a moment too soon, not a moment too late—he raised his eyes and found that hers were fixed upon him. He knew the question that they were asking well enough : "What of my cousin? What of Adolf?" He did not answer it.

In Tala's overwrought, excited state of mind, the keen scrutiny of his look was too much for her. As once or twice before under that gaze, she felt as if she had betrayed herself—answered some question the very terms of which she did not know, and to her own dishonour. Trembling excessively, she rose, hardly knowing what she was about, and made for the door.

"What is the matter?" she heard him say, as if he were a mile off.

The spoken question restored her to herself.

"Nothing," she said. "The room was hot, that is all. I feel a little faint. I shall return directly."

Once outside, she blamed her own folly. Why had she been so ridiculous? What was the strange effect which this man produced upon her? She strove in vain to recollect Adolf's features; instead of them she saw only those fixed and questioning eyes. She would go back, and meet them again. She had but a confused remembrance of his last words. Perhaps he had been speaking of Adolf then—was speaking of him even now. The thought winged her feet.

By the time she reached the hall, one of those curious changes in conversation had taken place which make the unwilling witness of them feel as though an earthquake had violently upset the relations of all things.

She had left two friends, peaceably sitting over their wine; she returned to find them enemies. Her father's eyes were gleaming fiercely under his rugged brows, as she had never seen them but when he was roused to stern indignation ; the Baron's forehead wore that look of high, quiet, and intense scorn, which

13

had chilled her blood on the night of Adolf's arrival. Each was apparently so well occupied with the state of his own sensations that neither perceived her return, and she sat down unnoticed.

"You do not believe what you say," cried Carl de Geer.

"I should speak accurately, if I were to say that I had never believed anything else."

"Change the Constitution!" exclaimed the old party leader. "He would not dare. Why, it was his own work, confound him, and, bad as it is, to alter it would mean ruin!"

"He will alter it, nevertheless; and in my opinion he is quite right."

"You have taken office under the Crown, I suppose?" said the old man, with a bitter sneer. "I should have thought that you knew his ways."

"Had the King himself been a Royalist, I should never have taken the opposite side. I saw that the Constitution of 1772 was unworkable. It was far too democratic a measure. The King denied himself the very power to exist. He has found out his mistake by now, and he will remedy it at the approaching Riksdag."

"Do you mean to say that he will turn the Government of Sweden into an absolute monarchy?"

"Yes."

"And you, *you*, Baron Essen, can speak tolerantly of this?"

"I do not tolerate, I approve. It is the only way out of an *impasse*. The King and the Constitution cannot exist together. The Constitution is paper, and the King is a man. We cannot abolish the King, therefore we must abolish the Constitution—the sooner the better."

"Not while I live!"

The Baron slightly shrugged his shoulders.

"There are Four Estates in the Riksdag," he observed. "The nobles only constitute one."

"The clergy will never pass it."

"The archbishop is an old washerwoman. The

Bishop of Wexiö is becoming more and more absolute every day, and he is hand-and-glove with the King."

"Pfui! the fellow talks too much. I am not afraid of him."

"What say you to Nordin, then? He never talks at all. He also is hand-and-glove with the King."

"A paltry, under-bred fellow, that had not five dalers in his pocket when he came up to Stockholm!"

"I daresay not. However, he has five hundred thousand now; and his lightest word is obeyed, as if he were the pope. So much for the clergy! The peasants are the King's men always. So are the burgesses. They may make what exertions they please, the nobles cannot secure a majority; and besides, they are bound to make themselves unpopular by defending Hästesko."

"If we can do nothing else, we can resist to the death," said Carl de Geer, his face darkening.

"And then," said Essen, bowing gracefully over his glass, "you may be thankful to have one friend in high places."

Tala held her breath; she had never before heard anyone address her father in this way.

Carl de Geer made no answer for a minute or two; then he replied, somewhat grimly—

"No doubt."

His eyes were not flashing now, they were dull and set.

"If you come to think of it," pursued Essen, with unchanged urbanity, "it is useless to struggle against the King."

"He has the devil's own luck, I grant you that," said de Geer between his teeth.

"When has he ever failed? The nobles tried it in 1772. He was young and inexperienced then, a mere dissipated weakling, as everyone thought. They were powerful; their prestige was so great that they had never been beaten. Who won? The King. Who won upon the brandy question? The King. Who won in the war with Russia—against overwhelming odds too? Why, the King! Who won the other day, at Gothenburg, without generals, without troops, with scarcely a personal attendant? The King."

"And who will lose, when he makes war upon the liberties of his own subjects? Why, the King!" cried de Geer, raising his hand solemnly to heaven.

"He will lose in one case and in one alone," said the Baron emphatically; "if he dies. He may die, of course."

"Die!" said Carl de Geer. "Yes, die like a dog! I would he might! His death would be the saving of us."

Tala leant forward with a cry.

"Father! Father!"

Both men started.

"You too!" said Carl de Geer. "My child, my only one! I did not know that you were here. Well, you have heard enough to betray me," and, with a smile, he stretched out his hand towards her.

She bent down and kissed it with fervour.

"Why must we always, always go against the King?" She spoke tremblingly. "He has saved us from the Danes. All the people love him. They would do anything for him about here. I know. I have met them upon the mountains and talked to them. Father, if we were all his friends"—

But her voice broke. She had spoken too suddenly of what lay nearest her heart; she seemed to be pleading for Adolf and herself.

"There! there!" said her father gently, "we have had enough of that. I know what it means, to be the King's friend. Happily, you do not, Tala; you never will. But the harsh words frightened her, poor little dove! There was nothing in them. Hate him as I may, as I do, the King's life is as sacred to me as yours, my child. Will that satisfy you?"

"It does not satisfy me," said Baron Essen gravely. "You must understand, sir, that I can no longer remain in a house where such things are said. I quit your roof immediately."

"Sir, you anticipate my dearest wish when you threaten to do so."

"Father!" cried Tala. "You used to love the Baron. He is our guest. And you"—she turned to him—"you know as well as I that he did not mean what he said just now."

A miserable fear oppressed her; she was afraid of Essen's friendship, but she dreaded his enmity past all expression.

"The little one is right," said de Geer, after an awkward pause. Hospitality was one of his first principles, and this Tala knew. Any reflection cast upon it troubled him. "You are my guest, sir; I am sorry that the tidings you brought caused me, for a moment, to forget it."

"It is a very small matter to me, sir, that you should forget that I am your guest. But one thing I must ask you to be kind enough to remember, which is, that I brought you no tidings. It is merely a private conjecture of my own that the King will act in this manner."

De Geer looked up at the ceiling.

"Believe it or not, as you list," continued Essen coldly. "I suppose that I may rely upon the honour of one whom I counted my friend to keep the matter secret?"

De Geer nodded.

"I have but one thing more to ask before I leave. May I request five minutes' conversation alone with your daughter?"

"I can answer for my daughter, sir, as for myself. She is not in the habit of granting audiences to gentlemen alone."

The implied insult was too much, after all that had gone before. Baron Essen let go his self-control. He played a card that he had not intended to play at this juncture.

"Indeed!" he observed drily. "As I knew that she had granted one to young Count Ribbing, some time since, at midnight, in the summer-house on the Reindeer's Crag, I thought that an older friend might perhaps be allowed to claim the privilege."

"Tala," said de Geer, looking at his daughter in blank amazement, "is this true?"

"What?" said Tala, who had not understood the accusation.

"That you spent the night, or any part of it, alone with Adolf Ribbing, upon the Reindeer's Crag?"

"Yes."

The Baron covered his face with his hands.

Tala looked in bewilderment from one to the other. Essen's astonishment was hardly less than de Geer's. The words had escaped him in an unguarded moment, when he was worn out with the long wrangle, and he regretted them as soon as they were uttered, expecting instant and angry denial.

For the first time the conviction of her perfect innocence dawned upon him. Tala, she knew not why, breathed more freely.

"Father," she said, "you do not want me to say more?"

Her father made no reply whatever.

Slowly, as she stood there by the table, she began to realise what was passing in his mind. She had appeared pale before, but now her lips and cheeks were marble; the only living thing about her was her auburn hair, on which the lamplight fell resplendently. Essen was terrified.

At length the rigid lips parted, and a long sigh came from between them.

"Speak to him!" she said, in a voice so unlike her own that he did not recognise it. It seemed as if the evil thing he had thought her were speaking, not she herself. "I have no mother. You said it. Tell him it is not true."

All that was best, all that was worst in Essen's nature, leapt up at the words.

"Baron de Geer," he said (and Tala started at his voice, because, for the first time, it sounded soft and beautiful), "your daughter is innocent. I made no charge, remember. She has more than justified herself in my eyes. I desire to prove it. If she will do

me the honour to accept me, I will make her my
wife."

De Geer raised his head, and looked once more at
his daughter.

"You hear what he says, Tala. If there is no
reason why you should refuse to be an honest man's
wife, you will obey my commands and accept him.
After your confession he does you great honour."

"I feel it," said Tala, without moving a muscle; "I
shall not forget Baron Essen's conduct towards me. I
cannot marry him, father."

"Why not?"

"Because of Adolf," she said, a smile flitting across
her lips, as though, even at that moment, the utterance of the name made her proud.

De Geer frowned.

"Adolf cared little enough for your reputation when
he allowed you to hazard it in that way. Baron Essen
asks for your hand at a moment when any other man
might well have dropped it. Which is the true
lover?"

"It was not Adolf's fault. I went to him," said
Tala recklessly. She was beginning to feel that she
did not care what anyone thought of her; only
she clung with desperation to her own belief in
herself.

"We will not discuss it further," said de Geer
haughtily. "Whatever happens, Essen, you have
earned my warmest gratitude. I shall remember.
You wished to speak in private with this wayward girl
of mine. I will no longer interrupt you. Good-night."

He rose and moved towards the door.

But Tala sprang to him and laid her hand upon
his arm.

Unable to resist, he kissed her hastily, and went
out.

"How did you know of it?" she said, turning to
Essen, as soon as the door had closed. "Did he—did
Adolf tell you?"

The real solution of the enigma did not so much as
cross her mind.

Essen made no reply. He had found it prudent before now to leave questioners to answer their own questions—women especially.

"I must tell you everything," Tala went on hurriedly. "If Adolf has trusted you, that means that I trust you too," and she gave him a radiant smile. "It was the night of the dance. He would not come in, you know, because my father was angry. I could not have left him out there in the cold, with nothing to eat; how could I? I took him some food. That was all. I meant to have told my father; I do not know why I did not. I would have trusted you before, but I thought that you were against us. Now I feel sure that you were jesting. You did not know that my father would take it as—as he did. You were provoked because you wanted to speak to me, to tell me something that would help me. Oh, how good, how noble it was of you, when you saw what you had done, to speak to my father in that way!" She blushed. "It made him happy at once; he understood. And now tell me—tell me. Is it a letter from Adolf?" and she held out her hand.

"I have no letter," said Baron Essen.

"A message from him then?"

"He sent no message."

"One word—one single word? Oh, do not keep it back!"

"I cannot keep back what I have not got," said the Baron.

Her face fell.

"After all, there are other people in the world besides young Count Ribbing."

"Not for me," she said, quite simply.

"The King, for instance."

"What has the King to do with it?"

"Only this much, that he has sent Count Ribbing on a secret mission to France, with Axel Fersen. He charged me to tell you this, in case I should find—as, to my sorrow, I have found—that it was impossible for him to visit this castle in person."

"To France?" said Tala slowly. "But he will write."

"His Majesty asked me further to explain to you, that Count Ribbing, after some demur, had given him a solemn promise that he would not endeavour to communicate with you in any way before his return. It was of the utmost importance that he should go. His whole career may be influenced by his conduct in Paris. The King wished you to know this. He told Count Ribbing that he would speak to you himself."

"Is that all?"

"To the best of my recollection."

"I do not understand why," said Tala.

"It is simple enough, nevertheless. The King wants to win over Baron de Geer to his way of thinking. Count Ribbing wants to win over the King for his own advancement. His Majesty is well enough affected towards him, but he will not do anything to anger the Baron. If a letter from him fell into your father's hands, as might easily happen, your father, knowing his devotion to the Royal cause, might imagine that he had the King's consent; and you can see for yourself that this would not tend to raise 'the royal charmer' in his estimation. If he wished to rise, Count Ribbing was bound to submit to the King's conditions. He is a very promising young man. His conduct during the siege was admirable."

"My father will not change," said Tala mournfully. "He hates the King more than he loves me."

"I would not make too sure of that. The King's powers of fascination are great, when he wishes to please. Make your father come to Stockholm this winter. Tell him that you wish to go."

Tala shook her head.

"I will try; but it is of no use," she said, with sudden dejection. "How did my cousin look when you saw him last?"

"I never saw anyone in better health or spirits."

Tala stood silent. Was this the end of the interview on which she had built so many hopes? Was there nothing more?

"Good-night," she said at last.

All that night the words "To France!" rang like a knell in her ears.

All that night, when thoughts of Ribbing came between him and his sleep, Essen said to himself over and over again, "To France!" and the words were as a marriage bell. He rose before the dawn and went his way, leaving a letter for the Baron.

CHAPTER XXVII

AT STOCKHOLM

WHAT it was that Baron Essen wrote to her father Tala never learnt; but de Geer made no further allusions to his proposal nor to her rejection of it, and she set this down to some recommendation which the letter must have contained, and felt grateful, deciding in her own mind that she had wronged Essen before and must now make all the amends that lay in her power. She was generous and enthusiastic by nature; if it was any way possible, admiration was always her first impulse, criticism the last. She rejoiced to feel that she was not afraid of Essen any more; the wind blew more freely, the sun shone brighter for it! In the solitary leisure of her mountain life many a fancy sprang up around the few barren facts of his visit. Soon she came to look upon Essen as an ally whose every word and action must be a veiled benefit. Nevertheless, being at a loss for the motive of Adolf's supposed confidence in him—a confidence which had greatly startled her at first— at a loss also to account for Essen's sudden change of front in politics, she framed a romantic theory to the effect that Adolf had succeeded in enlisting his sympathies on the King's side, and then trusted him with the knowledge of his own private affairs. She took Essen's insinuation in perfect good faith, believing that he had been provoked into it by her father's refusal to let her speak with him alone—that he had felt almost as surprised and bewildered as she herself at the horrible misinterpretation. If this were so, then his proposal was a mere blind ; he knew that she must decline it ; he knew at the same time that it would disarm all suspicion.   Accordingly, he sacrificed himself and came to her rescue.   She had been brought up to have a high regard for chivalry ; she thought that he had behaved like a knight of old.   Besides, having always heard the King reviled by her father and his friends—by everyone whom she knew, in fact, except Adolf and the peasants—it seemed to her the height of chivalrous conduct to go over to his side, when the whole strength of the class to which Essen belonged was ranged on the other, and in the teeth of this gathering storm about the Constitution.   It never struck her that his altered opinions could be of any material advantage to him.

To her no small astonishment and delight, a few weeks later her father proposed, of his own accord, to spend the rest of the winter in Stockholm.

Stockholm was the centre of the Swedish world ; she was far more likely to get news of Adolf there than at the Castle.   Essen, she recollected, had advised her to go.   She would see the King ; she would be present during the Riksdag.

So the month of January 1789 found them settled in the beautiful Venice of the North, and a life which was not like any that she had known hitherto began for Tala.

She was in a strange position.   Surrounded by all the avowed enemies of the Crown, hearing nothing but what was evil of the King, unable, from her youth and inexperience, to contradict what was said, she still clung desperately to her faith in him, still held to the belief that he was right against all the world.   The vehement, exaggerated speech of the men and women who frequented her father's house disgusted instead of convincing her.

The high-bred courtesy of manner of the elder Count Fersen was charming, in spite of the violence of his opinions, and, from the first moment that she saw her, she entertained a passionate, girlish admiration for his beautiful niece, Aurora ; but she disliked the rest—

especially an old, white-haired man called Pechlin, who came oftener than anyone else, and paid her extravagant compliments. His boisterous geniality failed to put her at her ease, and she was haunted-by an uncomfortable feeling that he knew far more about her than she would have wished him to know. It surprised her to observe that, although he was deep in all their councils, neither her father nor any friend of the family spoke of him with respect. He had strange ways of getting information, Carl de Geer said once, when she questioned him on the subject.

During the first days of their sojourn she thought of many an innocent plan for the fulfilment of her wishes. The King paid great attention to Baron de Geer. He was invited to Court, asked to the State banquets, cajoled and flattered in every way. Tala hoped much from these meetings; but as time went on her hope grew less and less. Her father, who had confided absolutely in her, whose wont it was to tell her all that happened, maintained a grim, unbroken silence as regarded everything that went on at the palace, and refused to take her to the State ball, alleging as an excuse that the courtiers were all wearing the Polish costume, in deference to the King's ambitious designs upon Poland, and he was too old to change his clothes. The manner in which it was said made Tala drop her entreaties. After that the royal invitations became less frequent, and at last ceased altogether.

But if she did not go to the State ball, she went to many others—and to three or four given by the Duke of Sudermania, the King's brother. His lively little Duchess was a great favourite with all the different parties—even with her brother-in-law, who liked wit wherever he found it; she appeared to be as popular as her husband was the reverse. Tala conceived a great dislike for this person the first moment that she saw him. He complimented her on her beautiful chestnut hair and her brow of marble. All the while he seemed to be trying to see something that he could not quite see, trying to hear something that he was not intended to hear. The expression of his features was dull and thick; they never lighted up, except now and again with a flash of cunning.

"Why does he wear a blue and red uniform?" she asked her father.

"Because he is head of the Ninth Masonic Province and the vicar of Solomon," rejoined de Geer gravely.

"Solomon was not the wisest of men if he dressed like that," said Tala, laughing.

Her father laughed too and patted her cheek.

"But you must speak with more respect of His Royal Highness," he said. "I assure you, my dear, that he is not so foolish as he looks. If he does very little, he has most wonderful dreams."

"Does he talk to everyone about them?" said Tala.

"Yes. Three years ago, he dreamt that a very great friend, Colonel Reuterholm, came into his room, dressed in black, and said, ' *Tout est fini.*' Behind him stood the nobles, begging Duke Charles to take the regency and save his country. And so he did—in his dream."

Tala sighed, and wished that her father had not told her the story; she had a strong vein of superstition. She fought against it, knowing Adolf's contempt, but she was often unable to sleep for thinking of Noorna Arfridson's prophecy; and the dream recalled it to her mind. While she was at home she had seldom been troubled, but here, where the air was thick with plots and conspiracies, it oppressed her like a nightmare.

Her longing for some definite news of Adolf became intensified. She went to routs and assemblies, to the theatre, to the opera—everywhere where she fancied that there was any chance that she might meet somebody who had come from Paris. The capital of France was in a most dangerous state, and things were going from bad to worse there every day. She was assured of this on all sides.

Of the women whom she saw, the only one for whom she cherished a real affection was the gentle, brown-eyed wife of that Colonel Hästesko who was now in prison for his refusal to follow the King to St. Petersburg at the beginning of the Russian campaign. It was the fashion among the so-called "Patriots" to go and see her and condole with her. She, poor lady, understood nothing whatever of politics! she simply worshipped her husband with a love which knew no reason and no restraint. When he was taken from her, she was like a fragment of seaweed torn from its rock. Tala was drawn to her at first by the indifference which repelled her would-be comforters. They were full of suggestions to console her. One offered the loan of her country house. One brought her the works of Molière. One said that she herself, during a period of affliction, had derived great benefit from the use of quinine, and ordered a small bottle of it for her to try. One entreated her to go every Friday to hear the archbishop preach. All joined together to abuse the Government and the King—bell, book, and candle. She would not leave Stockholm. She would not read. She could not be induced to take quinine or to enter a place of worship. Gradually most of the good ladies who had been so anxious to assist fell away, one by one, and left her alone. It was of no use, they said. Tala, however, who had not dreamed of being of any use, continued to go, and in time the weak, despairing creature became fondly attached to the girl and clung to her impulsive, unpolitical, unpractical sympathy—feeling it the more that Tala could seldom express it in words. They were alike in nothing but in their power of absolute, exclusive devotion to one person.

As to the conduct of Colonel Hästesko, and the probable issue of the trial which was about to be held, there were many conflicting opinions. The Court party maintained that he and the officers under him were secretly in the pay of Catharine of Russia—that his mutinous behaviour in the face of the enemy had imperilled the whole country.

De Geer's friends, however, warmly applauded this act of flagrant insubordination. The King, said

cunning old white-haired Pechlin, was really ambitious
to the verge of madness ; only the patriotic resistance
of the Colonel had saved Sweden. There would be
terrible revelations at the Riksdag.

The country, others declared, was all but bankrupt.
Victory ? Yes, if you like, the King had been victorious,
but where was the money to come from ? Frietzsky,
the great Frietzsky, the greatest minister of finance
whom the eighteenth century had known, was in
despair ; so said Count Brahe, the senior peer of the
realm, in tones of absolute triumph. Even Frietzsky's
credit was almost exhausted. There would be terrible
revelations at the Riksdag.

Besides, who was the King that he should accuse
his own officers, and shake the very pillars of his throne
in the person of the nobles ? This was the cuckoo-
cry of Count Fersen, Axel's magnificent and stately
father, who condescended not to any lower form of
accusation.

The King had corrupted even the Church itself. On
the door of St. Michael's he, Count Fersen, had seen
this text, printed in large red letters under a rude chalk
drawing of the three leaders of the Opposition struck to
the ground by lightning : *Because they came not to the
help of the Lord, to the help of the Lord against the mighty.*
Abuse of the first gentlemen in the kingdom was stuck
up in every church porch. It was no longer safe to go
to the *bourgeois* playhouse even ; the most trifling
allusions were caught up by the audience and flung
in the teeth of their superiors, with hisses and groans.
Whose doing was this ? Hideous rumours of the
proceedings of the Court had gone abroad. There
would be terrible revelations at the Riksdag.

Tala listened with silent indignation. Was there no
one to say a word on the other side ? Where was
Adolf ? Why did he not come back ? The opening
of the Riksdag was fixed for the 2nd of February.
Surely he would return in time ! Baron Essen, who
was still at Linköping, her father told her, meant to
be present. It seemed to her that, wherever she
looked for Adolf, she found Baron Essen.

The sympathy that she needed so much came to her at length from a different quarter.

At a gay supper-party, given by the Duchess of Sudermania on the last evening of January, she happened to sit next to the younger Count Horn, whose father had been one of Gustav's warmest supporters in 1772. He was a great favourite at Court; but his poetry and his music made him extremely popular in other circles besides that of the King. Tala had felt some curiosity, —more especially as she remembered Adolf's praises of him in earlier days,—and she was not disappointed. They began to talk about Gluck's opera of *Iphigénie,* which she had seen for the first time that night.

"Ah, well," he said, with the air of a connoisseur, "they give it even better at the Grand Opéra, of course. I have just come from Paris."

Tala started.

"From Paris? Did you see any of our fellow-countrymen there?"

"One or two. De Staël, for instance, and Adolf Ribbing."

"Adolf Ribbing is my cousin," said Tala, trying so hard to speak as if he were nothing else that her voice sounded cold and harsh. "Can you tell me how he is getting on?"

"Very well indeed. He bids fair to be as popular as his handsome friend, young Count Fersen, in time. But he is too much with Madame de Staël."

"Does he ever speak of coming home?" said Tala abruptly.

Horn shrugged his shoulders.

"Not so far as I know."

"Why do you say that he is too much with Madame de Staël?"

"She is a Republican at heart. I dislike Republican ladies."

"Do you?" said Tala. "All the ladies that I know are Republican—almost all."

"But you are not?" he said quickly.

"No."

"Who made you a Royalist?"

14

"My cousin."

A light of comprehension passed over Clas Horn's face.

"I am so glad," he said. "I love—I worship the King. I would die for him."

Tala's eyes filled with tears.

"It is a long time since I have heard anyone speak like that, and it is the way that I speak in my heart," she said.

The other guests were rising from table. In her hurry to overtake them, she dropped her fan. Clas Horn picked it up, and handed it to her with a bow.

"May I come to see you, and we will talk of this again?" he whispered.

CHAPTER XXVIII

THE KING AND HIS COUNCILLORS

CLAS HORN did not confine himself to a single visit. The frankness of Tala's confession—for it was nothing less—had touched and pleased him, and he was quite ready to give her tidings of Adolf Ribbing. They became good friends almost at once. It was from his lips that she heard, for the first time, a full account of the incidents of the siege of Gothenburg.

From him also she learnt the politics of the other side—which was in truth her own—for Count Horn the elder belonged to the Royalist section of the Diet, and the father and son were deeply attached to each other and had no secrets. Clas was given to look at public affairs from the picturesque point of view, but she took little heed of that, being too simple-minded herself to find out that his interest in them was half dramatic, half poetical, and by no means sincere. Indeed, it was not altogether his own fault ; Gustav had made a brilliant confusion of thought the fashion amongst the younger men. Once or twice she felt annoyed when her father entered the room, and Clas, instead of upholding her in some gallant attempt to support the Government, sat silent, or changed the conversation.

As regarded Carl de Geer, he seemed to take a resolute pleasure in ignoring the difference of opinion between his daughter and himself. To her he was tender and affectionate as he had ever been, but she shuddered when she heard the strong expressions that he used in company with his friends; especially when, from time to time, he threw out a mysterious hint to the effect that he knew of a piece of treason on the King's part, worse than anything that they could imagine.

No one succeeded in fathoming these mystic utterances; no suspicions had been aroused as yet. Listen as she might, she could never hear a single word that led her to think that there was any idea abroad of an impending change in the Constitution. Yet every time she felt as if the secret were imperilled by the bare mention of it.

As the day for the opening of the Riksdag drew nearer and nearer, all Stockholm began to share in the excitement.

Furnished lodgings were provided, at the King's expense, for the peasant deputies, and eating-houses, where they might take their meals gratis. These were the subjects of most unfavourable comment in Carl de Geer's circle.

"An evident bid for the popular vote," said Fersen the elder, in tones of silvery contempt.

"There is no knowing to what lengths the King will go now," muttered old Pechlin.

Tala shivered, and wondered to what lengths he himself was capable of going. She could not bear the old man.

There were clubs for the peasants too—clubs for the clergy—two large clubs for the nobles; but on the very day when the existence of these was officially announced, Carl de Geer gave out that he intended to keep open house for all the poorer members of his class, and they, for the most part, availed themselves of the invitation. He was also instrumental in the formation of a committee of seven, for the practical management of the Opposition, and this committee met, day after day, in Frietzsky's study.

Great agitation was caused by the announcement of the names of the *talmen*, or speakers, of the Four Estates, who were all chosen, as usual, by the King. On the evening when these were made public, de Geer (whose eyesight was not good) asked his daughter to read them out to him.

"The marshal of the Diet, Count Carl Lewenhaupt."

"H'm! Over seventy, and half an idiot at that," said he. "Practically, the King will be marshal of the Diet."

"Dr. Troil, speaker for the clergy."

"No one can count on a fat archbishop. He has the gout, whenever Church and State are not in accordance. The King will be speaker for the clergy."

"Alderman Anders Lydberg, speaker for the burgesses."

"The mace could not be in the hands of a greater fool. Mark my words, Tala, the burgesses will have no one to lead them! They will vote for the King to a man."

"Olaf Olsson, speaker for the peasants."

"A nobody from Ostrogothland. I never heard his name before to-day. I had to ask who he was. Upon my soul, the King has done well! Practically, he has not appointed a single man capable of opposing him."

Tala laid down the paper and ran away to her own room. She hated all these manœuvres. Why were they needful? Her father accompanied her to a ball that night; and there she met Clas Horn, who could not say enough in praise of the brilliant wit of the King and his "collection of idiots."

Tala had many deficiencies; one of the worst of them was that she did not know how to laugh to order.

"What is the matter?" said Clas.

"Why does it amuse you?" she cried passionately.

"I see," he cried, stopping short. "You are right."

"No, no," she exclaimed, with even greater vehemence, "I am wrong. I wanted you to tell me that I was wrong. You never do."

And Clas Horn pondered over the strange ways of women.

A few days later, the Session opened with a grand State service at the cathedral, and a sermon from the

Bishop of Wexiö, on the text, *Eschew evil, and do good, seek peace, and ensue it.* Carl de Geer, and many another with war in his heart, sat listening grimly, and was candid enough to admire the soothing eloquence of Sweden's most eloquent preacher.

Tala recollected the morning, because, through a mist of hopes, fears, and fancies, she saw the King for the first time, as he rode by. He seemed much bigger than he was. In after days, when her views of his character somewhat changed, she recalled her impression with wonder.

The sermon over, the Four Estates withdrew to their separate hall of assembly.

The three Lower Estates at once agreed to the King's demand for a secret committee. They were full of gratitude to him for the energetic measures which he had taken to stop the war, and their votes were unanimous in favour of an address that should express their sentiments.

Very different was the reception of the King's message in the Riddarhus, where sat the nobles. There, Count Fersen lost no time in proposing that it should be "laid on the table,"[1] and Carl de Geer seconded his speech by moving that the King be petitioned to proceed summarily against the unknown and anonymous persons who had libelled the nobles and the officers of the Swedish army, and that the three Lower Estates be invited to second this petition.

The debate lasted three days. Violent language was used on both sides. Some members even forgot themselves so far as to draw their swords. The Lower Estates refused to support the Riddarhus. The Riddarhus refused to send delegates to the secret committee.

On the 9th February, the marshal of the Diet, weary of endless procrastination, condescended to entreat the nobles to proceed to the election of these delegates.

Fersen, waiving the appeal aside, continued to insist

[1] Indefinitely postponed.

on the necessity of sending a deputation to the Lower Estates.

The marshal refused to put the motion, declaring that it was against his oath, which bound him to consider the prerogative of the Crown as well as the privileges of the House.

In a moment, howls of rage and fury resounded from every part. Fersen and de Geer were loud in their outcries. Fists were clenched, swords drawn. The frantic members behind urged on those in front of them, and there was a wild rush for the marshal.

"Infamous scoundrel!"

"Death to the traitor!"

Trembling, in his excitement, like the leaf of an aspen, waving his white handkerchief as though it were a banner, Fersen fought his way up to the table behind which Carl Emil Lewenhaupt was standing, and tried in vain to make his voice heard above the tumult.

At length his hoarse shouts arrested attention.

The motion was put and carried, and the deputation was sent. In vain.

The Lower Estates refused to come to terms. They stood by the King.

Neither the nobles nor the King showed the least sign of yielding.

What the next move would be, who could say?

Still, not a word was breathed as to the change of the Constitution; and Tala herself began to think that the idea was a baseless conjecture of Essen's. She saw his name among the names of forty nobles who witnessed a note by the marshal, in which, with bitter complaints of ill-usage, he appealed to the King against the tyranny of those whom he was set to rule. But Essen did not come to see her. She supposed that he avoided the house on account of her father's views.

A very different sort of man from Clas Horn! He would not be all things to all men; he would not blow hot and cold; he would not serve two masters. The difference caused her to like him better, and the better she liked him, the more she felt his apparent neglect.

As for the appeal of the marshal, it was most graciously received at Court ; but no one, except Tala, felt much surprised to learn that his health failed suddenly at that moment, and he became incapable of presiding. His place was filled by the senior peer, Count Brahe.

Her father was present, as in duty bound, at the famous meeting of the Four Estates in the Rikssaal, when the King and his brothers appeared, surrounded by senators robed in purple and ermine, the King wearing his crown and carrying the silver sceptre of Gustavus Adolphus.

Everyone who heard the magnificent and indignant speech from the throne, noted his high colour—the sword-like gleam of his flashing blue eyes.

"If ever *War* was written on any human countenance, it was written on his," said Clas Horn, that evening.

Yet, of all those present, he was the only one who retained any pretence of composure.

The tones of his voice were cold as ice, hard as steel, when he called upon Fersen and de Geer by name, commanding them to withdraw, with their fellows, to their own especial hall of assembly, the Riddarhus, there to arrange and themselves conduct a deputation, headed by the first count of the realm, whose mission it should be to apologise to the marshal of the Diet, Carl Emil Lewenhaupt, and to see that the registers of the factious debates of the 7th and 9th February were erased from the record.

Fersen rose, in extreme agitation, requesting leave to speak.

The King bade him be silent.

Carl de Geer kept his seat.

Gustav struck the table with his sceptre to enforce attention, and once again, using an expression of contempt even more galling than the imperious command, ordered the nobles to retire.

"He told us to leave the room, as if we had been his valets," said Clas Horn, relating the circumstance.

Not one of the nine hundred stirred. Their hands were on the hilts of their swords, their eyes were bent upon Count Fersen.

General Duval attempted to speak. He was on the King's side; but he saw that for once the King had gone too far. He was a soldier, and he knew to what extent troops may be relied on.

Some of the nobles gathered round Count Brahe.

Fersen, however, had the wisdom to see that resistance would be useless and undignified.

" Let us go, gentlemen," he said, giving his hand to the Count.

The rest followed quickly.

In five minutes the King was left alone with the Lower Estates. He thanked them in touching terms for their devotion, and then withdrew, under cover of loud protestations of loyalty.

Meanwhile the nobles, left to themselves in the Riddarhus, passed a resolution that they "found it impossible to obey His Majesty's gracious command to apologise to the landmarshal."

Brahe placed the document in his hands that afternoon.

Then—in the velvet chamber—the storm burst.

Gustav read aloud, for the first time, the draft of his proposed Act of Union and Security, the provisions of which secured to Sweden a Government which was not far removed in form from the most absolute monarchy.

It came like a thunderclap.

His warmest admirers remained speechless with horror. They separated without coming to any decision.

Tala alone, in the midst of all her anxiety, rejoiced that the mask was off, the game declared at last. Diplomacy seemed to her, in her impetuous youth, only another name for lying.

She had expected that Clas Horn would agree with her, and she was vexed to find that he was agitated and full of gloom. His father, he told her, could no longer conscientiously support the Crown. She became indignant. He assured her that she did not

understand the vital principle underlying the whole
question; and they parted more coldly than usual.
The effect of the interview was to make Tala desire
Count Essen's presence still more. He was cool-headed,
wise, full of judgment, she said to herself. At a time
when no one dreamed of such things, he had foretold
this crisis—he had insisted that the King was right to
bring it on.

Next day the archbishop had a bad fit of the gout,
and found himself unable to attend the deliberations of
the clergy, although he was well enough to go and see
the King in the morning. These sudden illnesses were
becoming remarkable. Sudden deaths would be the
fashion next, somebody said.

Alderman Anders Lydberg, the third out of the four
talmen, still contrived to retain his health, but he
stated that the burgesses would not accept the Act of
Security.

The King announced his resolution to submit it to
the Estates in congress.

Thereupon, the Lower Estates sent a joint petition,
in which they humbly implored him to use his royal
authority to "set the Riksdag going again." He lost no
time in assuring them that he regretted the obstruction
as sincerely as they did, and was ready to do all that in
him lay to "quell the headstrong, and to chastise
frowardness."

CHAPTER XXIX

THE ARRESTS

IT was the afternoon of the 20th of February, and Tala was sitting by herself in the boudoir that she called her own.

Some of her acquaintance said that it was more like a young man's room than a girl's, presumably because it contained nothing that she did not want, and the chairs did not always stand in the same places. Yet a subtle design, not visible at first sight nor to everyone, prevailed in the decoration — a curious harmony of symbols. The carpet was of pale green, like the grass of the field, to signify the spring, when she felt hopeful. The walls were hung with dull blue, that they might remind her of her favourite mountains. The curtains— the *portiére* that covered the low door—were of a deep red, "Because," she said, when there was no one to hear her, "fire is red"; and at the thought her cheeks glowed. A single china vase of exquisite shape, of darker, more shining colour than the walls, adorned the mantelshelf. The chairs, the tables, the long, thin harpsichord were strewn with poetry and music. There were none of the little brackets, clocks, cabinets, and ornaments of every description in which women usually delight, for Tala wanted room to wander about, to fling herself down, to move freely and boldly, as though she were in the open air. Nor were there any pictures. When she was alone she was always thinking of Adolf; she needed no other faces to confuse with his. Herein she showed at least that she was feminine, if she was not, in the usual acceptation of the word, womanly.

Her father had gone to attend an important meeting
of the Opposition, at Frietzsky's house as usual,
promising to return at four o'clock and take her to
dine with the elder Fersen, whose favourite niece, the
lovely Aurora von Löwestein, was just then in his
house.   She and her three cousins were among the
most famous of the Court beauties in the earlier part
of the reign, and Tala, who had fallen in love with her
at first sight, was looking forward to the visit with
eager happiness.

They had met once or twice in society, and Aurora,
finding that she was related to her cousin Axel's
intimate friend, young Count Ribbing, was gracious.
Therefore Tala chose out her prettiest white dress
and white ribbons, and a cloak edged with the soft
white fur of which she was fond, and sat waiting,
in a flutter of pleased excitement.   She had made up
her mind to ask questions about Axel Fersen ; she
longed to know more of him.   Perhaps she might even
ask a question, such as pride would not allow her to
ask of a man, concerning this horrid Republican,
Madame de Staël.   Perhaps Aurora might ask her a
question about Adolf Ribbing.   After all, he was her
cousin.   And she blushed and smiled to herself, and
gathered a few snowdrops from the little *jardinière* that
stood in the window, and stuck them into her bodice,
to make believe that she was thinking of something
else.   She was very frank with other people ; she had
these coquetries with her own heart.

Four o'clock came, but the Baron did not return.
He was, as a rule, more punctual than the gold clock
on the stairs.   However, Tala was not uneasy.   He
had warned her that the meeting would be a long one ;
he might have been kept.

It was not till the clock struck half-past four that
she began to feel greatly surprised at his non-
appearance.

It was growing dusk now.

She rang for a lamp, and questioned the servants.

No ; they knew nothing.

The Baron had not come in; there was neither note
nor message for her.

Five o'clock.

Still not a word.

She was becoming anxious.

She waited another hour; her fears increased every
moment.

The want of sympathy between her father and herself during the last few months began to take the
proportions of a crime on her part.   She thought of all
his love for her.   Had she lost it?   Would he never
come back?   What was this dreadful, oppressive
silence?

The streets were unnaturally quiet.   As a rule, they
were thronged at this hour of the evening.

For the last week, too, she had always heard the
newsboys calling out the political events of the day.

Regardless of the cold, she flung her cloak round her,
unfastened the window, and stepped out upon the
balcony to listen.

Not a sound.

What had become of all the people?

Suddenly there was a crash behind, and a noise of
falling glass.   Someone must have seen her.   Some
unseen hand had flung a stone at the window.   She
could discern no one.

Half terrified, half angry, she withdrew.

Her father's old servant came at her summons, but
could or would give no clue to what had happened.
Strongly suspecting that he knew more than he chose
to tell, and controlling her impatience as best she
might, she ordered him to go to Frietzsky's house and
inquire whether her father was still there.

Frietzsky's house was not far.   The answer came
back in a single word, "No."

Her fear was fast becoming terror.

There was one other chance.   He might have
forgotten her, and gone home alone with Count Fersen;
they had been much together of late.

She was about to send a message thither when
someone knocked softly at the door of the boudoir.

She ran to open it herself, and was surprised to see the Countess Aurora, in a dark morning-dress, heavily muffled and veiled. As she threw back the gauze that covered her face, Tala saw that her cheeks were pale —her lovely eyes dim, as though she had been weeping.

"My child," she said, as she seated herself on the sofa and drew Tala towards her in a caressing, sisterly manner, that was more sweet and soothing than many words, "do not be frightened. I have come to tell you."

"What is it?" said Tala, her hands tightening together, while her eyes shot the question, "My father?"

"No, no," cried the Countess. "He is quite safe."

"Then nothing matters," said Tala, fetching a long sigh, as if to float her care away on it. They sat silent for a few moments; Tala felt her own hand tremble with the trembling of the hand that held it, and woke out of her short trance of relief.

"What is it?" she cried again. "He is not safe. What has happened?"

Instead of answering, the Countess took a slip of newspaper out of her muff. On it was printed in large capitals: *Arrest of the Leaders of the Opposition— Count Brahe, Count Fersen, Count Horn, Baron de Geer, Baron Pechlin, Baron Sterngeld, Messrs. Frietzsky, Engeström, etc.*—twenty-one names in all.

"Yes," said the Countess, when she saw that Tala had finished, "even Frietzsky! It was thought that the King would be afraid to touch him, whatever he did to my poor uncle. But we were wrong. He was arrested in his own house, together with my uncle and your father. They were all under lock and key within two hours. The Guard of Burgesses carried out the King's order—what does it say?— 'promptly and efficiently.' Oh, the mean hounds! Liljensparre is at the bottom of this."

"I cannot understand," said Tala. "In a prison! My father is not in prison?"

"He is indeed," said the Countess, her grief getting

the better of her wrath again. "But your father is a strong man; he is better able to bear hardship. It will kill my uncle. His daughters are in despair. They went to the palace, to try and see the King"—

Tala rose instantly.

"I must go," she said. "I must see the King."

Aurora shook her head.

"My child, it is of no use. The King refuses to see anyone. My cousins stood in the Pillared Chamber till they could stand no longer. No one asked them to sit down even. Sophie was almost fainting. The King returned to his apartments by a back staircase, in order to avoid meeting them." And Aurora broke down altogether, and wept, helplessly and bitterly.

"What can we do?" said Tala.

The question seemed to restore Aurora's composure.

"Write at once to those whose duty it is to come and protect us," she said. "I am sending a courier to Paris, to my cousin Axel; he starts in half an hour. Your cousin, Adolf Ribbing, is with him. Will you not write to him at the same time?"

"Why?"

"For your father's sake, for your own sake. You have no brother? I think you told me that he was your nearest relation?"

"He could not come," said Tala.

Aurora smiled rather scornfully.

"The Queen of France stands in the way, I suppose," she said. "For my part, I have no sympathy with these sentimental guardian angelships, and so I shall tell Axel. His sisters have no one else to look to; he is bound to return to them. If your cousin has any manhood in him, he will do the same."

"How could he help my father, if he did?"

"He could spare him the agony of knowing that you are unprotected, at anyrate."

"I am quite safe," said Tala hastily.

"My dear child," Aurora said, drawing her closer, "you are *not* safe. You must come home with me to-night. You are but a degree better off with us,

for the house may be mobbed at any moment, but
you cannot stay here alone—indeed you cannot. What
will happen next, no one knows. It is rumoured that
the King has sent for the Dalecarlians. If so, Armfelt,
with all his influence, will not be able to restrain
them. The whole town will be at their mercy."

"Are you cold?" said Tala, noticing that she
shivered.

"No—yes. It is cold in this room. Why—what
has happened?" cried the Countess, remarking for
the first time that the window was broken.

"I stepped on to the balcony just now, to listen, and
someone threw a stone."

Aurora's face became a shade paler.

"Then it has begun," she said. "Surely yóu
do not think of delaying now? You must have
someone with you. Write to your cousin at once!
Your letter will go with mine."

"He and my father are not—are not agreed," said
Tala confusedly.

"So much the better!" cried the Countess. "The
more likely he will be to help you—yes, and your
father too—at this juncture! Is he not a great
favourite with the King? I am sure I have heard
Axel say so. My child, we are all in the greatest
danger; this is no time for trifling nor for coquetry.
In Heaven's name, if you think he has any influence
with the King, send for him—send for him at once.
Do not hesitate!"

Her words fell lightly on the girl's ear. Tala indeed
scarcely heard them ; but the strong, persuasive touch
was magnetic, and she had half risen from her seat, as
though to seek pen and paper, when the door burst
violently open, and Clas Horn rushed into the room
—his face white and haggard, his eyes wild. He
must have come straight from some banquet or festival,
for he was gaily dressed ; but he had not taken the
time even to fasten his cloak, and it was falling from
his shoulders. He stopped short, seeing that Tala
was not alone, recognised Aurora, and held out his
hand to her.

"I did not think that I should find you here, Countess," he said. "I came to offer my services to this young lady,"—he bowed to her,—"but I am happy to have been forestalled. Your championship will be far more efficacious."

"She stands in need of someone who has a nearer right to protect her than either you or I," said the Countess softly. "I have been trying to persuade her to send for her cousin, Adolf Ribbing, by the same courier who is going in search of Axel Fersen. Will you not help her to see that this is the only right course? She will spend the night with us,—she could not stay here undefended,—but our house is, after all, scarcely more safe than her own."

"The Dalecarlians will be here at midnight," said Clas Horn.

The Countess shuddered.

"It is true then?"

"The King has sent for them."

"The King?" cried Tala.

"We must be prepared for the worst then," said the Countess. "Is it possible that we could leave Stockholm to-night?" She spoke as though she were questioning herself, no one else.

"Impossible," said Horn. "The roads are guarded. Your courier will not be able to get through."

Aurora smiled.

"Indeed he will," she said, with some significance.

Clas Horn looked at her curiously.

"If you can get through in his place, I should advise you to do so, then," he said. "The Duke of Sudermania has just been proclaimed absolute military governor of Stockholm."

Aurora's face blanched.

"But he is on our side?"

"He is on the King's side at this moment—in fact, he has been for the last half-hour!" said Horn sarcastically. "He is on the side that is going to win."

"But"—

"I know what you mean to say. We number nearly a thousand."

15

" *We?*" said Tala, bewildered.

" *We*—the nobility," he said. "The Guard of the Burgesses could not stand against us for five minutes; they have but fifty Light Dragoons to support them. If we had struck immediately, we must have won; but precious time was lost, and the King availed himself of it. The town is no fit place for ladies now. They threaten us with a general massacre of all the prisoners. The Dalecarlians are on the road. Armfelt himself cannot restrain them, when they have the King's word. They will probably set fire to every house that they enter; and that is not the worst you have to fear. You understand me? Go, if you can."

But Aurora shook her head, and spoke with determination.

"No; that is impossible. All I can answer for is, that my courier will be able to get through."

"He has my best wishes. Farewell! Commend me to Jacques de La Gardie."

"Where are you going?"

"To prison."

"But the King?"— said Tala, and stopped.

"I have no king now."

The profound despair of his voice shook Tala to the depths. If this man's devotion were changed, gone, utterly transferred in a moment, what would become of hers—of Adolf's? Noorna's words rang louder and louder in her ears. Dared she recall him?

"What good can you do?" cried Aurora.

"I can offer to take my father's place. If they will not allow this, I can at least die with him."

"Nonsense. You had much better live and save him," said the practical Aurora.

"I quite agree with you, madame," he answered, with a haggard smile, "only it is, like your proposal to depart from Stockholm, impossible."

He took the hand that Tala held out to him, and kept it for a moment.

"Let me look my last on you as a free man," he said. "The walls are closing round me already. If I

see your father, what shall I say to him? That you
also have done with kings for ever?"

His wild eyes, gazing into hers, cut her like steel.
She shut her own.

"I—I cannot," she said.   "Tell him that I will do
anything to deliver him."

He dropped her hand.

"You love your King more and your father less
than I love mine," he said, in a whisper. "A general
massacre of all the prisoners—think of that! Farewell!
We shall not meet again."

He was gone before she could make an effort to
detain him.

"What a madman that is!" Aurora observed
coolly. "I am glad that he did not offer to escort me
home. But I must go at once—at once. Now, dear
child, take off that pretty dress; put on something
dark and ugly, which people will not notice, and come
with me. It is getting late."

"You are very kind," said Tala. "I will come with
you. I should like to come. But leave me—leave me a
little while to write." She put her hand to her head.
"I am so bewildered. I must be alone for a few
minutes—only for a few minutes, to think. Then I will
do as you bid me. You said an hour. I will be with
you before then, and bring the letter. Old Jakob will
take me. We shall be quite safe. Listen! there is not
a sound in the streets!"

There were reasons why, after the news which she
had just heard from Clas Horn, Tala's proposal
should not be inconvenient to the Countess. She was
a wise woman; she had gained her chief point, and did
not insist on a detail. Besides, the child would be as
safe with her father's old servant as with herself—safer.
And she had made up her mind to send for Count
Ribbing. Aurora also had heard of that prophecy.

"You are right," she said, after a minute's reflection.
"You will need a little time to change your dress and
pack up your jewels. I rely upon you to come within
the hour, dear child. Farewell till then!"

She drew her mantle closely round her, pulled her

veil down over her forehead, and left the house, closing the door noiselessly.

No sooner was she gone than Tala clasped her hands together, with an upward look of relief. She sat down by the table and buried her face in her hands, trying to think. The more she tried, the more impossible it became. Her brain was nothing but a clamour of contending voices. Accustomed to determine everything quickly, upon impulse, the tortures of irresolution found her weaponless. She was torn in two by her longing to send for Adolf—by her terror lest, if he came, some dreadful thing should happen. With an instinct that the sight of clear, definite words might help her to some decision, she took a piece of clean white paper and wrote upon it the one word *Come* and her name. The first look of it called up a hot flush ; then she shivered.

There was Noorna Arfridson.

But her father ?

Thinking became no easier.

She took a second piece of paper, and traced these lines—

" Do not leave Paris."

Again she paused.

Her heart cried out that it was hard if she must drive him from her when most she needed him ; she must have some one word to tell her that he understood, some sign, however small. Besides, where was the harm ? A message by word of mouth could not be called correspondence. Fersen would be sure to come ; the Countess made no doubt of it. He might be trusted. She racked her brains for some expression that would not compromise the absent one. At length she took up the pen again, and added to her note—

" Say by messenger, *I cannot come.* We are safe.— Tala."

But which to send ?

Now that she had both alternatives before her, the question was less plain than ever. Whichever way she looked, distracting images of horror bewildered her. And meanwhile time was passing.

Suddenly a thought struck her—a name. A face arose before her eyes that she had seen, cool and passionless, when the storm raged. She thought it was an answer to her prayer. Up the stairs she flew, and, without waiting to change her dress, she hastily slipped on over it a fur pelisse, drew the dark hood as far forward as possible, in imitation of the Countess, and slipped out into the silent streets, without a word to anyone.

She scarcely knew what she was doing. Her head was in a whirl. One moment she saw her father in prison, in danger of death, cut down by savage Dalecarlians. The next, she beheld Adolf there, by her arrested, by her condemned. Yet—if she saved her father?

It seemed as if a heavy thunderstorm were impending; even out in the streets, in spite of the bitter cold, she could hardly breathe. As she sped along, she felt as though she were the only living thing in a dead city. No light came, save from the dim oil lamps. All the windows were darkened. Now and then a hoarse, isolated cry frightened her more than the stillness. Were the Dalesmen coming nearer and nearer? Would the massacre in the prisons begin? At this, all other thoughts vanished. She ran as though pursued, careless who saw her. She observed no one, however, except, just as she was nearing the palace, the figure of a woman who closely resembled the Countess, just in front. The impression was so strong that she paused; no—it could be nothing but fancy!— and she ran on. The Countess was going straight home; had she not told her so?

Panting and breathless, she made her way up the steps, and sought admission at the door of the palace, asking eagerly for Baron Essen, whom, she said, she must see, on business of the highest importance.

The porter stared, but he admitted her at once on hearing her name, and a lacquey with powdered hair ushered her into a small room on the ground-floor, where she perceived the Baron sitting at a table covered with books and papers. He wore a coat of purple velvet, trimmed with exquisite lace. The room was very brilliantly lighted, and felt hot. The sudden change from cold and darkness without—perhaps also the gentle, considerate kindness of the Baron, as he rose from his seat and placed her in it by the fire, was too much for her, and she burst into tears.

His astonishment on seeing her enter had surprised even himself. He was glad of her weeping; it gave him a moment to reflect. The calm of his manner reassured her as nothing else could have done. She began to feel as if she had reached a harbour of refuge at last.

"I am in great trouble," she said brokenly, seeing that he waited for some explanation. "There is no one that I can ask. Nobody knows the truth about me, except you. You will not think it strange? I know you will not."

"To whom should we go, if not to our friends, Fröken Tala?"

She was glad that he used her Christian name. It made him appear older.

"My father—you have heard?"

"Yes, I have heard."

"Is it—will it be worse than imprisonment?" she said, trembling—turning away, the moment after, from the compassion in his look.

"Hästesko has very little chance of escape, I believe, but of course that is different. No one can possibly say what will happen next."

"Is it true that the Dalesmen are coming?"

"Armfelt has twelve hundred of them quartered at Drottningholm, and he is ready to march on the capital at a moment's notice." (Essen was well aware that they would not be called upon to do so, but he reserved this information.) "When you did me the honour to seek me out just now, I was on the point of going to your house to inquire what steps you had taken."

"Countess Aurora has asked me to go to her for the night."

"You could not do better," he said, with grave approval. "But the Countess's own position is not a very safe one. Have you no other plans?"

"They want me to write—to write for Adolf—to bring him back."

"They? Who?" said Essen sharply.

"The Countess. She is sending a message to her cousin, Count Axel Fersen, to come at once."

Essen pondered an instant. These last words of Tala's had startled him considerably, though his countenance did not change.

"Sending a message?" he repeated. "No one is allowed to leave Stockholm ; there are sentinels everywhere. The Duke of Sudermania has given orders"—

"I know," said Tala impatiently. "But she has a courier, and her courier is sure to get through ; she told me so. No, she did not mention his name ; but it is quite certain. Oh, tell me, shall I make Adolf come or not? I must write to him one way or the other. He will hear from Count Fersen ; he will not know what to do."

Essen, whose mind was still running on the first part of her speech, suddenly recollected a story, many years old now, to the effect that Aurora was one of Duke Charles's early flames. "But who can this courier be that is 'sure to get through'?" he said to himself. "Wrangel is the only person who starts to-night, and that is a secret. The Duke knows it, of course— Ah, I see !" Tala, who was watching his face with great anxiety, supposed that he was thinking over her question.

"Tell me, tell me !" she cried piteously. "You have made up your mind. Tell me at once !"

"Count Ribbing might have some influence with the King," said Essen.

"But the King told him not to come back."

"If it is for his own disadvantage, I think we may be certain that he will not return."

Essen watched closely to observe the effect, as he shot the first of his poisoned arrows.

"You are quite wrong," said Tala, with angry surprise. "He would come at once if I summoned him, no matter who stood in the way."

"At the risk of ruining his career?"

"At the risk of his life—of his soul."

"Ah, well," said Essen, with a smile, "there is, of course, no risk of anything so serious as that. A hasty return would, at the very worst, delay his preferment."

"Are you sure?" said Tala, looking at him as if all her future lay in the eyes that met hers.

He shrugged his shoulders.

"My dear young lady," he said, "we can be sure of nothing."

"Then you are not sure of my father's danger?"

"There can be no doubt of that, unfortunately."

"How do you *know*?" said Tala, again showing her impatience.

Essen did not answer at once; after a moment he said, as though unwillingly and because she pressed him to speak, "I have already tried what I could do, but His Majesty is inflexible."

A sense of her injustice smote Tala hard.

"Can you—will you forgive me?" she said. "I ought not to have spoken like that. I hardly know what I am saying. It is very good of you. But—if I write—will not Adolf be in the same peril? Is it to bring him back to death?"

He observed that she uttered the word without any reluctance when it referred to Adolf.

"The two cases do not in the least resemble each other. Your father has done all that in him lay to thwart and to embarrass the King's Government. Besides, he has used many unguarded expressions. In Stockholm walls have ears, you know. On the other hand, Count Ribbing's devotion is well known; and the King is afraid of him, not he of the King. The King *dare* not make him his enemy."

He spoke as if the words were of great significance.

The King afraid! Noorna's warning had never struck her in that light before. Suddenly, what had seemed to her thick darkness turned to a gleam of hope.

"Do you think he would listen to Adolf if Adolf came?"

"The King is more likely to listen to him than to anyone else."

"I will write," said Tala, making a movement as though to rise.

"You think that he will come?"

"No, I do not think—I am sure of it."

Essen laid a detaining hand on her arm.

"Have you heard from him lately?"

"He could not let me hear. He promised that he would not write—you told me so yourself. What do you mean?"

"Only so much—that he finds it very easy to keep his promise, apparently. He is always with Madame de Staël. If he cannot see her, he writes to her every day. Hear me out to the end! Why do you think I have avoided you all this long while? I knew that you would question me. I did not wish to destroy your happiness."

"Do not distress yourself; you have not done so," said Tala coldly, "except in one way. I thought that you were his friend—and mine. Honour might keep him from me, nothing else could; not honour itself if I called him. I shall write now, of course, and you will see how wrong you are."

She would have risen. This time he made no motion to hinder her; he only looked at her. She sat down again as if fascinated.

"I am your friend," he said quietly. "It is in the capacity of a friend that I ask you what you are going to do if Adolf Ribbing does not come?"

"There is no need for me to think what will happen if he does not come."

"Are you my friend?" he said, in a still lower tone.

"I do not know," said Tala. "I thought I was; but I am not the friend of anyone who thinks meanly of Adolf."

"If my eager desire for your welfare makes me unjust to him, I shall be only too happy to recall any expression that may have wounded you—so soon as it is proved untrue. I promise you this, as your friend. In the meantime, will you promise me, as a friend,—merely as a friend, remember,—that if he declines to come, you will give me the same right to protect you that he has now?"

"Oh yes!" said Tala, a mirthful sparkle in her eyes in spite of her trouble. "Oh yes! 'If he declines to come,'"—she mimicked Essen's expression,—"I will do anything—anything."

The Baron winced, but not perceptibly.

"You promise?"

"I promise," she said lightly; and this time she laughed. She did not think that she was cruel Her overstrained nerves had rendered her callous, and it was a relief to laugh when her eyes were still smarting and her throat was aching with kept-back tears. She felt more kindly to him also; his motive was, she thought, transparent. "I must go home now! I must take my letter to the Countess at once." There was a touch of defiance about her.

"Will you not write it here? My carriage is at the door; I would leave you at Fersen's house afterwards. It will be quicker. Besides, it is not safe for you to be out in the streets on foot to-night."

"No," said Tala; "I must go back. I do not want to write here." For some undefined reason she felt as if she could not. Yet she braced herself for her lonely walk with something of an effort.

"As you will!" he said softly. "At least let me take you home in my carriage and escort you as far as Count Fersen's door, after you have written. Do you not see that it will save time?"

She hesitated for a second. The thought of those desolate streets frightened her. Besides, it was growing late. That was the excuse she made to herself. In sober truth, she yielded because those strong eyes were upon her.

"The carriage is at the door already."

They drove off. The Baron accompanied her upstairs to her boudoir. Shyness overcame her. She did not like to tell him that she had written the note already; it seemed foolish. Yet she was not sorry that he followed; having made up her mind to send for Adolf, she dreaded to be alone again until she had done so, lest resolution should cool. She sat down at her writing-table and toyed with a pen. Essen leant against the harpsichord, watching.

" If you will follow my advice," he said, "you will write very shortly, and you will put no address and no signature. I do not know what precautions the Countess has taken, but it is conceivable that the letter might fall into wrong hands ; if it did, the fewer people implicated the better ! "

Tala made no answer. Once more a bewildering host of arguments on either side went sweeping through her brain. To send the message she was sending was to commit Adolf irrevocably. Must she do it ? Dared she trust Countess Aurora ? It struck her that she might have known beforehand that the Countess would say, " Let him come ! " Naturally, she would desire to bring about a formal break between Adolf and the King.

Tala put her hand to her head. A plaintive cry burst from her lips.

" I cannot tell what to do. I must write something. What shall I write ? "

She had not spoken to be answered ; it was merely a cry.

" Write to him not to come," said Essen, tincturing the words with a sort of half-scornful compassion, which seemed to imply, " He will not come, in any case."

Tala was stung. She had the motive she wanted now, and hesitated no longer.

" I have told him to come at once ; I had done so before I asked you," she said haughtily, as she folded the note without even looking again at it, so eager was she to prove her independence. " Will you light me a taper, please? I want to seal it."

" I am charmed ; but there is nothing with which to light the taper."

" This will do," she said, twisting up a scrap of paper and handing it to him.

" I would not use a seal with any distinctive mark upon it, if I were you," remarked the Baron, when he had done as she desired. " It is better not."

" How annoying ! " she cried. " I never thought of

that. No matter! My father has a plain seal in the library."

She ran downstairs to look for it, leaving Essen alone.

He had noticed that there was writing of hers on the paper when she twisted it up. He had been careful only to burn one end. Now, quick as thought, he untwisted it, and read the words: "Do not leave Paris. Say by messenger, *I cannot come*. We are safe.—Tala."

What was the meaning of this? To tear off the burnt end of the paper, to smooth it out, and fold it exactly as Tala had folded the other note, was the work of a moment.

He laid it where the first note lay, and, hearing her step outside the door, thrust the other into his pocket.

"I cannot find the seal," she said, in troubled accents.

"Allow me to lend you mine; it has neither name nor arms upon it," replied the Baron politely.

It did not occur to her to ask why he had not offered it before. In truth, his pulses were fluttering almost as wildly as hers; he was amazed at himself.

She sealed her letter at once, and they left the house together. As the carriage rolled along through the darkness, she softly kissed the wax that Adolf's fingers would break.

Essen stopped the driver at the top of the street.

"We will get out here," he said, "and I shall leave you at the door. I have the greatest esteem for the lovely Countess, but she does not reciprocate it. I will ask you not to mention to her the fact that you have honoured me with your confidence."

CHAPTER XXX

IN THE VELVET CHAMBER

BESIDE his love—beside his enemy—there was one person in Stockholm that night who pictured Adolf Ribbing as vividly as if he had been present.

That night, it is recorded of the Bishop of Wexiö, that he went into the Velvet Chamber, about ten o'clock, and found the King sitting at his desk, a paper before him covered with blots and scratches.

He was surprised. In general his master wrote as he spoke, clearly and fluently.

"What do you think of the arrests?" he asked.

The bishop had spoken the truth too long to be afraid to speak it now.

"I greatly deplore them," he replied.

The King left silence to answer.

Then he said, in a voice that would have been defiant but for its languor, "I mean to make the Estates accept the Act of Security to-morrow."

The bishop shook his head.

"Impossible."

"No matter. I shall try," said the King. "There is a man in Paris—not my brother Louis—who says, *Ne me dites jamais ce bête de mot.*"

But it was not spoken with the old confidence. The flashing eyes were dull and tired, as if they had looked upon too much and longed to close. He pressed his hand to his forehead and sighed heavily.

Wallqvist had never heard him sigh like this before. He had smiled when Denmark was thundering at the gates of the realm ; he laughed when Russia threatened to overwhelm him.

" What is it, sire ? " he asked, in great alarm.

" To-morrow I must introduce my proposal with a speech," said the King, "and I have been trying to jot down the heads of it ; but it will not come right, some-how or other.   Give me a suggestion."

The bishop was at his wits' end what to suggest. He did as best he could, however, avoiding any reference to the prisoners, and the King took down a few notes, and dismissed him.

" If Adolf Ribbing stood behind that curtain, with a loaded pistol in his hand," Gustav said to himself, when he was left alone, "and I saw him ready to fire, I do not think that I should move."

What had become of all the reforms that he had planned ? His strength was sapped by these un-ceasing contests ; there was none left to carry them on. Where was the fame that he had promised his country ? Far from ruling the other Powers of Europe, alas, she could not even control her own lawless and passionate sons !

One by one, his splendid dreams were failing him. He fell asleep at last. Only in sleep could he find them again.

CHAPTER XXXI

THE KING'S JUSTICE

THERE was not a trace of emotion on the King's features when he met the Estates in congress next morning, and assured the eight hundred and fifty gentlemen who stood in a solid phalanx to the right of the throne that he would be "the last to hold them responsible for the misconduct of a few of their number."

He proceeded to reinstate as landmarshal poor trembling old Carl Emil Lewenhaupt, who seemed to desire nothing less, and immediately begged, in a scarcely audible whisper, to be allowed to decline the arduous position. The King accepted the *bâton* placed in his hands without a smile, and forthwith bestowed it on another and stronger friend of the Crown, by name Liljehorn.

His secretary, the all-powerful Elis Schröderheim, who at that time combined the incongruous offices of clerk of the council, grand herald, and minister of public worship, then read aloud the Nine Articles of the Act of Security, the effect of which would be to confer equality upon all the King's subjects throughout the realm (certain offices about the Court being alone reserved for the nobles, who would thus be shorn of many of their most cherished privileges); to reduce the functions of the Senate to those of a Supreme Court of Appeal; and to give the Crown the power to lay questions before the Diet, to appoint public officials, and to make peace and war. A bolder combination of monarchy and democracy was never attempted.

"Do you accept the provisions of this Act?" inquired the King, turning to the Order of the Peasants.

Deafening shouts of "Ay, ay," made the roof ring again.

He turned to the Order of Burgesses, put the same question, and met with the same response.

He turned to the Order of the Clergy and to that of the Nobles. This time a confused uproar was the only result.

Three times he put the question. Three times in succession the same hubbub was raised—the nobles all vociferating loudly, "No," the clergy being divided.

Availing himself of a momentary lull, Count Hamilton rose, with a draft of the Constitution in his hand, and asked that the nobles might be allowed to deliberate in their own chamber, while he called attention to the fact that the forty-second paragraph forbade the adoption of any new law, unless it had been previously discussed by each Estate alone.

He reckoned without his host.

During the last Riksdag, the nobles, annoyed by the opportunity to prolong debate which this paragraph gave the King, had succeeded in forcing through a measure, according to which, any Bill that was passed by three out of the Four Estates became law without further discussion. Gustav did not mean to allow them to forget that.

"Gentlemen," said he, "the Act of Security has been passed by the Order of Peasants, by the Order of Burgesses, and by the Order of the Clergy. No further deliberation can therefore be permitted."

For the first time that day he smiled. It was sweet to him to pay his enemies in their own coin, to turn against them the weapon that they had forged for his destruction; but in the very moment of triumph he was shaken.

A young Royalist poet, Gudmund Göran Adlerbeth, the most intimate friend of Clas Horn, burst through the ranks of the nobles, and flung himself on his knees before the throne.

"Justice! Justice!" he cried. "Sire, you have given the right of free discussion to your people—are you the first to take it from them? Justice "—he stopped short, unable to go further, and covered his face with his hands, his figure swaying to and fro with the violence of uncontrollable tears.

There was silence throughout the hall. Every man looked on the ground. Who, out of all that great assembly, could have said that what he wanted was justice? Who wanted anything but to conquer? Adlerbeth was the King's most fervent partisan; his enthusiastic devotion was the laughing-stock or the admiration of everyone present, according to his different lights. The agony of disillusion in that wild outcry touched even those who had long ceased to be moved by anything but their own interest.

To the King it seemed as though his younger self knelt sobbing there before him.

"Gentlemen!" he said, after a brief pause, "I request that the nobles withdraw to their own chamber for the discussion of this Act."

He turned and left the hall abruptly. Not a single cheer followed, but one or two of those who best loved him drew a long breath of relief.

In the evening, Adlerbeth went as usual to the palace. It was a point of honour among those of his way of thinking to attend, for the *levée* had been much deserted of late. The King came forward through the green curtains to meet him, and embraced him with even greater affection than usual.

"You made the finest peroration I ever heard," he said in French. "Well," and he played with his sword, "you see that I know how to do justice."

"Upon my word, you have taken a fine step forward," said Baron Essen afterwards. "Were you one of our best actors, His Majesty could not have congratulated you more warmly."

Adlerbeth coloured; he felt the implied sneer.

"Can you tell me what has become of Clas Horn?" he said, to change the conversation.

"I wish I could," said Essen.

"You speak as if you were alarmed. Is there any cause?"

16

"Nothing has been heard of him since his mad attempt to get into prison last night. He seems to have disappeared. He did not return home, and I hear that his people are very anxious; they are afraid that he may have done himself a mischief. The shock of these arrests was too much for his brain. He was as true a Royalist as you—or I; but I am told that the expressions he used at the club regarding His Majesty were terrible."

Adlerbeth frowned.

"Heaven send him safely back to us!" he said, in a low voice.

"Amen! *À propos*, have you heard that two of the prisoners are to be taken to the fortress of Marstrand, without trial?"

The young poet's face fell.

"It cannot be," he said hastily. "You heard what the King said only a moment ago."

"*You see that I know how to do justice*," quoted Essen. "Yes,"—and he glanced at his companion,—"poetical justice."

"I will not believe it," said Adlerbeth, with impetuous anger. "It is not true. What are the names?"

"I do not know. For your friend, Clas Horn's sake, I can only hope that his father is not one; and for his daughter's sake, I can only hope that Carl de Geer is not the other."

"De Geer?" said Adlerbeth. "It was to de Geer's house that Clas Horn said he was going when I met him in the street last night. I was greatly surprised to hear it."

"De Geer's daughter is not of the same way of thinking as her sire."

"Why has she gone to the Fersens then?"

"She was quite alone. There was no one else with whom she could take refuge. But she enters the household of the Duchess to-morrow."

"What?" said Adlerbeth. "The little Duchess? Duke Charles's wife?"

"Yes."

" Is the Duke really one of ours ? "

Essen shrugged his shoulders.

" Has the poor young lady no relations of her own ? "

" Her cousin, Adolf Ribbing, is supposed to have some claim to protect her ; but he is in Paris."

" Where he is busy protecting Madame de Staël," said Adlerbeth. " I know that story."

" She believes that he will return, when he knows what has happened."

" Whether he does or no, she is like to need him. I hear that Carl de Geer is ill. The shock affected his heart."

" Indeed ? I am sincerely distressed to hear it. He seemed to be in perfect health two days ago. Do you know what bearing the arrests are likely to have on the judgment of Hästesko ? "

" Not in the least. In my opinion, Hästesko is a villain and he deserves to suffer. But everyone is sorry for that unfortunate wife of his ; and the King will never hold out."

" Are you so sure of that ? "

Adlerbeth stared politely.

" Do you not know that it is next to impossible to prevail upon him to sign a sentence of death ? Look at him now ! Is that the face of a man who could be relentless ? "

The King had taken the little Crown Prince upon his knee, and was playing cat's cradle with the Duchess of Sudermania for his amusement.

CHAPTER XXXII

BETWEEN TWO FIRES

IT was nearly a month before Baron Wrangel reached Paris, on his way to Florence. His consular appointment came under the terms of the new Act, and had therefore been conferred upon him by the King alone, without the consent of the Riksdag; so that it was desirable to get him out of Stockholm as soon and as secretly as possible. Aurora, after her interview with Clas Horn, on the evening of the arrests, had found it no easy task to persuade the Duke of Sudermania over again to let him carry her letter. It was only when she threatened to expose certain passages in the life of the Duke, with which she, and no one else, was acquainted, that he gave way. He knew that nothing could be less palatable to the brother whose cause he was just now espousing than the return of the younger Fersen and Adolf Ribbing, and he saw good reason to believe that this was what Aurora desired. They might refuse to come, of course. Fersen's chivalrous devotion to the Queen of France was well known, and many rumours had arisen at Court, no one exactly knew how, to the effect that Adolf Ribbing was the delighted captive of Madame de Staël. However, it was dangerous. On a question of secret influence, he himself would have backed Aurora against any queen or any ambassadress on earth.

Nevertheless, her calculations were thrown out by an unexpected and trifling incident.

Baron Wrangel caught cold on the journey, and was detained for some time at a little fishing-village on the coast. There further news of the progress of events was brought him—news which Aurora had not sent, and certainly would not have sent, unless with an injunction to keep it secret.

Pushing on as fast as he could, he reached Paris towards the middle of April, and went straight to Axel Fersen's *hôtel*, rue Matignon.

Fersen could not be found. He was only returning from Valenciennes, whither he had gone to visit his regiment, the Royal Suédois, that afternoon. Wrangel deposited the precious letter which the Countess had entrusted to him, left word that he would call again in the evening, and went away.

Adolf was at the opera that night, alone with Madame de Staël, enjoying the performance of Grétry's *Lucile*. His neighbour had been very brilliant at dinner-time, laughing and talking until the whole table followed suit. In that common mood with womanhood, when excessive mirth opens the door to melancholy, she was now silent, almost remorseful. Adolf, for once, forgot her. The thin, sweet melody set thoughts of home astir in him.

"Où peut-on être mieux
Qu'au sein de sa famille?
Tout est content, le cœur, les yeux,
Vivons, amis, comme nos bons aïeux ;
Les noms d'époux et de fille sont délicieux.

So sang the chorus ; Marmontel's words were musical as Grétry's music to his ear. He saw his white-armed Tala—wondered—craved to know when he should see her next.

"Tout est content, le cœur, les yeux."

A wave of longing for her swept over him. He closed his eyes, that he might behold her more distinctly.

"Les noms d'époux et de fille sont délicieux."

Madame de Staël laid her hand on his arm.

"I cannot bear this," she said huskily. "Let us go!"

At that moment the door of the box opened with a harsh creak, and Axel Fersen, accompanied by Baron de Staël, came in.

The ambassadress, preoccupied with her own emotions, observed nothing particular in his appearance.

He wore a suit of the pale lilac colour called *soupirs étouffés*. He was point device as usual, his hair curled and powdered, his lace ruffles in perfect order. Adolf, however, saw at a glance that the lines of his face were drawn, as at Gothenburg, on the night of their first meeting.

"I must apologise profoundly to you, madame," he said, with a low bow. "A private matter, of some importance to us both, compels me to interrupt my friend's enjoyment."

"Monsieur de Fersen wishes to speak to Count de Ribbing on business. I shall be happy to see you home, my love," remarked the Baron timidly.

"I have no intention of returning home before the end of the opera," she said, in icy tones. "I hope that you will honour us with your company, Monsieur de Fersen. If you have waited till so late at night to discuss business with Count de Ribbing, you can surely wait an hour longer."

She made an impatient gesture, and let her scent-bottle drop. Fersen picked it up, and restored it to her.

"I regret extremely," he said, "that I cannot accept your kind invitation. If my friend is not at liberty now, perhaps he will join me at the conclusion of the opera," and, with another low bow, he left the box.

Before he had reached the vestibule, however, an arm was thrust through his, and a scared face turned up to him. Adolf had braved the wrath of the Muse by abandoning her.

"In Heaven's name, Axel, what is it?"

"Bad news from home."

Adolf started as if he had been shot. He could think only of one person, of one thing.

"Dead?" he said inarticulately.

"Worse."

"Who?" It was a questioning sound, not a word.

"My father."

Adolf breathed again.

"I thought"— he said, the next moment, with a keen pang of self-reproach.

"I know," said Fersen, in the same toneless voice. "We cannot talk here. Wait till we are at home."

They hurried silently through the streets, which, at that period, were seldom deserted, even towards midnight, and reached the Hôtel Fersen, after walking—so it appeared to Adolf—a hundred miles. The courtyard expanded indefinitely, the staircase had many more steps than usual.

A lamp was burning in Fersen's study; in one vivid moment it reminded Adolf of the tower at Gothenburg—of the many evenings they had spent there, in a former state of existence, as it seemed.

"The King has arrested my father and twenty others—your uncle, Carl de Geer, among them," Axel said, as slowly as though he were pronouncing sentence of death.

Adolf sprang from his seat. The table, the lamp upon it, Axel himself, were dancing round him.

"Why?"

"Because they would not sign some Act—the Act of Security, Aurora calls it," said Axel, referring to a letter in his hand. "They were taken to prison by the officers of the Guard of Burgesses."

"By the officers of the Guard of Burgesses! Where was Armfelt?"

"Armfelt is at the head of the Dalecarlians, and the King has told him to be ready to enter Stockholm at a moment's notice. The King refused to see my sisters. They are ill—unable to write. The letter is from my cousin Aurora, but I can hardly read it—it is all blotted! They are in terror of their lives."

"Are you going?" said Adolf breathlessly.

"No."

A cry burst from him.

"I cannot," Axel said. "This is secret as the grave —but my regiment at Valenciennes is ripe for mutiny.

If I left, I dare not answer for it to the Queen. I have weighed it well, but I cannot go. It is against honour."

"Your sisters—your father?"

Fersen dropped his head on his hands without answering. The silence that followed made Adolf look up. Then for the first time Fersen raised his eyes, and in the midst of his own excitement, Adolf was struck to the heart by their lifelessness.

"I will go," he said, with quick determination.

"You cannot. You are bound to this doomed city just as I am. (Beneath the regret of the words Adolf knew that there was a dumb satisfaction in Fersen's heart.) You promised the King that you would not return without orders."

"The King has made perjury the fashion," said Adolf briefly. He was surprised to find himself so well able to speak.

"Hush!" said Fersen, laying his hand upon his sword. "If you were any other than the King's friend, you would have to answer for those words to me."

"One of us must go," said Adolf. He scarcely even noticed Axel's unusual tone. He was beginning to feel as if he could not stay five minutes longer in that room. Tala in danger! Who and what could compel him to stay?

"Have you considered? It may ruin your career."

"Is this a moment to think of such things?"

"It is not yourself alone. Another is involved. You cannot go."

"One of us two must," said Adolf. "I break a promise given in words if I go; it is no light thing. I understand what I am doing. You—if you go—must break a vow so solemn that it was never registered. Your place is here."

"You have given your word. You cannot," Fersen repeated.

Adolf choked back the rising passion, struggling hard to control his voice, that he might speak calmly.

"If the Queen were in Sweden now, would any oath to any king under heaven keep you here, Axel?"

There was no answer.

He put out his hand. Axel took it in his own and held it a moment.

"Who brought the letter?" demanded Adolf, his mind turning to practical details.

"Baron Wrangel. He has been made consul at Florence. Did not you know that? De Staël told me. He must be on his way to Italy. I had not come back when he arrived, unhappily, and he did not leave his address; but he said that he would return again later."

"Was there nothing but this?"

"You are right to ask," said Fersen. "I think I am losing my head. There was a note for you inside. Here it is."

Adolf tore open the cover.

"She tells me *not to come*!" he cried, as if he challenged the whole world to explain.

"Give me the note!" said Fersen.

It ran thus: "Do not leave Paris. Say by messenger, *I cannot come*. We are safe.—Tala."

The two young men were still seated, staring blankly at each other, when the door opened and Wrangel appeared.

"This is very kind of you, Baron!" said Axel, with his usual dignified friendliness. "You find Count Ribbing and myself in great agitation."

"I cannot say that you look as if the air of Paris agreed with you."

"We have only just heard of the arrests. Do you think that the latest news is of a character to raise our spirits?" said Adolf sharply.

"I do not know what you may have heard, Count Ribbing. I was delayed some time on the road, but the latest news that I got from Court was remarkably good. Oh, we have gone on at a fine pace since you left us! As for constitutional government, there is not a rag of it left. In fact, the King will make himself Grand Turk this time next year, I should imagine."

"The caprices of your imagination are, no doubt, interesting," said Adolf, in a tone the nervous asperity of which vexed Axel, "but my friend and I are plain, matter-of-course persons. If you could tell us the facts as they occurred, we should be much obliged to you. How did you leave our friends in Stockholm?"

"They were all in a state of panic when I came away," said Wrangel, whose good-humour it seemed impossible to disturb. "The Bishop of Wexiö told me himself that he was trembling every minute for the King's life. Feeling ran high. However, the speakers of the three Lower Estates signed and sealed the Act of Security, two days afterwards, and I hear now that, having waited three long weeks in vain, the King sent for the marshal, put a pen in his hand, and made him add his signature to the document on behalf of the nobles. It seems to be a wonderfully simple way out of the dilemma, when you come to think of it; as simple as the egg of Columbus. Of course the nobles are not pleased. When were they ever pleased? They have passed a special resolution that they will not have the marshal's portrait hung in the Riddarhus, like those of his predecessors. But the King is having it painted—at his own expense—and hung in the palace, among the Kings of Sweden. So how is Liljehorn the worse?"

"And the prisoners?" said Adolf.

Axel started as if the word stung him.

"The prisoners are enjoying a dignified retreat, with all the honours of war. No business to attend to, wine from the King's own table, all the delicacies of the season. We shall hear, to-morrow or next day, that the Diet is over and they are free. The King wanted to give them a fright—that was all."

"Is this certain?"

"I have it from Schröderheim himself. The King has given his word to release them, the moment the Diet is over. And the Diet cannot legally be protracted much longer."

"But how about the Dalesmen?" said Fersen anxiously. "My cousin writes that they are expected to enter the city."

"A mere myth. Armfelt has some hundreds of them at Drottningholm, I believe. 'The bonny general,' who fears nothing, is very much afraid of them himself; but the King knows what he is about far too well to tempt them into his capital. The Countess wrote on the evening of the 20th February last, when we were all in a state of over-excitement. I have received advices since. Everything is quiet again."

"Then that was the meaning of the note," said Fersen to Adolf. "Your correspondent knew that it was a false alarm, and feared that you would compromise yourself by returning."

"I cannot agree with you," said Adolf hotly. "I am far from feeling reassured by Baron Wrangel's account. I shall start for Stockholm to-night."

"You will do nothing of the kind," said Fersen, the gentle persuasiveness of his manner softening the imperative words. "Of what avail would it be? The Diet will be over before you arrive, and your uncle will be at liberty."

"How can I tell? The King has broken his word once. He may break it again."

Adolf was impatient — mad to be gone. Fersen's scruples were empty air to him. Fanned into flame by opposition, his dislike of Wrangel had grown rapidly, in the last few minutes, to hatred. He disbelieved every word that the Baron said. He could not endure to be in the same room with him.

"You are talking like a foolish child," said Fersen severely. "If His Majesty were about to take further proceedings, he would never have told Schröderheim that he meant to release the leaders of the Opposition. Of what advantage could it be to him to act in that manner?"

"I do not know," said Adolf, who saw a smile—of irony, he thought—on Wrangel's face. "I know that it is my duty to go at once to Stockholm, to protect my cousin."

"When—at her own peril—she writes to warn you that she does not wish it? Aurora says that she has honoured my father by accepting the shelter of his roof. She is not alone; she tells you herself that she is safe. In a day or two Carl de Geer will be with her

again. He has never favoured your suit ; you will be
farther off from her than you are here, seeing that your
disobedience to his orders will have alienated your one
friend, the King. How are you going to account to
him for your conduct ? "

"I do not know, I do not care ; but go I will ! " said
Adolf, clenching his fist.

"So would I, were I in your place ! " put in Wrangel,
reminded by Fersen's last words of a certain bet that
he had laid with Jacques de La Gardie.

Adolf pulled himself up short.

"You are right, Axel ! " he said abruptly. "I will
stay here."

Wrangel raised his eyebrows. Axel dropped the
note, which he was holding, into the fire.

"No," he said, as Adolf sprang forward to save it,
"her instructions were that it should be burnt."

"You have both of you become very dramatic since
you left Stockholm, gentlemen ! " said Wrangel, yawning. "I have seen too many *coups de théâtre*, however.
I am tired of them. I wish you good-night."

Adolf scarcely bent his head.

Fersen rose courteously, and ushered his guest to
the door. He did not return for some time.

"I have despatched a courier," he said, when he
re-entered the room. "I had to write to Aurora, of
course. I told the man that he was to find your
cousin, wherever she might be, and to report the three
words that she asked for as a sign that you had her
letter and understood. It was a very good arrangement. I wish Aurora had such a head. She is too
clever to be wise ; she always was."

"Yes, she was right," said Adolf, a sour little smile
playing round the corners of his mouth. "You were
right too, and I was wrong. To think that it should
take the approval of a thing like Wrangel to show me
that ! I despair of humanity."

Fersen had too much tact to make any comment
upon his friend's change of front. They had been
sitting silent for a long while when Adolf spoke again.

"I would give the world that this had not happened,"

he said. "I would rather Count Fersen and my uncle had arrested the King himself."

"A revolution? Heaven forefend!" said Axel. "We distrusted him far too easily. You are still so much excited that you cannot tell right from wrong. The nobles are not all chivalrous gentlemen like my father and de Geer. We cannot tell to what lengths they would go, if they had the King in their power. There is old Pechlin—one shudders to think of it!" He paused a moment, then added, in a tone of ringing confidence, "Now we know that *he* would not injure his enemies."

"Are there no injuries short of bodily suffering?"

Fersen did not answer at once.

"My father will never be the same man again," he said, in altered tones.

"Yet you uphold the King?"

"I have sworn to uphold him."

Adolf leant forward.

"Axel," he said, "you know that I love the King. You know that I would give life itself for him. I shall obey his orders as I have always done. It is as a man that I shall love him now. As a king he is dead. He has killed himself. I shall never speak of this to anyone; or, if I do, I shall defend it—even to the ambassadress. To you I cannot call black white. I dare not."

"You were not there," said Axel. "You do not know the details. You cannot judge."

"Perhaps not," said Adolf bitterly; "but I wish I had died before Wrangel brought you that news."

CHAPTER XXXIII

THE HOUSEHOLD OF THE DUKE

FOR Tala, shut up among the Duchess of Sudermania's ladies, the days passed heavily enough.
Freed from acute anxiety about her father (for it
was now recognised that the prisoners, with two
exceptions, had no hardship except that of restraint to
endure, and would be set at liberty so soon as the Diet
was over), she was, nevertheless, most anxious as to the
issue of the note which she had sent to Adolf.

That he would come she never doubted for one
instant. She used to smile at Aurora, who professed
to be sure of Axel Fersen, and sometimes twitted her
with uncertainty.

The weeks went on, and still no tidings reached them
from either of the two friends. Her confidence was as
firm as ever, but she began to weary of the long effort
of looking out, looking out always for something that
never arrived. Other troubles weighed on her too.
Her sleep was haunted by unrefreshing dreams. She
felt tired and listless. It was not so much that the
excitement of the last few weeks had been too much for
her, as that she could not bear the little life of cunning
and intrigue, in the meshes of which she found herself
caught. She pined to be back among the great, quiet
mountains, where people said what they meant and
did not smile when they were angry. The laughter of
courtiers and maids-of-honour jarred on her nerves;
she became painfully clever at detecting the emptiness
of it. She knew now when it was but the result of
some *ingénue's* nervousness over an indelicate jest,

254

which she was ashamed of not understanding—when people laughed because they were fond of showing their pretty teeth—when they were relieving the over-tension of their spirits in this manner.

It was indeed a period of unnatural excitement everywhere. The King's friends were not less anxious than those of the prisoners. It was known—suspicion was so strong as to reckon itself knowledge—that these would stop short at nothing, more especially as the King had taken a leaf from their book and shown that he was not above the temptation of using force. Each side was kept on the alert, fearing an attack on the part of the other. No one knew when he went to bed at night whether he would awake to find himself in the saddle or under the horse's feet.

The beauty of the bright spring weather contrasted with the gloom visible on almost every face throughout the length and breadth of the city. It was the first time that Tala had not felt her blood flowing more quickly, her pulses dancing faster, because the sun was bringing back the flowers. For the first time she had not been able to sing; her voice was too weak. All her joyous sensations seemed to have resolved themselves into bodily longing for the sight of Adolf's face and the sound of his voice. She had lost the government of her thoughts, and could not remember or look forward to anything else.

She saw very little of anyone except Aurora and Colonel Hästesko's poor little wife during these long weeks, for she had made few friends amongst the ladies of the Duchess. Her very loveliness isolated her—made her less attractive to them than she might otherwise have been. They did not understand it; red hair was not in fashion; they were inclined to be jealous, because the gentlemen of the household—quicker, as the way of mankind is, to appreciate beauty that is not according to rule—showed their admiration openly, whenever chance gave them occasion. Tala was unpractised in the art of conciliation, and a great sense of loneliness oppressed her. She was accustomed to want of companionship,—that was no intolerable

misfortune,—but she was not used to breathe an
atmosphere of cold dislike and disapproval, the reason
of which she could not even guess; it made her feel as
if she were herself a prisoner.

News from the outer world did not reach her often.
Almost all the ladies of Stockholm, except the King's
immediate relatives and those of his suite, declined
to appear at Court. There was great indignation
amongst them at the treatment which Fersen's
daughters had received, and they were determined to
show it. The merry little Duchess went seldom enough
—and came back with odd stories of the deserted
aspect of the white drawing-room, and the unusual
and ungentlemanly guests whom she encountered
there. Tala liked her well, and could enjoy listening
to her gossip, which was less ill-natured because
it was brighter and cleverer than that of her satellites;
but no confidences were encouraged in that quarter,
for the Duchess had learned by bitter experience what
the King never learned to the end of his life—that
a good ruler must make no favourites.

Whenever Tala saw the Duke, he paid her marked
attention; but she could not overcome her distrust of
him, and he only repelled where he sought to attract.

As often as she dared, she stole away to her two
friends, neither of whom could visit her, so long as
she remained in her present surroundings. Siri
Hästesko was more in need of comfort than ever.
She had no tidings of her husband; her health was
breaking down under the pressure of that terrible
anxiety, and she could neither eat nor sleep. Tala
forgot her own woes, for the moment, when she was
trying to lighten this dumb sorrow; but she would
come away feeling miserable and bewildered. Why
all this cruel delay, this needless suffering? She knew
that Hästesko had behaved ill. She clung desperately
to her old trust in the King. Everyone said that he
would pardon in the end; but in spite of herself, her
heart cried out against the interminable suspense.

Aurora was not slow to perceive this. In the
beginning of their intimacy, Tala had thought it only

honest to allude to the political difference between them ; but the beautiful Countess smiled, as if it were not worth mentioning.

She never tried to proselytise.

As time went on, she told the girl one or two of the false and hideous stories about the King, which she herself firmly believed, and left the venom to work.

Tala was horrified, indignant, utterly incredulous.

The Countess said no more for the time being.

Gradually slight suspicion crept into Tala's mind. If the King were in truth a monster of iniquity—if she and Adolf had both been deceived in him?— She hated herself for thinking such a thought, and yet, the more she hated it, the more persistently it returned. Again she longed for Adolf, to give her back her faith.

Essen could not do this. She saw him now and then, but she had convinced herself that he was wrong in one supposition, and as she no longer believed him omniscient, she went to the other extreme, and made up her mind that he knew nothing. He was always very deferential.

"Have you received your answer, Fröken de Geer?" he said one day when he chanced to find her alone.

"Not yet," she said.

"Let me assure you that you cannot be more impatient for the arrival of the messenger than I am."

"I am not impatient," said Tala proudly.

"Was that true?" she asked herself, when he had left her. "No." Then why was she not humiliated by the discovery that she had told a lie?

She would have liked to confess to Aurora, but something (she did not exactly know what ; certainly not the Baron's injunction to silence) always kept her from mentioning Essen. It seemed to her that she could not speak as freely of Adolf to her friend if she did so.

The shadows were falling black and thick about her ; she was fast becoming a mystery to herself. The great, silent mansion in which she lived was dark, and wanted air. It was full of crooked, tortuous passages,

17

lighted only by little windows set too high up for anyone to see out of them. The people in it moved and spoke softly, as if they feared to disturb the echoes. Strange things were done. The master of the house went one way, the mistress another.

The Duchess kept to her own apartments, which had a southern aspect, and were less gloomy than the rest. Here she often received the poet, Gudmund Adlerbeth, whose impassioned appeal to the King to allow freedom of debate had caused so great a stir, some weeks ago. His modest, refined manners delighted Tala, and she was glad when he came up to her, one evening, and asked her if she had heard anything of their mutual friend, Clas Horn.

"No," she said—ashamed to think that she had forgotten all about that young gentleman. "The last time that I saw him, he told me that he was going to join his father."

"He did actually make the attempt," said Adlerbeth. "It was unsuccessful, of course; and since that night no one has seen or heard anything of him. We are growing anxious. I thought that he might have communicated with you."

"If he does, I will let you know," said Tala. "But I am afraid that it is not at all likely. Why should he have let such a long time go by?"

"I cannot tell; but I am persuaded that he is in hiding somewhere in this neighbourhood. I am almost certain that I saw him this very evening, about dusk. I think he saw me too. He turned down a side street at once, as if he wished to escape notice; but though I followed him as quickly as possible, I could not trace him."

"That is just like everything here," said Tala impetuously. "You try to catch it, and there is nothing. It is all shadow and emptiness. Everyone is somebody else. It is horrible; I lose myself when I think of it."

Adlerbeth smiled.

"To lose oneself is to find heaven," he said.

The Duchess called him away before Tala could reply; but she pondered over the words.

The other ladies informed her that the young poet was the only person who found it possible to remain on good terms with the Duchess's husband as well as with the Duchess.

So far as the conduct of life was concerned, however, the Duke seemed to be altogether in the hands of his secretary, Reuterholm, a man of strong character and passions, whom Tala feared rather than otherwise, in spite of the pleasure which he expressed in her society. She preferred another inmate of the house, Colonel Silfverhielm, whose manners were less imperious.

The three were often closeted together for many hours of the night, in a little room which no one else, except Gudmund Adlerbeth, was allowed to enter.

What they did there, nobody knew; but it was whispered amongst the ladies, that Silfverhielm was an ardent disciple of the famous Mesmer—that if they slept, they slept with their eyes wide open. One lady, who occupied the room adjoining, had not been able to get any rest, because of the loud knocks against the wall, and the mysterious noises in the chimney.

" Why do they knock on the wall? " asked Tala.

"It is not they who knock, it is the spirits. It means that they are seeking to learn the future. Did you not know that spirits always announce themselves in that way? "

Tala felt that she had been rebuked for her ignorance. She asked Gudmund Adlerbeth about it one day.

"Yes," he said, without hesitation, "you are quite right. We do investigate the future. The Duke is a wonderfully good medium. You would be surprised if I ventured to tell you the results at which we have arrived. It has been going on now for years. Two or three of the events predicted have already come to pass."

Tala, had she been less simple, might have wondered a little why their coming to pass seemed to be of such slight importance, comparatively speaking; but she was ready of belief, and said with eagerness—

"Tell me about it!"

"I should think you would make a good medium yourself," he said reflectively, not answering her question. "I have seen you smile, now and then, when no one else was smiling; you are very sensitive, and quick to immaterial influences. Have you ever allowed anyone to throw you into a trance?"

"No."

"You must let me try some day. I promise to ask no indiscreet questions. By the way, there is a friend of yours,—at least he called himself so (I hope that he was not presumptuous),—Hans Henrik von Essen, who has wonderful power. I had only to show him a few passes, and he mastered Reuterholm — a man with whom neither the Duke, nor Silfverhielm, nor I myself could do anything."

"I do not like it. I wish I were away from it all!" cried Tala.

She shut her eyes; it seemed as if Essen were looking into them. Adlerbeth's talk had confused her, and made her feel as though her senses were not her own.

"Why should you say that?" he asked softly. "You can never be 'away from it all.' You are unhappy, Fröken de Geer,—anyone can see that,—but it is because you want to understand, not because you want to run away. If you would study the works of our great master, Swedenborg,"—he made a short, reverential pause,—"you would give up living for the flesh, and live, as we are humbly seeking to live, for the world of spirits alone."

"Where can I get them? I will read them at once," said Tala, moved by the quiet earnestness of his manner.

"Ask the Duke to lend you *Conjugal Love*," said Adlerbeth, "but"—he lowered his voice to a whisper —"do not let the Duchess know that you have asked for it. She laughs at these things."

Tala, however, spoke to her mistress first.

The Duchess laughed, and said, "My dear child, *ça n'existe pas*; but if you like to read a book about it, pray do!"

The Duke was pleased to find that she took an interest in his favourite hobby, and presented her with a copy of the work.

The fascination of the mind of the great mystic—who had died seventeen years before, when she was only a little child—laid hold of her like some living, clinging presence, with hands and feet. She did not understand one quarter of what she read, but she read, night and day. The sound of his magnificent phrases was music; she asked nothing more; she had heard nothing but noises for so long. She forgot the cackle of laughter all round, and heard only singing.

"Man in his perfect form is heaven."

"In heaven the angels are advancing continually to the spring of their youth, so that the oldest angel appears the youngest."

She learnt it by heart; she slept with it, and woke to it; and more and more she longed for Adolf, that she might instruct him also in this new learning.

And still the Countess watched and waited, and there was no sign, either of Axel Fersen or of his friend.

CHAPTER XXXIV

TALA RECEIVES HER ANSWER

MEANTIME, the King had not succeeded in imprisoning all his difficulties with the twenty-one captive nobles.

A fresh grievance had arisen.

The Act of Security having been allowed to drop,—not because the nobles were weary, but because, in their present leaderless condition, they were afraid to contest it any longer,—they became even more vindictive over the burning question of subsidies.

The King was in terrible straits for money, and the finances were utterly exhausted. If he could not obtain the grant that he asked for, his position would be precarious in the extreme.

Once more, after a great deal of friction, and not without the strongest personal inducement from the King himself, the Lower Estates passed a Bill by which the subsidies were granted to him indefinitely, that is, until the next meeting of the Riksdag.

Once more the nobles saw their opportunity—for on questions of finance the Four Estates were bound, by the law of the land, to be unanimous, and there was no avoiding discussion on the plea that three out of the four had consented. They refused to grant the subsidies for a period of more than two years.

The Riksdag had already exceeded the limited time for which it was called together, and everyone was grumbling at the inordinate length of the session.

Another crisis seemed to be at hand.

On the evening of Sunday, the 26th April, the

streets presented a very unquiet appearance. The public-houses were brilliantly lighted up, and bands of drunken men paraded everywhere, shouting at the tops of their voices, "Long live the King! Down with the aristocrats!" The only people who could not be seen in any direction were the guardians of the public peace.

Where was the terrible Liljensparre? What was that argus-eyed minister of police about? Could he be unaware of the state of things? people asked.

Nobody seemed to know.

During the earlier part of the day, when there was no disturbance, and she did not foresee any difficulty about returning, Tala had gone, as usual, to visit the Countess.

Aurora was, like herself, an ardent admirer of Swedenborg, and talking long together, and hearing the music of the spheres, the two forgot that it was growing late in the particular sphere to which they belonged. They were both surprised, therefore, when the door was thrown open, and the servant announced His Grace the Duke of Sudermania and Baron Essen.

They had come, they explained, for the purpose of escorting Fröken de Geer home. Baron Essen was calling on the Duchess, and had volunteered to accompany the Duke, at her request, as the streets were inconveniently crowded, and the mob did not always know friend from foe.

"Like some other people!" the Countess said.

The Duke also wished to offer the Countess a shelter in his house. Her cousins had left Stockholm, and she was living alone in Fersen's great deserted mansion. Tala glanced at her eagerly; but she declined the offer with a promptness which was not very flattering.

"It is a relief to me, to find that you are still here," Essen said to the younger lady. "The Duke was half afraid that you might have started."

"It is the Duke's fault that she had not," laughed Aurora. "What business had he to give the child Swedenborg to read? She thought time was

annihilated—and, for the matter of that, so did I, five
minutes ago. You will find your hood and cloak in
my room, dear."

Tala ran off to fetch them ; and the Countess said,
with some severity, rather as if she were asking a
question than making a statement—

" I have not had the pleasure of seeing you for a
long while, Baron Essen."

"Whose fault is that, madame ? " he asked, with a
dark smile.

The street in which Fersen's house was situated had
been quiet hitherto. Just at that moment there arose
a deafening cry of "Long live our gracious King!
Down—down—down with the nobles ! "

Aurora shivered, and looked nervously in the direction of the window.

"*A various thing is—man, and he changeth ever,*"
she said, putting into her tone the full significance
that she dared not give to her words. " You see, I
have confused the sexes. That is another remote consequence of the perusal of *Conjugal Love* ; but you are
not a reader of Swedenborg, I think ? "

"You do me wrong. I admire a certain work of
his very much."

"Essen is an occult philosopher himself," said the
Duke. " He is a marvellous fellow, Countess. He
can make you see what is going to happen to-morrow,
as if it had happened yesterday."

"Indeed ! " said the Countess, putting her hands
over her exquisite little shell-like ears, as another
piercing shriek rose from below. " I should be quite
content if he could make me see what happened
yesterday."

Her anxiety about Axel was suddenly multiplied
a hundredfold by her anxiety about herself.

" May I ask what it is that you want to know,
Countess ? "

"You may not ask, Baron Essen."

Aurora smiled.

" I think I can tell," said the Baron. He looked at
her attentively for a moment ; her smile faded.

"Why do you stare in that way?" she said, with rising colour.

"I can tell now.   You wish to know why a certain courier—a courier from Paris—has not arrived."

Aurora and the Duke both started.

"You see what he is," the Duke said.

The noise below the window was increasing.

"For Heaven's sake," cried Aurora, "if you know what has delayed him, tell me!"

"A misadventure of Axel Fersen's, probably.   My science does not go so far as to inform me what it is, but"—he glanced at Tala, who had just entered the room—"if that young lady would allow me to ask her a few questions, I might be able to find out.   A strong *rapport* exists between Fröken de Geer and Axel's great friend, Count Ribbing."

Again the Countess was taken by surprise ; so far as she knew, Tala had confided in no one but herself. Nevertheless, it required a strong measure of credulity to be sure that all this intimate knowledge of their affairs was due to second-sight.   Aurora, however, was not quite herself at that moment.   Tala's pale cheeks flushed and her eyes gleamed.

"Anything!   Anything!" she cried.   "Ask me any questions you will."

Essen would have been the last person in the world to avail himself of it, had he in truth suspected that there was any such thing as a spiritual *rapport* between Tala and Adolf Ribbing.   He was consumed by a jealous desire to hold her hand again, to look into her eyes, as he had on the night of the birthday dance at the old Castle, more than six months ago.   At the name of Adolf Ribbing, she was clay in the hands of the potter.   He was conscious of his power over her intellect ; he knew the wonderful influence of suggestion.   By a strong effort of will he abstracted his mind from his present surroundings, and forced it back to Paris, to Madame de Staël's well-remembered boudoir. If he could compel Tala to think she saw it—to think that she saw her lover there, certain consequences, highly favourable to himself, might ensue.

"Give me your hand," he said. "Fix your eyes on mine, and do not move your eyelids."

Tala did as she was told.

Aurora and the Duke sat watching.

The noise outside, the dead stillness within, made a strange contrast.

It seemed to Tala that all her senses were dragged away from her except the sense of sight, which was becoming preternaturally acute—though what she saw was nothing that she looked at.

"What do you see now?" asked the Baron, after some minutes.

"I see a little white room. It is all white, except for the roses and the pink Cupids on the wall."

"Is there anything in it?"

"There are branches of bay and laurel round a little china clock that stands on a bracket. The floor is polished; it shines; it reflects everything, like the gilt mirror. Everything looks double."

"I have heard of that room," the Duke said to Aurora in a hurried, frightened whisper, "Madame de Staël's boudoir. It is exactly as she describes."

"Is anyone there?"

"A tall, quick, dark lady, with bright eyes."

"Poor child!" whispered Aurora. "It is Madame l'Ambassadrice."

"Is young Count Axel Fersen there?"

Tala shook her head.

"Is Adolf Ribbing there?"

There was no answer, but the expression of the girl's face changed so that Aurora became alarmed.

"Stay!" she said hastily. "We have no right to ask her these questions. It is cruel. Besides, there is someone knocking at the door. Come in, whoever you are! Wake up, my child, wake up!"

The door opened; one of the servants came in with a note.

Essen—much annoyed, for his experiment seemed to be succeeding as well as he could desire—turned his head round for an instant, and Tala awoke with a cry.

"A courier from Paris has arrived, my lady," said the servant. "He desires to speak with you at once."

Aurora glanced at the Duke.

"Have I your Royal Highness's permission?"

"This is a matter that concerns us all," he said. "I hope that you will not object to my presence?"

Aurora—just and only just perceptibly—shrugged her shoulders.

"Let him come up!" she said, as she tore open the note.

Tala, in whose face terror and bewilderment had given way to stupefied exhaustion, crossed over to her side.

Aurora read the note through, and then, very neatly and deliberately, tore it up into long strips, as though for some reason or other this action were one that she enjoyed.

"The Queen of France!" she muttered, between her teeth.

"I beg your pardon," said Duke Charles, leaning forward. "I did not catch your words."

"My cousin will not return to Stockholm."

"Heaven be praised for that!" murmured the Duke to Essen, with a sigh of relief.

Essen smiled; if the Countess had irritated him before, he was duly avenged now.

"Have you any message for me, Antoine?" she asked, turning to the courier, who had just made his appearance. He was booted and spurred, and looked as if he had ridden hard.

"No, madame," he said in French. "My master told me to inquire of you where I could find the daughter of Carl de Geer. I have a message for her."

"I am she," said Tala, clasping her hands. "Speak!"

"Speak!" said the Countess. "We are among friends."

"The message was from Count Ribbing, mademoiselle. He bade me say to you only these words, *I cannot come*."

Tala looked furtively at Baron Essen.

"You were right," she said, putting her hand across her eyes. "Adolf is not coming. He never will come now. Take me home—home to the Reindeer's Crag, to the little house there—home—home!"

"She is ill," said Aurora, in sudden alarm. "All this has been too much for her. Come with me, dear child—come away and lie down. You are tired out— you want rest."

"You will come too?" said Tala, gazing up at the Baron with dull eyes. In those few minutes she seemed to have shrunk into a tiny creature.

He made a quick sign of assent, and she let Aurora lead her away.

All that night she lay very ill, wandering incessantly. Aurora, as she sat beside her bed, listening now to her wild talk, now to the shouts of the mob outside, made not a few reflections on the inconstant faith of man.

CHAPTER XXXV

TRIUMPH

NEXT morning, long before the King appeared, alone and on foot, in the great square outside the Riddarhus, it was thronged by a dense multitude, shouting and cheering in thick, drunken voices. He passed straight in, through the open door, and a moment later the whole building was filled with a crowd of these ragged adherents. They had made their way into the hall of assembly in considerable numbers, before anyone could stay them. The thousands who followed were only kept out by five or six resolute gentlemen, who undertook to guard the door with their swords.

Standing by the marshal's table, the King reminded those present that the Riksdag had already exceeded its lawful limits. The defence of the State called for his presence elsewhere.

As the first nobleman of the realm, he then installed himself in the landmarshal's seat, under the shield of Gustav Vasa, and beckoned Liljehorn to sit beside him.

The country, he continued, could not protect itself against Russia, unless the subsidies were granted until the next meeting of the Riksdag ; he would not answer for the consequences if these should be refused.

Here Count Wachtmeister interposed, saying that those who had the right to grant subsidies had the right to fix the period for which they were granted.

Nothing could have been more quiet, composed, and dignified than the tone of the King's answer.

He had not come thither, he said, to dispute the
rights of the nobility, but to ask them, on this single
occasion, to acquiesce in the decision of the three
Lower Estates, for the welfare of the whole realm.
Then, tightening his fingers on the arm of the chair,
he flung down his challenge—

"Do the nobles and gentlemen here present consent
to grant the subsidies until the next meeting of the
Riksdag?"

In the uproar that followed, it was impossible to
distinguish a single word.

"The Ays have it," the King said, still as composed
as ever.

Shrieks of *No* rent and pierced the air on every side;
they might have waked the dead. The King, however, did not hear them. Imperturbable as ever, he
thanked the whole assembly in the most cordial terms,
desired the secretary of the House to enter the result
on the books, and sent a deputation to the three
Lower Estates, to inform them that he had triumphed.

This was the final scene of the famous Riksdag
of 1789.

The prisoners were released the evening afterwards.

The Royalists heard the blast of trumpets, which
announced the closing of the Diet, with a relief which
they did not attempt to conceal. The rebels muttered,
"Wait till next time."

Fersen's proud heart was broken; he never appeared
in public again.

Count Horn looked in vain for the son who should
have been the first to welcome him on his return.

Carl de Geer hurried to his daughter's bedside, but
she did not know him.

What were such little things as these, when the
storm of revolution had been averted—the welfare of a
great country secured?

The King had won.

CHAPTER XXXVI

" FINE FEATHERS MAKE FINE BIRDS "

ABROAD, the events of the year 1789 were of such a nature that the public life of Paris absorbed, for a short space, the private life of all the men and women who dwelt there. It was, for the time, impossible to divide interests, for everyone had become a politician. The tragic struggle was quickening into fury. The chief actors were being thrust, insensibly, closer and closer, by the tremendous force of the opposing masses arrayed against each other. When they were once at close quarters, who could say what would ensue? Opinion had already turned to action; action was turning rapidly to combat.

Adolf threw himself into the fight, heart and soul.

News had reached him of the conclusion of the Diet and the release of the prisoners; not a word more concerning Tala. Axel's servant, cross-questioned on his return, said that he had delivered his message in person; that was all. Aurora, angry at her cousin's indifference, as she considered it, ceased to correspond with him.

For a long while afterwards, Adolf was troubled with frequent doubts as to the rectitude of his own course. He had ceased to approve of the King's methods; could it be honourable to stay where he was, as though nothing had happened, as though he were still a thoroughgoing Royalist? He wrote a long letter to his sovereign, begging to be allowed to return. Then, in a fit of hesitation, consequent on the sudden relief of having written it, he took counsel with Fersen, who gave him to understand that it would be the

blackest ingratitude, both towards the King and towards
the lady whom he hoped to marry, to think of sending
such a missive, not to mention that it would look as if
he wished to desert France in her hour of need. Fersen,
when he spoke, had three strong allies in Adolf's own
breast—his love, his ambition, his sensitive dread of
ridicule. All these pleaded so strongly, that the letter
was torn up at last. It became more and more the
habit of his life to be much with Madame de Staël, in
whose tumultuous presence he forgot his troubles,
intoxicating himself with her society, as another man
might have drunk wine. Madame de Staël was never
at rest for one moment. Wherever there was noise,
bustle, activity, the clash and clamour of contending
foes, there was she — and there was Adolf Ribbing,
in her train.

He was at her side, on the 4th May, by a window
gaily hung with flags and tapestries of yellow and red,
whence they could watch the procession of deputies
gathering for the solemn service before the assembly of
the States General at Versailles.

The day before had been rainy and dull. The morning
of the 4th broke radiant ; it was a perfect moment in
spring.

"See ! Now the sun shines on the Golden Age that
is coming ! " cried Zulmé, as the household of the King
trooped past to the roll of drums and the inspiriting blast
of trumpets—equerries, pages mounted on horses with
nodding plumes, falconers — their keen-eyed birds
hooded upon their wrists.

"The Golden Age indeed ! " murmured Adolf, as he
caught a glimpse of the gorgeous cloaks of the *noblesse* ;
even then he was somewhat inclined to be cynical, when
he saw the effect produced on his neighbour by clothes.
A brilliant medley of every colour of the rainbow
streamed past. The *Tiers État*, in two parallel lines,
led the procession, between the hedges of French and
Swiss guards.

Then came the white, waving feathers *à la Henri
Quatre* of the representatives of all the first families in
France.

After them, the violet *soutanes* of the clergy.

Next, the scarlet capes of the cardinals.

At this point in the procession, a loud shout from some of the crowd stationed in advance went up for the passing of the deputies from Dauphiné, whose action had been the chief cause of the assembly of the States. Madame de Staël could not restrain herself; she burst into loud cheers, waving her handkerchief. Adolf was about to uplift his voice also, when he was checked by Madame de Montmorin, the wife of the minister for foreign affairs, who was sitting on the other side of Madame de Staël. She now turned gently to the younger woman, with a look of grave and tender sadness that was almost reproach.

"You have no reason to rejoice. All this will bring great calamities both to France and to us," she said.

It struck a chill through Adolf, even at that hot moment. When—long afterwards, as men reckon in revolutions, but only a year or two later, as we count time—he heard that Madame de Montmorin had been sent to the guillotine, whither Madame de Staël was in imminent danger of following her, he thought of those words.

"Here comes Monseigneur the Archbishop!" cried the ambassador's wife. "You may talk about women's dresses! When men set their hearts on the pomp of this world, they are far more expensively attired. I should like to know how much the *aune* all that rose-coloured silk cost. Ah, but it makes a most exquisite effect against the young green of the trees!"

The archbishop was carrying the Host under a canopy, the ropes of which were held by the King's brothers, Monsieur and the Comte d'Artois, the Duc de Berry, and the Duc d'Angoulême.

Adolf, in his character of Northern Protestant, remarked that very few people knelt down or crossed themselves; one or two laughed audibly.

The King followed, in cloth of gold, embroidered with precious stones, bearing a huge wax taper. A loud shout greeted him. It ceased at once on the appearance of the Queen. When all the rest grew

18

dim, Adolf recollected that she wore crown imperials in her hair.

The sight was almost as brilliant on the succeeding day, when Madame de Staël had reserved a seat for her friend in the front row of boxes in the Salle des Menus Plaisirs. He was one of some two thousand onlookers—ambassadors, their wives and families, and others—who had come together to witness the opening of the session.

The draperies hung from the slender Ionic columns gave to the chamber something of the look of an enormous tent; the skylight was veiled in white silk; the floor was softly carpeted, so that the deputies hurried to and fro with scarce a sound. On a platform in the midst stood the throne, under a splendid canopy, an arm-chair for the Queen beside it, chairs for the princesses on the right, chairs for the princes to the left.

"That person standing at the foot of the throne is the Keeper of the Seals, and there is the Lord High Controller of the Household beside him," said Madame de Staël, pointing out various men whose names were already famous. Farther down was a long table, covered with purple cloth embroidered in golden *fleurs-de-lys*. Every seat had been filled for an hour or more.

"There are the secretaries of State. They have been sharpening their pens long enough; they must want something to sharpen their wits on."

To the left sat the councillors, the governors of provinces, the military commanders, resplendent in dazzling uniforms, the *maîtres de requête*. Among the ministers, one alone appeared without a sword; he was dressed in the snuff-coloured coat of a private citizen.

"My father!" cried Madame de Staël, in an agitated whisper, as the whole Chamber rose to applaud him with frantic shouts. Adolf, of course, knew well enough who it was, but she spoke because she could not restrain herself.

On the right were the deputies of the clergy, the scarlet cardinals again, the purple bishops.

Opposite them sat the nobles, in black this day, with gold-embroidered tunics, lace cravats, and white

stockings ; their powdered hair, their splendid mantles
and creamy feathers, contrasted with the flowing locks,
the short black cloaks, and plain three-cornered hats
worn by the members of the *Tiers*, who face the throne.
Cheers broke out again and again, as the Duc d'Orleans,
the deputy for Crépy in Valois, made his appearance
among these last, and, with ostentatious politeness,
yielded the front place to one of his poor colleagues, a
parish priest.

"I do not trust that man," muttered Madame de
Staël, between her teeth.. "Did you hear how they
applauded him yesterday because he alone of the
princes walked, not with the Royal Family, but with
the members of his *bailliage?* ''Tis an ill bird that
fouls its own nest,' say I. The Queen almost fainted
when she heard the shouts, poor woman ! They were
actually forced to hold her up for fear the procession
should be stopped."

"He dare to insult the Queen !" cried Adolf, flushing
crimson. "If I had only known I would have shot the
villain. I thought they were silent because "—

He stopped.

"Because what ?"

"Silence is the only homage we can pay the divine,"
he said in a low, troubled voice.

The ambassadress looked at him curiously.

"The Queen belongs to Monsieur de Fersen," she
said, with a certain dryness. "You are an Early
Christian in friendship, Monsieur de Ribbing. You
and your friends have all things in common, it would
appear. I have heard you say that you esteem only
one man more than the Count, and that is the King of
Sweden. Does everything that belongs to you belong
to His Majesty ? "

"What do you mean, madame ? "

"Oh, nothing ! I heard last night that he had given
away a piece of property which—so I gathered from
your conversation—belonged to you. But my in-
formant may have been wrong. In any case, he
begged me not to repeat what he said. I regret that I
mentioned it. Let us change the subject. Hark, hark !

how they are hissing and groaning! Do you see that great, fat, ugly barrel of a man over there, with eyebrows like Satan's on the stage? That is Monsieur le Vicomte de Mirabeau. Yonder, shaking his black hair like a wild boar, sits his brother, the deputy for Provence. Bah, how I hate him! But he will make you listen to him for all that. It is as if you heard Demosthenes. That thing with its throat all muffled up, standing beside him, is the deputy for Auvergne, Monsieur de Lafayette, who fought so well for America. Why a true patriot should have a sloping forehead that makes him look like a third-rate murderer is more than I can tell you or anyone else. I have sometimes wondered, though, whether it is any better to kill men in God's cause than in your own — seeing He made them. How tight Lafayette's pigtail is! Look well at the Bishop of Autun—pointed nose—slightly turned up. That is de Talleyrand-Perigord ; they say that he will make a name for himself. There is Sieyes talking to Bailly. Bailly's profile would do for a definition of a straight line, if he had not modelled his nose on Mont Blanc."

"You made me very anxious by something that you said just now, madame," said Adolf, as soon as he could get in a word edgeways. "I implore you to tell me what you meant."

It annoyed her to see that he had changed colour.

"I will tell you nothing," she said, with some asperity. "Everyone knows that I say more than my prayers. Do not regard it! If you want to talk about your miserable coal-hole of a country of Sweden, ask my husband. I give you fair warning that I will not be worried. I take no interest whatever in it. Ah, how tired of waiting I am ! When will the King come ? And what is to be the upshot of all this ? It cannot really affect us—they have no power to act. What will be the end of an Assembly which has nothing to do but talk?

"'De tous ces Etats, l'effet le plus commun
Est de voir tous nos maux sans en soulager un.'"

Adolf was compelled to hide his uneasiness as best

he might. A piece of property belonging to him? She had said it in the tone she always used when speaking of women whom she did not like, and he was completely mystified. Whether she meant to warn him or not, who could say? At anyrate, there was no getting anything further out of the ambassadress in her present mood, and he resigned himself to wait.

The King arrived at last, surrounded by all his household, and by the high officials of the Crown.

"He does not walk as if France belonged to him," said Adolf, who had risen and cheered with the rest, but rather coldly. "Our King steps out in a different fashion."

"His hat is very royal. See the big diamond in the centre!" cried Madame de Staël. "For my part, I think he looks like the toad with the jewel in its head.'

"Hush, hush, madame! That is *lèse-majesté*—they will shut you up in the Bastille."

"Here comes the real King!" she said, as the heralds cleared a passage for the Queen. "How well she does, to wear that heron's plume in her diamond fillet—only it should have been an eagle's. But the white petticoat, spangled with silver—the violet mantle over all! *Ma foi*, it is perfect!"

"How sad she looks!"

"She is only a little tired. After all, she has not had nearly so long to wait as we have," said Madame de Staël sharply.

When—more than a little tired after a speech from the King, a speech from Barentin, the Keeper of the Seals, a speech, three hours long, from the snuff-coloured Monsieur Necker—the Queen was preparing to follow her husband out of the hall, and there was no demonstration as she did so, Adolf stood up conspicuous in his place and raised a cheer. He was surprised by the faintness of his own voice. What was the effect of this great lady upon him, that he never could see her but a mist rose before his eyes? She heard, however, and, turning back with a look of grateful recognition, she curtsied low ; he could see the quick rise and fall of the silver spangles upon her breast.

In a moment, the whole Chamber was ringing with the shouts of applause of the excited deputies.

Adolf, who had felt ready to knock them down the moment before because they did not cheer, now felt ready to knock them down because they did. Perhaps his features showed as much, for Madame de Staël smiled with a look of superiority, and joined in a half ironical way that vexed him. He broke away from her as soon as he could, and returned to his lodging.

An hour or two after, as he was sitting in a low balcony that jutted out over the road, his mind full of the enigmatical words of the ambassadress, a young man of gentlemanly appearance saluted him from below. He returned the salute, dimly conscious that he had seen this person somewhere or other before, though memory did not bear it out, when he examined himself more closely. Leaning over the rail to try and identify the features, hidden as they were in the shadow of a great black, plumed hat, he heard these words, uttered in a low, clear voice, at the sound of which there arose before him that old vision of the room with twisted antlers and firelight playing on a branch of coral—

"Whatever rumours may reach you from Sweden, do not be uneasy. The Water Lily is safe. Stay where you are."

To climb over the rail—to spring to the ground, was the work of an instant; but the figure had disappeared.

CHAPTER XXXVII

EN ATTENDANT

A MONTH after the meeting of the States General, Adolf heard, with a pang of grief and surprise, that the Dauphin had breathed his last at Meudon.

"The first of the lights extinguished!" Fersen said. His friend had no heart to chide him for superstition; he thought of the wailing babe upon the knees of the lady in the crimson gown, and sighed.

The elder child was forgotten quickly enough. In the press of public events, this, which at an earlier period would have plunged all France into mourning, passed almost unnoticed. The deputies had talked to some purpose, it seemed, in spite of Madame de Staël's prophecy. By the end of the year no one, except perhaps the mother of the little thing, recollected his last hours as the saddest part of it.

The Oath of the Tennis Court was taken but a fortnight after her bereavement.

The Bastille fell but a month from that day.

Axel Fersen was at Versailles on the dangerous 6th October. Adolf saw the Queen glance at him when the mob shouted to her to dismiss her children — to return alone to the balcony. He never admired his friend more than when he read in Fersen's eyes the mute encouragement to do so.

Both young men went back to Paris with the suite of the Royal Family; but the captivity of the King and Queen was only just beginning when duty forced Axel to join his regiment, which was still in garrison at

Valenciennes and showed a disposition to give trouble.
His presence quelled the revolt immediately; the ring-
leaders were arrested and punished; and he remained
there, keeping the peace, until near the end of January
1790, when he had orders from Gustav to resume his
post of observation in Paris.

Adolf was glad indeed.   Madame de Staël continued
to fill his thoughts, but he had begun to know the need
of masculine friendship.   He sought her society, not so
much for its own sake, as to discover what he himself
was likely to do and say in her presence.   He was still,
to some extent, ignorant of his own character; he
was quite ready to give her what she invariably took—
the credit of knowing him best.   Yet, half unconsciously, he wanted someone who would sometimes be
of the same mind two days together.

Madame de Staël, on her side, had had her instructions from the King, and for a time she obeyed them
to the letter.   Her vanity led her to think that she
was making progress, until—in that jealous moment at
Versailles—she hinted at a report which had reached
her ears, to the effect that the King of Sweden was
anxious to bring about an engagement between Baron
Essen and the daughter of Carl de Geer.   By his silence
rather than from anything that he said when her name
was mentioned, she had been led to suspect that Adolf
loved his cousin.   He was bound by his promise not to
tell her, but he betrayed himself still further on that
occasion, as on many another, when she repented of
her imprudence.

She was in bad spirits just then.   Her adored father
was ill, and the doctors gave it as their opinion that
he could not live long.   All these circumstances led to
a certain strain in their intercourse, and Adolf became
restless, and was led to brood over the long duration of
his exile.

More than a year had passed, and why he was still
in Paris he did not know.   His country was at war
with Russia again.   On the first outbreak of hostilities,
he had written to the King, begging to be allowed to
rejoin his regiment.   All that he got in return was an

official document to the effect that his master required him to stay where he was.

Those who had any leisure to spare from the consideration of French politics criticised the King of Sweden's conduct severely. It was, they said, the act of a mere adventurer, to begin a war which he could not possibly have funds enough to sustain. He was inviting his own destruction. When they heard of his brilliant victory at Liikala, they changed their tune, however; and now the partisans of Russia began to look grave.

Adolf's longing for active service revived in all its force.

During the winter he felt it less. The King, who had come back through the enemy's lines, after his usual romantic fashion, disguised as a common sailor, remained quietly at Stockholm, and the guns were silent on either side. When the fighting began again in spring, Adolf opened his heart to Fersen upon the subject.

"When I first came to Paris, Axel, I believed that I was to be attached to the Swedish embassy. Here I am, in receipt of my pay, but I am doing nothing whatever to earn it. I cannot endure the want of regular employment. You know yourself how often I am at the house in the rue de Bac. De Staël has plenty of subordinates as it is, I suppose. He never confides anything whatever to me."

Fersen smiled.

"He has nothing to confide."

"Do you mean that he is not in the King's confidence?"

"How could he be? His wife betrays everything to her father. Look at me! Why do I remain in Paris, do you suppose? Why is Evert Taube here? You may take it on my authority, my dear Adolf, that the Swedish ambassadors do not all live at the Swedish embassy. No, no, be content! In a little while you will find plenty to do. As for fighting, we are bound to fight here, first or last, and you may as well be on the spot. The authority of the King is a mere word to the National Assembly; the National Assembly trembles before Paris; Paris trembles before forty or fifty bandits up at Montmartre. If Lafayette were anything but a popular hero, we might make them hear reason soon enough; but there are other signs. Money has disappeared. Everyone who has any is hiding it. For the last seven months all bonds have been cancelled; and we are losing six per cent. on our paper. That kind of thing cannot go on long. Wait, my dear fellow, wait!"

It was a long speech for Count Fersen.

So Adolf waited; and another year glided by.

CHAPTER XXXVIII

THE KING'S MERCY

ON the evening of the 7th of September 1790,—more than sixteen months after the closing of the Diet,—the cathedral church of the Riddarhus at Stockholm opened its doors at a season when those of all the other churches were shut. Rich curtains, splendid hangings of tapestry fell over them, after a fashion which was very unusual at that time. The ancient walls had blossomed into wreaths, hearts, and floral devices of wedded initial letters.

Garlands of white flowers hanging from pillar to pillar, white flags waving, tall white lilies arranged in snowy fence about the altar, foretold the approaching solemnity of a marriage. In spite of the numerous candelabra, everywhere pendent from the roof, the greater part of the vast building lay still in shadow, for as yet only a little lamp, here and there, had been lighted, seeing that it was full an hour before the time appointed for the service, and they must be eager guests indeed that would arrive so early.

One, however,—an old man,—was already in his place; and another,—a very young man,—wearing Court dress, came in soon afterwards, and stood close beside him, in the deep shadow of an arch. His face was pale and agitated; he would not sit down, although the other motioned him to do so. His eyes were fixed on the ground, and the least noise made him start.

"I am glad to see that you keep time," said the older man, with an approving nod.

Clas Horn—for he it was—looked up nervously.

"I have no wish to be here, Baron Pechlin," he said. "I only came because you would have it so. I shall probably leave before she appears."

"You will probably do whatever is most foolish. I am not concerned to deny it. There is one thing, however, which I wish you to understand. If you leave, you leave us for good and all. The way in which you behave, hiding from your most intimate friends, making a mystery of your simplest actions, is enough to bring suspicion on everyone. You will get the whole society into trouble, if you persist in this nonsense. In fact, you are not worth it. No, no, my dear boy ; you must do at Rome as the Romans do, or we dissolve partnership."

"What do you ask of me ? " said Clas passionately. "I cannot live two lives. I never in my life could wear a mask."

"You will have to now. Masking is all the rage. Your King sets you the example."

"Do you mean to say that I am to return to my father's house as if nothing had happened—to speak of the King as if I loved him—to "—

"Hush, not so loud ! The sacristan will hear—that little man with the red beard, over there ! But you exaggerate very much. Your father does not speak of the King as if he loved him, I imagine. Besides, the Count will not be here to-night. I ascertained that before I took the liberty of inviting you. I only ask you to go back to the place in which you can be most useful—to your normal position in society."

"How can I ? I have been away too long. Even my friends have given up all hope of my re-appearance."

"You are a poet," the old Baron said suavely. "The eccentricities of everyday men like myself are the commonplaces of a poet. You are driven mad so easily, *vous autres*. And no one thinks it strange that a poet should go out of his mind ; on the contrary, it is almost *de rigueur* that he should. The excitement of the Diet was too much for you. Well, that is not so far from the truth ! You have been out of your

mind for the last year and a half. You have been
wandering about sticking flowers in your hair, like
Dido in *Æneas at Carthage*. Now you are well again,
and you seize the joyful occasion of the marriage of
one of your old companions, in order to make known
the fact. Are you prepared to obey me?"

"I have no other choice," the young man said, half
stifling a sigh. "Out of my mind? Yes, I was out
of my mind before. I am sane now. Does Adolf
Ribbing know of this marriage?"

"He is completely ignorant."

"Why did you not tell him? He could have stopped
·.ıer. It is a wicked thing."

"Very wicked," said Pechlin complacently. "As
wicked as we could wish. Count Ribbing will never
forgive the King, and the King's favourite."

"That would have been the same, had you fore-
warned him."

"Not at all. Adonis would have found some way
of clearing himself from all complicity—let him alone
for that! Indeed, he has a legitimate excuse; he has
been misinformed by a certain wise lady in Paris, who
thinks that she has effected a conquest; he sincerely
believes that Adolf Ribbing has no longer any affection
for his cousin."

"And is it so?"

Pechlin shrugged his shoulders.

"I cannot tell. The young man is an enigma. He
has formed no other connection in Paris—that much
is certain. But I have not seen him since he left
Gothenburg, and it is hard to judge of such matters
from hearsay."

Clas Horn looked at him with an expression of
gathering mistrust.

"Surely you have seen him since then," said he.
"He came to Stockholm at the time of the arrests."

"You are mistaken," said Pechlin, genuine surprise
in his voice. "How could he come? The King had
not recalled him."

"No; but his cousin had."

"Are you sure of the truth of that?"

"Quite sure. I was with her when she made up her mind."

"It would explain many things," said Pechlin, nodding his head slowly, as was his way when he thought. "She sends for him—he does not come—she thinks he has ceased to love her—then she falls ill—her father dies—she is left alone—*faute de mieux*, she accepts Baron Essen. I own that I was surprised before at her docility—though I was very much pleased."

"But are you certain that he did not come?"

"Count Ribbing does not go from one end of Paris to the other without my knowledge. He never left that city for an hour."

"Then it is true, and he has ceased to love?"

"I do not know. It is nothing to me. But I am quite ready to explain the political importance of this wedding, if you desire it. Had Ribbing arrived beforehand, the King and Essen might have cajoled him easily enough between them. I do not say that they would have done so, for I cannot gauge the depth of his passion. I say they might. There is one thing, however, on which we may all reckon with certainty; that is his pride. It is ours to make the King break with him at any cost. If the King wounds him in that sensitive point, he will never forgive. When he returns and finds the marriage has been accomplished without so much as a word to him, whether he loves his cousin or not, he will be very angry. If he had been consulted, he might, or he might not have been furious. As it is, Heaven defend His Majesty! I know my gentleman well enough to know that. We could not fling the net more skilfully."

"Do you mean to send for him to-morrow?"

Pechlin's little thin old chuckle grated upon Horn's ears.

"To-morrow! Oh dear, no! He would suspect a plot at once. We wait until the King recalls him—as the King must some day or other—or until he breaks bounds of his own accord. That may not be for a year or two."

" Has he no idea—has no rumour reached him ? "

" If it has, I have taken care to dispel it. He believes that his cousin is faithful."

" Will you tell me one thing, Baron ? " said Clas. " Why are you so determined to have him on our side ? I have heard the silly story that is current ; but you are too well acquainted with me to think that I think you believe that."

" You are right, my son. To me it is nothing, but it is much to another man, and he is much to me. I cannot tell you anything further. See, they are beginning to light up. Have you any further questions to ask ? "

" Yes—one or two. I have been so long away, that I know nothing. What is the latest news of Colonel Hästesko—of the patriots of Anjala ? "

" Bad enough, except as regards Klingspor. He is a good example for you, by the way. He did very well for himself by going mad when he heard of the confirmation of his arrest. The King, who is very kind to mad people (he has a fellow-feeling for them, I suppose), ordered a respite, until he should recover his senses. You will not be surprised to hear that he is still mad, poor fellow ! Colonel Montgomeri and Count Leionstedt are yet at Frederikshof; nobody knows what will become of them. General Hatsfer has been relegated to his property in Finland."

" And Hästesko ? What of Hästesko himself ? "

" Sentenced to death," said the Baron.

Clas Horn sat down, unable to stand longer, and put his hand over his eyes.

" When ? "

" To-morrow."

" Can nothing be done to save him ? "

" It appears that nothing whatever can be done."

" When I was at Court," said Clas Horn, in a hurried, half apologetic tone, as though he were pleading the cause of someone of whose innocence he was only half convinced, " it was all that the judges could do to induce the King to sign the death-warrant of the meanest of criminals. I have known him refuse

over and over again, even when Nordin—even when
the Bishop of Wexiö assured him that it was absolutely
necessary for the sake of example; and if he had to
yield, he would be silent for hours afterwards, and
shut himself up alone in his room and take no food."

"So I have heard.   It was his cue then to be
sensitive, but matters are very different now.   Nordin
and the Bishop of Wexiö were with him from three
o'clock to five yesterday, endeavouring to persuade him
to show mercy; quite in vain!   He ate his dinner with
a remarkably good appetite afterwards; I heard that
from someone who was present.   It shows us what to
expect, if any one of us should be taken prisoner.
He may re-introduce torture next."

"No, no," cried Horn, with a shudder.   "It cannot
be.   It is impossible.   Hästesko has a wife, who only
lives for him.   I used to know her well."

"They have allowed her to see him to-night.   You
know what that means.   They say that she is heartbroken.   She had to drag herself out of her bed to go;
she fainted away when she reached the gate."

"Is there no chance of any last appeal?"

"The one chance lies with you," said Pechlin,
blinking.

"With me?"

"You are a great friend of the pretty bride's, are you
not?   They say that the King is much attached to her.
He had no great liking for her father; but perhaps,
when Carl de Geer died so suddenly, he felt bound to
show the poor child some kindness.   He is going to the
Duke of Sudermania's house to-night, to be present
at the banquet after the ceremony.   Tell her to ask
him then and there to forgive Hästesko for her sake."

"I will," said Clas eagerly.   "If there were any
hope of saving him, I would go to the Duke's, should
it cost me my life.   I cannot think that she could ask
for anything in vain—from anyone.   Besides, I do not
believe that the King means it — he will respite
Hästesko at the last moment."

"Hush! the people are beginning to arrive.   We
had best not be seen together, for the Court party

suspects me. Wait a moment, and then take some other place."

"How beautiful it looks in the half darkness! I never was here at night before. I never saw that gleam on the crests of the Knights of the Seraphim up above."

"They are all buried here," said Pechlin. "It is a fitting grave for the Head of the Order."

"When the time comes," said Clas Horn dreamily.

"When the time comes," said Pechlin, with an indescribable snap of his lips.

"What do you mean?" said Clas Horn, his voice taking a sudden edge. "Our object is, to make the King prisoner and to keep him prisoner until he promises to return to the Constitution of 1772—is it not? There is no thought of violence against his person? If there is, I will be no party to it," and he laid his hand on his sword.

"Why, what a child you are!" cried Pechlin. "The King must die some day, I suppose ; and when he dies, he will be buried here. It seems to me that even a courtier might make that remark, and not be hauled over the coals for high treason."

"I beg your pardon," said Clas, moving away. The trumpets which announced the King were sounding.

Many a look of wonder was cast at the young man, as with dogged defiance he took up his position close to the altar, in full view of the whole congregation. The shadow of his tall form, thrown upon the column against which he stood—for he remained standing throughout the ceremony—made him look even taller and paler than he was.

Keenly conscious of the attraction he presented, suffering from the artillery of glances directed at him, and yet determined to brave it out, he felt little except his own personal discomfort.

He left the church as soon as he could, but encountered Pechlin again outside the door.

"Whither away so fast, young friend? You are surely coming to the house. The Duke of Sudermania does not entertain every day."

19

"I cannot. I cannot endure those eyes all fixed upon me. I feel as if I were made of glass."

"And who is to intercede for Hästesko?"

"Intercede for him yourself!"

"I should be charmed to do so, but, unluckily, the Baroness Essen has a prejudice against me. I am afraid of her."

"You afraid?" Horn said incredulously; yet he retained an odd impression that Baron Pechlin had, for once, spoken the truth.

"Make what you can of it," said the old man, snapping his fingers. "Doves and serpents, you know, and all the rest. You are a poet. You understand that you are robbing Hästesko of his last chance?"

"You drive me mad," said Clas.

But he went.

The hall was cleared for dancing in the Duke of Sudermania's house.

At one end of it, the floor around her strewn with water-lilies, sat Tala, in a great golden chair of state, sometimes leaning forward a little, as though the weight of the bridal veil, fastened in her auburn locks by one of the same flowers, were too much for her slender strength to bear. Behind her, resting his arm on the back of her throne, stood Essen. It was hard to decide whether he were the more handsome—she the more beautiful; so people said.

The dance had not yet begun. Friends were coming and going around the bride and bridegroom, offering their congratulations. Shouts of laughter came from the other end of the hall, where the King was the centre of an ever-widening group of courtiers. Near him stood the little Duchess, to receive her guests; but she was not so merry as usual, and sometimes stole an anxious look towards the upper end of the hall. Presently she called away Baron Essen, and Clas Horn, taking advantage of a quiet moment, walked up to the golden chair, with an appearance of calm which was very far from being sincere.

"Do you still remember an old friend?" he said.

Tala, who had scarcely looked up the whole time, raised her eyes; there was no astonishment in them—only pleasure. The gratitude he felt would have been out of all proportion but that, to sensitive natures, it is harder to be an object of surprise than an object of anything else except pity.

"I am very glad to see you," she said simply. "Where have you been all this long while?"

"In many horrible places—I could not tell you. Where have you been yourself?"

"In the Valley of the Shadow of Death."

"Indeed! I am glad to see that it has such a cheerful exit."

She shrank away as if he had struck her.

"I am going deeper in," she said, with a frightened glance round, lest her husband should be within earshot.

"You do it of your own free will?"

"They say I do. I feel as if something had forced me."

"What villain"—

"Hush! It is not a man; I do not know what it is. Besides, how can it matter? There is no such thing as life for me now—only one way or another way of dying. I want to die at home. I cannot die among these dreadful people. There is no air; I cannot breathe, even to breathe myself out. Baron Essen knows; I have told him. But he is very good—he will take me home. He said I could not go except as his wife; and the King said so too. He has been very good since my father died."

"I was grieved to hear of your loss," said Clas Horn, troubled by her quiet voice. "When was it?"

"Oh, a long while ago—more than a year—before the battle of Svenskund; I have never cried since. But I was almost glad, because then I could not be married. Now they all say that I must."

He bent over her, whispering, looking straight down the hall.

"I loved him once. He was not worthy. I have forgotten my King. Forget yours."

"I cannot forget ; it is not in me. Do not speak of
it ! " she cried, with a dash of her old vehemence, which
died away immediately.

"You will be better when you get out of Stockholm,"
said Clas, hardly knowing what to say.

"I shall be well enough to die ; that is all I want. I
want to be quiet among my mountains. Hark ! there
is that laughter again ! " She put her hands up to her
ears, shivering.

"Yes, they are very gay down there," said Clas
bitterly. "And all the while one of our finest soldiers
lies in prison under sentence of death, and a woman is
breaking her heart because this is his last night on
earth."

"I have heard nothing," Tala said. "I do not know
to whom you allude."

"To Colonel Hästesko—to his unfortunate wife."

"I used to know her. I used to see her often, when
first I came here. I loved her dearly."

"They have allowed her to see her husband to-night
for the last time."

"And we are dancing here ! Horrible ! Why did
they never tell me ? "

"You may make it an occasion to save him," said
Clas hurriedly, for he saw that the group at the other
end had broken up, and that the King was coming
that way. "Speak to His Majesty—say that it is your
wedding-night—ask him to pardon ! "

Tala gave him a rapid look of intelligence as he
moved off.

He watched the King go up to her and offer her
his arm. She took it, but still the dance did not begin.
She was speaking quickly, eagerly ; he saw her clasp
her hands together as she looked up into her partner's
face ; then he whispered in her ear something which
seemed to reassure her.

"There is no chance," said Pechlin's voice, close at
his side.

Horn turned round angrily. The presence of this
man was like an intrusive thought ; he could not free
himself from it. That poisoned breath withered the

hope of grace in a moment; but he would not allow that it was so. "She has promised to speak to the King," he said, with all the confidence he could muster.

"She has spoken, and spoken in vain. He never listens in that way when he means to grant a request."

"I think you are mistaken. Look!"

Tala was radiant, her face transfigured.

Pechlin laughed that peculiarly disagreeable laugh of his, which always gave the impression that nothing amused him so much as the least sign of trust in another person.

"We shall see."

The minuet over, Gustav conducted Tala back to her chair of state, remained talking with her for a few moments, and then joined Schröderheim and Silfverhielm, who were standing together in one of the recesses formed by the great window-seats.

"You are a happy man, Count Horn. The bride does you the honour of asking you to fetch her a glass of lemonade; she feels the heat of the room," said Colonel Ehrensvaerd, as he passed, throwing into his voice more significance than the request demanded, and not waiting for any answer.

"Well?" Clas could not help saying, as he offered Tala the glass of lemonade. The atmosphere of the room was indeed very oppressive.

"He has given me no promise, but I am sure all is well. He did not wish to speak of it at first, but I told him that I could think of nothing till I had asked. Then he listened to everything that I had to say. I told him that the Colonel's wife had been a dear friend of mine when we were happy—that I should never ask him for anything again, because I should soon be far away, out of it all. You cannot think how kind he was. 'We have both of us our parts to play for this evening,' he said. 'You are not a girl now but a bride, and I am not the King but a guest. Let us act it out. Be certain that I will weigh carefully every word that you have uttered. When it is time for us to part, I will let you know my decision—not

before.' And then he said the most beautiful thing—
I shall never forget what he said. Did you see his
face? Do not be anxious any more! He could not
look like that, if he did not mean to forgive."

Clas went at once to seek Pechlin.

"Our mediatrix is certain that she has gained her
point," he said triumphantly.

"Has the King promised her the life of Hästesko?"

"No—not yet; but he will, by the end of the
evening."

Again Pechlin laughed, and Clas wished suddenly to
kill him.

He longed to break away from all these faces and
voices—to hide himself in the night. But he could not
leave before he knew the issue, and that he could not
know before the King left; so he stayed on and on,
miserable, and yet afraid to put an end to his misery.

Several officers of his acquaintance were there. The
glorious Peace of Värälä, consequent on the war with
Russia, had been signed only three weeks before,—this
was the first great social gathering since their return,—
and conversation turned largely upon the campaign in
which they had taken part, and the behaviour of the
chief person interested. It was now acknowledged on
all hands that the first battle of Svenskund had been
converted from a victory into a defeat of the Swedish
arms by the King's rash interference. He himself
never sought to deny it. The man who, in the second
battle, had annihilated the Russian fleet, was strong
enough to bear even such a reproach as that. Liikala—
the battle of the Viborg Gauntlet—was in everyone's
mouth too. At Svenskund, Gustav had risked everything on a single throw, and success was the more
dazzling. He had the devil's own luck, they said.

For the moment, however, everything else was
eclipsed by anxiety as to the fate of Hästesko.
Speculation was rife among the guests. Older men
looked grave and uttered words of serious disapproval;
even the younger officers were not, as usual, unanimous
in favour of the King's decision. One or two spoke
doubtfully of the effect on the troops. Most of them

were of opinion that a reprieve would be granted at the last moment.

"He cannot pardon now. He has gone too far," said Reuterholm. "After all, Hästesko is the biggest traitor between the two seas."

The word sounded ugly in Clas Horn's ears.

"There are many who are tarred with the same brush, if it comes to that," said Jacques de La Gardie. "What has he done more than the others, that he should be made an example of? It is only one of His Majesty's surprises. I daresay we shall hear to-morrow that the fellow is respited. The King has done with Russia now. He talks of nothing but France—France—France—*cette pauvre France!* I am sick of the subject. Let France go to hell her own way, say I, and Heaven send back all good Swedes—my cousin, Axel Fersen, among them! Adolf Ribbing too! What merry days we used to spend together in the old time!"

"They are well out of the way to-night," said Adlerbeth, who had greeted Horn with much warmth. "They would not have approved of this wedding. Your cousin, the Countess Aurora, has not seen fit to grace it with her presence. I think Axel Fersen would have had a word to say about to-morrow's execution also."

Clas Horn glanced again in the direction of Tala. She smiled, as though to reassure him; he could not believe that she had failed. Yet whenever he saw Pechlin's face—and Pechlin took care that he should see it often—his doubts revived. If the King had decided in favour of mercy, why did he stay?

This evening, that seemed to Clas interminable, passed like a flash for others. The King seemed to have thrown aside all his preoccupations. He never allowed their gaiety to flag for a single instant. He made no allusions to France; it was remarked, as a strange thing, that he did not once mention the Feast of Federation—a word that had been on his lips perpetually for the last month. He jested—laughed—danced. The former days were come back again, said those who had known the Court before the Diet of 1789.

It grew later and later. Here and there a lady began to look weary and pale. Here and there an officer stood more stiffly than he was wont. People with less to think of might grow tired, but not he ! As the night wore on, he grew only more animated. It was he who proposed the bride's health at supper, in words the tenderness of which remained for ever in the hearts of those who heard them. Then—as if alarmed lest he had roused feelings of a nature too delicate for such an occasion—he threw himself once more into the quick spirit of mirth and revelry, and the fun waxed faster and more furious than ever.

It was two o'clock in the morning before he went to bid farewell to the young Baroness.

She was tired and bewildered. When she rose from her chair, it seemed as if she could scarcely stand ; but Clas observed that her face brightened again as he approached. A crowd of people came between them ; he could not see what happened. When it divided, the King came swiftly down the centre of the hall and passed out, still laughing and talking rapidly to Secretary Schröderheim, on whose arm he was leaning. There was a general rush of all the guests to accompany him to the door, and Clas made his way, fighting against the stream, to the place where Tala stood, motionless as a statue. He was too much agitated to note that Pechlin was following in his wake.

" It is of no use," said Tala slowly, as if she were a mere echo. " He cannot change the sentence. He can forgive every crime except a crime against Sweden."

" We will remember that another time, eh ? " chuckled Pechlin. " There are other people besides Sweden's King who can forgive every crime except a crime against Sweden."

" Good-night ! " said Tala. It was as if a marble image had opened its lips to speak.

" Good-night."

Clas vanished into the darkness.

CHAPTER XXXIX

THE ROAD TO VINCENNES

MEANWHILE, Adolf chafed restlessly at his detention in Paris. If the conditions of life had been the same for Axel Fersen, he could have borne it better; but it was clear that, however heavily the want of serious employment might oppress him, Axel was very far from sharing that affliction.

He owned to no occupation, and he was by birth and breeding too much of a *grand seigneur* ever to have the air of being busy. The ambassadress and others besides took him for a mere courtier. What it was that he did, his companion knew no better than he had known at Gothenburg; but he was out from morning to night and sometimes from night to morning. No reason was ever mentioned—not so much as a hint was dropped as to the motive of this frequent absence. Adolf, who felt his own inaction the more keenly, once asked him in jest whether he were preparing to blow up one of the bridges across the Seine and would want a friend to light the match by and by.

"No," said Fersen, "you are more likely to help me to build a bridge this time"—a saying which made Adolf thoughtful.

One night towards the end of January, when he was returning home late after a supper-party, he met Fersen coming out of the Tuileries. Was it a bridge from the Tuileries that they were going to build? His heart beat high with the hope of it. But the days went on, and nothing was said.

Shortly afterwards, however, Fersen altered his mode of life completely.

Adolf, who always lodged in the *hôtel* in the rue Matignon when he was in town, observed with surprise that he now made a point of being at home for every meal, of accounting for every hour which he passed in different society. He seemed to spend many hours at the house of a certain Baroness de Korff, a Russian lady, of whose name Adolf grew tired. She lived an inconveniently long way off, in the northern quarter, rue de Clichy, and Axel went there in season and out of season, and never had time to go anywhere else.

It was not that Adolf resented his independence; he had, of course, a perfect right to take his own line. Nevertheless, a friend had also the right to feel a little wearied with the monotony of this particular line (when he had taken it for three months), a little angry at the preciseness with which his actions were always explained—perhaps a little jealous of the lady. She was a charming creature, Axel assured him. Axel assured him so often that she was a charming creature, that Adolf became sick of the sound of the words.

"I do not care how charming she is or is not," he said crossly. "For what do you take me Axel? For a spy in your house? If you choose to honour with your attentions the ugliest ballet-girl at the Opera, what business is it of mine? I do not understand you. Is it necessary that you should mention the fact to me, every time that you go to Madame de Korff's house?"

"It *is* necessary," said Axel, an inscrutable smile flitting over his features. "There are many things, my dear Adolf, which I should wish you to know, but which I cannot possibly tell you. You are clever enough; a thousand times cleverer than I. Let me talk to you about Madame de Korff!"

Adolf whistled.

"Sits the wind in that quarter?" he said.

"It is blowing from the north-east to-day, I believe. Are you inclined for a walk?"

"Perfectly, my dear friend."

" We might go to Jean Louis, the coach-builder."

" We might—only there is no reason why we should. I am not building a coach, nor are you."

" Pardon me, I am greatly interested in one which is being built there at present—for my friend, Madame de Korff. She is about to return to her native country."

" I am delighted to hear it," said Adolph, with strong emphasis.

" Ladies are very helpless as regards travelling," continued Fersen. " She has asked me to superintend the affair. She is quite indifferent as to expense, but she requires all the most modern improvements, as she is taking her two daughters with her and does not wish to expose them to more fatigue than is necessary. I thought you might be able to suggest something. That is why I proposed that we should walk in this direction ; but it is not of the slightest consequence, if you have anything else to do."

" Your business is mine, *mon ami !* "

And forthwith Adolf wondered what he was going to do with this coach.

" It is a berline, you see," Axel said, when they had reached the coach-maker's yard.

" There is no need to explain that, my dear Axel. If you had said that it was the most magnificent berline the world has ever beheld, you would have come nearer to an original remark. I never saw so perfect a thing."

He examined the dainty little morocco cushions—the silk cords and tassels of the net for the imperial—the portable pockets on the doors—with exclamations of delight and astonishment.

" It was done from a model."

" It is a model for all the berlines present and to come. It might have been made for a queen."

Fersen appeared to be much gratified by his friend's enthusiasm.

" There is a new kind of skid," he remarked. " It is said to act well going downhill."

" Upon my word, they will want a skid that acts

well. I should not care to drive such a huge Noah's
Ark down one of our Swedish hills, I know that!
What is the use of these great iron-shod forks?"

"To steady it on the slope."

"What an idea!

> ' Voyager si loin
> Donne le tintouin.'

I see that it has a peculiar kind of axle-strap also."

Fersen illustrated, from a technical point of view,
the advantages of the peculiar kind of axle-strap.

"Madame la baronne must be blessed with an
enormous family, if she requires such a patriarchal
conveyance as that. Has she a child for every day of
the year, like Augustus the Strong?"

"No," said Fersen, "only two daughters; but they
are very delicate."

"Two daughters!" said Adolf to himself, "h'm!
Lamps with reflectors, too!"

"They want to start at night, on account of the
heat. There is a leathern canteen at the back of the
imperial. I am proud of that contrivance; it holds
eight bottles of wine."

"Eight!"

"Russia is a long way off, you see," observed Fersen.

"What, in the name of Heaven, is this great chest
under the box-seat?"

"A case of tools, for fear there should be an accident."

"There is quite sure to be an accident."

"Why?" said Fersen anxiously. "Do you detect
any flaw in the arrangements?"

"None. That is why I say it is certain to come to
grief."

"What if we were to take it for a trial? I thought
of sending for the horses. We might test the affair
for an hour or so, on the road to Vincennes?"

"By all means," said Adolf, with enthusiasm.
"How many horses will be wanted? Three or four,
I suppose?"

"Oh no; we must have the full complement of six.
Come with me to the livery stables, on the other side

of the road. You did not know that I had turned
horse-dealer? I want to see whether you will approve
my choice."

"What superb animals!" Adolf said, as his friend
showed him, one after the other, six vigorous coal-
black horses, one and all in perfect condition.

"I am glad you like them."

The horses were harnessed to the berline, and off
they set, Axel driving, Adolf seated beside him.

It was a soft summer's evening.

They went quietly enough through the streets; but,
no sooner were they clear of these, than Axel broke
into a gallop, whipping up the horses as though he
were possessed by a fury.

Adolf began to enjoy himself with that element of
fear which changes pleasure into excitement. He
knew that his friend was an excellent driver, but he
had never seen such a reckless performance as this.
Up hill and down dale, round corners, racing over the
level ground they swept. The huge, lumbering vehicle
whirled after them as if it were a mere feather-weight.
The trees flew by on either side. Adolf had barely
time to perceive the end of one long vista after another,
as a turn in the road disclosed it, and they had reached
the goal—had passed beyond.

"Halt! Halt!" he cried at last. "There is a
carriage in the way. We shall go smashing into it.
Pull up!"

Axel obeyed the warning just, but only just, in time,
and drew up his horses, panting and quivering with
their exertions, by the side of the road.

"Who is it?" he said. "I cannot see."

"The Duke of Orleans, of all people in the world,
driving with Madame de Buffon!"

"Then we had better go on!" said Axel, gently
touching the leaders.

But they were not to escape recognition. Fersen
had used his ticket of entry to the Tuileries pretty
often of late, and the Duke, who was in an open
carriage, knew him at once, and ordered the driver to
stop, while he shouted out—

"Are you mad, my dear Count? You are likely to break your neck at that game."

"I do not want to break my carriage on the road, monseigneur."

"Why have you got such a big one? Is it to carry off the whole of the Opera chorus?"

"Oh, monseigneur," said Fersen, smiling and lifting his hat, "I leave you the chorus!"

The Duke laughed.

"Adieu. Bon voyage!"

"I do not think there will be any accidents," Fersen said, when they had finished their wild career, and were at home again, safe and sound.

"It was hardly your fault that there were none to-day," laughed Adolf. "I thought we had both looked our last on that berline four times at least. The deceased Jehu was the steadiest of hackney coachmen compared with you."

"Ah well," said Fersen, with a sigh of content, "a man can only do his best. I shall have the berline brought into the courtyard of my *hôtel* to-morrow. It wants another bolster or two. Do you think that your friend, Madame de Staël, would care to come and inspect it?"

"She would be charmed," said Adolf gravely. "No doubt she will command one, exactly similar—for Monsieur de Staël."

On second thoughts, Adolf did not ask his friend, Madame de Staël, to go and inspect the berline, although it stood, for some days, in the courtyard of the *hôtel*, rue Matignon, where every passer-by could see it; nor did Axel repeat the invitation. Madame de Staël had heard that he was about to leave Paris—that he had a most wonderful carriage—that he drove it in a most wonderful way. Adolf thought that she had heard quite enough (and perhaps this was also his friend's opinion). He felt sorry when the Baroness de Korff claimed her own, and it was removed to the rue de Clichy. It was a riddle on wheels, the attempt to decipher which amused him.

While it was still in the courtyard, Colonel de

Choiseul, an old friend of Count Fersen's, happened to call, and he was taken down at once to examine it.

"I did not know de Choiseul was in Paris," Adolf remarked, with some surprise, later on. "I thought he was on duty."

"So he is," said Axel. "He is only here in a private capacity—to see his children for a day or two. Do not say anything to the ambassadress. He is not going about just now."

"Dear me!" said Adolf. "Since when has it been considered disreputable for a father to visit his children?" A question which Axel did not think required answering.

The only other guest who came to the *hôtel* in these days was Monsieur de Moustier. Through him Axel obtained an introduction to the Russian ambassador, Simoulin, and procured a passport for Madame de Korff. She seemed to be a very helpless person, incapable of doing anything whatever for herself. Fersen was now much occupied about a postchaise, also to be provided by Jean Louis. The Baroness, it appeared, had maid-servants as well as daughters, and the berline—large as it was—was not large enough to contain them.

"It is all very well to talk of the chorus at the Opera," remarked Adolf; "the Baroness must be going to carry away half Paris."

"She is carrying away more than that."

"Is it the whole of France?," said Adolf. "And, by the way, are you her dressmaker as well as her coach-builder?"

"You credit me with too much ability. Why do you ask?"

"Why did you leave the door of your bedroom open two days ago? I saw a short brown cloak and a charming gipsy hat on the bed, as well as the prettiest little frock imaginable. Oh, do not be frightened! It did not compromise your reputation in the least. No lady over the age of six could possibly have worn it."

"Have you anything particular to do this evening?" asked Fersen, somewhat irrelevantly.

"Madame de Staël has a supper-party."

"You do not return till after midnight when that is the case."

"I can go away earlier; if you want me"—

"Oh no! I merely wished to learn the hour, because I may have something to say to you when you come in."

"I will be sure to leave the house by twelve o'clock," said Adolf.

"That will suit me perfectly."

Madame de Staël's house was, however, by no means an easy one to leave. In spite of every effort on Adolf's part, it was twenty minutes later than the hour he had mentioned when he found himself on the steps. Vexed and distressed—for he knew Fersen's love of extreme punctuality—he looked up the street and down, in search of a conveyance.

There was only one, and that one was not a hackney coach, but an ordinary fly. The driver held up his hand interrogatively, scenting his fare.

Adolf looked this way and that, and, seeing no other sign of assistance, held up his hand also, got inside and drove off.

"After all, the horse goes very well," he said to himself. "I could hardly have done better."

He sprang out on the threshold of the gate in the rue Matignon, tossed the jarvie his money, and, putting his latchkey in the lock, was about to enter when he was stopped by the man's grumbling voice.

"*Hé l'ami!*" said he, in hoarse, half-tipsy accents, "do you think I drive a fly for my own amusement—or yours—at this time of night?"

Adolf was going to remonstrate, annoyed by his insolence, when he caught sight of Fersen's German coachman, Balthazar Sapel, standing inside the court-yard.

"Send that jarvie away, Sapel, will you?" said he. "I am in a hurry. But do not give him one sou more. He has quite as much as he is entitled to get."

Sapel advanced to the horse's head. The jarvie leapt from the box with remarkable agility, considering that he was half-seas over, and clapped Adolf on the shoulder, crying again, "*Hé l'ami, me v'là donc !*"

"I'll thank you not to call me your friend, sir," exclaimed Adolf, indignantly trying to free himself.

"Will you?" said the low, musical voice of Fersen. "Come in," he added, pushing open the gate which Adolf, in his amazement, had allowed to close again. "Good-night, Sapel! Go to bed immediately. We join the regiment at Varennes to-morrow night. You will need all your strength for the drive."

"Am I dreaming, or are you mad, Axel?" said Adolf, as they crossed the courtyard.

"Feel my pulse," said Fersen, stretching out his wrist. "I was never more sane in my life."

Madame de Korff must be qualifying for a lunatic asylum then! Has she commissioned you to get her a fly as well as a postchaise and a stage coach, and then to drive them all three about Paris in the middle of the night? I never knew before that you could give the Opéra Bouffe points and beat them at low comedy, among your other accomplishments."

"You overrate them," Fersen said, pausing at the foot of the staircase to light a candle.

Adolf looked at him in complete bewilderment. He was of course still in the cabman's costume; in other respects, it was a transformation. How could the commonest clothes have disguised that figure? He burst into a fit of laughter as he recollected his impression that the fellow on the box was immensely stout.

"Again, Axel!"

"No," said Axel, smiling. "It is quite enough to make a fool of yourself once in the twenty-four hours. Be quiet! The servants will hear. If I can deceive your sharp eyes, I can probably deceive a brother jarvie—that is all that I wanted to make sure of. Wait for me in my room here! I shall come down in a few moments."

Adolf threw himself back in an arm-chair, crossed his legs, and pondered deeply over the situation. Underneath his amusement a vague feeling of alarm had begun to stir.

20

Who was this mysterious lady? Had she any real existence? If she had, did she live in the rue de Clichy? And if she lived in the rue de Clichy, why did she want to go to Russia *viâ* Varennes? She was, of course, some secret friend of the Queen's. But who?

The Duchesse de Polignac? She was in the Netherlands.

The Princesse de Lamballe? She had gone to England.

Madame de Tourzel, the governess of the Dauphin? They would not dare! It was as much as a man's life was worth to suggest the departure of so small a thing as a kitchenmaid from the Tuileries. The terrible excitement of the mob when the King's poor old aunts chose to leave Paris was still fresh in everyone's mind. Fersen was playing a dangerous game, whatever it might be.

Yet it was difficult to feel sure of this when he was once more seated opposite, dressed in his ordinary black velvet coat, his face as calm and placid as if he meditated nothing more serious than what was then called a *pique-nique* for the morrow.

The room in which they sat was on an upper storey. Down below twinkled and murmured the great town. Up above hung Corona, faintly golden. The still, close heat seemed to have dimmed even the stars. Ah, how the fresh night breeze must be blowing on the mountains of Sweden! When would they be back there together, Axel and he?

"Are you bound in honour to tell me nothing more of this affair?" he said at last, breaking the silence. "If you are, I give you fair warning that I shall do my utmost to find out for myself. I do not like it, Axel."

"You are quite at liberty. If I undertake an adventure, that is my own business; I have no right to involve you. This consideration alone would keep me dumb. Still, though I cannot confide in you, you may surely—dear friend—confide in me. You know that I fight only in one cause."

"You are about to run some great risk for it, I am certain of that," said Adolf, chafed by this exhibition of superior wisdom. "Are you sure that the gain is in proportion to the risk?"

"Would there be any risk if I were?" said Fersen, smiling.

Adolf made a last, desperate appeal.

"Are you going to condemn me to stay here and do nothing, while I know you are in danger? That is not like your friendship, Axel."

"On the contrary, there is one thing that I am very anxious that you should do. There is a certain risk, but it is worth running, I think. You have quite made up your mind that you do not wish to remain permanently in France—that you would rather return to Sweden?"

"How can you ask?" said Adolf, resenting the question.

"I ask because the step that I am going to suggest may make it impossible for you to stay. I want you to meet me on Thursday evening at the *Belle Etoile*, on the Paris road, just outside Arlon."

"Arlon?" said Adolf, in great surprise. "Then you are not going to join your regiment at Varennes?"

"Sapel thinks I am; there is no need that you should think so."

"But will it take you all that time to get to Arlon?"

"I leave home to-morrow for one night," said Fersen, not answering the question directly. "I shall come back again on Tuesday, in all probability, but only for a few moments, as I am starting at once for the Netherlands, on a mission to the Archduchess Marie Christine. The hour of my return cannot be determined beforehand, and I do not wish to inconvenience you, so we will make our arrangements now. The King—yours and mine—is at Spa. He came on purpose to be near the frontier. The Queen has sent him a golden sword; it has *For the deliverance of the oppressed* engraved upon it."

"Do you mean to say that he has resolved to enter France?"

"Hush! Do not be so excited. We are a long way from that, I fear."

"Still, no one knows what may happen. He gallops where other people crawl. Are you going to him?"

"Not at present; but I shall have a very important despatch to send him from Arlon; it is one of my dearest wishes that you should be the bearer of it."

Adolf looked up, bewildered with sudden joy; an honour, the greatness of which he could but guess in the present imperfect state of his knowledge, was about to be conferred upon him.

"I shall see the King," he said, drawing a long breath.

The old feeling of joyful awe swept over him. How would it be to stand again in that presence? His brows drew together. Had he forgotten? Was it to be as though the arrests had never been? Had he not sworn that he would no longer make an idol of the man who sold his power for a tyranny!

The two thoughts shook him in their fierce grasp. And suddenly between them shone Tala's face.

"Axel, will the King let me return?"

He would have given anything to recall the words directly they were uttered. How boyish—how undignified, to think of his own private affairs at a national crisis! But Fersen only laughed.

"I think he will. Everything depends on the character of the despatch. If it be what I hope"— He did not finish the sentence. "You have had a long time to wait," he concluded.

Adolf sat silent; his eyes shone like two stars; even Fersen's were not, at that moment, more beautiful. Fersen watched him with a grave and gentle interest, touched by compassion. At length he spoke abruptly, as was his way when reluctant.

"One word before we say good-night. I have told you that I do not think that any accident will occur. So far as I know, it cannot. But we are in the hands of a higher Power; often, for His wise purposes, He puts to rout our wisdom. Here is the key of my private bureau. Will you keep it for me? If, between this and Thursday, you hear that I have been killed"—

The change which he had dreaded to provoke came over Adolf's face.

"If," pursued Fersen steadily, "you hear this on good authority, unlock my drawers and burn all the papers you will find there. If you hear that I am a prisoner, burn. If, when you reach Arlon, I am not there, and you hear nothing of me for the next twenty-four hours, so soon as they are over—not before—ride back as if you were riding for your life, and burn. After that, fly—fly anywhere out of France. You understand?"

"Perfectly," said Adolf, and took the key, with a strange sensation of the tremendous responsibility that little shining thing conferred on him.

CHAPTER XL

ADOLF dreamt too vividly to sleep well that night. When he came down, haggard of eye and exhausted, soon after seven o'clock, he saw Axel, fresh as ever, get into the carriage, which stood waiting at the door, and heard him call out—

"To Jean Louis', the coach-maker's!"

That everlasting postchaise again! Its wheels seemed to make a comic refrain to the winged words of the ballad of flight that was singing in Adolf's brain.

Axel returned, after no long interval, and shut himself up in his own room, which he did not leave till it was time for breakfast. They spoke, as usual, about indifferent topics; he ate with a far better appetite than Adolf, who found material life difficult just then.

"I am going to the Swedish embassy," Axel said, when they had finished. "De Staël called on me this morning. I had told the porter that I would not see anyone, and he was refused admittance. To my certain knowledge he never called upon me before. It is most annoying. I shall have to pay him a visit, or he will suspect that I have left Paris. Will you come too?"

"No, thank you. It is too soon. I saw Madame l'ambassadrice last night, and she wants me to go with her to the theatre this evening. She thinks you have got some official position in Russia. She cross-questioned me very closely, but I told her that you had visited the Russian ambassador, a day or two ago, to get a passport for a friend of yours, and as you said nothing about one for yourself, I did not think you could be going."

"Spoken like one of the sages ! *Au revoir, mon ami!*"

"*Bon voyage!*" Adolf said lightly.

He yawned, as he turned back into the pleasant library; his wakeful night was revenging itself. He had an engagement later in the afternoon, and he was anxious to finish an abstract of Montesquieu before he started; but weariness made him slow. He could think of nothing but Axel's words the night before, and even these seemed to have no immediate meaning.

As he sat by the window, a blank sheet of paper before him and a pen in his hand, his eyes wandered down to the courtyard below. It was full of bright sunshine; the pink and white oleanders, set out in pots along the wall, stood stiffly, straight and motionless against the unclouded blue; the leaves of the orange trees in the green tubs on the flight of stone steps leading up to the door reflected a thousand little points of light, and made a dream-like tracery of shadow. A cat was washing her face below as if she had eternity to wash it in. It was all very suggestive of going to sleep, and very still.

He had already begun to feel drowsy when he was disturbed by the clatter of wheels over the paving-stones. There was a hackney coach coming in at the gate.

What for?

Axel was out. He himself had not ordered it, and nobody sat inside. He half expected to see Axel on the box; but it was an unmistakable jarvie who sat there this time, with a big red bottle-nose. He drove up to the flight of steps, and then waited, as though he had come by appointment. He waited a long time.

In another part of the courtyard, down by the gate, the butler and one of the grooms, a man named Antoine (the same who had been sent to Stockholm), were busy coming and going about a ramshackle old wooden shed in which the gardener kept his tools. They never remained long within, but they must have made a fire

there, for wreaths of smoke were issuing from the door.
The smoke lay still upon the air, as if there were not
enough to waft it skyward.   What could they want
with a fire on such a blazing day as this?

The same thought seemed to strike the jarvie, who
accosted them in a friendly manner, and asked them
what they were doing.

A curtain hid Adolf from view; all the windows
were open, and in the great heat it seemed as if no
medium at all, not even of thinnest ether, divided him
from the voices.

"*Sapristi!* is everyone deaf?   What are you doing?"
repeated the jarvie.

"Melting lead," said Antoine.

"Melting lead?   The devil melt you!   What for?"

"You may well ask!   To load seven pair of double-
barrelled pistols with ball."

"Seven pair of double-barrelled pistols?"

Adolf, though he neither exclaimed nor swore, felt
almost as much surprised as the jarvie.

"What can your master want with so many?"

"It is my master's mistress who wants them.   She's
going to Russia.   Russia is a long way off."

"That is so," said the jarvie; "and she won't get
there in a hurry, if she's as long loading as you are."

"All very well to jeer, but the work's enough to kill
a fellow on a day like this.   You might come and take
a ladle instead of sitting up there, grinning like a
donkey."

"Well, men are brothers!   It's all one whether I
roast inside or out," said the jarvie good-naturedly;
and humming—

> " Quat' gentilshommes y avait
>   Dont l'un portait son casque,
> Et bon, bon, bon, dondi dondon
>   Et l'aut' ses pistolets,"

he drove across the courtyard, fastened his horse to the
outer gate, and entered the shed.

The work went on merrily after that, as would appear
from the shrieks of laughter that broke the tranquil

atmosphere—loudest of all when, one of the pistols going off by mistake, a ball passed clean through the hackney coach, and nearly killed a passer-by.

Presently, Axel's valet brought down a handsome English saddle and bridle, much admired by the jarvie from a professional point of view, and stowed them away under the seat.

Two large boxes appeared next, after which he went upstairs again, returning with a case, made of sheet iron, about ten inches square. He tried in vain to open it, for a few minutes, using much profane language the while, and then asked the jarvie if he could force the lock. This complacent person, who was apparently a jack-of-all-trades, and enjoyed lead-melting and lock-breaking quite as much as the more peaceful occupation of driving a horse, did as he was desired, and a sudden flash of silver illuminated the court.

Adolf leant forward, scarcely breathing. The valet took from one of the other boxes a beautiful little cup, made of the same metal, and curiously chased. As he held it up in the bright sunshine, turning it about every way, that the jarvie might properly admire the work-manship, Adolf wondered where he had seen it before. The look of the thing recalled to him firelight—Axel's face—the wail of a child—a stately lady dressed in crimson. Yes, yes, and yes again! He knew now. It was all that he could do to prevent himself from screaming out to the man to hide it immediately. Here was damning evidence indeed.

The jarvie having satisfied his curiosity, the little cup was packed with the rest of the silver, and transferred to the hackney coach. Not till the lid was screwed down did Adolf breathe freely again.

The valet clambered in.

"Where am I to go to?" cried the jarvie.

"Rue de Clichy!" he shouted, and they drove off.

Having allowed time for the men in the courtyard to disperse and go about their business, Adolf, who was so thoroughly awake that he felt as if he could never in his life sleep again, sauntered leisurely down to the stables.

There he found Sapel, smoking a big Munich pipe.

"At what time does the Count start to-night?" he inquired.

"He goes late, to avoid the heat," said Sapel gruffly.

"I know that," said Axel, who did not know it at all, "but I want to make sure of finding him before he starts."

No reply.

"He will be at the house in the rue de Clichy, I suppose?"

This was a bold move, for Adolf had no definite reason to suppose so whatever; but it had the desired effect of making the cautious German think that he was aware of the Count's plan, and the answer came readily.

"He will be there between six and seven."

"To see that everything is right about the berline, of course?" said Adolf, with confidence.

Balthazar Sapel nodded.

"He trusts no one but himself to drive that," Adolf went on.

"You are quite wrong, sir. The Count knows I can drive," said the old fellow, in a huff.

"He knows that you can drive his own carriage admirably, but he would not entrust you with Baroness de Korff's. Come, come, you do not tell me that!"

"Indeed I do," cried Sapel testily. "If he can't trust me, why have I got to leave my bed, and go to the rue de Clichy at half-past eleven to-night, to take the blessed thing to meet him at the barrier of Saint Martin?"

Adolf strolled out, if possible still more mystified than when he strolled in.

He had quite determined on one thing; he would see the departure of this berline, and he would ascertain who went in it, no matter who tried to prevent him.

He would walk to the rue de Clichy now, and reconnoitre, making sure he knew the house, so that

he could return at night. It was true that he had
an engagement with some friends, to go and see a
man of undoubted science descend to earth on wings
from a balloon, but there was still time; if he
walked quickly, he could do both. He was much
interested in the experiment; for he thought it quite
possible that men might learn to fly.

The little dress that he had seen on Fersen's bed
puzzled him more than anything else. How could it be
necessary to take such a young child? If there were
any motive for keeping the affair secret, it would more
than double the chances of detection.

Pondering over the various items of his knowledge,
attempting vainly to combine them, he reached the rue
de Clichy sooner than he had expected, and suddenly
remembered that he did not know the number of the
house for which he had come to look. It was extremely tiresome. He did not like to ask; an instinct
that he might repent it if he did kept him silent.

He scanned the houses one after the other.

They were all candid, open-eyed dwellings, and
very much alike. None had the mysterious air which,
so it seemed, the house that sheltered the mysterious
Baroness de Korff ought to have.

In one of these she had her abode.

In which one?

Who could say?

There was nothing for it but to go, and to return
about six o'clock, when, if fortune favoured him, he
might see Fersen entering, or coming out again.

And fortune did favour him, for the experiment
which he desired to witness fell through; the aëronaut
said it was too hot. Whatever birds might do, men
could not fly in hot weather.

"Carriages are, after all, more dependable than
wings in the present condition of human knowledge,"
said Adolf to himself, as he pursued his strange
quest.

He had gone by a short cut, through the mews at
the back of the rue de Clichy, and was about to take a
turning that led to the main thoroughfare when he

heard two voices, one of which he recognised at once, behind a little iron gate in a blank wall.

"My man, Sapel, will come for it to-night, at half-past eleven," said the voice that sounded like Fersen's.

"Very well. The porter will let him in."

The second voice had an extraordinary accent, like nothing in the world except that of a gifted American Irishman, who had once been heard by Adolf at Madame de Staël's talking what he considered French.

"Is the *bœuf à la mode* ready?"

"Quite ready. I put it in myself."

The voices were coming nearer. Adolf hastily bent down behind a waggon that happened to be standing there, with the shafts on the ground.

"Good-night, madame!"

"Good-night!"

Fersen walked away in the contrary direction. The other speaker was still in the gateway, looking after him, when Adolf peeped out. She was a stout, homely woman, between forty and fifty, by no means beautiful.

Surely this was not the charming Madame de Korff? If it were, never again could he rely upon the word of man. At the end of a minute or two she went back to the house; he saw that she closed, but did not lock the door behind her.

"Can you tell me who lives in this house?" he inquired of a passing milkman.

"Madame Sullivan."

She had an Irish name, then, to match her Irish accent?

"Is she quite alone?"

"Monsieur le Colonel Crawfurd comes sometimes—no one else;" and the milkman went on his way.

Colonel Crawfurd! Madame Sullivan! he could not remember that he had ever heard the names before.

His investigations had brought him no nearer to Baroness de Korff so far. Instead of one mystery, there were three.

He had promised to accompany Madame de Staël to the theatre that night, but there were several others of the party, and he found it possible to invent an excuse to slip away after the second act.

"Come to me to-morrow morning at eleven," she said impressively. He promised and escaped.

His first thought was for the little gate in the wall. He had been charmed by that little gate directly he saw it; it was a friend to him. Sure enough it yielded at once, and he found himself inside before he had quite made up his mind what to do when he got there.

He was standing in a very large stable, only lit by one small lantern, placed on the ground, and by the lamps of the berline, in all their glory; the sight of the enormous vehicle gave him a subtle comfort, for it seemed to justify his suspicions.

The horses were champing and chafing in their stalls, and the odd noises that they made afflicted his spirits. The long, ghastly shadows all about reminded him of the shadows he could never forget in the Black House. A mouse, running over his foot, made him start and tremble. He felt that he was a conspirator, without even the satisfaction of knowing what the conspiracy was about. These restless horses knew more of it than he did—this great, winking berline, that stood there spick and span and silent, and kept its secret.

"See the thing out I will!" he said to himself. "Why are there four horses—not six? I suppose I had better hide. The hero of low comedy I saw to-night would not have thought twice about it," and he got into a corn-bin, so disposing a bundle of hay that he could bring it down all over him at the shortest notice.

It was not a very pleasant place in which to sit, and he had been there long enough to think about getting out again, when the near sound of footsteps warned him to keep still.

Balthazar Sapel came in, ushered by an obscure person, whom Adolf took to be the porter; it was certainly not Madame Sullivan.

In perfect silence the horses were harnessed, and the coachman, taking the lantern in his hand, mounted to the box. The light flashed, for an instant, on the face of his companion, as he also climbed up, and to his extreme bewilderment, Adolf recognised Monsieur de Moustier.

"The great gates are open," muttered Sapel.

"*Alles toujours!*" rejoined de Moustier, speaking low ; and one of them put out the lantern.

What! Was there no Baroness de Korff at all? Were these two going alone?

He could not stay here, driving himself mad with shadows and conjectures. Come what would, he must see the end of it! Without taking a moment for reflection, he sprang lightly from the straw, and jumped into the rumble. The lantern had been extinguished a minute before. The horses were making too much noise for either of the men on the box to notice the slight sound.

Away they went.

It was the work of a second for Adolf to jump out again, when they reached the barrier of Saint Martin, and to conceal himself in a ditch by the side of the road ; but although the period of waiting in the stable had seemed long, it was nothing in comparison with the long delay that occurred here.

Half an hour.

An hour.

An hour and a half.

The horses' hoofs beat the ground with ever-growing impatience. The poor beasts were mad with impatience to be off—and small wonder! Adolf said to himself. The two figures on the box sat motionless, neither speaking a word.

De Moustier got down at last, walked some way back along the road, and returned with slow steps.

"Is it possible that anything can have gone wrong?" Adolf heard him mutter to himself.

"Does your master generally keep you waiting like this?" he said aloud to Sapel.

"The Count comes to the moment, always," said Balthazar severely.

If you hear that I have been killed—the words recurred

to Adolf, with terrible persistence, in the hot, stuffy
darkness

They had been waiting for an hour and three-quarters
now.

If it went on much longer, he could not bear it, he
must speak to de Moustier! They would go in search.
They must—

Hark!

What was that coming along the road?

The sound of whirling wheels, of galloping horses.

There were sparks in the darkness. The dust flew
into Adolf's eyes and mouth, and nearly choked him.

"Thank Heaven!" said de Moustier, with a deep
sigh of relief.

The fly in which Adolf had driven home from
Madame de Staël's the night before drew up on the
other side of the road. There was Axel in his dusty
surtout, his fair face a little flushed with hard driving—
otherwise, composed as ever.

"I thought you would never come!" de Moustier
said, grasping his hand as he sprang from the box.

"We were delayed. She lost her way."

"Where is the postchaise with the maids?"

"It will meet us at Bondy. Quick! let us get them
out! Bring the berline up close to the fly, Sapel.
Give me the lantern—here!"

Then and there did Adolf, craning his neck out of
the ditch, behold six persons—a man in the dress of
a valet, wearing a large wig, three ladies and two
children—pass in rapid succession from one carriage
to the other, without setting foot on the ground. The
lady who went first he did not know, nor the second
lady. The sight of the third set the blood tingling in
his veins.

She wore the gipsy hat, the short brown cloak that
he had seen lying on Fersen's bed; she wore them as
only one woman could. His heart beat madly against
his breast, crying, "The Queen! The Queen!" Others
might disguise themselves—for her there could be no
disguise.

The elder of the two girls he did not recognise; the

tiny creature that Axel lifted in his arms had the face of the little Dauphin, whom Adolf had seen that winter's night, long ago, when his brother was alive and he was but a baby.

It was all over in a moment.

Axel took the horses he had been driving by their bits, and turned them round, so that the back of the fly came just opposite Adolf.

What was he going to do?

He was forcing them backwards with all his might.

In a flash of perception, Adolf divined that he meant to upset them all, carriage and horses, into the ditch, and leave them there.

He had only just time to get out of the way. As it was, in the heavy crash that followed, when the fly went over the edge, dragging the horses with it, something—he did not know what—fell on his right leg, sending a thrill of agony straight from the ankle to the brain. He hardly suppressed a groan.

"When these good people awake in the morning, they will see there has been an accident," he heard Fersen say, in his quietest tones. He heard de Moustier's low laugh.

Sapel, who had been sitting on one of the horses, dismounted and got into his place ; they followed, without the loss of a moment.

"Quick! Drive fast!" cried Fersen, cracking his whip, and the berline rumbled ponderously but swiftly away into the distance.

CHAPTER XLI

ADOLF'S first care was to disentangle himself from the *débris* and to scramble out of the ditch as best he might. He did not think that he was badly hurt, but the pain in his ankle was still severe, and compelled him to limp.

One of the horses had cut its knees, and was still struggling violently; the other lay quite still. As soon as he had examined his own bruise, he went to them; but there was little he could do except to cut the traces, for he dared not call anyone.

The dawn was just breaking. The wind-stirred coolness, the gentle noises of early morning had succeeded the silent, airless heat of the night. Adolf stood up as well as he could, stretching his cramped arms, drawing in long breaths of the delicious air, rejoicing to think that it tasted like freedom to the poor prisoners of the Tuileries. How could anyone be set free at night? Night itself is a prison.

The great palace was empty now—robbed of its jewel. Often, when he went past it before, he had looked up with reverence at the walls that held within them so beautiful a queen. Now they were common stone.

The city lay still asleep. Among the thousands of dreamers there, no one dreamt of the thing, more strange than any dream, that was happening. What would it be when they awoke and found the King had fled? *The King had fled! Flight* and *a King*—the words went ill together. His King—the King of Sweden—

21

would have had people say *died* rather than *fled*; so
much he knew. He blushed for Louis XVI., and felt
glad that he was not a Frenchman. That was the
King, he supposed—that stout person in a wig? And
Adolf chid himself for the reflection that, after all,
he looked the part of the valet best.

Whither was he going?

To Bondy. Northwards! Across the frontier, no
doubt—to meet Gustav at Spa. The Knight of the
North—as many people had begun to call him of late
—would come with fire and steel to reinstate the
masters of France.

Would he, Adolf Ribbing, see these things with his
own eyes? Was this why Fersen had summoned him
to Arlon? Wild conjectures appeared to be no more
than probable, since this flight had become sober truth.
The solid fact on which he anchored his impatience
was the indisputable one that the day after to-morrow
was Thursday. Tuesday had dawned already; was it
so long to wait?

Now and then his brain was urged to frantic activity
by the pain in his ankle. Fancy and pain seemed to
be running a race together; then pain won, and the
rest was a blank. He reached the *hôtel* about four
o'clock, and went straight to his room.

By half-past six, Paris was ringing with the news.

At midday he received an ultimatum from Madame
de Staël. Had he forgotten his promise to visit her?
If he did not appear at her house within the next hour,
let him beware! Something unexpected would happen.

The note alarmed him not a little.

He had meant to avoid her altogether, sending an
excuse later on; but what did this mean? Did she
suspect anything? Had she got private information?
He dreaded her impulsive ways at such a critical time.
She was capable of descending upon the Hôtel Fersen
at any moment; and if she came, Heaven only knew
when she would think fit to go! No; there was
nothing for it but obedience.

He dragged himself up from the bed on which he
was lying; contrived, though with some difficulty, to

get down the steps and across the courtyard, and drove to the rue du Bac.

"What has happened to you?" said Madame de Staël, as soon as she saw him. "You look as if you had seen a ghost—or as if you were on the high road to become one yourself. Give me your handkerchief!" and, snatching it out of his hand, she poured half a bottle of lavender water over it, and upset the rest on her *fichu*.

Now Adolf liked a little scent, but not much.

"I am feeling the heat," he said. "We have more air in Sweden in the summer months."

"You say truly. Paris is too hot to hold people of your nation just now. Take my advice; leave it!"

"I would do so with all willingness, madame, but for one reason."

"Ah!" she said, tapping the floor with her foot, "your eyes speak the truth even when your lips cannot. You are eager to leave me."

"Do not say so! I am eager to see my country."

"It is the same thing; a man's country is the woman he loves. Your friend, de Fersen, thinks that France is his. Let him take heed! Unluckily for him, I am not the only person here that can put two and two together. I know, as well as if you had told me, that it was de Fersen who helped the Royal Family to escape last night from the Tuileries."

"You are then better acquainted with Monsieur de Fersen's plans than I, madame," said Adolf, shrugging his shoulders.

"Well parried! You never lied to me before, but you have attempted it twice in the last five minutes—very successfully too."

"How can madame think so? The first condition of a successful lie is that it should impose on the person who hears it. Granting, for the sake of argument, that I told you a lie, it is not successful. You do not believe me."

Adolf was trying to decoy her off this dangerous ground on to her favourite metaphysics. She laughed —with a grain of malice.

"Whether I believe you or not, you had better believe me when I tell you to warn de Fersen. I ought not to do so perhaps; but, after all, I was a woman before I became an ambassadress. I am sorry for the poor Queen. I wish him well. He hates me; but he is none the less a noble heart. You and he between you have taught me that there is such a thing as truth amongst men. But do not trust the King of Sweden."

"Do you know of any reason, madame, why I should not?"

"Were not last year's arrests reason enough? He is a king no longer. He has defied the Constitution. He is a mere tyrant."

"I once thought that you knew of another argument?"

She shook her head vehemently.

"You were mistaken. But no sane man would place his confidence where once he has been deceived."

Adolf was silent.

"You no longer confide in him," she said. "That is well. One word before you go! -Something about your mouth tells me that you are going much farther than the rue Matignon. Promise me that you will not return to the King of Sweden."

"I have no intention of doing so at present."

"I think you have. I think you are going to him now," said the ambassadress, not as if she were asking a question, but only stating a fact. "Well, I have no power to change your resolution. As a woman, I am nothing to you. If you could care for me as you do for de Fersen, it might be different. That is impossible; not because I am a woman, but because you are a man. But there is one thing I can do, and he cannot. I am no saint. I can forgive. Remember that!"

"Is it too presumptuous, madame, to hope that I may never need to ask your forgiveness?"

"I may need yours," she said lightly. "We will put it that way. I am wretched enough—how wretched may you never know! I want to find out where I stand with you. You are quitting us at an awful

moment. The times are dangerous. I do not think
that they will kill me. I feel that I am meant to live
for a hundred years *et quand même*"—she paused, as
though she challenged eternity itself to destroy her.
"Still, we may never meet again."

Adolf took no pains to contradict her. A spirit
within him laughed, as if he had broken a chain;
another spirit uttered a sigh.

"You and I have been friends," pursued Madame de
Staël, and her voice took the ring it had when another
woman would have softened or lowered hers. "Shall
we be friends always? Or is it only that your eyes
have been the friends of mine—your fingers of mine?"

"Let us be friends always!" said Adolf, lifting her
hand reverently to his lips. He had never kissed it
with any real emotion before. It struck him, for the
first time, that there might be, somewhere or other, a
man who loved this woman.

"You will write to me?" she said. "Farewell,
then! And tell Monsieur de Fersen that he and his
berline had better not come back to Paris just yet." .

CHAPTER XLII

FAREWELL, FERSEN!

AS he made his way home through the hot, hard, crowded streets, Adolf began to be strongly of Madame de Staël's opinion. His anxiety concerning Fersen became acute. The people were beside themselves with panic. Business was at a standstill, the shops were neglected, the public places were thronged with vagrants, rendered dangerous by their own fear. The savage threats that he heard uttered on every side of him, by men with gleaming eyes and clenched fists, against any and all who had helped the King to escape, filled him with alarm.

What madness possessed Axel to return to Paris at this moment? As yet suspicion had no leisure to choose a victim. The one and only thought of the National Assembly was, how to overtake the fugitives; it would be time enough to inquire into the manner of their flight when once it was arrested.

Of course Axel would not dare to appear before nightfall; but it would be far wiser for him to stay outside. He could not know of the terrible excitement which now prevailed in Paris. It was the duty of a friend to warn him, if possible.

With some effort, for the pain in his ankle was still severe, Adolf made his way as far as Bondy, hoping that he might hear something of him there; but the people at the inn did not know the name, and he was afraid to make inquiries.

He went to the rue de Clichy, but the house was

shut up. Madame Sullivan had left for Ireland only an hour or two since, the porter said.

When he came back to the *hôtel*, it was only to learn from the servants, who suspected nothing unusual, that Fersen had returned in the interval, taken some refreshment, and started again without leaving any message.

Clearly, the wisest thing that he could have done, but very provoking. Axel's unalterable wisdom was the one quality in him with which Adolf found it hard to have any patience. The reflection that his friend had probably avoided him on purpose, because he deemed it safer, annoyed instead of consoling.

He must have something to do. He would not be treated like a child. He must be in the scheme or of it, some way or other ; it was impossible to stay here idle. He would ride to Arlon at once.

A gentler mood came over him, as he looked his last on the house in which he had been so happy and so sad. He tried to note its angles, its doors, its ornaments, as though familiarity had never taken the edge off them all, as though he were seeing it for the first time. He wondered whether, by the end of the week, it would still be standing. He took a sentimental farewell of it, as of one doomed to die. Every chance man and woman whom he had seen that day was its enemy. How could it then escape? In his imagination, the leaping flames surrounded it already ; but Axel was safe—the Queen free—the King of Sweden at hand. Behind the vision of the burning house hovered visions of golden glory—the French monarchy restored — Sweden at the head of all the nations of Europe—Axel high in office—he himself leading Tala to the altar, while the King bestowed on him the new grade of the Order of the Sword, as a recompense for his heroic exertions during the last campaign.

So fancy flew away with him, while reason lagged far behind, hiding her head.

Yet, now and then, uneasy questionings disturbed his dream.

Madame de Staël's ardent championship of an ideal

Republic had influenced him more deeply than he knew at the time ; and the doubts which he entertained of the righteousness of a monarchy at all, unless it be strictly constitutional, were to return, with over-whelming force, later on.   He could not believe in Gustav, as a political leader, any more ; his faith had not recovered from the shock of the arrests ; the bitter agony of the moment when he discovered that the King could stoop to violence was still vivid in his recollection.   Authority was not the law of his life as it was of Fersen's.

The ambassadress had forced him to shape clearly the dim conviction of his inmost heart.   There was a cry in him for truth ; she had made it articulate, by her mistakes as well as by her genius, as the human creature that she was, even more than as the oracle that she desired to be.   He asked himself now whether it was right to go back.

All the time he knew well enough that he would go. Ambition demanded that he should.   Love would take no denial.   Did truth demand the sacrifice of these ? One voice in him said *Yes*.   He would perhaps have listened but for Tala's.

He made a compromise with it at last.   He would not of course accept any political employment.   So long as he declined that, his hands were clean.   As a soldier, nothing to the prejudice of his country could be demanded of him.   The King was confessedly one of the captains of the age.   Adolf would hardly have been a young man at all, if the brilliancy of Gustav's exploits in the war with Russia had not, for the moment, dazzled his imagination.

Still, as of old, on his solitary ride, the King, and he alone, divided his dreams with Tala.   His thoughts were for Fersen, and they were long and anxious, but he had not indulged his northern love of reverie for a long while, and it was good to find again, with a quiet pleasure that surprised himself, the enchantment of that borderland between memory and reflection.

He had put aside Madame de Staël for the present, though he sometimes composed parts of a long and eloquent letter, which he meant to write to her, full of interesting theories about the difficulties of practical government, and the character of friendship between a man and a woman. He rode slowly, and spent two restless, wakeful nights on the way—afraid of Axel's quiet smile if he were to arrive long before the appointed hour.

As he neared Arlon, every other consideration vanished, like morning mist, in an eager desire to learn what had happened after the departure of the Royal Family from the barrier of Saint Martin. His naturally hopeful disposition never admitted so much as a passing suspicion of failure.

In spite of all his reckoning, he had arrived much too soon, and there was little in Arlon to distract him. The hours dragged heavily enough until the sun set, burning gold, at the end of a long, thin alley of poplars.

"Ah, not a moment earlier, for all my impatience!" he laughed to himself, as he shook his fist at it from the window of the inn parlour. He was in high spirits ; they rose higher and higher, as the time at which he might reasonably expect Fersen approached.

It was very quiet.

The glory of the sunset was quick to fade. A waft of cloud lay, like a folded wing, across the sky. The cocks and hens in the yard outside had gone to roost. The last rooks had circled, cawing, to their nests in the elm trees beyond, long ago. In this tranquil hour it would be good to hear the flaming news, and start again at once, to carry it post-haste, through the starlight, to the King. His horse was standing, saddled and bridled, in the stable. He had ordered it to be got ready five minutes before the sun sank, for now Axel might come at any moment.

He waited until hunger refused to wait any more, and then supped alone. Not feeling in the least unhappy as yet—for twenty-four hours was a broad margin, when you came to consider, and some sort of delay almost inevitable in an affair like this—he took out *L'Esprit des Lois*, when he had finished, and set to work on it with great resolution. But he had never closed his eyes the night before — not often, the night before that; he fell asleep and slept for several hours.

Just as the church clock of Arlon was striking twelve, he awoke with a start.

There, on the opposite side of the table, sat Fersen, scribbling in his blue pocket-book. He did not raise his eyes, but wrote busily.

Not thus had Adolf pictured their meeting, though he had pictured it a thousand times. Something made it impossible for him to speak.

Axel looked up, but he did not answer the terrified questioning of his friend's face.

"Read that!" he said, tearing a leaf out of his pocket-book. Adolf's hand shook while he read: ·

"MIDNIGHT, *June* 23, 1791.

"SIRE,—The whole plan has failed. The King was arrested sixteen miles from the frontier and brought back to Paris. I am going to see M. de Mercy, and am the bearer of a letter from the King, asking the Emperor to take steps on his behalf. I will come and see your Majesty from Brussels.—I am, with the most profound respect, your Majesty's very humble and very obedient servant,

"AXEL FERSEN."

There was nothing to be said.

Desperate admiration, pity, anger, were tearing Adolf's heart to pieces, but he was quick to perceive that Axel could bear nothing but silence just then. He was deadly pale; his eyes had lost their light, even their colour, it seemed; the dumb suffering in them was suffering that no words could reach.

"Were they all arrested?"

Adolf spoke after a long pause, during which Axel sat motionless, gazing before him.

"All! They were overtaken at Varennes. You were right when you said there would be an accident. The details are not known yet. Bouillé told me, a short time since. He was to have joined them with the soldiers."

"Our hope is in the King."

Fersen shook his head.

"If the will to help were everything—but he has not the power. Give me that note."

"Are you not going to permit me to take it, after all?" cried Adolf, in blank distress.

"There is no merit in being the bearer now. Best let me find someone else!"

"No," said Adolf. "I said that I would take it, and I mean to."

"As you will," said Fersen indifferently.

For a moment Adolf's heart failed him; he felt as if he could not speak again; but there was one thing that must be done.

"Here is your key!" he said. "But—Axel—you will not return to Paris now?"

"No, not now. I rescued all the papers that I wanted on Tuesday."

"And you will come to Spa? I shall see you again there?"

"Yes."

They bid each other good-bye under the stars. There was speech in the touching of their hands, though their lips could not utter it.

CHAPTER XLIII

BAD NEWS

THERE were other people besides Adolf, as he stood watching the golden ball behind the poplars, who thought that the sun sank to rest very slowly on the night of the 23rd of June.

Among the miserable little band of French emigrants, whom chance, or the hope of relief from the eccentric friendly power of Sweden, had brought together at Aix-la-Chapelle, a vivid though indefinite expectation of some great event immediately about to happen kept many eyes awake.

These people, when they left their homes, had parted with almost everything that made life dear. They were oppressed by the direst want. Excepting on those days of the week when Gustav kept open table for a hundred guests, their fare consisted only of milk and potatoes; such a diet, when he is not accustomed to it, sharpens a man's wits. No confidence had been reposed in them; but they had seen the tears in the King's eyes, when women and children stretched out their arms to him, beseeching him to take them back to France; they had seen the golden sword, sent by the Queen, *Pour la défense des opprimés*, and they read the signs of the times. When the King moved to Spa, that he might be as near Paris as possible, many of them accompanied him; their feverish impatience made suspense even more difficult to bear than usual for one of his fiery and sensitive temperament.

It was chiefly in order to escape from the dumb

interrogation of thin, worn faces, that he had elected to walk alone, the evening after the 23rd, on the high road, outside the gates of Spa. Too restless to stay in the apartments provided for him, too much preoccupied to desire any company until the longed-for courier from Axel Fersen should arrive, he paced up and down, his eyes fixed now on the distant horizon, now on the watch that he held in his hand. Since midday he had been counting the hours ; now, he said to himself that he might lawfully count the minutes. If his calculations were right, the courier must arrive before dark.

The sun was like the sinking monarchy of France ; the crimson battlefield of clouds lay all around it.

He saw the Imperial troops entering by Flanders, the Swiss by Franche-Comté, the Sardinians by Dauphiné, the Spaniards crossing the Pyrenees, himself Generalissimo of the forces at the head of twenty-two thousand Russians and Swedes. The thought of the terrific effect of the wild dress of the Cossacks pleased his fancy, and he dwelt long on it.

But there was still no cloud of dust on the horizon, and the galloping horseman, upon whose speed the fate of all these millions hung, came not.

The sun disappeared, the stars shone out, and he was forced to return.

Whatever might be about to happen, it had not happened yet—so much the exiles gathered from the silent, reserved manner of their host at the banquet that evening. The courtiers looked grave also, and gave short answers to those who questioned them, not because they knew anything, but because they did not care to have it thought that they were ignorant.

Together they talked more openly.

"When will there be an end of this suspense ? " said Jacques de La Gardie to a friend of his, Fabian Wrede by name. He had thought much of Paris lately, in connection with Adolf Ribbing. Wrangel had more than once solicited the payment of that debt, but Jacques declared that Adolf was still a favourite.

Wrede shrugged his shoulders.

" Important news from France is on the road ; I am quite sure of that," continued Jacques.

"What makes you think so?"

"I saw him when he thought that he was alone this evening. He was walking on the Paris road. Every few minutes he pulled out his watch and looked at it."

Wrede made no reply.

He did not go to bed that night.

Before the dawn was well begun, he ordered his horse and rode out of Spa at a gallop, coming back even faster than he had gone.

Curious faces met his, round the gate, on the stairs, and in the passages of the house where the King lodged, but he said nothing to anyone. He went straight to the King's door and knocked loudly. The King sprang from his bed and opened it himself.

" News ? "

" News, sire ! "

He snatched the note in Fersen's writing from the hand of his equerry, and read it eagerly. His face fell.

" Did Count Fersen himself give you this ? "

" No, sire. I had it from Count Ribbing."

The King looked up quickly.

" From Count Ribbing, did you say ? "

" Yes. He would have brought it in person, but he has had a slight accident, and is laid up at a village about seven miles from this place."

The King seemed to reflect.

"What is that?" he said, as a rush of feet was heard outside.

Suddenly the door opened. A rumour of Wrede's expedition had spread through the village, and some of the leading exiles, unable to control their impatience, stormed the King's apartment in a body, and fell on their knees before Gustav, imploring him to tell them what had occurred.

There could be no need to make a secret of what was by this time public property all over France.

"The King has been arrested on his way to the

frontier, and taken back to Paris. All hope of escape is at an end."

Some wept in silence ; here and there a man sobbed aloud. Gustav himself broke down.

Wrede, though he was inwardly in a state of great self-satisfaction, pulled out his handkerchief and held it before his eyes. It was indeed a heartrending scene, that might have melted the heart of any but a courtier.

As soon as the room was clear, Gustav turned again to his equerry.

"What is the matter with Count Ribbing?" he said.

"It is but a very slight hurt, sire. He sprained his ankle, a day or two ago ; hard riding, heat and fatigue inflamed it, and he had just been obliged to dismount, when, by good luck, I encountered him and persuaded him to give me Count Fersen's note. The horse was utterly spent, and he was unable to walk as far as the next village. I put him on Black Woden, and took him to the inn myself, where he lies, awaiting your Majesty's pleasure. He begged me to say that a few hours' rest would quite restore him. Does your Majesty wish to see him to-morrow?"

The King stood in deep thought. Was this face always to rise before him, at every crisis of his life? A powerful aversion made him shrink from the sight of it.

But if he sent the boy back to Paris, it was certain death. Fersen was too well known there ; no friend of Fersen's could escape. He thought of Delaunay, torn in pieces by the *sans-culottes* in the Place de la Grève. The recollection had haunted his dreams of late. He had no mind to be haunted more vividly.

"What do you think of sudden death, Wrede? Is it a blessing in disguise?"

"I must own, sire, that I have not considered the matter," said Wrede, surprised at the abruptness of the question. He was a feather-headed young fop, with little to recommend him except his good looks and a certain officiousness which made him do the wrong thing nine times out of ten, and the right thing once in a way.

"I have had to consider it often—very often," Gustav said. "If I have to face it, I pray that it may be on the scaffold, not by the hand of a Damien or a Ravaillac. No, I do not wish to see Count Ribbing to-morrow. It is much better that he should rest. Ride back at once, and take him half a dozen bottles of the best wine in my cellar. Tell him that I commend his zeal and regret the hurt that he has sustained. Express to him my regret that I cannot have the pleasure of inviting him here, as I have just issued an edict for the immediate recall to Sweden of all Swedish officers now in France, and dare not make an exception. Say that I shall hope to welcome · him back to Stockholm shortly. You may add that the Court is under orders to leave Spa at once. And, Wrede—a word to the wise! Do not mention his name to anyone here; say that you had the good luck to meet Fersen's courier, and that he went straight back to his master. If they know that he is only seven miles from this place, the poor boy will be besieged by the *émigrés*. May I rely on you in this matter?"

Much flattered by such a proof of the confidence that was reposed in him, Wrede gave the required promise, and withdrew to execute his commission.

When he had gone, the King took from the mantelpiece a letter from Baron Essen, which he had received that morning, and pondered over it for some time.

"Poor child!" he said to himself, with a little shrug of the shoulders. "Poor child! I must go as soon as I return. At anyrate, he was quite unworthy of her. I wonder how far his intrigue went with Madame de Staël?"

CHAPTER XLIV

THE RETURN

SOME weeks later, Adolf was on his way to the old Castle by the lake.

His hurt proved more serious than he thought for, and completely prevented him from walking or riding for many days ; but, except for his growing impatience to see his cousin again, the time had not passed unhappily. The kindly message from Spa pleased and flattered the young man, and, in his joy at the permission accorded him to return, he saw in it only a proof of the willingness of his sovereign to grant him his heart's desire as soon as possible, after long delay.

He had a sharp struggle with himself, before he decided not to write to Tala ; but the spirit of romance prevailed. Having waited so long, it was worth while to wait a few days longer for the ecstasy of her surprise and joy. He was a lover of the unexpected, and had often deliberately risked total disappointment for the sake of a brighter thing than mere pleasure. It was possible, of course, that Tala might have left the Castle ; but he did not think it likely, for her father was almost as securely rooted to the soil as one of his own fir trees, and nothing short of the assembling of a Diet ever brought him to Stockholm. No further report having reached him, after the news of the release, he imagined that his uncle, like the old Count, had gone back to his estate, and would probably never leave it again. Axel's correspondence with his family had been much interrupted of late, and Adolf had no other sources of information, for his mother was now unable to write,

and he only received occasional bulletins of her health
from her attendants.

He often pondered over the few words Tala had sent
him. Was she yet loyal to the King? Had she
changed? The message made him think that she was
perhaps aware of circumstances which were not known
to him. There might be another side to the question.
Still, the fact of the arrests remained; nothing could
change that. The knowledge of it hung on him like
a weight. Could it be honourable, he asked himself,
to serve under the King again?

During the long hours in which he lay tossing to and
fro, while Wrede carried his message to the King, he
had made up his mind that—whatever post he might
be offered—he would accept it only on condition that
it did not involve him in any of the political measures
of a Government whose methods he could not approve.
Some appointment the King was bound to give him
after his faithful service at Gothenburg and this long
interval of waiting. A certain relief blunted his disappointment, when he found that the interview with
his sovereign was put off. If he were to stand again
in that magnetic presence, he owned, with a feeling
akin to shame, that he could not answer for himself.
The adjournment allowed room for a faint hope to
spring up, that perhaps Tala might be able to throw
some light on the occurrences of the past year—to
prove that what looked like treason against the Constitution of the land could be otherwise interpreted.

And yet, how could it? As well hope that two and
two would not make four! Could it be well to accept
anything from one whom, in his secret heart, he must
regard as a despot?

He stifled the question as soon as it arose. There
could be no dishonour in receiving the promotion that
would enable him to marry. That was the due reward
of service rendered long before this last fatal Diet.

It was after dark when he came once more to the
familiar country. His heart was full of the love of
home. The rough music of his own language, the
sight of his compatriots, of the lakes and hills and fair

cities that it was his birthright to see, had so bewitched him with the sweet novelty of things old and forgotten, that he was ready to take a vow that he would never travel more.

He had so arranged his journey that he could not arrive before sunset, because he remembered with minute remembrance every sensation of that night of his life, the last minutes of which had been spent with Tala upon the Reindeer's Crag. He fancied that, if he showed due regard to time and place, each would return to him with something of its original poignancy. Therein he reckoned without experience. Two and a half years of Paris had aged him considerably, but he was not yet old enough to know that the stupidest of us can never do the same thing twice over. The passion of delight in life—the sudden fear—the extraordinary quickening of the senses, physical and spiritual, by which the most insignificant sights and sounds were transfigured—these it had been given him to feel once, when for the first time he had stood face to face with death and come off victorious ; but if he lived to the age of a patriarch, if he escaped as great a peril twenty times, life would not repeat the gift.

Therefore he passed the avenue that led to the Black House and felt nothing. His own want of emotion bewildered him. The village was a common village ; what had become of the fantastic oddity of those first cottages ? Was the outer world disenchanted ? Was existence less wonderful now ?

It was very hot, the air burdened with coming storm. All his limbs ached with weariness, and the thunder-calm tired his head as though it were noise ; but he gave little heed to that.

As he came within sight of the wan shimmer of the lake, the nearness of his joy overcame him. Behind those walls was she whom his heart worshipped. It was almost three years since he had seen her face ; the three years seemed to him shorter than the few minutes that must yet pass before he kissed her again.

What if she should be dead ?

He smiled. There had been a time when he never

came near the Castle walls without asking himself that
question ; but he was older now.

Or absent? Absence would be death for the moment.

No ; there was a light in the Castle. He saw it
gleaming from the windows of the great hall, which
was never used except on State occasions. What were
they doing there ?

He recollected the dance music, that had sounded in
his ears like a dirge, when he climbed the hill. There
was no music now. He could not even hear the sound
of the lake water lapping against the rock. Everything
lay in profound silence. The gate at the foot of the
hill was open, as though someone were expected.

The great door stood ajar ; a brilliant ray of light
streamed through, cutting the darkness like a sword.

Some instinct warned him to go no farther. He got
down from his horse and stood listening. All was
quiet.

What was that? A woman sobbing? Mad with
terror, he pushed open the door and went in.

A lamp hung in the entrance ; otherwise the hall was
in total darkness, except for a little island of light at
the farther end. What was that white figure, lying
straight and still on a stiff couch, in the centre? The
auburn hair on the cushion was Tala's hair.

" Who is this ? " he said stupidly.

Someone from beside the couch rose up.

" My wife," said a grating voice that his ears knew
again.

Someone with the features of the King laid his finger
on his lips.

"Thank Heaven ! " said a sweet voice, broken with
tears, " he has come at last. Now she can go in peace."

Then, with a rush of horror, he understood. He
made one step forward, bending as though to take the
little thin hand lying open on the coverlet, but he could
no longer see it. Oddly shaped patches of black
seemed to be falling, with tremendous swiftness,
between him and the couch. He covered his eyes that
he might shut them out ; they went on falling inside
the eyelids ; he opened his lips as though to speak, but

could not form a word—reeled—and sank blindly to the ground.

At that, the figure on the couch opened its eyes, and sat up, with a little weak laugh. He heard it speak.

"You said he did not love me. See! He is dead."

CHAPTER XLV

ST. BRITA'S CROSS

"WHERE are we going?"
"To St. Brita's Cross."
"Why?"
"You will know soon enough."

It was an odd sight—if anyone had been there to see it—the young, daintily dressed gentleman, arm-in-arm with a white-haired beggar, whose rags scarcely covered him.

"Are we to wait here?"
"Yes."
"Is it safe under the trees on a night like this?"

The lightning played like a live sword amongst them. The beggar shrugged his shoulders.

"Beeches are never struck. Choose a beech, if you will!"

"What are we waiting for?"
"For Adolf Ludwig Ribbing."

The young man started.

"We must send him on at once to the Castle," he said, grasping his companion's arm. "Countess Aurora told me, three days ago, that the only chance of her recovery lay in the sight of him. I have done my utmost to find him, without success. You will send him to the Castle at once?"

"There is no need. He will be coming from the Castle."

"The devil he will!" said Clas.

They sat silent for a long time. Presently, drops of rain began to fall, and there was a roll of distant thunder. The wind rose without a moment's warning; the stillness turned into a wild confusion of bending and breaking trees and cracked branches. In the middle of it all the beggar began to sing.

"What are you about, Pechlin?"

Clas thought that his companion had suddenly gone mad. The shrieking wind made a more human noise. It was impossible to catch the words, except that there seemed to be a doggerel burden of—

"There passed us a woman with the West in her eyes,
And a man with his back to the East."

He had only sung a bar or two when, to Horn's astonishment—almost to his terror—he heard a high, clear voice echoing it. For all the noise of the storm, the old man had detected the sound of hoofs, and now he dashed into the road, and seized Ribbing's horse by the bridle.

"Who sings my song?" he cried.

"One of the King's enemies."

"Where have you been?" he said.

"Killing a man."

"And watching a woman die?"

Ribbing made no answer. It was too dark to see his face. Clas Horn could hardly believe that it was he, for the voice was not like his own.

"No alms of life to-night from the Black House," said Pechlin. "No alms of love from the Three Water Lilies. The Knight of the North has refused both. What are you now?"

"Why, a Beggar—a Beggar like you," said Ribbing, "and the King's enemy."

"That is well. The Beggars are all the King's enemies. Will you be one of them? Will you swear?"

They spoke together for a few moments, but Horn could not hear what they said for the wind.

CHAPTER XLVI

CLAS HORN'S VISITOR

" IF Captain Anckarström should call, say that I am not in."

Clas Horn was seated in an easy-chair by a tall blue and white china stove, of Dutch construction, in one of the comfortable rooms of a large house in the most fashionable part of Stockholm, where he now lodged whenever circumstances required his presence in that city. A rich old bachelor uncle had died in the course of the last year, and, to his nephew's great surprise (for they knew little of each other), left him the heritage of Hufvudstad, a beautiful place in the country, at some little distance, on the express condition—mysteriously worded in his will—that he should continue his present mode of life. This he was very willing to do, but he continued it more luxuriously than of old, and with less absolute conviction. Conspirators are, as a rule, poor.

A violin lay on the table, and various old instruments hung round the walls, where these were not covered by bookcases, and pictures of Cupids, and shepherdesses in hooped petticoats. It was winter, and the Dutch stove heated the room very agreeably. Clas, who had just come in out of the frosty air, warmed his hands at it for a minute or two, yawned as if the sudden change of atmosphere had made him drowsy and he were half inclined to fall asleep, and lay back in his chair with closed eyes. The persistence of one thought, however, hindered him from sliding into unconsciousness. He roused himself at last, and rang the bell.

"Captain Anckarström has not called?"

"No, sir."

"If he should come, say that I am at Hufvudstad."

The servant withdrew.

Horn glanced out of the window. It would be some time yet before darkness fell. The thought was in some vague sense consolatory. He had never seen the person against whose approach he was taking precautions, except at night. Nevertheless, he walked away from the window, as if he feared to be noticed there.

He had just opened a music-book, which lay on the table beside the violin, and was studying a concerto by Viotti, when the servant brought him a note. He tore the wrapping in his impatience to get at the contents; but there was nothing inside, and he was about to exclaim, when he caught sight of a mark in the corner, which, to the uninitiated, would have looked like a mere blot.

"The falcon's foot," he said to himself, as he scrutinised it more closely. "Yes, there is no doubt. The number of the smudges is right; they make the claw."

"It is not Captain Anckarström?" he demanded hastily: then added, as if ashamed of the suspicion, "Ask the bearer of this to come up at once."

He leant his elbow on his knee and his head on his hand, and sat musing.

"It is not Anckarström. He has no need to make a fool of himself with signs in that way; he would never consent. It is not Anckarström."

None the less did he give a start of relief when the door opened gently and he beheld upon the threshold a very different person—one whom he had not seen for the last two years—with whom he had no associations but those of pleasure.

"What! Pontus, Pontus Liljehorn!" he cried, rising and going to meet him with both hands out, in all the effusion of welcome poured forth for him who is not only welcome in himself, but because he is not somebody else.

The fair, delicate-looking young man whom he addressed showed no corresponding emotion, only raising his eyebrows slightly, as though he were surprised.

" I never was more amazed in all my life," said Clas, setting a chair for him near the stove. " You one of the Beggars! I can scarcely credit my senses. But you sent me the falcon's foot ? "

" The falcon's foot ? Yes."

" You—Pontus Liljehorn—a Beggar! And may I ask who told you that one of those unfortunates lived here ? "

" Baron Pechlin. He gave no name of course."

" It is like old times to see you."

" Is it ? " said Pontus vaguely, his wistful grey eyes roving over the walls. " I never think of the old times now."

" How you used to play then ! " (A kind of nervousness made Clas go on, though he divined that the subject was not one which pleased his visitor.) " Many's the night that I have sat up with Jacques de La Gardie until the stars were almost gone, to hear you play that sarabande of Corelli's—do you remember ? " He hummed the air.

Pontus waved his hand towards the old mandolines on the wall.

" There is no more music in me now than in these," he said sadly. " It is all gone."

" I thought you lived for your violin and for nothing else," said Clas. " I thought you never heard any sound that was not music. How did you come to know of the existence of such a discord as this Society of the Beggars ? "

" Through Baron Pechlin."

" That old rat is at the bottom of every dark hole. May I ask what led you to join them ? "

The grey eyes of Pontus Liljehorn flashed.

" I loved the King, and he gave me no love. I am like that. I can only love or hate. There is nothing between."

" I loved him too," said Clas, " as Brutus loved

Julius Cæsar." He had thought about Brutus and
Julius Cæsar very often of late. "But I loved my
country more."

"I have always wondered what was meant by my
country," said Pontus. "I thought I understood
what was meant by my King; it seems that I was
mistaken."

"You were disappointed of preferment, were you
not?" said Clas drily. "That makes it hard to
understand."

"You may call it so, if you like," retorted Pontus,
·shrugging his shoulders. "All your ancestors held
high positions about the Court, I believe."

Something in either young man began to irritate the
other. Each in turn had been the King's favourite,
and though they were now of one mind in hatred,
neither cared to believe that the other's affection for
him had been real. Absurd as it might seem, each
was jealous; yet, at the end of a moment, they felt
that it was silly of them to quarrel.

"Perhaps I ought to tell you," said Pontus, "that I
have been made Captain of the Blues since my return
from France."

"Indeed! I congratulate you. It was because
Liljensparre suspected the fidelity of the Blues that he
persuaded the King to enrol the Blacks, was it not?"

"The Blues are not suspected now," said Pontus,
his lip curling.

"And yet the Blues are with us to a man, are they
not?"

"To a man."

"Surely the Blacks must have some suspicion?
Duels are more frequent than ever; they are all the
talk of the town. The Black-and-Silver never meets
the Blue without insulting him; an acquaintance of
mine was challenged three times in one week. Do
they suspect nothing?"

"I do not think they do. Of course there were
great objections to the formation of a second regiment
of the Life Guards, and the Blacks, who are mere
bourgeois, are very unpopular everywhere except at

Court or in the public-houses. That is quite enough
to account for the friction."

"It is an odd state of things," observed Clas
thoughtfully. "If the rumour be true and we are to
have another Diet soon, it is ten to one we shall see
some strange sights. You were not present at the
close of the last Diet, if I remember right?"

"No. I was in Paris at the time."

"Ah! I had not long returned from Paris myself.
I saw one or two of my fellow-countrymen at Madame
de Staël's house when I was there, but memory
does not serve me. Had I the pleasure of meeting
you?"

"I am afraid not. I was not the friend of Madame
de Staël."

"Someone else, who hails from our part of the
world, was, then. I never went to visit her but I
found that young scamp, Adolf Ribbing, in her
boudoir."

"It was about Adolf Ribbing that I desired to
speak," said Pontus, with a sudden change of manner.

"Why? Are you a friend of his?"

"I may say that I am; he does not know me, but
that makes little difference. I saw him often, when I
was in Paris; since he left, I have heard nothing
beyond the bare fact of his return to Sweden. I am
very anxious to know what has become of him. Baron
Pechlin told me that I should find in this house someone who could tell me?"

"I cannot deny that he is right. But a word or two
before we begin. Why were you in Paris? Why did
I never meet you there?"

"I was there as a spy for the Beggars. Some of
my family are English, and I can speak the language
well, so that I passed for an Englishman. I went into
society often enough, but I had to avoid all my own
country-folk, for the sake of keeping watch over one."

"And that one?"

"Adolf Ribbing."

"Singular!" said Clas, with rising interest "He
was heart and soul for the King at that time; surely

they could have had no idea that he would change?
Why did they have him watched?"

"Have you never heard of Noorna Arfridson's
prophecy, that the King would fall by his hand?"

"No one speaks of that now."

"Because everyone thinks of it."

"He has not thought of it himself," said Clas,
hurriedly and nervously. "I never met anybody who
had—except once; and then the man was a fanatic."

"Fanatics are dangerous people," said Pontus, with
an uncertain ring in his voice. "They are the only
ones who act as they think. What was he like?"

"He is a very dark man — pale — insignificant
features—dead, fishy eyes."

"I thought so."

"You know him then—Captain Anckarström?"

"Ah!" said Pontus, and he gave a long, shuddering sigh. "That is his name?"

"He seems to have great influence among the
Beggars," Clas went on, still in the same flurried
manner. "Old Pechlin sent him to Hufvudstad,
about a fortnight ago. I told him that I would have
nothing to do with any scheme of blood; that we were
banded together merely to take the King captive and
to hold him in captivity until he consented either to
give us back the Constitution of 1772, or to resign in
favour of the Crown Prince. I think that I convinced
him."

"Oh!" said Pontus, very slowly, "you think that
you convinced him, do you? Well, he it was who
insisted that Adolf Ribbing must be watched, protected
against all danger, and on no account allowed to
return to Sweden before the moment was ripe, because
the King's fate depended on him."

"Protected! Why was he in danger?"

"Paris was likely to become hot enough for any
friend of Axel Fersen's just then. Not that he was
involved in that business of the King's flight. Fersen
is a cautious fellow; he gets no one into trouble, not
even himself. But Ribbing lived in his house, and I
was never free from anxiety"

"Why was he not allowed to return, then?"

"It was feared that the King would favour his marriage with Carl de Geer's daughter, and so bind him for ever to his cause. They were quite right, it seems. The King profited by his absence to marry her to Baron Essen, and so make sure of that uncertain piece of goods. But, if I know anything of Adolf Ribbing, he will not have taken it quietly."

"You are right," said Clas Horn. "He has joined the Beggars."

"Heaven be praised!" cried Pontus, with some fervour. "I always dreaded Pechlin's villany. Are you quite sure of that?"

"I am indeed. I was with Pechlin when the old wretch went out to catch him."

"Pray tell me!" said Pontus Liljehorn earnestly. "I have heard nothing."

"It happened about five months ago, one dark night in the beginning of August," said Clas. "I had been staying at a little village near the Castle of Carl de Geer. You remember? You must have been there in old days."

"I remember very well. It stands above the lake."

"The Baroness is a most dear friend of mine," continued Horn. "It was thought at that time that she would not live."

"She was engaged to Count Ribbing for a long while before her marriage with Baron Essen, was she not?"

"It was said at Court that Count Ribbing had forgotten her, and fallen in love with Madame de Staël."

"I think that is not true. Whilst I was in Paris, I once heard Madame de Staël, who is very unguarded, let fall a hint as to Fröken de Geer. He would have acted upon it at once, but that she recalled the words the moment she had said them, and I—in accordance with instructions received from Stockholm — found means to reassure him. I had my orders from Baron Pechlin, who wished him to remain in Paris. I did not then suspect that the information was false."

"I do not know how that may be " said Clas,

instinctively taking the side of Tala, as his visitor had taken that of Adolf. "I know that when her father was arrested and she was left quite alone, she wrote, urging him to come to her; and he refused. This happened more than a year before her marriage; she never heard from him again."

"She took the Baron out of pique, I suppose?"

"Far from it! The girl was heartbroken after her father's death, which followed hard on his release from prison. He could not survive the disgrace." Clas paused. "My own father has never got over it," he said in a low tone, as if reminding himself of something that he half feared to remember. "She believed that she herself was on the verge of the grave. She married Essen simply because he promised to take her back to her old home, and she wanted to die there."

"If she had been heartbroken, she would have had something else to attend to. Was she indeed so very ill?"

"You must not ask me to talk of that," said Clas, turning away.

"I have no interest in the Baroness Essen, alive or dead," said Pontus coldly. "Her doings are a matter of complete indifference to me, unless they happen to affect Count Ribbing. You were going to tell me, I think, how it was that he joined the Beggars?"

"He was enrolled at a deserted house, in the neighbourhood of St. Brita's Cross—the Black House, they call it. What is the matter?"

"Nothing. I happen to have heard of it, that is all. Go on."

Clas told him everything as it had happened that August night.

"Pechlin made me administer the oath of secrecy to him then and there," he concluded. "I do not think that he understood a word of what he was saying."

"How did he look?" said Pontus.

"As if he came out of hell."

They were both silent. Outside a sledge flew past along the road, the bells jangling merrily.

CHAPTER XLVII

THE MAN OF ACTION

"WHAT did he mean by saying that he had killed a man?" asked Pontus at length.

"He and Essen fought in the avenue, I believe. It was given out next day that the Baron had fallen downstairs as he was on his way to the hall, where his wife was lying, and hurt himself severely; but Pechlin told me afterwards that he had been wounded in the chest. For a long time they thought the case desperate."

"Why did I never hear anything of this? It must have made a stir at the time."

"Not Liljensparre himself ever got wind of it."

"That is a good thing. There would have been short work with both gentlemen had it come to the King's ears."

"It was the King who hushed it up," said Clas, in a low voice. "He was there."

Pontus leant forward, holding his breath.

"Essen is hand-and-glove with him; and he is fond of the Baroness. He came there *incognito*, that he might see her before she died."

"And Adolf Ribbing?"

"I do not know. I have not met him since that night."

"What is that? Someone knocked."

"Oh no!" said Clas, who liked the sound of his own voice, and seldom heard any other noises when he could hear this.

"I am sure that I heard someone," repeated Pontus.

As he was speaking the door opened, and Adolf Ribbing came in. He had lost every trace of colour. His eyes looked as if someone had set fire to them.

"Well," he said, as he stood still in the middle of the room and laughed, "you two behave as if I had committed murder. Perhaps I have. You can tell me, Horn. You must tell me indeed, for you are a brother of mine; at least so I'm told."

"Essen still lives," said Clas, startled into answering directly.

Adolf snapped his fingers.

"Do you think I care that much whether he does or not? Is she dead?"

"No."

He drew a long breath, put one hand to his throat as though to free it from some deadly coil, and with the other steadied himself against the table, closing his eyes.

"I must ask you to forgive me," he said, his steely tone changed into quivering softness. "I have been very ill. I am only now recovering."

"Sit down," said Clas, bringing forward a chair for him.

He obeyed, his thoughts evidently somewhere else, his body following the first suggestion made to it by the will of another.

"This gentleman is one of the brotherhood as well," said Clas, indicating Pontus Liljehorn.

"We have met before," said Pontus. "Do you remember me?"

Adolf looked long at him.

"No," he said at length, with a shake of the head. "I have forgotten everything, except two faces. It is because I was ill. Everybody I meet now seems to have one of those two faces. You look like the King, but I know you are not. I think I have not seen your eyes before; but I have seen you sit, just as you are sitting now, your chin in your hand."

"You have. It was a long while ago, at the Black House."

"Ah!" said Ribbing indifferently.

23

"It was a long while ago," put in Clas, alarmed by his manner, and nervously anxious to divert the conversation from the personal course that it seemed to be taking. "Things have changed very much everywhere in the last few years—ever since you left Stockholm, Pontus. For instance, you find the Court much altered, do you not?"

"I should not have known it again," said Pontus, following his host's lead. "No one attends the *levées* now. I hear that they are to be given up altogether. The King is going to try a series of public masquerades in the Opera House, but those who are best informed are not at all confident of success. It is very strange. Do people think that the white drawing-room is infectious, I wonder?"

"I cannot say. Other friends have told me that it has been more and more empty of late. But people began to fall away after the close of the last Diet. The ladies of Stockholm—the Fifth Estate, as Armfelt used to call them—have never forgiven nor forgotten the insult to Fersen's daughters at the time of their father's arrest; they speak of it still."

"It is not the Court alone. I do not know what has come over Stockholm. I scarcely recognise my native city. I went to the theatre the other night; it was only half full. As for the opera, La Gardie tells me that no one ever thinks of attending it now."

"No one has any money," said Clas, in the comfortable tone of a man who can afford to express that opinion. "So long ago as the victory of Svenskund, the rejoicings had to be cut short for lack of funds to carry them on."

"The King appears to have plenty. I drove out to Haga with him a week since, to see the foundations of the new palace. It is as if the Sphinx had laid them—I never saw such vast masses of stone. One of the suite asked him when it was likely to be finished. He said that, if he reached the average age of humanity, he hoped to dwell in it a few years before he died "

"Before he died?" said Adolf, rubbing his hands together slowly.

Pontus glanced up at Horn, but he carried on the talk at once, without any sign.

"These perpetual journeys to France also! Persons of that rank do not travel for nothing. There is great irritation. Even the peasants have begun to see at length that it is not all beer and skittles—or brandy, rather. Do you know what the national debt amounts to now? Forty-three million riksdalers!"

"Indeed? I suppose that is why it is rumoured that we are to have another Diet almost immediately. The taxes are not likely to go down at that rate."

"I should think not. There is a deficit of nine hundred thousand. Frietzsky is at the end of his resources."

"And yet they declare that another war is imminent! Gyllenstierne was in the King's private room, the other day; the table was covered with maps of Norway. He made some allusion to it, but the King turned the whole thing into a jest and changed the conversation."

"Norway! What will he take in hand next? We all know that he had designs upon Poland. The Gothic Crowns and Lions will never rest till they have quartered the White Eagle and the Horseman of Lithuania among them. But Norway too! And when he is all but embarked upon a war with France!"

"France?" said Ribbing dreamily. "Yes. He must fight for the Queen. We must all fight for the Queen."

"He will not find it so easy as he imagines. They are beginning to find him out in the army. The men have been paid in notes the value of which is depreciated, and they are very angry. The sailors are furious. There would have been a mutiny at Carlscrona, but that Toll went down at once and put a stop to it."

"Pechlin thinks we should strike while the iron is hot. It is certain that the Beggars have never been so popular. They are numbered by hundreds now. It used to be a distinction to belong to them ; nowadays it is quite the reverse."

Pontus smiled politely, as if the jest did not amuse him. Adolf still sat silent ; whether he even heard what the other two said, they could not tell.

"The new Constitution is almost ready," pursued Clas. "Engeström has been at work, night and day, drafting it. You are about the Court, Pontus. You have many opportunities which are denied to us poor devils. What do you think of the present disposition of the King?" He was feeling his way. He looked hard at his neighbour, as he spoke, but the words seemed to produce no effect upon Ribbing.

"He is very much altered," said Liljehorn. "I sometimes think it is not the same man. I have not once heard him laugh since my return."

"Wallqvist is always with him, is he not?"

"Wallqvist—and Nordin. He might almost as well be in a monastery."

"That is a change indeed. It looks well for us. Do you think he sees the error of his ways? Do you think it possible that he might be induced to grant the new Constitution without a show of force?"

Liljehorn shook his head.

"No. In that respect he is unalterable. He will go no man's way but his own. If the new Constitution depends on his signing it peaceably, it will never be signed at all."

Clas gave a heavy sigh.

"Pechlin was right then, I suppose? We shall have to get possession of his person and compel him to grant it, or to resign in favour of the Crown Prince. Some attempt must be made, and that soon?"

"Yes," said a new voice, striking into the talk with a note of decision which it had lacked hitherto. Adolf had been too much absorbed in his own thoughts and the other two in their own conversation to heed the entrance of this fourth person.

"Captain Anckarström !" exclaimed Horn, concealing his intense annoyance under a show of welcome, while Pontus deferentially made room for his superior.

"Your servant told me you were at Hufvudstad. I knew that he was wrong."

"Stupid fellow!" cried Clas, flushing ; "how could he make such a mistake ?"

"Mistakes are common enough. I was not mistaken, however, in the conviction that I should find Count Ribbing here. I am come, in the first place, to congratulate our new brother."

As though compelled by some magnetic influence, Adolf, who had taken no notice of him hitherto, raised his head slowly and looked up at Anckarström. The bright light that had shone in his eyes the whole time went suddenly out, and they became dull and stonelike. Once more he was in that room full of the shadows of twisted horns and antlers ; once more the ruddy glow of the fire fell on the little branch of coral. There it was, hanging still on its owner's watch-chain. He rose—stood for a moment as though uncertain what to do—and then bowed low.

Anckarström, who had not taken his eyes off him, returned the salute, to the astonishment of Clas, and even more of Pontus, who had never seen him bow in his life before.

"Will you not be seated ?" said Clas.

Adolf sank back again into his chair. Anckarström, who was leaning against the table, his legs crossed, declined, with a careless gesture.

"We must proceed to business," said he. "We cannot afford to waste such an opportunity as this. You were speaking of the attempt on the King."

"Pechlin is of opinion that it should be made early in January." Clas spoke unwillingly and yet hastily, as if some outside force were constraining him to utter the word.

"It is too early," muttered Pontus, with a shake of the head. "Nothing will succeed before March. March is the King's fatal month. I have heard him say so."

Clas Horn raised his eyebrows.

" He used not to say that kind of thing when I was at
Court. If he said it, I should think that a guarantee
that he did not mean it."

"Why January rather than December?" inquired
Anckarström.

"Because," said Horn, still reluctantly, "he will be
at the château de Haga then, for the festivities at the
New Year. It would be easy to surprise him there.
I know every twist and turn of the ground as well
as if it were my own garden."

"I will be at the south gate, at half-past twelve at
night, on the 3rd January," said Anckarström. "I
cannot risk being seen by daylight; if you are well
acquainted with the ground, that does not matter.
We will reconnoitre; we will see whether anything can
be done."

" Is there any other scheme afoot?" asked Pontus.
"Would it not be well to have more than one string to
our bow? Do you hear anything of this new fancy to
buy up the whole town of Gefle?"

"What can you mean?" said Clas, with some
irritation. "The King has no interest in Gefle that
ever I heard."

" It is his own borough, you know. He has taken
several houses there of late, and he is in treaty for
more. Some acquaintances of mine, who were going
there for the winter, are very indignant. They had
hired apartments, and the lease was cancelled to please
the King. Others have been put to inconvenience in
the same way."

"Was any explanation given? It seems quite
insane."

"Nothing has been vouchsafed officially; but old
Pechlin thinks that he means to hold the Diet there
instead of at Stockholm. If so, the burgesses will be
furious; that is another point in our favour."

"Upon my word, it sounds likely," said Clas, in
great excitement. "He would lodge himself in the
old castle of Gefle, I suppose. Would it be possible
to seize him there?"

"I do not know. We can count on the Blues;

Silfverhielm will not be able to restrain them. But someone told me privately that Armfelt is coming."

"He means to use the soldiers in good earnest this time then, depend upon it."

"If he does, nothing further can save the country. Arbitrary laws—the press gagged—secret police—open force—and a despotic monarchy. To be sure, we have these things already. If ever strong measures were needed, we need them now."

"It will be no good till you get rid of Gustav III.," said the harsh voice of Anckarström.

Adolf shrugged his shoulders.

"God knows when that will be," he said.

"I would do it, *if I only had the chance*," said Anckarström.

"Do it? Do what?" cried Horn.

Adolf burst into a fit of contemptuous laughter, in which Horn joined shrilly, Pontus with the ease of an accomplished actor. The instruments all round the wall, jarred by the noise, gave back a wiry echo. It was growing too dark for any one of the four to see the faces of his fellows.

"I mean what I say, gentlemen," said Anckarström, rising to his full height. "You do not doubt it?"

He left the room abruptly.

Adolf, still laughing, went out after him.

"What do you think of Captain Anckarström's intentions now?" said Pontus, as soon as the door had closed.

"He cannot be allowed to speak in that way. We must put a stop to it. Do you know where Pechlin is?"

"Pechlin will drive him on rather than hold him back," said Liljehorn. "Anckarström is a terrible man. Pechlin is not a man, but a devil."

CHAPTER XLVIII

THE KING AT THE WINDOW

THE beautiful château de Haga lay, clear and still, in bright moonlight.

The year was still young, and a large party had assembled there, to do it honour ; but they were all gone now, some in coaches, some in sledges, some on foot, back to Stockholm. The household had retired to rest ; the windows were darkened.

Now and then gusts of wind passed with a sighing sound through the branches of the snow-laden trees, and shook something of their burden in thick flakes to the earth,—lowered a white mound here and raised one there,—but they fell again almost immediately, and left the night to her sombre silence.

Of the two men who were cautiously threading their way through the labyrinth of paths leading from the park which bounded the King's property to the castle, one was at home in the darkness and one a stranger to it. One dreaded the fall of his own footsteps, and breathed as quietly as if he feared the roots of the trees under the ground would hear him—the powers of night seeming to know and to resent his want of confidence, so that, however cautiously he moved, something crackled or broke. One took no precautions whatever, but forced his way through the brushwood boldly and quietly, making no noise because he was afraid of making none. The younger man spoke often, in a nervous whisper, beginning sentences that had no end. The elder never spoke at all ; but he was telling his companion eloquently with every step and every gesture a thing against the knowledge of which his whole disposition struggled in dumb revolt.

It was one of those hours, Clas Horn imagined, flying with desperate haste to fancy, as a relief from thought, when, to her human children, Nature appears to will her own loneliness—to resent their intrusion. She will not drown the little stir of their presence in one of the innumerable harmonies at her command ; her trees are still and she withholds her storm ; she will not veil them with her leaves, nor let her darkness cover them. She is no mother, but an outraged queen who may not retaliate on the invaders of her privacy— with cold indifference looking on while they betray themselves.

The other man was following, not leading, for Clas Horn knew the way and he did not ; but it was he who had the aspect of the leader. From time to time, when they reached a clearing where two or more paths met, Clas turned and silently pointed out some landmark by which the right course might be determined. Anckar- ström nodded, and they went on. In the days when Clas belonged to the Court, he had been wont to wander hither and thither at will, alone, or with some charming companion in the sweet sunshine, while the birds sang gaily and the water splashed and leapt and fell in rainbow spray from the fountains. If Anckar- ström had fallen cold and stiff at his feet that moment, he knew that he would have cried out for joy. He was beginning to own the dreadful ascendency exercised by this man over all who came near him. For the living light of day there was the wan light of the moon, quiet and terrible, like the smile on the face of a woman who has ceased to breathe. The birds had flown, the trees were shrouded skeletons, the fountains ice. Where of old sprang the green grass the snow lay heavily. The statues of nymphs and fauns, fantastically draped in white, were cold, unmoving ghosts—the empty belve- deres and summer-houses ruins without the grace of a ruin. The windows, that he had never seen before but they flashed and gleamed, were like blind eyes now, sunk and rayless. The hand of death was on it all; the whole garden was dead, the white palace dead.

And the master?

Was there no way of escape? Could he not flee—he, the pursuer? He did not know, he did not understand to what he had pledged himself. And all the while a loud voice, making no sound, cried in his heart that he knew it well.

"When you told Pontus that you had persuaded Anckarström to give up all thoughts of violence, you hoped that the belief of another might win you to believe yourself," it said. "You cannot go back now. There is no escape."

And another voice whispered ever more and more faintly, "There is time yet. Nothing has happened yet. You may flee yet."

"The great sycamore, there in that clump of bushes, will shelter us, if we can reach it. Once we are there, I will show you a little door leading to the King's apartments. We could seize him and hurry him off through the shrubbery, by the way we have come. No one else knows it. Two men would be enough. Another night"—

Anckarström stopped, looked hard at Clas, and spoke for the first time.

"I do not intend to carry off the King," he said; "I mean to kill him. If you wish to save his life, take mine. You have only to raise your voice and call. The servants would hear you at once; they sleep lightly that sleep within the walls of a palace. Come; have the courage of your opinions. Shout!"

"I will not be a party to the murder of any man," said Clas, trembling in every limb. "I tell you I dare not. It is not safe to cross the lawn. The moon is bright; if anyone looked from the windows, we should be seen at once. We will return another night. Come away!"

For all answer, Anckarström strode out into the open. His long shadow looked no darker than he. Clas hesitated, but followed a moment after. They had just concealed themselves in the thicket when a bar fell, a shutter was pushed back, and a light flashed in one of the windows on the ground floor.

Clas with difficulty repressed a cry. Even Anckarström started.

The next moment his hand stole to the pocket of his coat. This time Clas heard the pistol cocked, with a nightmare sensation of trying to scream and finding himself voiceless.

It was the King himself, wrapped in a long fur gown. He put his hand up to his head, as if he would remove some heavy weight upon it, and stood quite still, gazing out mournfully at the fallen snow. There was something stately and sad beyond all words in his attitude, as he stood there alone, showing the weariness, that he let no one see, to the night. Was this the despot before whom free men trembled—the tyrant dispensing life and death at his capricious pleasure? Was it indeed this tired and lonely man, outworn with watching?

A passion of remorse and pity made Clas shake like a leaf.

The King moved languidly to his writing-desk and sat down. Suddenly his head fell forward upon his chest—his eyes closed. He was sitting full in the moonlight. Was it that, nothing but that, which made him look deadly pale? Was it possible that one man could kill another by the sheer hatred of his eyes? There had not been a sound. Horn glanced in terror at his companion. Anckarström remained motionless, still holding the pistol.

"The hand of Fate!" he said.

"Of God!" said Clas.

He took off his hat and remained bareheaded in the biting air. He scarcely knew what he was doing or saying.

There was a slight rustle in the bushes. It might have been only the wind. He did not stay to think.

"Fly! Fly!" he whispered.

Slowly, and without the least change of countenance, Anckarström turned the pistol against himself, touching with his other hand the little fork of coral that hung on his watch-chain. The instinct of self-preservation—it was nothing more unselfish—made Horn seize his wrist. The touch awakened him; he let his arm drop at his side.

Without hesitating a moment, Clas darted across the lawn. Anckarström followed quickly and quietly, without so much as another look at the window.

To Clas, as they fought and trampled their way back again, the garden was as the garden of Eden. Birds sang among the desolate branches. Flowers of snow hung from them in great clusters. The moon was a white swan, sailing across the blue lake of heaven.

They walked back to Stockholm in silence. Clas was about to bid his companion good-night, when Anckarström said in a low tone, as if he feared to be heard—

"You have forgotten. We must go first to Ribbing."

"I do not know where he lives."

"I know."

To Horn's surprise, he found that his companion was taking him down a street that he had much frequented two years ago. He said nothing, however, till they stopped in front of a carved door. Then he exclaimed—

"Carl de Geer's house!"

"It was. It is Ribbing's now."

Adolf seemed to have been expecting them, for he opened the door himself when they knocked, and led the way, after the briefest possible greeting, up the dark, uncarpeted stone staircase straight into the boudoir that Tala had been wont to call hers. Here also the walls were bare, the floor uncovered. All the disorder and the charm was gone. The curtains had been pulled down. The chairs stood in a rigid row as if no one ever moved or disturbed them now. The long, thin harpsichord had vanished. The only relic left was a little blue vase that stood forlorn upon the mantelpiece. The fire had gone out, and the chill stuffiness of the atmosphere wrapped them round like a heavy covering without warmth.

A large table in the centre of the room was strewn with pieces of paper, on which Adolf had been drawing, or trying to draw, over and over again, something that looked like a sharp-pointed dagger. Sometimes the hilt was of one shape, sometimes of another, and the blade was now long and fluted, now short and curved—never quite straight. He sat down at once, without any word of invitation to his guests, and began to draw again. Clas, remembering his courtly manners of old, wondered.

"The King is dead," said Anckarström, as he laid down his pistol.

Adolf took it up and looked at it curiously.

"If the King be dead why is this loaded still?" he said.

Clas Horn described in a few words what had happened.

"If you did not kill him," Adolf said, looking at Anckarström, "he is not dead. It was an attack of faintness. I have seen him like that before. It does not last five minutes."

Anckarström reeled and leant against the wall to support himself.

"Then I have failed," he said.

"I thought you would."

"I was as close to him as I am to you now."

"The time has not come," said Adolf, as he carefully shaded the under side of his dagger.

"I thought the time was come," said Anckarström in a voice of agony. "If it has come—and passed—I am undone."

"It has not come," said Adolf. "It will not come till March. You are trying to do my work. He will fall by my hand, by no other."

The young man spoke in a quiet, matter-of-fact way. Clas wondered if he had heard aright.

"It is my work," said Anckarström fiercely. "No one has a right to take it from me. If fate appointed you to share in it, that is another thing.

That I can well believe. It was for that I preserved you."

"You tell me that you could have done this deed to-night," said Adolf. "You were close, close to the King—as close as you are to me now. Yet you did not."

Anckarström sat silent, his brow contracted. At last he said—

"Are you willing to submit to the arbitrament of the lot?"

"Yes," said Adolf, with a shrug of the shoulders.

"The lot will fall to me," said Anckarström.

He took up one of the pieces of paper that were lying about, tore it into three strips of equal size, and wrote a name on each in his small, close hand. Then he signed to Clas to bring him the vase that stood on the mantelpiece, dropped them into it one by one, and shook them together.

"Draw!" said he, giving it back to Clas.

Clas knew the name which would be written on his slip before he drew it out, and read aloud tremblingly, *Jakob Johan Anckarström.*

"Go where you will!" said Adolf, "I stay. While I remain in Stockholm, the King is safe everywhere else. When you have failed come back. You will find me here in the month of March."

Anckarström rose and went out without a word.

When he had gone it seemed as if the room grew colder still. That man of ice had yet some fire in him apparently; there was not left one spark in Ribbing. Clas would have gone too, but he felt as if his feet were frozen to the bare boards. A stupor of inaction, the result, it might be, of excitement beforehand, held him dully fixed in the same position. Adolf went on drawing. Clas was not even sure whether he knew that he was not alone. He coughed to attract attention, but Adolf took no notice. At last, he said with a shiver—

"It is as cold here now as it was in the streets of Gothenburg that night."

Adolf started, and dropped his pencil.

"When?" he said; "I forget."

CHAPTER XLIX

THE SCARLET COAT

ADOLF was, at this time, completely possessed by one idea.

Life was no longer of value to him ; and by a strange turn of the wheel, the deprivation of all that made life precious had deprived death also of interest ; he ceased to contemplate it. In the days of his happiness the thought had been with him constantly, now as a shapeless horror, now bright with glory. In these days it was no more beautiful nor terrible ; it had become dull. Only one reflection gave his blunted feelings an edge. He had—for a single moment—tasted sweetness, when he saw Essen fall by his hand.

He ate little, and sleep was almost impossible. Night after night he lay awake, empty of all power of connected thinking. He was unable to read ; the words arranged themselves in spiral columns instead of running straight across the page. The slightest sound excited him to a frenzy of irritation. He saw but few people, for he did not visit any of his former friends, and those who presented themselves were denied admittance, with one exception—Pontus Liljehorn —to whom he had an indefinite notion that he owed something. Clas kept away ; so did Anckarström and the rest. Pontus came often enough, and brought him news of the outer world, which, for the most part, he cared little to hear.

Nearly a fortnight had slipped by in this manner, when Pontus said one day—

" The Court is buzzing with rumours about this Diet

at Gefle. They say the King has been to Noorna
again ; he always consults her before the meeting of
Parliament. The old witch told him to beware of a
man in a red coat. Did you ever hear anything more
absurd ? Red coats are as much out of fashion now as
lilac. I suppose there is not a man in Stockholm who
wears such a thing ? "

" Is there not ? " said Adolf carelessly.

Yet this one phrase he heard, though all the rest
passed by him like wind ; and when Pontus was gone,
he donned his hat and cloak and went to look for the
shop of a costumier, whom he had known well enough
in old days, when acting was all the rage at Court.
Here he asked to be provided with the uniform of an
English officer.

" For the approaching masquerade, if we may
venture to suggest ? " inquired the vendor. "We
have what will just suit your Excellency. The uniform
is quite new—has not been worn at all, in fact."

Adolf ordered it to be taken home immediately,
hastened back, put on the brilliant scarlet coat, and
went and stood in the bright sunlight near the gate of
the palace.

He could not have told what made him do this
childish thing.

The sunshine and the free air were pleasant after his
long sojourn within doors. It was with an old man's
enjoyment of a holiday that he loitered there hour after
hour, sometimes walking briskly up and down to keep
himself warm, sometimes standing still, in spite of the
cold, to watch the traffic. A wheel that was always
going in his brain had stopped for the moment. He
knew that it would begin again directly he entered the
empty house in which he lived, and he put off the
moment as long as possible. Once, as he was tramping
up and down, he stopped—his eye caught by the word
Masquerade placarded in an advertisement on the doors
of the Opera House, which was but a few minutes' walk
from the palace. A masquerade ? Where had he
heard of that before ? Ah yes ! It was the costumier,
who thought that he ordered his scarlet coat in order

to appear at it. A masquerade was announced for the 21st January. Nothing was said about February; the Court would be absent at Gefle during that month; but lower down came the advertisement of a second masquerade on the 2nd March. Adolf noted that. But the effort to read had been too much. All the images of his memory were lost once more in a vague blur. He had almost forgotten why he came thither— if indeed he ever had any clear conception of his purpose —when the great gates were thrown open, to admit the King on his return from an excursion to the château de Haga, and Pontus, at the head of a detachment of the Guards in blue and silver, rode swiftly past. He was followed by the royal carriage, which was open as usual. Adolf came forward, standing upon the edge of the kerbstone. He was sure that the King saw him; a glance of recognition flitted across his face, but he made no sign as he bent over to the other side of the carriage to speak to Essen, who was sitting opposite.

Essen turned his head and looked.

For an instant the fire of hate flamed up in Adolf, as though revenge had never, even for a second, extinguished it.

The carriage entered the great gates, and another detachment of the Guards closed in behind it.

Adolf walked slowly homewards. A black door had shut again on the sunshine.

Some two hours later a parcel was brought, addressed to him in a hand that he did not know. It proved to contain a coat of worn purple velvet, with soiled lace ruffles. It was rubbed and spotted in many places; here and there almost in holes. There was a note pinned to the tail of it. As Adolf held it up to the light, that he might read this, a scrap of paper fell to the ground from one of the pockets.

The note ran thus—

Count Ribbing, perhaps, is not aware that the fashions have changed since he was last in Sweden. Red is no longer worn. He is advised to try a more sober hue, if he would find favour in the eyes of his King.

24

Adolf unpinned the note, wrote on the back these words—

Count Ribbing is much obliged to Count Essen. He has, however, old clothes enough of his own.

and fastened it on again.

Then he picked up the scrap of paper, meaning to put it back. What was his stupefaction, when he read in well-known writing his own name and the two words—

Come.—Tala.

It was as if a voice from the dead had reached him. He forgot Essen ; he forgot the King.

For a long while he sat there. The sounds in the street, that had annoyed him so of late, fell on his ear unheeded. At length someone in the opposite house threw up a window, and the shrill notes of a caged bird singing there roused him.

"In March," he said, with a little sigh. "Not before. She has waited long enough, but she must wait longer. In March."

And all at once a vision of spring passed before him—the grim trees dotted into leaf—the timid first flowers—the calling of rooks in the boughs of tall elms and oaks.

"I shall see it once more," he said to himself, "and then not again."

CHAPTER L

FOR some time after this Adolf resumed his former way of life.

A certain practical power had come back to him. He consented to see Pechlin, and listened, or seemed to listen to his proposals. Once or twice he went out with Anckarström. They were at the masquerade on the 2nd of March together. There was to have been one the following week, but this was postponed. The last of the season was announced for the 16th. He would go to that, he said to himself. Arrangements for it were much discussed among the conspirators. As to his own part, he was confident; he troubled himself little about that of others. He was still unable to sleep.

All this time, though he had kept Tala's note close to his heart, he had never ventured to look at it again. On the afternoon of the 15th, however, he permitted himself to do so. Once more, at sight of the letters that she had traced, feeling stirred within him. He saw strange visions. At last, with a loud cry, passion awoke.

He started from this trance, the length or the shortness of which he could not measure, hung the coat over his arm, and, still holding the little note clasped in his hand, set out for Essen's house. What had he been doing all this time? Had he been wasting golden moments? Was it too late? Surely not. Several of the city clocks struck as he went along. It was a singular mark of the disturbance of his mind that, though he heard them, he could never count the strokes right.

"Tell the Baroness Essen that an old friend wishes to speak to her," he said quietly to the servant who opened the door.

He was shown into a great drawing-room on the first floor. Tala was not there. A thick blue curtain hung at one end, dividing it from a smaller room beyond. He heard a light footstep moving there. In that one moment he was nearer madness than he had been yet. The curtain was drawn aside.

She flew to him like a bird—she flung her arms round him.

He felt no surprise—nothing but the delight of nearness. Neither spoke for a while. They stood there, holding each other.

"Tala, my own!" he whispered at last. "Look up. Let me see you."

"Will you promise to see me—not as I am now—but as I was three years ago!" she said, still keeping her face hidden.

"Yes, yes," he said impatiently. "Look at me. Let me see you."

She stood back a pace or two, with drooped eyelids.

"Your eyes," he said. "I want your eyes. Look at me."

She raised them.

"You will never remember me now!" she cried, turning away with a quick gesture of despair. "Why—why did you come?"

Adolf held out to her the scrap of paper in his hand. She made a movement as though to take it.

"No," he said quickly. "I keep that."

"Two years ago? Before my marriage."

"It is but a little while since I received it."

Her face changed.

"You never heard from me before?"

"Yes—once—when I was in Paris. You told me not to come—to send word that I could not come."

The colour fled from Tala's face. She stood quite silent, her hand to her breast, as if she were trying to breathe less heavily. Adolf saw her glance in the direction of the curtain. Thinking that she needed help, he sprang towards it.

"No, no," she cried, stretching out her arms as she fell back on a couch by the window. "Come, come! I may come to you now."

Adolf sat down opposite her, trembling in every limb. He dared not go nearer. There was one thing that he feared now more than her death. A sudden terror was between them. She waited, with hungry eyes, on the other side of it.

"Tell me!" she said. "How did you get this?"

"Tell me one thing first. Do you love your husband? If you do, do not ask."

"I ask you once again to tell me," she said.

"I am no longer a favourite at Court. A short time since, your husband saw me by the gates of the palace, dressed, as he thought, unbecomingly. When I returned home a parcel was brought me, containing an old coat of his, which he proposed that I should wear when next I came before the King. This note fell from the folds of it on to the floor. See!"

"I remember that purple colour," she said. "Where have I seen it before? The night the Dalecarlians were coming—yes, I remember—the night I wrote to you. He wore it then."

"Do you mean that he intercepted this note? For Heaven's sake, Tala, speak!"

"Yes," she said, a dangerous light in her eyes. The fierceness of them made Adolf shrink; he had never seen her look thus before. Her voice had lost its girlish, silvery ring—it was like her father's. "Let me look at the note—quick!"

The fire died away as fast as it had flashed out. The sound of tears, that cannot rise and come to the surface, made her voice soft again.

"You had the wrong note," she said. "I wrote two. I was beside myself. He watched me all the time. I was never out of the room except for one moment. He must have changed them. He must have kept this back."

Again that quick glance at the curtain.

"I had one note from you," said Adolf. "I sent the answer you desired."

"*I cannot come*," she said. "Ah yes! I remember."

"You thought it was the answer to this — you thought I had forsaken you?"

"Yes."

"Essen"—

"Hush, hush!" she interrupted. "I have wronged him enough. It is wicked to feel so—but I am glad that he has wronged me. I am glad, I say."

"Do you ask me to be glad also?"

She turned her head away.

"After all," he said bitterly, "if I had come, we should have been happy. No one has any right to be happy now. It is a crime that we are saved."

She made no reply.

"I should never have done my duty if you had married me."

Her lips moved; they seemed to form the word "Cruel!"

"No. It is your duty to live; it was mine to die."

"Yours is the easier then," she said, not looking up. "You think that now, Adolf, but you will not die. I thought that I should—and I am here. When I knew that you loved me, I had to live. I am glad that you came now. It is better for us to speak. I want you to know that somewhere or other—some time —not here, not now — you and I will keep house together yet." She began to speak quickly. "It is a long while to wait—as I do. I know. You must marry. If you have a child, think that I love it. I would love your wife too, but I cannot. Only do not forget that I told you to marry."

"You can say that?"

"Some day you will be glad that I did."

"Perhaps," said Adolf, "you will suggest that I should be your husband's friend?"

"You shall not be his enemy," she said. "When I thought that you had killed him— If you had, I could never have looked on you again. Dead people are strong. I would have disobeyed my father living; when he was dead, I could not."

"Will you keep faith with me when I am dead?" said Adolf. "I will not send your husband where alone, as you say, he could claim your obedience. So much I promise you."

"You are laughing. You think there is no hope. Why did you come?"

"Because I am dead. Are you afraid of ghosts?"

She looked at him, horror and rapture fighting in her eyes.

"It is not true?" she said. She laid her hand on his, and quickly drew it back again.

"Do you think that I should have dared to see you else? It is so true that in a week from to-day the hand that you have touched will be lying under the earth somewhere."

He opened his fingers in a fan, and watched them curiously, as though they moved of themselves. He seemed to have forgotten her.

"You mean to kill the King," she said, facing him full.

His cheek blanched.

"No word of yours told me. No word of yours could unsay it. Remember, I believe no denial."

He rose unsteadily.

She had reached the door before him—locked it—possessed herself of the key.

He turned towards the curtain.

"Adolf!" she called after him, "that door leads only to my bedroom. There is no way out."

Her voice was firm. She repressed a nervous desire to say the words twice over, and met his questioning eyes boldly. The habit of belief in her was too strong for him. He turned back

"Tala, you must let me go."

"Not yet," she said, her fingers clutching the key. "Promise me that you will not go to the masquerade to-morrow night."

"And what if I have promised that I will?"

"Adolf—you will not touch him?"

" I have told you already that he is safe from me."

" No, no ; not Essen—the King ! "

" Who talks of hurting the King ? "

" Why will you jest ? " she cried.   " Adolf—your word !   You will not touch the King ?   Give me your word—promise ! "

" Betray me if you will ! '' he said, shrugging his shoulders.

" I will—unless you promise."

He stood silent.

They heard the rasping voice of Essen on the stairs, asking whether the Baroness were at home.

Tala's white face grew whiter.   She put the key in the lock and turned it.   She glided across—pushed aside the curtain—signed to Adolf to follow her.

" If you will not promise, I let him come ; I let him find you here.   I will tell him all.   It was not true. The door of my room is open.   You can escape that way.   If you take one step forward before you promise, I call him."

The passionate entreaty of her eyes belied her threatening words.

Adolf had followed her as she bade him, but he still stood doggedly silent.

The drawing-room door opened.

" Is my wife in her room ? " said Essen.

Tala's whole attitude changed ; she shrank, as if in mortal terror.

" If you kill him, you kill me."

" I have no longer any power to harm you or to help you, Tala."

" You have, you have ! " she whispered, putting her hand before her eyes, while the colour rose like flame in her cheeks.   " I am not lost yet.   I am fighting hard.   But if you kill the King, you kill my honour. You ruin me, body and soul.   I will fight no more. Why should I keep myself for a murderer ? "

CHAPTER LI

"AT midnight."

"Why not earlier?"

"We should not be sure of him. He is going to the French Theatre to see *Les Folies Amoureuses.* Baron Essen is invited to sup with him afterwards at the Opera House."

"He must come. This is the last masquerade of the season."

It was Clas Horn who spoke, Pontus who questioned, writing busily the whole time, as he sat at the table in Horn's luxurious room, the mellow light of three great lamps clear and soft round him. He wrote only a few words on each piece of paper, as he took it from the quire on his right hand; no signature, no date, no address. His work seemed to be merely mechanical. He and Horn had been much together of late, and by this time they had almost forgotten their old enmity.

"I have no great confidence in these masquerades," he said. "Anckarström and Ribbing have been close at his heels twice before; nothing came of it."

"That was not their fault; the ball was too thinly attended. To-morrow there will be a great crowd. All the people who were disappointed when the entertainment was postponed last week will be there. Besides, old Pechlin has worked like Hercules. He has summoned every one of the Beggars now in Stockholm. They will be there to the tune of a hundred and fifty."

"Is he coming himself?"

"Not he! He is too well known. It would bring suspicion on all of us. But we are to dine at his house to-morrow, to hear the last details before we start. Armfelt will be at the ball too. The Second Life Guards are on duty that evening. Once we are safe he is to be arrested, and the Crown Prince proclaimed, with a regency. Engeström swears by his new Constitution."

"What are the Beggars to do at the masquerade, if there is no one to lead them?"

"Ribbing will lead them. He has undertaken to divide them into two bands. He is to head one—you the other. Directly the King appears in the grand saloon, you are to rush at each other from opposite sides, that he may be caught between you."

"Ribbing will have enough to do without that, I should think."

"Oh no! Did you not hear? It is Anckarström who is to fire."

Pontus laid down his pen.

"Ribbing was set to do it when last I saw him."

"He was set to do it until to-day. Pechlin told me an hour ago that he had resigned his claim to Anckarström—why, no one knows. I thought you must have heard."

"How should I? I have been writing here since two o'clock. Pechlin knew nothing of it this morning. Have you seen Ribbing himself?"

"I saw him coming out of Essen's house. He was in one of his black moods. I dared not speak to him. Still, à vrai dire, I am glad it is not he."

"And I am sorry."

"Why?"

"Because," said Pontus, writing away more busily than ever and speaking hardly above a whisper, "because, Clas, Ribbing might have missed fire."

"No, no," said Clas eagerly, seizing his hand. "Anckarström may miss—Ribbing could not. I was standing by when Anckarström was as close to him as you are to me; but Anckarström could not touch him. If it is not Ribbing who fires, he is safe. Remember Noorna's prophecy!"

"I believe in the prophecy of deeds, not of words,"
said Pontus shortly. "Every one of Anckarström's
deeds is a prophecy; that is the sort of prediction that
comes true."

He spoke with an intensity of significance that
was not lost upon Clas, but the latter shook his
head.

"I have seen what I have seen," he said. "Anckarström has no power. Besides—even if you do not
believe Noorna—he has not the same motive. Ribbing
worshipped the Baroness Essen; she was lost to him
through the King."

"Maybe. But have you never seen the bit of coral
that Anckarström wears on his watch-chain?"

"I have noticed it often. What a strange fellow
you are, Pontus! You spring from one subject to
another. What of that? I never saw one like it
except in Italy."

"It comes from Italy. The famous *danseuse*, Carlotta
Bassi, gave it to him nine years ago, when he was one
of the Blues. He wanted to marry her. The King
could not permit one of his officers to make such a
mésalliance; Anckarström would take no denial. The
lady was seized at night, as she was coming home from
the opera, and sent back to the coral country whence
she came. So runs the story at least."

"Do you believe it?"

Pontus shrugged his shoulders.

"I have sometimes thought that it might be true.
I tell you only to show that there are those who hold
Anckarström as well entitled to revenge as Ribbing—
better, indeed; for you have only to look at Ribbing
to see that there are many women in the world for him,
whereas there could be only one for Anckarström. Still,
if you ask me in sober earnest, I do not believe the
tale. Let him believe it that will! I think that
Anckarström is as much a destructive force of nature as
a thunder-bolt or a flash of lightning. He has no
personal responsibility. Why, the King remitted a
sentence against him for seditious speaking only the
other day! Gratitude weighs heavy with some people.

An ordinary man would have paused. Did he hesitate
for one moment? Not he! It made no difference."

"He was quite right," said Clas hurriedly. "It is
not for private reasons that we do this. We have no
business to consider ourselves when our country is
perishing."

"Yet," said Pontus, "you were a Royalist until he
put your father in prison; Ribbing was a Royalist until
Fröken de Geer married; I was a Royalist until another
was preferred before me."

"Our eyes were opened in different ways; but he
is, nevertheless, a bad King. He must go."

Pontus read out the last words that he had been
writing.

A minuit il ne sera plus. Arrangez-vous sur cela.

"This is the fiftieth time that I have written those
words," he said; "yet I cannot believe them."

"We shall capture; we shall not kill—I also am
certain of that," said Clas uneasily. "I am so sure,
that I have undertaken to give the signal."

"What signal?"

"Anckarström is afraid of himself! He declared
that he should not know the King in a domino. I am
to clap him on the shoulder and cry, *Bonjour, beau
masque!* Then we shall see what we shall see—it will
not be the death of the King, Pontus!"

"What? Did Anckarström really demand a signal?"

"He did indeed."

"Upon my word, I begin to believe you. Did you
say that you saw Ribbing leave Baron Essen's house?"

"Yes."

"That seems strange. Well, I must wish you
good - night. I have to leave these letters at
Pechlin's door, that they may all be posted to our
allies in the provinces at the same time to-morrow
morning."

"I have another batch to write," said Clas, taking
his place. "Farewell till to-morrow. A white mask
and a black domino—you know the order?"

Pontus walked quickly home.

"There is something wrong," said he to himself.

" Ribbing has begun to hedge. The fair Baroness is, no doubt, at the bottom of this."

After some reflection, he wrote another and a much longer letter on a piece of paper which he carefully soiled first among the ashes in the grate. He was equally careful to write very ill; no one would have recognised the hand.

He slept with this letter under his pillow, went about with it close to his heart all the next day, and took it about ten o'clock at night to a restaurant near the Opera House, where he was in the habit of supping.

A baker's boy had just brought in a consignment of hot rolls, and was resting his tray on the little table at which Pontus usually sat.

"You do not generally bake so late at night?" said Pontus to this youthful person.

" No, sir, but His Majesty the King—God bless him! —sups to-night at the Opera House, and he must have fresh rolls. I am to help carry in the dishes, as far as the bottom of the grand staircase."

" Hark ye, a word in your ear!" said Pontus. "Can you get speech of one of the King's pages? If you can, your fortune is made. Give him this letter. Tell him to present it to His Majesty at once! Say *it concerns His Majesty's life*. Be secret. Do you understand?"

Two gold pieces seemed to make it quite easy for the baker's boy to understand; he had no difficulty whatever.

CHAPTER LII

THE MASQUERADE

THE King had spent a pleasant day, that sixteenth of March.

All the morning he was out in the park at the château de Haga, inspecting the foundations of the new palace. The sight of visible bricks and mortar gave him delightful assurance that his castles were not all in the air. Afterwards he drove in his sledge to the pretty little village of Brunswick, where a large sledging party was assembled. Many of his personal friends were there, and nearly all the members of the Opposition ; for once they were rivals, not enemies, in the races they ran. Gustav watched them pass by the park in long procession, and followed them to see the sport ; the air rang with their laughter. He had looked grave and worn since the beginning of the year, but it gratified his dramatic nature to observe that a common amusement drew together those whom the most serious interests of their country could not unite ; and for the moment he threw aside anxiety and was as gay as the gayest.

George Löwenhjelm, a sentimental, lover-like young equerry, something of a favourite with his master, who was in attendance that day, wearied of the endless jests and the monotonous applause that always greeted them ; but the King knew no fatigue. They returned to the château for dinner, and immediately afterwards drove in to Stockholm, to the French Theatre, to be present at a performance of Regnard's *Folies Amoureuses*. It was a good lesson for Löwenhjelm, said the King, for Löwenhjelm was deeply enamoured of one of the

actresses, who had promised to meet him later on at
the masquerade in the Opera House.

Thither they went accordingly, as soon as the play
was ended, and found the chief equerry, Baron Essen,
waiting for them in the little room reserved for the
King when he chose to take supper there.

They were still at table, when one of the pages
entered with more haste than usual, bringing a letter.
Löwenhjelm politely turned his head the other way,
that he might not seem to watch as his master opened
it. He noticed that the boy looked pale, and, seeing
that the King was now quite absorbed, he peeped
over his shoulder. The missive was written in pencil,
in a large round hand, and bore no signature. The
King read it through twice, with some attention—
smiled—put it in his pocket. He said nothing, and
Löwenhjelm dismissed the matter from his mind.
The charming actress of the *Folies Amoureuses* must have
finished her supper by this time. She was probably
waiting for him below stairs.

"Shall we put on our masks now?" he cried,
springing up from the table.

The King laughed good-humouredly.

"Run away to your little sweetheart!" he said.
"You will find her at the foot of the steps, I make
no doubt. Baron Essen and I are not in such a
hurry."

Löwenhjelm hurriedly donned his mask and his blue
domino, and departed.

"Now that we are alone, read that!" said the King.

The letter had been written in bad French—apparently
by some very illiterate person, for almost every word
was spelt wrong. The writer stated that, if the un-
lawful and violent measures sanctioned by the recent
Diet of Gefle had been actually resorted to, he for one
should not have hesitated for a moment to take up
arms against the King and his mercenaries, though he
detested crime and had no wish to charge his conscience with regicide. He desired to warn His Majesty
that, unless he changed his present mode of government, some terrible calamity would follow. He

adjured him by everything that he held most sacred not to appear at the masquerade that night.

Essen gave the letter back, and his expression was grave.

"Do not go, sire!" he said.

Gustav stood leaning with one hand on the table. Even the practised dissembler who was now playing the part of his friend thought, as he looked at him, how little the King needed a mask. It was impossible to divine what he was thinking of.

"Do not go, sire!" he said very earnestly. "Ribbing is about again. There may be some plot."

Always that face—always that name!

"I wish I knew whether or no he were at the ball," said Gustav.

"He is here," said Essen, with great eagerness. "I trust, sire, that you will not expose yourself. Ribbing is here."

"How do you know? You cannot tell. Masquerades are republics; one mask is just like another. How was he dressed?"

Essen hesitated.

"You see," said Gustav, rather impatiently, "you do not know."

"I do know, sire. Count Ribbing recognised me as I was entering the Opera House. He lifted his mask, and bowed. It was a white mask."

"Are you sure that you saw him?"

"As sure as I am that I see you here before me. Sire, do not go!"

"If he had not been here, I would perhaps have returned home," said the King. "If he is here, I shall go. I desire to speak to that young man."

Essen, who had played the trump card in his hand, was taken aback.

"May I entreat you, sire, to reconsider."

"Enough! I am not such a fool as you seem to think," said the King. "Where are the dominos?"

"If you are resolved to go, sire," urged Essen, with still greater insistency than before, "will you at least put on the coat of mail that "—

The King burst into a fit of laughter.

"Your nerves are not what they were, my dear Baron. Married life does not agree with you. You will have to consult my physician. Here is my coat of mail; what do you think of it?" And he threw over his shoulders a cloak of light venetian silk.

"I think," said Essen, "that the decorations on your Majesty's breast can be seen very plainly."

"Much as the chin on His Majesty's face can be seen very plainly, eh?" said the King, choosing from amongst a heap a small half-mask that barely covered his eyes and the bridge of his nose. "Where is my three-cornered hat? There! Now we are ready. Italian noble, *tout complet*. If it's a stabbing affair, the costume is perfect. Give me your arm! We will go first to my box."

"Not there; I implore your Majesty!" said Essen, now seriously alarmed. "If you have made up your mind to appear, let us go downstairs and mingle with the crowd. Standing up in the box, your Majesty is an easy mark for any madman that may chance to be in the house."

The King shrugged his shoulders, as though disdaining to reply, and pushed open the door of the box, which communicated with the room in which they had supped.

He stood in front, quite motionless, Essen beside him. From the position in which he was placed, he commanded the whole of the grand saloon. A group of men in black dominos came surging through a door at the opposite side just as he stepped forward. Was it mere imagination on his part that they raised their heads simultaneously and looked at him, seeming to whisper together? He thought it was, for in an instant they had all dispersed. Faintly, behind the loud strains of the orchestra, he heard the bells of every church in Stockholm striking three-quarters after midnight.

"Come away now, sire!" said Essen. "You have shown yourself. That is enough. Come out!"

But Gustav did not offer to move; he still stood gazing down intently upon the throng. It seemed

25

as though he were searching for somebody amongst
the crowd—for some one face among the undis-
tinguished and indistinguishable thousands.   He
looked to find the one face that he feared.   If it
had not been there, he would have yielded to Essen's
entreaties and gone home, he said to himself that
night.   It was quite true that there was matter of
suspicion in this warning.   But to go home because
the voice of fear bade him—impossible!   Even if he
had wished to do so, the fact that Essen knew that
face and would have traded upon his fear of it kept
him chained to the Opera House.   No!   Not that
night.   Not till the last dancer had gone.

It was a strange conflict that he waged with himself,
as he stood there for full a quarter of an hour.   The
rigid calm of his outward demeanour gave not a token
of it.   Adolf, from the far corner where he had
stationed himself, looked up and felt a sudden glow of
admiration.   The King's attitude was perfect in dignity.

" He cannot look grander when he is dead," muttered
Clas Horn.   " He does not know fear."

" No," said Adolf, "he does not know fear," and
turned away, unable to bear the sight.

" How many white masks there are !" said Gustav.
" It is a dance of ghosts."

The voice within him was crying ever more and more
loudly, "Go!"   It drowned the music.

" I will not stir from this box till I hear the clock
strike again," he said to himself firmly.

If once he could see that face—if it once became
visible, tangible, human, he should fear it no more.
His bright glance hovered over the vast assembly, and
rested here and there, and flashed to and fro, under the
lights, over them, everywhere, and never saw the eyes
fixed upon his.   The dancing had begun now in good
earnest.   The centre of the grand saloon was a broken
rainbow of gliding, eddying, whirling masqueraders,
the tints of their dresses blended into one complex
harmony.

" It is growing late, sire," said Essen, consulting his
watch.   " One o'clock.   Is not your Majesty tired ? "

The King did not answer directly. Was it the far sound of the clock for which he waited?

"They have lost a good chance of shooting me," he said, as he turned round. "Come, let us go down! How gay it is! Well—this is the last time, and they are right to make the most of their opportunities. Let us see whether they will dare to kill me!"

Still leaning on Essen's arm, he made his way out. They found Löwenhjelm sitting, as he had predicted, in a sheltered corner formed by the winding of the stairs, his arm round the waist of a slender pink domino. Two figures, wearing the prevalent white mask, with ordinary cloaks of black, followed them. They stopped, when the King stopped a second in passing and bent down to murmur in the ear of the pink domino—

"The pretty mask should be very gracious to her cavalier there, for he was quite in a hurry just now to run away from me to her!"

When he moved on they moved on also, and when he disappeared into the green-room with Essen, intending to speak to some of the actors who were gathered there, they waited among the side-scenes just outside.

Neither Essen nor the King noticed them.

Again they fell in close behind, when he opened the door and came forth.

A murmur of *There is the King!* went round the theatre.

Gustav heard it.

He had been on the point of retreating. It was the hardest battle that he had ever fought, to stay in this place; but the sound of applause delighted him like the flashing and roaring of the great guns at Svenskund. For the moment he had no fear. The fight was over— the triumph about to begin.

There is the King!

Often as he had heard it, he seemed to hear it that night for the first time.

"*En avant! Marche!*" he said to himself, and took a step forward, walking with his head high, his hand on the hilt of his sword.

In an instant the crowd thickened and darkened

round him ; in whatever direction he looked, he could see nothing but black dominos — white, ghost-like masks. They seemed to be swarming, raging, rushing together from opposite sides. He could not get through them ; he was half stifled for want of breath.

"*Bonjour, beau masque,*" said a loud voice in his ear, and someone tapped him lightly on the shoulder.

There was a flash and a report.

Still the King did not fall.

"Drop it!" whispered Adolf; and to himself his whisper sounded like a shriek. "Drop it!"

For Anckarström still stood amazed, holding the pistol.

The King had taken off his mask ; he was deadly pale.

"The true face at last!" Adolf found himself saying. Suddenly he saw the figure reel and fall back into Essen's arms. By a supreme effort of will the King fought back the faintness that was creeping over his senses.

"I am wounded. Arrest the man. Do not hurt him."

He put his hand to his side, his brow contracting with agony. The dancers had noticed nothing. The orchestra was still playing merrily. Anckarström's pistol was wrapped in wool, so that the sound could not penetrate far.

At that moment Löwenhjelm rushed in. He had heard a muffled report where he was sitting close by under the stairs.

"What has happened?" he cried.

"Some villain has shot the King!" exclaimed Essen. "Help me to get him out!"

The crowd was denser than before. Without a word, Löwenhjelm drew his sword and drove them before him as if they had been sheep. One of the Guards, following his example, urged them back in the same manner. Essen—a clear space round him now—half dragged, half lifted his master to the door.

Adolf, the only one who had not retired before the Guardsman's sword, stood leaning against a pillar, breathing deep with excitement. He could have wept like a child ; he was on the alert, with all the practical sense of a woman, not to be captured, not to let Anckarström be captured. They must be taken in the end—that he knew—but not yet.

Above the din he heard two voices, one loud and clear, one wild, half hysterical.

"Close the doors !" exclaimed one.

"Fire ! Fire !" screamed the other.

It was Anckarström.

"Fire ! Fire ! Fire !" echoed Adolf, still standing composedly where he was.

The cry was taken up by every white mask there. True to the order of their adjutant, however, the sentinels had closed the doors.

CHAPTER LIII

THE END OF THE BALL

A SCENE of utter confusion followed. The cries of "Fire!" were hissed and hooted down. The orchestra continued to play, as if nothing had happened, the executants supposing that it was a mere practical joke. Some of the women were still shrieking "Fly! Fly!" and endeavouring to force their way past the sentinels. Others continued to dance as if they were mad. One, very extravagantly dressed with peacocks' feathers stuck all about her, rushed up to Adolf, crying—

"Dance with me! Dance with me! There is room now."

He tightened his mask, looked at his watch, and seized her hand. He was a free man as yet, for he had promised not to leave the theatre within twenty minutes of the firing of the pistol. The four leading conspirators had agreed beforehand that they would be careful not to approach each other—that Clas Horn (who would naturally be conspicuous as the one who gave the signal) should make his escape directly after the words were spoken—that Pontus Liljehorn and Ribbing should find their way out, if possible, ten minutes and twenty minutes later respectively. As well fill up the time with a gavotte! Was that Gluck's music? Outside lay the vast prison of the world. Within, the sword hanging by a thread over his neck, he was still free.

"You are not keeping time," he observed to his partner.

"Stop the music! Unmask — unmask, I say!" exclaimed the same voice that had ordered the doors to be closed. Adolf knew it well. It was the voice of young Captain Pollett, one of the adjutants. He bowed lightly to the peacock lady, whom his words had offended, and walked towards the other end of the Opera House. As he went, Löwenhjelm crossed his path, looking for the Guardsman who had assisted him to keep off the crowd.

"Go at once to the sentinel at the stage entrance, and tell him to let you through!" Adolf heard Löwenhjelm say, in low, authoritative tones. "Warn Liljensparre. Order out fifty dragoons of my regiment; they are to be present here under arms as soon as possible. Inform the foreign ministers — especially Monsieur D'Escars—of what has happened. Find Lieutenant Reuterskjöld,—I saw him just now over there by the orchestra; his dress is green and silver,— tell him to say to the Duke of Sudermania that the King requests his presence immediately, and desires him to see that the gates of Stockholm are barred until further notice."

The Guardsman departed on his errand. Löwenhjelm was hurrying back when Adolf stepped forward, mask in hand, and accosted him.

"How is His Majesty now?"

"His Majesty charged me to tell anyone who inquired for him that his wound is a mere scratch," replied Löwenhjelm.

"Thank God!" said Adolf, using the word that he only used in moments of deep sincerity. Then, recollecting the part he had to play, he added, "I trust the murderer may be brought to justice."

"Amen!" responded Löwenhjelm, with fervour.

His little pink domino was weeping, forlornly and rather loudly, close at hand, all by herself; but he did not so much as look at her, and hastened back.

Urged by an impatient longing to know how matters really stood—for the instinctive sensation of relief, caused by Löwenhjelm's words, was contradicted by his tone and manner directly afterwards—Adolf followed him as far as the narrow antechamber between the grand saloon and the King's apartment. It was only lit by one candle; the dull, faint glimmer was restful after the glaring chandeliers. On the floor by the stove sat a very young page, his head in his hands, his whole form shaken with violent sobs. Adolf, leaning against the wall, watched him curiously, wondering why anyone wept for the death of anyone.

Outside, the rough voice of one of the porters exclaimed loudly—

"You may go in, General, but you will not be allowed to come out again!"

There was a noise as of some hasty scuffle, and then a muttered explanation.

"It is Armfelt!" said Adolf to himself. "Is it possible that he does not know?"—

The next moment Armfelt opened the door and staggered in, pale as death, his knees tottering under him. He did not see Adolf.

"Where is the King?" he gasped, shaking the page by the shoulder; but the child could not speak.

"In there, on the red divan," he said at last, brokenly.

"Wounded?"

"Yes."

The General passed in without another word. In his agitation he forgot to shut the door after him, and Adolf heard the King speak.

"Who would have thought, my friend, that I should be wounded from behind!"

The tone was clear and distinct—not like that of a dying man.

"Do not be so alarmed, my dear Armfelt!" the voice continued. "You know from experience what a wound is. I feel no pain."

Again there was silence.

"He always thinks of others—not of himself," sobbed the page. Adolf could have shaken him. It was his own thought.

"Have the surgeons been sent for?"

"No. *A quoi bon?* They would only tell me that I

am going to die, to have the credit of making me well
again. For once you are mistaken in your tactics,
dear friend! *Le Médecin Malgré Lui* is not the title of
this piece. Well! if you must go—come closer—stoop
down to me—send and see whether La Perrière is at
home. He was not acting to-night. I fancied that I
recognised him in the crush just now. He is a
Jacobin."

Adolf started. Fortune seemed to favour the conspirators. The King had taken it into his head that
this was a French plot. General Armfelt strode
through the room and was gone.

He was absent only for a few minutes. In the interval, the Russian ambassador, Stackelberg; Liston,
the English envoy; and Duke Charles of Sudermania,
followed by several others, passed through the antechamber.

"They are all wearing their white masks," Adolf
said to himself.

Suddenly a cry arose from within.

"Air! Give the Duke air! He is fainting," and
the door was flung open.

Quick as thought, Adolf ensconced himself behind it.
Not much was to be seen through the chink, but the
sofa on which the King lay happened to be near, so
that he heard much better than before. The royal
pages seemed to be holding the Duke up.

"Give him some water to drink," said the King a
little contemptuously. "Ah, there is Armfelt! Let
him come to me!" and the others made room for the
favourite.

"La Perrière was not well this evening. He went
to bed at nine o'clock, sire, and has been there ever
since."

"So much the worse! It is a Swede then, after
all," murmured the King, a note of bitter disappointment in his voice. "We will not talk about it any
more now. There is something for you to read!"

"Ha! what can that be?" thought Adolf. He was
profoundly touched, in spite of himself.

A startled, impassioned cry followed.

"Sire, sire, in spite of such a warning, to have exposed a life so precious to your country — to Europe!"

Such a warning! From whom? Tala?

"Thank you, dear Count!" the King said, "but when a madman has made up his mind to sacrifice his own life to obtain yours, he must succeed in the long run!"

A fussy little fat man was ushered in.

"Room — room for the surgeon — room for Professor Hallman!" was echoed on all sides.

"See how my portly Hallman puffs and blows!" whispered the King to Armfelt.

The surgeon proceeded to examine the wound at once. No one spoke. Even the page's sobs were hushed.

"Well?" said Gustav carelessly.

"I can give no opinion, sire."

"Nay!" said Gustav, with some sharpness, "a King should know his danger. You have no business to hide it from him."

"I cannot tell, sire, till I have probed the wound with proper instruments."

"The coach is at the door. If your Majesty would submit to be carried down?"— said Armfelt.

"I am quite able to walk."

He rose from the sofa, but could not stand upright— went forward a few steps irresolutely — then, with a feeble smile, beckoned to Armfelt to support him, and allowed himself to be placed in a sedan-chair and carried out through the crowded hall.

"I go like the Holy Father, borne in procession from the Vatican to St. Peter's; do you remember, Essen?" he said, making an effort to laugh as he saw the grave faces all round him.

Adolf tried to slip out with the rest, but he was turned back immediately, as was everyone else who had been present at the masquerade, except Baron Essen.

The police, who had assembled in force by this time, bade all the guests return to the grand saloon, and massed them at the farther end. Two files of soldiers, with fixed bayonets, made a long, hedged-in road down the centre. Near the grand entrance sat Liljensparre, at a table furnished with pen, ink, and paper. Each man was required to pass between the rows of soldiers, that he might give his name and address to the minister of police before he was allowed to leave. The sight appeared grotesque enough. Most of the women were weeping.

Adolf was the last but one to go out. Having looked in vain for any trace of his fellow-conspirators, he was inclined to believe that they had all escaped, when, to his dismay, just as he had given his own name and address, he heard Anckarström's voice close behind him.

"You will not suspect me, I hope?"

"Why you more than others?" said Liljensparre, and his searching eyes rested on Anckarström's face for a moment with an expression that Adolf did not like.

Nothing further was said.

CHAPTER LIV

THE examination of the masqueraders had taken a long time; it was five in the morning when Adolf left the Opera House.

He could not have explained, even to himself, the shiver of disgust which made him refrain from any speech with Anckarström.

Strong excitement still kept him from feeling any of the weakness of fatigue, and the air was like fiery wine. Every street seemed a mass of blackness made solid, slit with crude light from windows here and there, where someone watched late or waked early. The great square of the palace was pierced with them through and through.

A longing for some place where there was no light, for some natural sound after the wild music that still went wildly in his brain, possessed Adolf. He walked down to the docks, and thence on and on until he came to an old deserted pier, a favourite haunt in the days of his first coming to Stockholm. Here he clambered down among the wooden beams and supports to a place where he had been used to moor his boat, and seated himself on the topmost step of a stone stair, slimy with thick, gummy-brown, grass-green seaweed, and spiky with mussel shells. The soft, resistless, constant murmur at his feet soothed him, as darkness soothed his eyes. For, except upon clocks, morning had not begun yet; only the foam at the edge of the waves glimmered, asserting itself as whiteness will in the absence of any ray. The burden of mental

existence was gone; there was no need to think.
What he meant to do next he knew very well, and
what would be the consequence he knew as well as if
it had happened already. The cold numbed him to
sleep. His last piece of consciousness was a dim
wonder whether, if he yielded to it, he should wake
again; and as he wondered he yielded, for he was very
tired.

A splashing of the spray in his face, as the tide rose
and shook the wooden beams, awoke him. The chill
banners of dawn were in the sky. With difficulty (for
the weary frame was thirsting for rest) he pulled
himself up from his cramped position, and walked in
the direction of his home. He found a different city
from that which he had left. The bells were tolling.
Every church door stood wide open. Pale women,
anxious men were crowding in. The corners of the
streets, at every one of which a great placard was
posted up, were thronged. Adolf stopped at the first
to which he came, and read as follows:—

" To the Citizens of Stockholm !

" 25,000 riksdalers ! ! !

" The above reward will be given to any one person
furnishing such information as may lead to the arrest
of the dastardly assassin, who last night attempted His
Majesty's life in the Opera House, or to that of any of
his accomplices. Particulars to be sent in at once to
the head of the police at the police office. Every hope
is entertained of His Majesty's complete recovery. Men
of Stockholm, pray for your King ! "

Anckarström was still a free man then, and the
King was not dead.

Twenty-five thousand riksdalers ![1] It was a large
sum.

" Will you kindly let me pass ? " said an impatient
voice. The anger in it expressed the desperate irritation of someone impeded upon an errand of life or

[1] £2000.

death. Adolf looked up, surprised, and recognised
his former acquaintance, Jacques de La Gardie.

"I beg your pardon, my dear Ribbing!" said
Jacques, astonished back into his natural courtesy.
"I took you for one of this vile crowd ; it is impossible
to get along for them. Yes, yes ; I own that I have
been to church! One ought to be ashamed of it,
perhaps, but after all—you have not been able to sleep
either? You too have prayed for his restoration?"

He seized Adolf's hand feverishly.

"*Every hope is entertained of His Majesty's recovery,*"
said Adolf, with white lips, pointing to the placard.

Jacques made a gesture of frantic rage.

"A lie !" he cried. "A lie ! They only put that up
to keep the people quiet. I have just come from the
palace ; there is no hope. Farewell !"

"I shall be going to the palace in an hour or two.
We may meet again in the guard-room," Adolf said,
scarcely knowing what he said.

"You will never meet me again. Give me your
hand a moment. Good-bye !"

"What do you mean?" said Adolf, forcibly detaining the young man.

"I am about to lose the only friend I have. I am
going where he is going, that is all. Let me alone !
Heavens, Ribbing, who would think, to look at you,
that you were so strong! Let go, I say!"

"I am stronger than you think. You shall not stir
from this till you have told me what you mean."

Something in La Gardie's face, reminding him of
Axel Fersen, appealed powerfully to his affection ; as
the boy's eyes questioned his, a faint glimmer of hope
began to shine in them.

"Well, I will tell you !" he said, ceasing to struggle.
"Why should I not? You are a man of honour. You
will understand. The King had promised only yesterday to help me. Without his help I am ruined ; and I
can never ask him now."

"Are you very deeply in debt?"

"I owe Wrangel seven hundred riksdalers. He
presses for it. My father will not lend me another

penny. My friends are all as poor as I am. If the money is not sent by to-morrow, Wrangel has sworn to expose me. I cannot face that."

"Could you not borrow from Axel?"

The uncertain hope in La Gardie's eyes vanished instantly.

"I would rather die," he said. "I thought you knew Axel."

Ribbing was silent.

"You see yourself," said Jacques at last, "there is nothing else left for me. A jump from the old pier cancels all. Let me go, Ribbing!"

"Not yet," said Adolf. "I cannot lend you this money. I wish I could. But it would be as safe for you to borrow from the King's assassin as from me. Before nightfall I shall have lost everything."

La Gardie stared at him in amazement. Everyone in Stockholm knew that young Count Ribbing was rich.

"Nevertheless," he continued, "I can tell you how to earn that sum—and more."

"I should owe you more than my life," La Gardie said fervently.

For all his answer Ribbing pointed to the placard.

"Twenty-five thousand riksdalers. You have but to obey those instructions."

"Are you mad? How should I know that accursed villain, or any of his damned accomplices?"

Adolf bowed.

"One of them stands by your side."

The despair in La Gardie's face changed to blank horror as he withdrew his arm.

"Ribbing," he said, "I do not believe you. If I did —do you think that I am fallen so low?"

He turned away.

Adolf laid a hand on his shoulder.

"Listen!" he said authoritatively. "I shall give myself up to-day, whether or no. That is why I cannot lend you the money. You are not betraying me. I shall betray myself in any case. I will never mention to anyone that you are concerned. Liljensparre will keep your name secret. Nobody is the worse—and all your debts are paid. Look here!" He took a piece of paper from his pocket—a facsimile of one of the notes written by Pontus the night before. "Take that to Liljensparre. Tell him that you picked it up outside my house—on the steps—in the hall—anywhere."

"I cannot."

"Nonsense. Think of your honour."

La Gardie made a movement as if to take the paper, but stopped himself.

"Are you a demon, Ribbing, to tempt me like this?"

"Your guardian angel rather! What were you praying for in church just now? That you might meet a man who would put seven hundred riksdalers into your hand."

La Gardie coloured high. Twice he yielded, and twice he changed his mind again. Adolf still stood holding the paper. At length Jacques' fingers closed on it.

"Nothing would induce me to do this, if I did not believe that you are perfectly innocent."

"Of course I am," said Adolf. "You did not think that I meant what I said just now. It did not deceive you for a moment. But we can mystify the Government between us, I should hope. Let me alone for that! For me it will be only a few days' inconvenience, and you will get the reward."

La Gardie laughed rather nervously.

"Your hand!"

Adolf gave it him.

"Ribbing, I dare not express to you my thanks for "—

"No gratitude, I beg!" said Adolf. "It is a *bourgeois* virtue. I hate it."

He leaned against a pillar to watch La Gardie walk slowly away. Something that was not the best part of him laughed.

.   .   .   .

Between two and three o'clock he went to the guard-room at the palace, as he had told La Gardie that he should. He was surprised to find himself still free to do so. For some reasons he would have preferred to be arrested in his own house, but he considered that he was bound to keep his word. At any other time his reappearance would have provoked some comment among the officers and nobles gathered there, as usual, to hear and to discuss the latest political event; on this day, however, nothing surprised anyone, and they made room for him at once, accepting his presence as a matter of course. General Armfelt was there, pale and dejected after his sleepless night; Silfverhielm too, darker than ever—and Tala's friend, Adlerbeth, his great eyes dim with watching. In a corner sat Wrangel, who had just returned from Italy; but he made no sign of recognition. Count Brahe, lately one of Gustav's fiercest opponents, shook the new-comer warmly by the hand. Adolf liked this man, and was not surprised at the look of real distress on his countenance.

"Well, and how is His Majesty?" he inquired, seating himself in the chimney corner.

"He has passed a very bad night, but he is all himself. He told Armfelt here that he did not wish to know so much as the name of the man who wounded him."

"As nobody knows that at present, it is fortunate that His Majesty's curiosity is not aroused."

"We are pretty sure to hear soon. The idiot let fall his weapons. They were found on the floor directly the grand saloon was cleared. A pair of pistols—an enormous dagger of the most extraordinary shape. Anyone who made that must know it again."

Anckarström had no chance then. Adolf found it impossible to stay in one position. He rose.

"The pistols are English—so I heard; but they were probably bought in Stockholm. All the armourers have been ordered to appear before Liljensparre."

"The King believes it is some Frenchman. He is sure that no subject of his would ever have conceived anything so dastardly."

"Everyone else is taking a great deal of trouble to find the assassin among the gentlemen of Sweden. It

26

is some rascal of a Frenchman, no doubt!" said Adolf, speaking that language.

"I, for my part, think that it is some rascal of a Swedish gentleman," said Armfelt, answering in the same.

At that moment the door opened, and the head of the police appeared on the threshold, his little blinking eyes smaller than usual with satisfaction.

"Gentlemen," he said, "the assassin has been discovered!"

A storm of questions burst upon him. Adolf alone among the crowd stood perfectly silent, warming himself, his back to the fire.

"When I can hear myself speak, I will speak," Liljensparre said.

The storm was lulled in an instant.

"Kaufman knew the pistols again. He repaired them, only two months ago, for Captain Anckarström, formerly of the Guards."

"The dagger has been traced to him also?"

"And the design to someone else," said Liljensparre, holding out a piece of paper, "someone to whom this note was addressed. Count Ribbing, I arrest you in the King's name."

CHAPTER LV

DE LA GARDIE TO THE RESCUE

EVEN as he stood in the Opera House and Anckarström fired, Adolf had been conscious of the sudden extinction of the spirit of revenge within him. He was himself once more; the black cloud had lifted, and the madness was gone. On the old pier, out in the bitter cold, among the waves, excited, exhausted as he was, he had slept and no dreams troubled him. During the hours of suspense that followed, he was upheld by the certainty that they would not be long—that they could only end one way. To him whose soul had been in hard captivity imprisonment was nothing. In the light of its approaching freedom from the bondage of life he could see things clearly. Justice was satisfied. No remorse vexed him; he felt convinced that what had been done was for the good of his country and for her sacred law. As for his own private wrongs, forgiveness came easy enough. He was done with this world. He had but to wait for death.

He thought constantly, almost incessantly, of the King; of Tala not so often. Had she died on the night of his return, he would not have forgotten; but she was living, and like to live. It was the dead—above all, the dying—to whom his thoughts turned now.

In body he was weak from the long strain of the previous months, so that he slept all night and half the day. In his eager boyhood he had often rebelled against the necessity for taking rest; life was short

enough, without having to shorten it in that way.
Long nights of awful, uninterrupted self-consciousness
taught him to think otherwise. Now, though the end
was near, he rejoiced in forgetfulness. Winter had
come again, repulsing the first attack of spring ; and
but for this perpetual drowsiness, he would have
suffered from the cold. Little by little, sleep invaded
him, took him captive, body and soul. Something of
its indifference grew upon him, even in waking hours.
He had looked forward with keen excitement to his
trial—had busied himself much with the composition of
a scaffold speech in the manner of Rousseau—with the
details of his toilette even, when he should make his
brave last appearance before the headsman, and overwhelm that functionary by the generous gift of five
pieces of gold. Now he cared nothing at all.

On the eleventh night after his arrest, he was roused
by a violent shake. Opening his eyes stupidly, he was
bewildered to see, by his prison bedside, Jacques de La
Gardie. The jailer's lantern stood on the floor.

"Upon my soul, Ribbing, you do not sleep like
a guilty man!" said Jacques, with nervous lightness
of manner. "Wake up! Be quick, I say! Every
moment is precious. Put on your clothes, and come
with me!"

"You are very kind," said Adolf stiffly, "but it is
not consistent with my dignity to escape."

La Gardie stamped upon the floor in his impatience.

"Who wants you to escape? Nobody has the
slightest ambition to play Crito to your Socrates. I,
for one, have given my word that you will be back in
this cell before seven o'clock to-morrow morning. But
if you are wise, you will do as I bid you and ask no
questions. More depends on it than you can possibly
imagine—both for yourself and for another. Be quick,
man, be quick!"

Another? Tala? Was it a message from her?

"That is a different matter," said Adolf, rising at
once. "You understand that I have pledged my word
to return?"

"You have no choice," said La Gardie, shrugging

his shoulders, "and—I am sorry—but you must allow
me to blindfold you."

Adolf's presumption that he was to be taken to the
Hôtel Essen became a practical certainty.   He submitted
without the least demur.

"One word!" he said.   "Is the King still alive?"

"Yes, but in very great danger.   Do not speak
again till I speak to you."

Jacques tied a handkerchief over his eyes, pulled his
hat over it, and hurried him down the stairs into a
carriage, which drove quickly away.   After a few
minutes they alighted—he was urged up some steps,
then up a flight of stairs and through a door, that La
Gardie shut carefully behind him.   All this time he had
not said a word.   Adolf, by some sympathetic instinct,
divined that he was hesitating now.

"Speak out, La Gardie!   Am I going to be
murdered?"

"Hush!" said La Gardie.   "No one speaks above
his breath here.   Ribbing, I owe you much—you must
let me owe you one thing more.   I have been tormented
by remorse ever since your arrest.   It is far worse
than I thought.   Personally, I am sure that you are
innocent; but you have not a chance.   I have heard
them talk.   They are only waiting until the breath is
out of the King's body to inflict death—worse than
death—torture.   The one hope lies here.   Listen!   It
is my turn to watch to-night behind the screen in the
King's room.   You must take my place.   You are just
my height—if you are careful, no one will observe.
By and by, when everything is quiet, choose the right
moment, go in to the King—speak to him.   He will
forgive—I know he will.   All I beg is that you will
not mention my name.   I shall return for you while it
is still dark, between six and seven."

As he spoke he unfastened the bandage that covered
Adolf's eyes.   They were in an antechamber that he
remembered well.   In the first rush of disappointment,
when he found that he was not where he had hoped to
be, he had scarcely taken in the sense of Jacques'
words, but now he forced himself to think   The

mysterious circumstances of his introduction had
revived his love of adventure, of any plan that had a
spice of risk in it ; and this rendered him more docile
than he would else have been.

"You are a fool, La Gardie !" he said good-
humouredly. "It would be as impossible for the King
to grant as for me to ask what you propose. If I had
known that this was what you meant, I never would
have come. You are endangering yourself for a thing
that can be of no service to me. Nothing, it seems,
will make you understand that I have not even a wish
to avoid the extreme penalty of the law. As for yourself, a babe unborn is not more innocent."

" I cannot feel it," said Jacques, in a voice of agony.
"If you would undertake this watch, I might feel it
again."

"My death would be on my own head then, I
suppose ? As you will !" said Adolf, with a gentle
sigh of contempt ; for, although he had not for an
instant contemplated the refusal of this strange offer,
he thought Jacques a poor creature. "Only, if the
King calls for assistance, I cannot present myself."

"He will not," said Jacques eagerly. "I have never
known him call. But when you are left alone, you
will go to him. I know you will."

And again La Gardie stood looking this way and
that, the picture of miserable indecision.

CHAPTER LVI

THE KING'S RULING

"WHERE does he lie?" said Adolf, with an effort.

The stillness of the palace made him feel as though he were blind and deaf. It was far more silent than the prison. He caught sight of his own thin face in the tall mirror on the stairs, and shivered.

"In the great state bedroom, towards the centre of the first corridor," said Jacques, leading the way. "Take off your shoes. Carry them in your hand. We always do. He cannot bear a noise."

The vast chamber which they now entered was divided into three parts by two high screens, one drawn round the bed of the sick man, the other round a table in the corner at the upper end, that was kept for the consultations of the doctors. It was cold and full of draughts — colder even than the corridor out of which they came. The row of stone pillars down the middle gave it the aspect of a vault. Here and there a patch of light—sickroom light, carefully shaded—made the great sea of shadow visible. Solid shadows sat in the corners — leant against the wall—stretched themselves on the bare floor. No one spoke nor moved.

Notwithstanding the huge fire that burnt on the central hearth, every one of these waiting figures was wrapped in his fur cloak. Almost all were asleep; one or two stirred uneasily, when they passed, as though restless with dreaming. Adolf thought of the Black House.

La Gardie sat down in a tall, stiff-backed chair, some way from the first screen, rather apart from the rest, and signed to Adolf to do likewise.

" Does he never sleep ? "

" Never."

" Is there always someone with him ? "

" Not always. Last night he told me to clear the room—he thought that he could sleep if they would go."

" And did you ? "

" No ; I was afraid. I sat down just outside the screen, in case he should need anything. Then I heard him groan softly over and over again. He never does that except when he thinks that he is by himself."

" Can he speak ? "

" Yes ; but it is the same thing over and over again. He is always asking the time."

Adolf remembered how he had watched the minutes pass once, when he thought himself within half an hour of his death.

" There is a clock on that pillar."

" Yes ; but I do not think he can see it. His eyes are too bright. He is all dead but his eyes."

Adolf sat meditating.

" I never saw anyone so patient," said Jacques, in a still lower voice. " If you knew "—

" Does he ever speak of his wife ? " interrupted Adolf.

For some undefined reason, he could not endure to hear that the King was patient.

" Not often. "

" Of religion ? "

" Alas, no ! "

" Why alas ? " said Adolf in a fierce whisper. " They do not feel it most that speak of it."

A white handkerchief fluttered over the top of the farther screen.

" Wallencreutz has ended his watch," said La Gardie. " Come, it is our turn now. Pull your cloak over your face ! "

It was very dark behind the second screen, for there was neither lamp nor candle—only the light reflected from beyond on the ceiling. A few sheets of paper lay on the table, as the last doctor had left them after writing his prescription, and a chair or two had been pushed back from it. Jacques drew the paper to him, and scribbled these words with a pencil—

"Wachtmeister will be there for the first hour. If, later on, the King should want anything, do as I am doing now, and make a sign to me. I shall be close at hand."

Adolf nodded assent, and Jacques, having pocketed the paper, went out noiselessly at a low door in the wall.

For some time there was no sound at all.

Only, now and again, the wind sighed mournfully, raised its voice to a wail that was almost human, and sank again.

"Women moan like that!" Adolf thought to himself.

It rattled the windows in their frames, and through the chink below the door an icy draught rushed in, so that his feet were half frozen. Then it gathered its strength together, and seemed to shake the very foundations. Was the house itself trembling in sympathy with its master? He recollected what someone had told him of birds loosening the mortar when death was near.

"What time is it?"

Adolf started—not because he knew the voice, rather because he did not know it. Were these the tones that rang out like a trumpet among the hills of Mora?

He did not catch the answer.

"Is my brother Charles in the palace?" asked the same voice.

Someone, whom Adolf took to be Wachtmeister, replied—

"He is, sire."

"Bring him to me!"

Again there was silence.

A sudden gust of wind warned Adolf that the great

door at the farther end must have been opened and shut; from a movement of shuffling feet he conjectured that the watch without stood up as the Duke entered.

"Are we alone?" said the thin voice again. "Is La Gardie near, in case I want anything?"

"La Gardie is in his usual place, sire."

"Good. No one else is within earshot?"

"No one else, your Majesty."

"That is well. Leave us!"

Adolf listened intently.

"I wished to speak to you, Charles," the voice continued, "on a subject that we have hitherto avoided."

The Duke put on a manner of abnormal importance.

"Do you desire that the Bishop of Wexiö should be sent for, brother?"

"No."

For the first time Adolf felt that it was the King who spoke.

"I desire to be told the names of the chief conspirators in the plot against me—the *chief* conspirators, mind! No one else."

"Captain Anckarström, formerly of the Guards, Baron Pechlin, the young Counts Ribbing and Horn. Your old favourite, Pontus, was deeply implicated, and"—

"Enough!" said the King. "More than five chiefs they cannot possibly have had, or they would never have been successful. A constitutional monarchy has taught me that, anyhow. As for Pontus, he repented before the act. It was he who sent me that warning letter. Liljensparre traced it to his address. I have given directions that he should be pardoned. What is the judgment of the Court likely to be, in the case of the others?"

"Surely your own judgment must tell you that, Gustav."

"You think that they will be sentenced to death—beheaded, like Hästesko?"

Adolf held his breath.

"I think not. They have forfeited that last right of

gentlemen," said the Duke grimly. "Hästesko was no assassin, after all."

"You mean that they will be hung?"

Was it the cold that made the listening man shudder? He had thought to die by the axe.

"Hung to a dead certainty," said the Duke, with dry satisfaction. "On a gallows forty feet high."

What was the ugly word that La Gardie had uttered? *Torture.* Something in the Duke's voice brought it back.

"Pechlin is old," said the King. "I used to call him the first Republican of Sweden, before I came to the throne."

"He must be seventy at least."

"Why, he might be my father! I will not have him hung, I tell you! Are there no fortresses in this country? Shut him up in the Varberg, if you like! As for the others, they are too young. Liljehorn has my full pardon. Let the rest be set free!"

Free? For the only time in his life, the word fell upon Adolf's heart like lead.

"Charles, you will be Regent for my son. Will you promise me this?"

"He cannot promise," Adolf said to himself. "His brother—his own brother. He cannot."

"Gustav, it is impossible."

"Why?"

"Have you not heard what the people did to Horn's father, the General? They robbed his house. The Dragoons had to pretend that they were taking him prisoner, and we were forced to give him quarters in the palace, to protect him."

"Well?"

"What chance would his son have then—and those who are even guiltier than his son? The populace would tear them limb from limb; their lives would not be worth a minute's purchase in Sweden."

"Send them out of Sweden then, as quickly as possible!"

Adolf could tell, from the King's tone, that he smiled.

"I cannot make you that promise," said the Duke, with sombre indignation. "Do you think yourself that the Guards would undertake such a duty? It is enough to say that I could not fulfil it."

"It is enough that I desire it, Charles. As your monarch I command—as your brother I beseech you to obey me; and you shall answer to me before God, if you do not!"

This was the voice that Adolf knew at last—the voice that he had never been able to resist. Pray Heaven the Duke held out! And yet—how could he?

There was a long silence. The Duke sighed heavily twice or thrice. Then he broke down altogether, and Adolf caught the sound of a stifled sob.

"I could promise," he said at last, low and unwillingly, "for all but one. You would not have the murderer set free to slay the son as he has slain the father?"

The King seemed to reflect a moment. It was the thin, strange voice that spoke again now, in utter weariness and exhaustion.

"For all the rest you promise—before God?"

"For all the rest I promise," repeated the Duke, as if the words were dragged out of him.

"Before God?"

"Before God!"

Adolf was fiercely torn in two. Had he stood in the Duke's place, he must have yielded—he knew that; yet he despised him. His brother—his own brother—and he could let him go thus lightly! Must he, Adolf Ribbing, accept his life from such a fellow as this?

"You have talked more than you ought. Goodnight, brother!"

"I am better. The cough is gone. I shall sleep now. Good-night!"

The Duke stole out, with hushed footsteps.

The wind had fallen suddenly, as it does sometimes before dawn, and the circles and patches of light upon the ceiling did not waver. To Adolf's fancy, their steadiness made the quiet room quieter still. It seemed to him that long hours ebbed away. If sleep depended upon silence, surely the King must sleep. The painful sound of his breathing had ceased altogether.

A chill struck home to Adolf's heart. Was he dead? He could not stay there. He must look.

He rose, and peered cautiously round the screen. By the subdued light of a little silver lamp, covered with a paper shade, he saw the great bed, smooth and white, and the shrunk face on the pillow. The bed-clothes were in perfect order. The hand that lay half open on the coverlet looked scarcely like a human thing. Ah, what a ruin of a man was this!

Adolf came a step forward.

His youth rushed back upon him. He remembered only that this man, of all men that he had ever seen, was the bravest. He would have fallen on his knees and kissed those waxen fingers.

At that moment the King's eyes opened. He raised himself upon his arm, with a look of indescribable terror—then fell back, putting his hand to his heart. Tala had spent herself in vain. It was not Adolf's hand that fired the shot, but it was none the less Adolf who killed him.

"I am not afraid of you now," he whispered. "Come nearer! Have you forgiven? Will you let me sleep?"

He looked up. There was no fear in his eyes. Adolf saw this—and he could see no more for tears

CHAPTER LVII

FREE !

FREE !

Adolf had believed as deeply as he believed anything, that there would never be a moment in life when that word failed to shine in him like light. Yet now he had a sense that his young body alone rejoiced in the clearness and stir of day, while his spirit lay once more dark and in bonds, indifferent—since the passions that once possessed it were gone—whether he lived or died. He rode along heavily, looking neither to the right nor to the left, thinking of all that had happened since his arrest.

Jacques de La Gardie, who had been, so far as he could see, the main instrument of his deliverance, told him that it was due to the secret intervention of a lady—an *illuminée*. Who she was he did not know, having heard of the incident only at second hand, through Colonel Silfverhielm. She assured the Duke of Sudermania that "the master" (by which name Swedenborg was known among his disciples) had appeared to her when she was in a trance, declaring that Adolf was innocent in the matter of the King's death—that every hair that fell from his head would cost a day of the Duke's life. Her report had strangely coincided with the arrival of a letter, enclosing the memorandum taken by Adolf on the 14th September 1788. Thereupon, the Duke, who had been urging on the trial, forgetful of the promise made to his dead brother, stopped it short with a suddenness which bewildered the judges, and, as soon as he dared, gave orders for the private release of the young Count, passing upon him sentence of perpetual exile.

Anckarström had been beheaded, a week since. He died well and firmly, La Gardie said, having endured with great courage the dreadful ordeal of the three days before, when he was driven to three different quarters of the town, set in the pillory, and scourged with rods.

"If it were to do again, I would do it," he said, as the axe was about to fall.

"I could have prophesied that those would be his last words," mused Adolf.

He could not help it—he breathed more quietly because this man was gone. The thought of his fate moved horror—no regret.

Pechlin was shut up in the fortress of Varberg, never to reappear.

As for Clas Horn, he had shown great penitence during his imprisonment, insomuch that all the gentle hearts in Stockholm were touched by his sorrow. Sentence of perpetual banishment had been passed upon him, as also upon Pontus, and they left the city of their birth under a feigned name. The Duke was very unwilling to let them go ; but it was represented to him that he could not treat them with greater severity than Ribbing, who—so his jailer said—had exhibited no repentance at all. Pontus was, like his companion, sincerely convinced of sin ; besides, did not he write the warning letter ?

Whither they had gone Adolf did not know, nor in truth did he care to know. Jacques de La Gardie proposed to him to change his name likewise ; he declined absolutely, and without a moment's delay. He had been cautioned not to show himself near the capital, where his features might be recognised—for portraits of the chief conspirators were everywhere in circulation ; but it was scarcely for this reason that he rode forward without stopping. He was not reckless nor inclined to defy Fate ; he felt certain that at this moment life was too dull for her to have any designs upon him.

In broad daylight, in the midst of a populous village, it occurred to him that he was tired (he had been on horseback since early dawn), and he dismounted to rest himself. The sun was turning into diamonds the clear water of a trough formed by a hollow tree split open, that lay across his path, and the brilliant dance of the diamonds pleased his eye. He made a cup of both his hands and drank. Then he let his horse drink also, and stood waiting.

A walnut tree spread its fragrant branches over the trough, and while he waited he busied himself idly, plucking the large, light-coloured leaves, pinching them to make them smell sweeter, and sticking them into his hat.

All at once the listlessness in him quickened, his muscles tightened, the blood in him ran fast. Along the road, in the contrary direction from that by which he had himself approached the village, two horsemen came. The nearer of the two he did not know. Every pulse in him thrilled with recognition of the other. There was but one man who could sit his horse like that. It was Axel Fersen.

Adolf stood still, one arm flung round his horse's neck, holding his hat in his hand. He did not care even to shield his face.

Obviously the travellers had come a long way, for their steeds were hot and covered with foam, and they were only going at a foot's pace.

"Good-day to you, young gentleman!" observed the stranger.

"Good-day!" said Adolf, louder than usual.

The stranger looked more closely at him, and then spoke very kindly.

"You are young, sir," he said, "probably inexperienced. Do not take it amiss, if I warn you that you should be more careful how you expose that handsome face of yours. The expression is, of course, totally different, but otherwise your features bear a very marked resemblance to those of the odious and generally detested Ribbing—eh, Fersen?" and he touched his comrade's elbow.

"I do not know Count Ribbing," answered Fersen; and for the space of a moment he and Adolf looked each other full in the face.

"Thank you, sir, for your warning," Adolf said. "I shall remember."

And they were gone.

Adolf had been directed to spend the midday hours at a French convent—one of the very few that existed in Sweden for the purpose of teaching the daughters of the nobility to speak that language. Here he would run but little risk of discovery, and he could partake of some refreshment and rest his horse. He was to reach the coast that night, and to embark at a little fishing village under cover of darkness. The Duke had thought that this would be quieter and safer than an attempt to leave direct from Stockholm, on account of the difficulty about passports. The Duke was very much concerned for his safety, Adolf reflected, with a smile.

It was not long before he reached the straight, narrow, red brick house that had been described to him. It stood back from the road, divided by a terrace and three great grassy steps from the chapel, which was almost equally narrow and high, with an odd, slender little round tower, scarcely peeping above the roof.

There was not a man to be seen anywhere. Girls of different ages, some of them not more than eight or nine, some of them sixteen or seventeen perhaps, were sitting all around, on the steps, by the door of the chapel, on the grass, on the low wall of the terrace. Each wore a hood of pure white, edged with blue, and several of the elder ones were attired in long white cloaks down to their feet. They looked like birds, he thought, clustered together.

He seemed to be expected. A youthful portress took his horse and led it away to a stable at the back. The Lady Abbess came forward immediately from among her scholars, and gave him her hand in token of greeting. She was a girl, too, though somewhat older; her figure was still young and graceful, her way of moving lithe and abrupt.

27

"God sends the guest," she said sweetly, in her native tongue. "Will monsieur excuse me an instant? The bell is ringing for Sext. I cannot have the pleasure of waiting on him"— There was a touch of half-questioning appeal in her voice.

"If I may come with you, madame?"— said Adolf, unconsciously catching the note.

She bowed her head, and he followed the long procession of girls and nuns into the chapel. One carried a golden cross in front. The service was very short. He waited until they had all filed out again, and then joined his hostess on the terrace.

"We are glad to see you," she said. "His Royal Highness the Duke of Sudermania sent word to us to expect a friend of his about midday. We do not often have the pleasure of entertaining those guests who, we are told, are angels unawares. And monsieur has the most perfect French accent. Ah, what a joy to me, poor exile, to hear my own tongue again!"

"I am afraid that I can lay no claim to be an angel unawares," said Adolf hastily. The youth, the innocence and girlishness of everything around touched him; he dared not deceive. "My name is Adolf Ribbing."

"It is doubtless an old name in this country," said the Abbess politely; it was clear that she had never heard it before. "One can see that in monsieur's face. Monsieur has ridden far?"

"From Stockholm," said Adolf. "You have heard, madame, of the King's death?"

"Ah yes!" she said, with absent-minded sympathy. "It is, of course, a great grief to everyone living there—to monsieur in particular? The poor King! If he had but belonged to our holy faith— If monsieur will excuse me, I will go and speak to the housekeeper about the collation. Monsieur will, I hope, find something to occupy him in the garden? It will be ready in an hour. Or in the parlour? We have books—
The Lives of the Saints?"—and on the wings of her shy suggestion she glided away.

Adolf went out into the garden, bright with tulips of all colours, and seated himself on a stone bench. Four

of the younger girls were playing battledore and
shuttlecock on the grass. They were playing well,
and the hollow, regular thud on the battledore half
mesmerised him, as any recurrent sound was apt to do,
so that he sat for a long time, idly watching the
shuttlecocks, as they tossed to and fro, little pieces of
flying foam against the azure sky.

"The poor King!" That it should come to this!
The careless word of pity moved him with dull amazement. He had known many who loved the King,
many who hated him, but anyone who ventured to pity
him and to think of something else the next minute—
never! It troubled him like an insult. Was everything so soon forgotten? Was there no such thing in
the world as fame—good or evil?

His heart was sore too.

"I thought you knew Axel!" he said to himself
ironically, repeating the words of Jacques de La
Gardie.

And it was true. He had known always that it
must be as it was; he had known it as a man knows
he will die. It did not make the recollection of those
stony eyes less bitter. The gentle looks and words
that met him here had been as balm to a wound. Yet,
for all that, he might have felt less absolute dejection
now had he been spurned and hated. They only
welcomed him because they did not know.

The shuttlecocks fell at last, and the little maidens
went back into the house, except the youngest of them
all, who came deliberately and seated herself beside
him. Adolf was very much afraid of children, not
knowing in the least what to say to them, and his
instinct was for immediate flight; but before he had
time to put it into action, she said, in clear, distinct
tones—

"I came on Ascension Day."

"Did you?" said Adolf stupidly.

"You have got a beautiful horse," she continued.
"I went into the stable to see him after chapel."

"Did you?" said Adolf again.

"May I sometimes ride him whilst you are here?"

"I am afraid I shall want to ride him myself, as soon as he has had a rest."

"But you are not going to-night?"

"Indeed I am."

"When you come back then?"

"I shall never come back."

"Why not?"

"If I did, a man in Stockholm would take a big, bright sword, and cut off my head."

"Then had you not better go at once?" she said, not with any alarm, but in a shrewd, wise way, as if she had thought the affair well over. She was not a pretty child; yet he began to think she was.

"My horse is too tired. He would drop down on the road."

She reflected a moment.

"Why do they want to cut off your head? Have you been wicked?"

"Yes."

"What did you do?"

"I tried to hurt someone who hurt me."

"We are called naughty, if we do that; but when it's grown-up people, it's wicked."

"Are you ever naughty?" said Adolf, who began to think that it was his turn to question.

"No. I am good; at least, not always quite, but generally. If I am naughty, I say I am sorry. Are you sorry?"

"Yes."

It seemed to Adolf as though he had let fall an overwhelming weight in that one word.

"I wish I had a horse like yours."

"See here!" said Adolf. "I am going to Paris. I will send you a little horse."

"Will you?" she said. "Have you got money enough?"

"I think I have."

"Thank you!" she said demurely.

The Lady Abbess summoned him indoors, and carried off the child.

"I am so sorry that you have been troubled.

Children are very annoying.   She knew quite well that she ought to be at her lessons."

He did not see her after that, but this slight incident remained in his memory, and bore fruit years and years afterwards.

He thought of many things as he rode down to the coast.   Never again should he love anyone as he had loved Tala—never again rejoice in any leader as he had once rejoiced in the King—never again confide in such a friend as Axel.   He was the last of his race, and he was going forth, over these wide, grey waters, not to return.   He thought also of the old stories of the house of Ribbing—how, in its darkest hour, a child appeared, and there was hope again.

And he remembered that he was only twenty-three.

THE END

PRINTED BY
MORRISON AND GIBB LIMITED
EDINBURGH

Telegrams :
'Scholarly, London.'

41 and 43 Maddox Street,
Bond Street, London, W.,
September, 1907.

Mr. Edward Arnold's
List of New Books.

FROM THE NIGER TO THE NILE.
By BOYD ALEXANDER,
LIEUTENANT, RIFLE BRIGADE.

Two volumes. Large Medium 8vo. With Illustrations and Maps.

36s. net.

It may be doubted whether any exploring expedition of modern times compares for interest and romance with that led by Lieut. Boyd Alexander from the Niger to the Nile in 1904-1907. The distance accomplished was about 5,000 miles, and among the many remarkable results of the expedition was the demonstration that it was possible to go almost the whole way by water ; in fact, the steel boats which conveyed the stores were only carried for fourteen days out of the three years occupied by the journey.

The book is packed with adventure, much of it of a kind unusual even for Central African explorers. In one famine-stricken village young girls are offered to the party for food ; elsewhere the people, fleeing before them, throw down babies in the hope of staying their hunger, and so stopping their advance. In contrast with these cannibals, we find other populations engaged in the arts and industries of a comparatively high state of civilization. Two of the party—Lieut. Alexander's brother and Captain G. B. Gosling—died of fever at different stages of the journey. The survivors had countless escapes from death by disease, poisoned arrows, hunger, lightning, and drowning. The numerous exciting hunting-stories include the capture of an okapi after a weary search. There was a good deal of fighting with natives in the earlier stages of the journey, but on the whole the people, when not shy, seem to have been well

LONDON : EDWARD ARNOLD, 41 & 43 MADDOX STREET, W.

disposed. Lieut. Alexander's observations on the manners and customs of the natives are extremely curious and interesting.

The story is fully illustrated by nearly 200 striking photographs, and there are several maps.

MEMOIRS OF MISTRAL.

Rendered into English by CONSTANCE MAUD,
AUTHOR OF 'WAGNER'S HEROES,' 'AN ENGLISH GIRL IN PARIS,' ETC.

Demy 8vo.   With Illustrations.   **12s. 6d. net.**

The charm of this autobiography of the celebrated Provençal poet may be judged from the enthusiastic reception accorded by critics to the work on its original appearance. Thus, the *Revue des Deux Mondes* speaks of 'these pages all vibrant with the sunshine of the Midi,' of 'the graphic language, full of energy, freedom, and richness of expression,' in which the author of 'Mireille' records the impressions of his early years, while the *Semaine littéraire de Genève* says: 'This is an exquisite, healthy, joyous, cheering book. This delightful picture of the Midi, with its honest country life, its ancient manners, preserved by a passionate attachment to the ancestral soil and example, calls forth laughter, smiles, and tears. It is, perhaps, the most purely joyous, moving, and charming work that France has given us for a long time.' And it adds: 'A ceux qui cherchent en vain, dans la littérature triste ou compliquée de notre temps, la joie et la santé de l'esprit, nous pouvons dire en toute confiance: Lisez les souvenirs de Mistral!'

TURKEY IN EUROPE.

By SIR CHARLES ELIOT, K.C.M.G.
('ODYSSEUS').

A New Edition, with an Additional Chapter on Events from 1869 to the Present Day.

Large Crown 8vo.   **7s. 6d. net.**

Although the identity of 'Odysseus' has for some time been an open secret, it is satisfactory to be able at length to reveal definitely the authorship of this important work. The additional chapter contains a valuable review of the present position of the Turkish question, and brings up to date a book that is already regarded as a standard authority on its subject.

MEXICO OF THE TWENTIETH CENTURY.

By PERCY F. MARTIN, F.R.G.S.,

AUTHOR OF 'THROUGH FIVE REPUBLICS OF SOUTH AMERICA.'

Two volumes. Demy 8vo. With Illustrations and Map. **30s. net.**

In view of the immense amount of interest which is being taken in Mexico by investors both great and small throughout the world, there is clearly a place for an authentic and trustworthy book by a competent observer, which shall give an accurate picture of the country and its industrial condition at the present time. Mr. Martin has devoted fifteen months to examining the country and its resources from end to end, and the result is not only an extremely readable account of the Republic, but a mass of information relating to every aspect of its business existence which should form a standard work of reference on the subject. To show the thoroughness of Mr. Martin's method, it may be mentioned that he includes a particular description and history of every mining district, including many of the separate mines and the actual amount of work done and being done; a complete history of banking, with full information about the native and foreign banks; insurance matters; the commercial code; mining laws; railway laws, etc. There is a detailed description of every railway in Mexico, with minute particulars as to management, finance, etc. All other matters of interest are dealt with in due proportion, and the whole work is abundantly illustrated.

ACROSS PERSIA.

By E. CRAWSHAY WILLIAMS.

Demy 8vo. With Illustrations and Maps. **12s. 6d. net.**

Mr. Crawshay Williams is an enterprising traveller and a very keen observer. His book contains the most recent account of a region which is vitally important as the meeting-place of Russian and British interests in Asia. It is written in a lively and entertaining fashion, with a shrewd eye to the political situation, and is well illustrated.

THE
GROWTH OF MODERN NATIONS.
A History of the Particularist Form of Society.

Translated from the French of HENRI DE TOURVILLE
by M. G. LOCH.

Demy 8vo. **12s. 6d. net.**

The articles which are here presented in the form of a volume were contributed by the author to the French periodical *La Science Sociale* over a period of six years ending in February, 1903. His death occurred within a few days of his completing the work. M. de Tourville, after showing that the transformation of the communal into the particularist family took place in Scandinavia, and was largely due to the peculiar geographical character of the Western slope, traces the development of modern Europe from the action of the particularist type of society upon the fabric of Roman civilization.

OUT OF CHAOS.
A Personal Story of the Revolution in Russia.

By PRINCE MICHAEL TRUBETZKOI.

Crown 8vo. **6s.**

Succeeding at the age of twenty-three to considerable position and wealth, Prince Trubetzkoi was early impressed by the desperate condition of the Russian lower classes, and began to interest himself in schemes of reform. He quickly discovered that open methods had no chance of success, and it was not long before an experience of prison and exile led him to abandon his social career and fling himself with all his heart into the arms of the revolutionary party. Throughout his unceasing struggles on behalf of liberty Prince Trubetzkoi has ever held up the ideal of Peaceful Regeneration as the result of education and self-sacrifice, and has opposed the anarchical violence which can only impede the cause of reform. His book, which is a nightmare of spies and passports, of underground printing presses and smuggled literature, of hideous anxieties and hairbreadth escapes, gives a lurid picture of modern Russia from the reformer's point of view.

RAILWAY ENTERPRISE IN CHINA.

An Account of its Origin and Development.

By PERCY HORACE KENT.

Demy 8vo.   With Maps.   **12s. 6d. net.**

The history of railway enterprise in China covers a period of rather more than forty years.   It reflects at once the main characteristics of the Chinese official classes and the tendency of the Far Eastern policy of foreign Powers.   This book, in recording the origin and growth of Chinese railways, and describing the present situation and its development, aims at providing a succinct and unbiassed account of an enormously important aspect of what is known as the Far Eastern question.   Each railway is dealt with in detail with the latest information obtainable, and as the appendices contain copies of the more important railway contracts, the book should prove a valuable work of reference.

PICTORIAL ART IN THE FAR EAST.

By LAURENCE BINYON.

8vo.   With Illustrations.

This important work, which is only rendered possible by the immense additions to our knowedge of Far Eastern art during the last decade, brings out and establishes the high interest of Chinese painting, hitherto practically unknown in Europe, and of the older schools of Japan, the subsidiary schools of India, Persia and Tibet being also glanced at.   The author's aim has been to treat his subject not merely from the technical historical side, but as a theme of living and universal interest, with its background of Oriental thought and civilization.

IN OUR TONGUES.

Some Hints to Readers of the English Bible.

By ROBERT HATCH KENNETT,

CANON OF ELY, AND REGIUS PROFESSOR OF HEBREW IN THE UNIVERSITY OF CAMBRIDGE.

Crown 8vo.

THE LIFE OF THE SALMON.

Wíth Reference more especíally to the Físh ín Scotland.

By W. L. CALDERWOOD, F.R.S.E.,
INSPECTOR OF SALMON FISHERIES FOR SCOTLAND.

Demy 8vo. With Illustrations. **7s. 6d. net.**

The Salmon's life presents so many remarkable problems—some of them, owing to the difficulties attending scientific observation, almost insoluble—that a considerable literature already exists on the subject. It is only in the last few years, however, that anything like a systematic investigation has been carried on in Scotland, and, from his acquaintance with the operations of the Fishery Board, Mr. Calderwood is able to speak with special authority. He traces the history of the fish from its youth up, and has most interesting chapters on the results of marking, on scales as records of a fish's journeyings, and on the effects of changes of water-temperature upon the growing fish.

MY ROCK-GARDEN.

By REGINALD FARRER,
AUTHOR OF 'THE GARDEN OF ASIA,' 'THE HOUSE OF SHADOWS,' 'THE SUNDERED STREAMS,' ETC.

Large Crown 8vo. With Illustrations. **7s. 6d. net.**

Rock-gardening appears to have a peculiar fascination for its devotees, and certainly in this book the attractions of the art find a very able exponent. Mr. Farrer is a recognized authority. His rock-garden at Ingleborough is well known among those who share his love of the subject, and he has been a remarkably successful exhibitor at the London shows. His pages, though conceived for the most part in a light-hearted vein, contain an abundance of practical information on sites and soils, and his amusing glimpses of the joys of the successful collector in Switzerland and Japan will make a responsive echo in the breasts of similar enthusiasts. The book, which describes the making of the garden as well as the innumerable things which, with luck, it is possible to grow in it, is illustrated by a number of excellent photographs.

A GALLERY OF PORTRAITS.

Reproduced from Original Etchings.

By HELLEU.

With an Introduction by FREDERICK WEDMORE.

Crown Folio. **25s. net.**

M. Helleu's exquisite portraits may be regarded as the French counterpart of the art of Gibson in America. Readers of *The Illustrated London News* will remember the delicacy and charm of the portraits which appeared in that periodical. This set of reproductions, to which Mr. Frederick Wedmore has written an introduction, forms ŗ singularly attractive 'gallery of beauty.' In the case of a considerable proportion, a dash of colour heightens the effectiveness of the portrait.

MODERN STUDIES.

By OLIVER ELTON, M.A.,

PROFESSOR OF ENGLISH LITERATURE IN THE UNIVERSITY OF LIVERPOOL.

Large Crown 8vo. **7s. 6d. net.**

Among the contents of this volume of literary essays are : "Giordano Bruno in England," "Literary Fame: A Renaissance Study," "A Word on Mysticism," and Essays on Shakespeare, Tennyson, Swinburne, Henry James, George Meredith, and living Irish literature.

THE GOLDEN PORCH.

A Book of Greek Fairy Tales.

By W. M. L. HUTCHINSON.

Crown 8vo.   *With Illustrations.*   **5s.**

This is a book for young people on the lines of Kingsley's 'Heroes' and Hawthorne's 'Wonder Book.' Among the contents are 'The Favourite of the Gods,' 'The Prince who was a Seer,' 'Peleus and the Sea-King's Daughter,' 'The Heavenly Twins,' 'The Pansy Baby,' 'The Lad with One Sandal,' etc. Miss Hutchinson is a former Fellow of Newnham College, and combines a wide knowledge of the Classics with a lucid and attractive English style.

AN INTRODUCTION TO CHILD-STUDY.

By W. B. DRUMMOND, M.B., C.M., F.R.C.P.E.,
AUTHOR OF 'THE CHILD: HIS NATURE AND NURTURE.'

Crown 8vo.   **6s. net.**

Recognition of the value of the science of child-study is extending rapidly among those who have to do with the training of children. It is not always realized, however, that, in order to be fully profitable, and for the avoidance of pitfalls, the subject must be approached with caution and with a certain amount of self-preparation on the part of the investigator.   Upon the importance of this caution and self-preparation Dr. Drummond lays considerable stress; then, after describing methods of study, he passes on to treat in detail of the facts of growth, the senses and the nervous system, health, fatigue and over-pressure, instincts and habits, forms of expression in speech and drawing, and moral characteristics.   He has an interesting chapter on the question of religion as a suitable subject for the child's mind, and concludes with a reference to peculiar and exceptional children.   The book will be found invaluable by the parent or teacher who wishes to get the best possible results from this important study.

THE CHILD'S MIND : ITS GROWTH AND TRAINING.

By W. E. URWICK, M.A.

Crown 8vo.   **4s. 6d. net.**

The author believes that the theory of education, which has been in the main dependent upon the philosophical system of Herbart and Froebel, stands in need of revision in the light of the scientific developments which have taken place since the days of those eminent writers.   The genetic method, which deals with the process of growth, is the one most successfully followed in the sciences— biology, physiology, and psychology—which have most to do with modern ideas on education.   Hence this book aims at setting forth some results already obtained from a study of mind-growth as an organic process, and establishing a clear and definite connexion between the natural processes of learning and the methods by which the mind should be taught and trained.

THE MYSTERY OF MARIA STELLA, LADY NEWBOROUGH.

By SIR RALPH PAYNE GALLWEY, Bart.

Demy 8vo.   With over 20 Illustrations and a Photogravure Frontispiece.
7s. 6d. net.

The strange story of Maria Stella is one of the most interesting of unsolved mysteries. Whether she was Princess or peasant, a Bourbon of France or a humble Chiappini of Tuscany, is a problem still unsettled, and upon its issue depends the real identity of the child who afterwards became Louis Philippe, King of France. The whole of the evidence is carefully worked out by the Author, and his view is clearly that Maria Stella was a daughter of Philippe Egalité.

NEW FICTION.

Crown 8vo.   6s. each.

HIS FIRST LEAVE.

By L. ALLEN HARKER,

AUTHOR OF 'THE INTERVENTION OF THE DUKE,' 'WEE FOLK, GOOD FOLK,' 'CONCERNING PAUL AND FIAMMETTA,' ETC.

It is often made a subject of reproach to our novelists that they rarely introduce children into their stories, probably because of the difficulty of drawing them 'to the life.' Mrs. Harker's skill in this direction has already been shown in the portraits of Paul and Fiammetta, and although 'His First Leave' is a much more 'grown-up' book, the pathetic figure of little Roger, the child whose sweet nature triumphed over the ill-effects of a mother's neglect, is indispensable among the dramatis personæ. The principal part, however, is played by Herrick Wycherly, and this charming character of a girl, slightly unconventional but always delightful, proves that the author can portray a grown-up maiden no less successfully than a child. The love-story of Herrick and Montagu provides the main current of the book, complicated by the baleful intervention of Mrs. Reeve ; but the windings of the current and its final issue must be traced by the reader in the pages of this entertaining novel.

Crown 8vo.   6s. each.

THE DESERT VENTURE.

By FRANK SAVILE.

This is a good stirring story, reminding one of the late H. Seton Merriman in its power of introducing a series of exciting adventures which, but for the author's skill, might seem almost too extraordinary for the twentieth century. As we read these pages, however, we feel that there is no reason whatever why an enterprising European should not even to-day attempt to carve out for himself a new little empire in the heart of Africa, why he should not have to confront all sorts of intrigues culminating in most sanguinary fighting both with natives and European rivals ; while the chain of circumstances which takes out Eva, the heroine, to follow the fortunes of 'Uncle Dick' and her cousin Arthur in the hinterland of Morocco seems the inevitable result of an ingeniously-contrived situation. An interesting and exciting book, which arrests attention and retains it.

THE ELECTION OF ISABEL.

By RONALD MACDONALD,

AUTHOR OF 'A HUMAN TRINITY,' 'THE SEA-MAID,' ETC.

It was inevitable that the claims of the 'Suffragettes' should afford material for a novel, but few authors could have attacked the subject in a lighter or happier vein than Mr. Macdonald. Lady Isabel Fenchurch, the daughter of the Duke of Hounsditch, is depicted as a perfectly charming woman with an infatuation for the 'Feminist Movement.' She marries Charles Lawless on the understanding that it is merely a matter of convenience, that he will supply her with funds for 'the cause,' and give her absolute freedom. He hopes in time to win her love, and accepts half a loaf as better than no bread. Then follows a host of difficulties arising from the situation, all treated most humorously, and culminating in an election, in which Lady Isabel and her husband are rival candidates. It would not be fair to reveal the *finale ;* the book should be read mainly for its amusing qualities, but here and there are glimpses of a more serious appreciation of this burning question.

FAMILIAR FACES.

By HARRY GRAHAM,

AUTHOR OF 'RUTHLESS RHYMES FOR HEARTLESS HOMES,' 'BALLADS OF THE BOER WAR,'
'MISREPRESENTATIVE MEN,' ETC., ETC.

Medium 8vo. With 16 *Illustrations by* GEORGE MORROW. **3s. 6d. net.**

In this volume Capt. Graham treats of fifteen types of everyday people—the Actor Manager, the Gourmet, the Dentist, the Faddist, the Colonel, and so forth—in the singularly facile and ingenious verse for which he is well known. His poetry is often irresistibly comic, and its spirit has been well caught by the artist who has illustrated the book.

NEW TECHNICAL WORKS.

ELECTRICAL TRACTION.

By ERNEST WILSON, WHIT. SCH., M.I.E.E.,

PROFESSOR OF ELECTRICAL ENGINEERING IN THE SIEMENS LABORATORY, KING'S COLLEGE, LONDON ;

AND FRANCIS LYDALL, B.A:, B.Sc.

NEW EDITION. REWRITTEN AND GREATLY ENLARGED.

Two Volumes, sold separately. Demy 8vo.

Vol. I., with about 270 *Illustrations and Index.* **15s. net.**

Vol. II., with about 170 *Illustrations and Index.* **15s. net.**

In dealing with this ever-increasingly important subject the authors have divided the work into the two branches which are, for chronological and other reasons, most convenient, namely, the utilization of direct and alternating currents respectively. Direct current traction taking the first place, the first volume is devoted to electric tramways and direct-current electric railways. In the second volume the application of three-phase alternating currents to electric railway problems is considered in detail, and finally the latest developments in single-phase alternating current traction are discussed at length. There is a separate Index to each volume, and in Volume I. an Appendix giving Board of Trade Regulations, Procedure, etc. In the case of both tramways and railways there are chapters on the financial aspects of these undertakings.

A special feature of the book are the illustrations, which are exceptionally numerous and absolutely up to date.

A TEXT-BOOK OF ELECTRICAL ENGINEERING.

By Dr. ADOLF THOMÄLEN.

Translated by GEORGE W. O. HOWE, M.Sc., Whit. Sch., A.M.I.E.E.,

LECTURER IN ELECTRICAL ENGINEERING AT THE CENTRAL TECHNICAL COLLEGE, SOUTH KENSINGTON.

Royal 8vo.   *With* 454 *Illustrations.*   **15s. net.**

This translation of the 'Kurze Lehrbuch der Electrotechnik' is intended to fill the gap which appears to exist between the elementary text-books and the specialized works on various branches of electrical engineering.   It includes additional matter which is to be introduced into the third German edition, now in preparation. The book is concerned almost exclusively with principles, and does not enter into details of the practical construction of apparatus and machines, aiming rather at laying a thorough foundation which shall make the study of works on the design of machinery more profitable.

HYDRAULICS.

By F. C. LEA, B.Sc., A.M.Inst.C.E.,

SENIOR WHITWORTH SCHOLAR, A.R.C.S.; LECTURER IN APPLIED MECHANICS AND ENGINEERING DESIGN, CITY AND GUILDS OF LONDON CENTRAL TECHNICAL COLLEGE, LONDON.

Demy 8vo.   **18s. net.**

This book is intended to supply the want felt by students and teachers alike for a text-book of Hydraulics to practically cover the syllabuses of London and other Universities, and of the Institution of Civil Engineers.   With this end in view, and to make the work as self-contained as possible, the earlier chapters are devoted to the consideration of fluids at rest and the stability of floating bodies. For the chapters on the flow of water, in pipes and channels, and through orifices and over weirs, the latest experimental work has been carefully consulted, and it is believed the résumé given of that work will not only be of use to students and teachers, but also to practical engineers.   The construction of modern hydraulic machines is shown by a number of examples.   A chapter on the resistance of ships' models is inserted, and the method of determining the still-water resistance of ships from that of the model is given.   The work is completely illustrated, and the methods of using the formulæ given are shown by worked Arithmetical Examples.

WOOD.

A Manual of the Natural History and Industrial Applications of the Timbers of Commerce.

By G. S. BOULGER, F.L.S., F.G.S., A.S.I.,

PROFESSOR OF BOTANY AND LECTURER ON FORESTRY IN THE CITY OF LONDON COLLEGE, AND FORMERLY IN THE ROYAL AGRICULTURAL COLLEGE.

New Edition, Revised and Enlarged and profusely Illustrated.

Demy 8vo. **12s. 6d. net.**

Of the many thousand different kinds of wood, the author deals with some 750 of those which are practically known in general commerce. The book is divided into two sections. The first describes the structure and development of trees, followed by chapters on the recognition and classification of woods, selecting, seasoning, storing, defects, methods of testing, etc. The second section, comprising more than half the book, gives condensed accounts, with physical constants, when these are known, of the different woods of commerce, and will prove most valuable for purposes of reference.

In an appendix will be found nearly fifty full-page illustrations of magnified sections of all the principal woods of commerce.

ORGANIC CHEMISTRY FOR ADVANCED STUDENTS.

By JULIUS B. COHEN, Ph.D., B.Sc.,

PROFESSOR OF ORGANIC CHEMISTRY IN THE UNIVERSITY OF LEEDS, AND ASSOCIATE OF OWENS COLLEGE, MANCHESTER.

Demy 8vo. **21s. net.**

The book is written for students who have already completed an elementary course of Organic Chemistry, and is intended largely to take the place of the advanced text-book. For it has long been the opinion of the author that, when the principles of classification and synthesis and the properties of fundamental groups have been acquired, the object of the teacher should be, not to multiply facts of a similar kind, but rather to present to the student a broad and general outline of the more important branches of the subject. This method of treatment, whilst it avoids the dictionary arrangement which the text-book requires, leaves the writer the free disposal of his materials, so that he can bring together related substances, irrespective of their nature, and deal thoroughly with important theoretical questions which are often inadequately treated in the text-book.

A HISTORY OF CHEMISTRY.

By Dr. HUGO BAUER,

ROYAL TECHNICAL INSTITUTE, STUTTGART.

Translated by R. V. STANFORD, B.Sc. LOND.,

PRIESTLEY RESEARCH SCHOLAR IN THE UNIVERSITY OF BIRMINGHAM.

Crown 8vo.   **3s. 6d. net.**

In the course of the historical development of chemistry there have occurred definite periods completely dominated by some one leading idea, and, as will be seen from the contents, it is upon these periods that the arrangement of this book is based.

CONTENTS.—PART I.—I. The Chemistry of the Ancients (to the fourth century, A.D.); II. The Period of Alchemy (from the fourth to the sixteenth centuries); III. The Period of Iatrochemistry (sixteenth and seventeenth centuries); IV. The Period of Phlogistic Chemistry (1700 to 1774).

PART II.—I. The Period of Lavoisier; II. The Period of the Development of Organic Chemistry; III. The Chemistry of the Present Day.   Index.

BOOKS RECENTLY PUBLISHED.

A STAFF OFFICER'S SCRAP-BOOK

During the Russo=Japanese War.

By LIEUT.-GENERAL SIR IAN HAMILTON, K.C.B.

Two Volumes, Demy 8vo.   With Illustrations, Maps, and Plans.

18s. net each.

LETTERS FROM THE FAR EAST.

By SIR CHARLES ELIOT, K.C.M.G.,

AUTHOR OF 'TURKEY IN EUROPE,' 'THE EAST AFRICA PROTECTORATE,' ETC.

Demy 8vo.   With Illustrations.   **8s. 6d. net.**

SOME PROBLEMS OF EXISTENCE.

By NORMAN PEARSON.

Demy 8vo.   **7s. 6d. net.**

MEMORIES.

By Major-Gen. Sir OWEN TUDOR BURNE, G.C.I.E., K.C.S.I.

Demy 8vo. With Illustrations. **15s. net.**

A PICNIC PARTY IN WILDEST AFRICA.

Being a Sketch of a Winter's Trip to some of the Unknown Waters of the Upper Nile.

By C. W. L. BULPETT.

Demy 8vo. With Illustrations and Map. **12s. 6d. net.**

TIPPOO TIB.

The Story of his Career in Central Africa.

Narrated from his own accounts by Dr. HEINRICH BRODE, and Translated by H. HAVELOCK.

Demy 8vo. With Portrait and Map. **10s. 6d. net.**

THE PRINCES OF ACHAIA AND THE CHRONICLES OF MOREA.

A Study of Greece in the Middle Ages.

By Sir RENNELL RODD, G.C.V.O., K.C.M.G., C.B.,

AUTHOR OF 'CUSTOMS AND LORE OF MODERN GREECE,' 'FEDA, AND OTHER POEMS,' 'THE UNKNOWN MADONNA,' 'BALLADS OF THE FLEET,' ETC.

2 Volumes. Demy 8vo. With Illustrations and Map. **25s. net.**

THUCYDIDES MYTHISTORICUS.

By F. M. CORNFORD,

FELLOW AND LECTURER OF TRINITY COLLEGE, CAMBRIDGE.

Demy 8vo. **10s. 6d. net.**

MEMORIES OF THE MONTHS.
FOURTH SERIES.

By the Right Hon. Sir HERBERT MAXWELL, Bart., F.R.

Large Crown 8vo.   With Photogravure Illustrations.   **7s. 6d.**

A HUNTING CATECHISM.
By COLONEL R. F. MEYSEY-THOMPSON,

Author of 'Reminiscences of the Course, the Camp, and the Chase,' 'A Fishing Catechism,' and 'A Shooting Catechism.'

Foolscap 8vo.   **3s. 6d. net.**

SIX RADICAL THINKERS.
By JOHN MacCUNN, LL.D.,
Professor of Philosophy in the University of Liverpool.

Crown 8vo.   **6s. net.**

CHURCH AND STATE IN FRANCE
1300-1907.

By ARTHUR GALTON,
Vicar of Edenham, and Chaplain to the Earl of Ancaster.

Demy 8vo.   **12s. 6d. net.**

THIRD IMPRESSION.

THE NEXT STREET BUT ONE.
By M. LOANE,
Author of 'The Queen's Poor.'

Crown 8vo.   **6s.**

THIRD IMPRESSION.

AT THE WORKS.
A Study of a Manufacturing Town.
By LADY BELL,
Author of 'The Dean of St. Patrick's,' 'The Arbiter,' etc., etc.

Crown 8vo.   **6s.**